“ANNE
FOR P

The Perfect Waltz

“Duty vs. love [are] brilliantly battled.”

—*Midwest Book Review*

“[O]ne of the best Regency-set historicals I’ve read in years, with a beautifully developed love story at the center.”

—*The Romance Reader*

“A definite keeper . . . one of the best romances I have read in a long time.”

—*All About Romance*

“If you haven’t already discovered the powerfully moving romances of Anne Gracie, I can’t urge you strongly enough to hunt [for] them.”

—*Romance Reviews Today*

“I can’t remember the last time I enjoyed a book so much.”

—*Fresh Fiction*

The Perfect Rake

“Contains bushels of humor, a tiny bit of farce, a generous dollop of romance, the right balance of sweet and tart, a dash of suspense, and, for spice, a soupçon of retribution.”

—*Romance Reviews Today*

“Near perfect.”

—*Midwest Book Review*

“Hysterical to read. Gracie’s humor is as engaging as ever.”

—*All About Romance*

continued . . .

Praise for the other novels of Anne Gracie

An Honorable Thief

"She's turned out another wonderful story!"

—*All About Romance*

"A true find and definitely a keeper." —*Romance Reviews*

"A thoroughly marvelous heroine." —*The Best Reviews*

"Dazzling characterizations . . . Provocative, tantalizing, and wonderfully witty romantic fiction . . . Unexpected plot twists, tongue-in-cheek humor, and a sensually fraught battle of wits between hero and heroine . . . Embraces the romance genre's truest heart."

—*Heartstrings Reviews*

How the Sheriff Was Won

"Anne Gracie provide[s] pleasant diversions."

—*Midwest Book Review*

"An excellent story with an engaging plot and well-rounded characters." —*Romantic Times*

Tallie's Knight

"Gracie combines an impeccable knowledge of history, an ability to create vibrant and attractive characters, and an excellent story-telling ability. *Tallie's Knight* is far and away the best Regency romance I have read in a long time."
—*The Romance Reader*

"Gracie's writing style is charming and wonderful, and the love scenes are very sensual . . . A special book with excellent writing and characters that touch the heart."
—*All About Romance*

Gallant Waif

"A great heroine . . . This is as polished a piece of romance writing as anyone could want."
—*The Romance Reader*

"I loved everything about it."
—*All About Romance*

A Virtuous Widow

"A wonderful, warm, emotionally stirring Christmas story of love found, wishes fulfilled, and promises kept."
—*Romantic Times*

Berkley Sensation titles by Anne Gracie

THE PERFECT RAKE
THE PERFECT WALTZ
THE PERFECT STRANGER
THE PERFECT KISS

THE Perfect Kiss

Anne Gracie

BERKLEY SENSATION, NEW YORK

THE BERKLEY PUBLISHING GROUP
Published by the Penguin Group
Penguin Group (USA) Inc.
375 Hudson Street, New York, New York 10014, USA
Penguin Group (Canada), 90 Eglinton Avenue East, Suite 700, Toronto, Ontario M4P 2Y3, Canada
(a division of Pearson Penguin Canada Inc.)
Penguin Books Ltd., 80 Strand, London WC2R 0RL, England
Penguin Group Ireland, 25 St. Stephen's Green, Dublin 2, Ireland (a division of Penguin Books Ltd.)
Penguin Group (Australia), 250 Camberwell Road, Camberwell, Victoria 3124, Australia
(a division of Pearson Australia Group Pty. Ltd.)
Penguin Books India Pvt. Ltd., 11 Community Centre, Panchsheel Park, New Delhi—110 017, India
Penguin Group (NZ), Cnr. Airborne and Rosedale Roads, Albany, Auckland 1310, New Zealand
(a division of Pearson New Zealand Ltd.)
Penguin Books (South Africa) (Pty.) Ltd., 24 Sturdee Avenue, Rosebank, Johannesburg 2196,
South Africa

Penguin Books Ltd., Registered Offices: 80 Strand, London WC2R 0RL, England

THE PERFECT KISS

A Berkley Sensation Book / published by arrangement with the author

PRINTING HISTORY
Berkley Sensation mass-market edition / January 2007

Cover art by Voth/Barrall.
Cover design by George Long.
Interior text design by Kristin del Rosario.

For information, address: The Berkley Publishing Group,
a division of Penguin Group (USA) Inc.,
375 Hudson Street, New York, New York 10014.

ISBN: 978-0-425-21345-2

BERKLEY SENSATION®
Berkley Sensation Books are published by The Berkley Publishing Group,
a division of Penguin Group (USA) Inc.,
375 Hudson Street, New York, New York 10014.
BERKLEY SENSATION is a registered trademark of Penguin Group (USA) Inc.
The "B" design is a trademark belonging to Penguin Group (USA) Inc.

PRINTED IN THE UNITED STATES OF AMERICA

10 9 8 7 6 5 4 3 2 1

ACKNOWLEDGMENTS

With thanks to Christine, my wonderful editor.

Thanks also to my writing friends Linda, Jenny, Theonne, Kaye, and Trish, who give me advice, support, and laughs when I need them most, and to Dave, an endless source of symptoms and diseases.

Prologue

DEREHAM COURT, NORFOLK, ENGLAND. 1814

"YOU ARE AN EVIL LITTLE GIRL!" THE OLD MAN BELLOWED.

Eight-year-old Grace Merridew stood braced against the corner of the room. Her grandfather's tirade pounded her with spittle-flecked waves of hatred.

"You'll dwell in misery and filth, alone and unloved, and when you die, even the worms will disdain your corrupt flesh!"

"I will *too* be loved," Grace muttered defiantly. "My mama promised."

He swore. "That whore of Babylo—"

Grace wasn't sure what a whore was, but she knew it was something bad. She planted her fists on her hips and shouted furiously back. "My mama was *not* a whore! She's an *angel*, an' she's watching over us now, and before she died she promised all of us—me and all my sisters—that we'll find love and laughter and sunshine and happiness and so we will, so we will, and you can't stop us, Gran'papa, because an angel is stronger than a horrible old man who spits and swears and smells!"

His eyes filled with a terrible light. He loomed over her, his big, gnarled hands clenching and unclenching. Grace was glued to the floor, shaking, shocked by her own temerity. He was going to kill her, she knew. She'd never before defied him like that. She braced herself for the blows she knew would come, the rage that would inevitably break.

The silence stretched unbearably.

When he finally spoke, it was all the more frightening because he wasn't shouting. He spoke softly, almost tenderly. "Your bitch of a mother may have promised your older sisters love and happiness, Grace, but she never promised it to *you*."

Grace shook her head in denial. She didn't remember her mother, but her sisters had told her often about Mama's promise. "She did, too," she muttered.

"No. She couldn't have. The others, yes, but not you." He said it with flat, unnerving confidence.

A trickle of uncertainty ran through her. She unclenched her fists. "Why not me?"

She flinched as he laid his hand on her head in a horrible parody of affection. "Because you killed your mama, Grace. A woman doesn't make that sort of promise to the daughter who killed her."

She stared, unable to take in what he was saying.

He repeated it with horrible relish. *"The daughter who killed her!"*

Cold fingers clutched at her heart. "I didn't kill my mother! I didn't!"

"You were a baby and don't remember, but you killed her all the same. You killed the whore of Babylon and came to Grandpapa. That makes you my creature, not your mother's." Long, twisted fingers caressed her hair.

Grace jerked her head away, knuckling her fist into her mouth to stem the welling horror. It couldn't be true, it couldn't. "I'll ask my sisters. I didn't kill her, I wouldn't."

"Do you think they would tell you the horrid truth? Upset their darling baby sister for no reason? You can't bring Mama back, can you?" He gave a raspy laugh. "Of course they'll tell you I'm lying. But I'm not, little Grace, I'm not."

Grace thought she might throw up, she felt so sick and shivery.

"You killed your mother, Grace." He smiled, a rictus of stained and broken teeth. "And for that you'll die alone and unloved . . ."

Chapter One

Happy the man whose wish and care a few paternal acres bound,
content to breathe his native air in his own ground.

ALEXANDER POPE

SHROPSHIRE, ENGLAND. 1826

HE RODE INTO THE VILLAGE OF LOWER WOLFESTONE WITH COLD revenge in his heart. On a huge black steed streaked with sweat and dust he drew all eyes, feminine and masculine alike. He was indifferent to their interest.

Spying the faded sign of the Wolfestone Arms hanging motionless in the sultry heat, the man nudged his horse in the direction of the tavern. A weary white-and-liver-speckled dog followed, her ribs heaving, her tongue hanging low.

Three old men sat on the bench outside, shaded from the afternoon sun by beech trees whose leaves were a mix of gold and green and russet.

A ragged, skinny child came running out. "Can I help you, sir? Fetch you an ale, mebbe? Water for your horse? For your dog?"

"Which road do I take to Wolfestone Castle?"

"The castle, sir? But Mr. Eades, he's bin gone—"

"Ach, Billy Finn, don't bother the gentleman wi' village

tattle-tale!" A large man shoved the boy aside and gave the gentleman an obsequious smile and a half bow. "A drink for yer honor p'rhaps? I've got some good ale, cool from the cellar, will slide down y'r honor's parched throat, a treat in this weather. Or if you're hungry, my missus makes a meat pie that's famous in three counties."

The stranger ignored him. "Boy, which road?"

The boy, who was giving water to the dog, glanced at the landlord, then pointed at the right fork. "Along that road, sir. You can't miss it."

The landlord shot the lad a warning glare and began, "There be nobody—"

But the stranger flipped a silver coin at the boy and rode on.

"Well, I'll be beggared," the landlord exclaimed. "What would the likes of 'im want up at the castle?"

The oldest of the old men, a wizened, bright-eyed gnome, snorted. "Ye never did 'ave a noticing eye, Mort Fairclough. Didn't you recognize him?"

"How could I? I've never seen him before."

"Didn't ye see 'is eyes? Golden bright and cold as an hoarfrost they were. With eyes like that and hair as black as sin, there ain't nobody else he could be but a Wolfe of Wolfestone!"

A murmur ran around those gathered.

One of the girls sighed. "He's right handsome, for a lord. I do like a lovely, big, stern-looking man. He could have his wicked lordly way wi' me any day."

The venerable ancient said severely, "The important question is, which sort o' Wolfe is he?"

"What d'ye mean, which sort?" the boy piped up.

"There's been Wolfes at Wolfestone for nigh on six hundred years, young Billy," the old man explained. "And

Wolfes come in only two sorts—good or bad. The fate o' the village depends on 'em."

His bright old eyes took in the listeners and he added, "We've had bad for as long as most of you can remember. But when I was a lad, ahh." He shook his head reminiscently. "The old lord then was a good 'un. One o' the best." He drank the last of the ale in his tankard and gazed mournfully into its emptiness. "So, I wonder what this 'un's like."

"He be a good 'un," said little Billy Finn confidently, clutching his sixpence tightly.

The landlord shook his head. "Openhanded don't mean good, lad. The old lord was free enough wi' a tanner when it pleased him, and he was a bad 'un for sure." He spat in the dust.

"We must hope for the Gray Lady," a bent old woman with white elflocks and black button eyes stated with an air of authority.

Billy Finn fetched a stool for her. "Who's the Gray Lady, Granny?"

Granny Wigmore eased her old bones onto the stool with a nod of approval. "She's the guardian o' this valley, Billy. She be the harbinger o' good times for us poor folks. When the Gray Lady rides, the Wolfe be a good 'un. She hasn't ridden in many a year."

Grandad Tasker added, "My mam saw the Gray Lady once when she was a girl. All in gray and on a white 'orse, she was, ridin' at dawn and bonny as the mist."

"When the Gray Lady rides, the Wolfe be tamed," Granny repeated.

The landlord gazed down the road the stranger had taken and shook his head. "I don't reckon any lady—gray or otherwise—will tame that 'un. I never seen such bright, cold eyes on a man before. Devil's eyes, I reckon."

"Wolfe eyes," the old man said. "Old Hugh Lupus had just such eyes."

"Hugh Lupus?"

"Don't ye know nothing, lad? Hugh Lupus be the first lord of D'Acre—came over with the Conqueror, he did. A mortal fierce man, old Hugh, with gold-hard eyes that could freeze a man's blood." He leaned back against the wall and added, "Storm be a'comin. I feel 'un in my bones."

THE HIRED TRAVELING CARRIAGE RATTLED ALONG AT BREAKNECK speed. Dust rose in clouds from the narrow country road, drifting through the open windows of the carriage and settling on the passengers inside. It was too hot and sultry a day even to think of closing the windows. Besides, dust was but a small part of their miseries.

They bounced and bumped as the carriage lurched and jolted over ruts and potholes, remaining on their seats only with the aid of the leather straps that hung from the sides of the carriage.

"I'll have that insolent fellow dismissed when we get back to London!" Sir John Pettifer muttered peevishly. He'd already reprimanded the postilion twice about the excess speed when they'd stopped to change horses, but the postilion and coach were hired for the journey, and he was not much inclined to listen to a fussy, elderly gentleman in old-fashioned clothes who'd already proved himself a miserly tipper.

Grace Merridew hung on to her leather strap and gritted her teeth. The problem was more than mere insolence. The postilion had been refreshing himself at intervals from a leather flask. And the more he drank, the wilder he rode and the wilder the coach swung and bounced.

Not far to go, Grace told herself. It was not for her to complain. She was supposed to be invisible on this trip. She was only here because her best friend, Melly Pettifer, had begged her to come.

And because she must have been insane at the time.

But she'd never seen Melly so desperate, so distraught. And indeed her plight seemed fantastic when she'd first broken the news to Grace.

"I won't have to be a governess after all. Papa arranged a marriage for me!" But as Grace started forward to congratulate her, Melly burst into tears. Bitter, scalding tears. Misery, not happiness.

The carriage hurtled around a bend, swaying dangerously, and Grace braced herself. Melly clung miserably to the window frame opposite her. Poor Melly. Her complexion was green. She'd thrown up three times already on the journey. She hadn't expected to enjoy the trip but this was worse than anyone could have imagined.

Melly's bridal journey. To be married in a few weeks to a man she'd never met. Grace couldn't imagine what that would be like. She could barely believe it. Melly could barely believe it. As it turned out she'd been betrothed to marry Dominic Wolfe, now Lord D'Acre of Wolfestone Castle, since she was nine years old. And nobody had told her until now.

Apparently Dominic Wolfe had returned to England for the first time in more than ten years. He hadn't even come for his father's funeral. But Sir John had heard he was back and had contacted him about the betrothal.

It was legal and binding. According to Sir John, Melly had no choice in the matter. He and the old Lord D'Acre had cooked up the agreement years before. Documents had been signed and a large sum of money had changed hands—money that Sir John had spent long ago and had no hope of ever repaying.

No wonder Sir John had been so miserly about spending money on Melly's coming-out. The Pettifer money problems were well known. Why go to the expense of launching Melly on the marriage mart when it was already a done deal, signed, sealed, and the bride ready to be delivered?

Sir John's main worry had been that it looked as though the new Lord Wolfe would never come to England. Or that he'd married abroad. But he'd arrived in England still a bachelor and so the wedding was on.

The news had shocked Melly badly, but slowly she had come to terms with it. It wasn't as if she had any other suitors. You didn't when you were poor, plain, plump, and intensely shy. And at least the new Lord D'Acre was young.

What a strange homecoming it must have been, Grace pondered, to return to claim your inheritance and discover you'd also inherited a bride. He'd been only sixteen when the contracts were signed.

That was the problem. Dominic Wolfe didn't want a bride. Melly wasn't sure what had gone on: her father and the family lawyer had journeyed up to Bristol, where he was staying. He had interests in shipping.

Sir John was determined Melly would not be done out of her rights. The contract was legal and would stand. And the only way Lord D'Acre could inherit the property of Wolfestone was by marrying Melly. It was in his father's will—he would inherit only after he had married Melly, or should she be dead or otherwise unable to marry, he could inherit the property only if he married a bride who met with Sir John's approval.

Lord D'Acre's legal advisers had examined the will for loopholes, but it was watertight, apparently. At that, he'd agreed to marry her, but in a letter two days ago he'd coldly informed Sir John that it would be a white marriage—a marriage in name only. He and his bride would part at the church door. He owned a fleet of ships and had no plans to live in England.

Melly was distraught. "It means I'll have a house in London and lots of money but I'll never have babies, Grace. And you know how I've always wanted babies. I l-l-love babies." And her soft, plump face had crumpled with despair, and tears had poured down her cheeks.

"Your papa loves you—he won't force you to marry a man like that," Grace had told her. "Just refuse to go through with it."

"He can, he can! He's utterly adamant! I've never seen him like this before." Melly had scrubbed at her red eyes with a mangled handkerchief. "Help me, Grace, I beg you."

And because she'd been protecting Melly from bullies ever since they'd met at school—and because insanity ran in her family!—Grace had found herself promising she would do what she could.

That was how she now found herself on this frightful journey dressed in drab gray clothes, wearing horrid sensible leather half boots, and disguised as Melly's hired companion, of all things. She could have been packing for a thrilling trip to Egypt with Mrs. Cheever, a wealthy widow and cousin to Mr. Henry Salt, the British consul general in Egypt and expert on Egyptian antiquities. With such wonderful connections, Grace had expected to have a splendid time. Egypt had been her passion since she was a little girl.

But there would be other opportunities for Grace to travel to Egypt, if not to stay in the house of the consul general.

Once Melly was married, it would be forever.

The coach jolted and swayed. There was a sudden thud and a burst of terrified squawks and cackles. Feathers drifted through the open window. The wretched man had driven through a flock of chickens; he hadn't slowed the carriage in the least and from the sound of that thud at least one of the poor birds had been killed.

It was the last straw! Grace thrust her head out of the door and shrieked furiously at the postilion to slow down. He pointed at the sky and yelled something back at her. Grace couldn't hear what it was, but the ominous bank of swollen, dark gray clouds ahead of them told their own story.

He was trying to beat a storm, racing to get to Wolfe-stone Castle before it hit. The road was bad enough when it was thick with dust. Once the rain came it would become a muddy quagmire. Coaches got bogged all the time. Reluctantly she pulled her head in.

Sir John shook his head at her. "Greystoke, Greystoke, Greystoke! It is not your place to interfere!" he told her wearily. "Lady Augusta expects us to teach you to behave in an appropriate manner, and I'll tell you now, no lady would *ever* thrust her head out a carriage window!" He gave her a minatory look. "Nor would she shriek like a banshee!"

"Yes, Sir John. Sorry, Sir John," Grace forced herself to say meekly. He gave her a stern look, then nodded as if satisfied she'd taken his words to heart and closed his eyes again.

It was very hard to remember she was Greystoke now, playing the role of one of her Aunt Gussie's orphan girls in training to become a hired companion. Calling herself Greystoke in case Melly forgot and called her Grace.

Sir John would never have let Miss Grace Merridew, of

the Norfolk Merridews, and darling of the ton, come on this shabby, shameful journey but when Melly's maid had left—having found herself a situation that paid wages regularly—the girls saw their opportunity. Melly needed a female to accompany her on this trip and since Grace was supposedly an orphan-in-training whose services came free, Sir John had leapt at the opportunity.

Grace looked at Sir John. He was leaning against the cracked leather squabs of the hired coach, his eyes closed, his skin sallow and clammy-looking. He looked nearly as ill as his daughter. Good, she thought angrily. He should feel sick, too, for what he was doing to Melly.

Grace didn't understand it. From all she'd heard, all Melly had told her at school, he'd always seemed a loving, indulgent father. As an orphan, Grace had eagerly listened to tales of other people's parents. She and Melly had always believed it was lack of money that had prevented Melly's coming-out. But now she had to wonder.

What sort of father would do this to his only daughter?

Poor Melly, who had never had a suitor, was—unless Grace could help her—doomed to a loveless, childless marriage to a man who didn't want her.

Grace pondered the unfairness of life as she clung to her strap and stared out at the countryside rushing past the window. It couldn't be said that she'd never had a suitor. Plenty of offers had been made for her hand. Mostly they'd wanted her for her face and fortune. A few men might have wanted her for herself, she supposed.

The trouble was she hadn't wanted any of them.

She'd tried to fall in love—some of the men who had offered for her were very nice—but there was always something missing, something stopping her. And it wasn't just a lack of . . . magic.

A big part of the problem was having faith.

Grace just couldn't manage to achieve the unshakable belief in love that her older sisters had. Prudence, Charity, Hope, and Faith all had memories of the great love their parents had shared. Even though they'd just been children, they'd *felt* it, felt its warmth, its power. They never questioned it. Grace's sisters *knew* love was real and tangible and all-powerful. They all believed in Mama's dying promise; that each of her daughters would find love and laughter and sunshine and happiness. Grace didn't.

Grace had no memories of her parents. She'd grown up in a cold, gloomy Norfolk mansion, not a sunny Italian villa. And unlike her older sisters, Grace had no guarantee, no promise of love from her dead mama to protect her.

Grace had watched each of her sisters fall in love. Their happiness was real and enduring. And her sisters assured her repeatedly that it would happen for her, too, one day.

One day a man will kiss you and you'll know . . .

Mama's promise, they'd remind her. *Mama's promise.*

Grace had tried, so hard, to believe, tried, so hard, to fall in love, but she just . . . couldn't.

So she flirted and parried men's advances, lightheartedly and with humor, ensuring that nobody would get hurt. And that nobody would suspect.

The old man's words would come back to haunt her whenever she was feeling sad and blue-deviled, whenever she'd failed—again—to feel more than a spark of attraction to some nice man. She couldn't marry a man, even a nice one, whose kisses left her cold.

It didn't matter, she told herself for the thousandth time. Plenty of people managed to live without love. She could still make a perfectly good life for herself. More than good—she was determined it would be splendid!

She was her own woman now—almost! She was almost one-and-twenty and about to take control of her own personal fortune. Once she had her fortune she could live how she liked, where she liked. She could have the splendid adventures her soul had craved all her life: travel to Egypt and Venice and Constantinople, see the wonders of the world, ride on a camel, cross the Alps in a basket as her parents had done—and she wouldn't have to ask permission of anyone.

If she married, her body would belong to her husband and so would her fortune. The carriage jolted and swung. No man's kisses could possibly be worth that . . .

"Tidy yourself, gel. You are all blown about!"

"Yes, Sir John." Grace's hands rose to tidy her hair and again she got a shock as she felt the harshly dyed locks. Nobody would recognize her as Grace Merridew now.

Under Grace's instructions, Aunt Gussie's maid, Consuela, had cut Grace's hair shorter and dyed it dark brown. And in a stroke of genius, she'd used henna to paint indelible freckles all over Grace's face and hands and around her neckline. The henna paste stained the skin and even washing failed to remove the false freckles.

They would fade, Consuela had assured the horrified Aunt Gussie. Grace would need to redo them every so often, but in the meantime, the shortsighted Sir John would never suspect that brown-haired, heavily freckled Greystoke was in fact Miss Grace Merridew whose red-gold hair and pure, peaches-and-cream complexion was famous. He had only met Grace a few times since the girls had left boarding school. As herself, and in the right context, he would probably recognize Grace, but not, she'd gambled, like this. She was right.

She felt a pang for the loss of her long, red-gold hair. *Melly's babies*, she reminded herself for the umpteenth time.

Grace didn't share Melly's passion for babies. She liked children, but only after they'd started walking and talking and had become small people. But Melly adored babies, even the doughiest, dribbliest, smelliest ones.

Melly's dreams were simple. She didn't want a lord or a fine London house or lots of money. She just wanted a nice man who would love her and marry her and give her lots of babies. It was what every girl dreamed of, Grace believed.

Every girl except Grace.

Which is why she was so determined Melly's dreams would not be sacrificed. Cutting off her hair was nothing. Hair grew back. People's dreams didn't. Dreams shattered, and sometimes, so did the people.

Lord D'Acre, Dominic Wolfe of Wolfestone Castle, could take his moneybags and his cold-blooded travesty of a marriage elsewhere.

Grace would rescue her friend. She was Grace Merridew, knight-errant! She pondered the term. Knightess-errant, perhap?

DOMINIC WOLFE RODE THE LAST FEW MILES SLOWLY, HIS HEAD bowed against the wind that had just sprung up. Gray clouds boiled slowly, darkening the sky. Summer storms were all sound and fury: lightning and thunder.

He'd reach Wolfestone before it hit, he thought.

As always, the thought of Wolfestone made his jaw tighten. He'd wanted never to set eyes on the place. Blast the Pettifers and their sudden decision to come here! He should have made it clearer to Sir John exactly what their bargain entailed.

Probably the daughter imagined she was inspecting her future home. His mouth hardened.

There was a jagged flash of lightning, and thunder rumbled in the distance. He glanced down at the dog trotting at his side. Her ears were flattened unhappily. Sheba was terrified of thunder. Dominic bent and scooped her up, settling her in front of him on the saddle. Both horse and dog were well used to Sheba riding so.

It had been a long journey. If he'd had more notice he would have used a carriage. He'd tried to stop the Pettifers leaving London but his messenger had returned with the information that they'd already left. By that time Dominic's only option, if he was to arrive before them, was to ride from Bristol.

Not far now.

He caught a glimpse of a turret through the trees. Wolfestone. He felt a strange frisson at the sight. Dread? Anger? Anticipation? Perhaps even a shred of the yearning he'd done as a child, in those far-off naive days when he'd longed to see Wolfestone. A tiny piece that seemed to have survived his coming of age, his *knowing*.

He dragged his gaze away. There was a bitter taste in his mouth. Wolfestone. The place for which his mother had been sold.

And now himself.

Ten minutes further on he found himself in front of a huge pair of iron gates, one hanging at a slightly drunken angle. They were supported by two imposing stone gateposts on each of which was mounted a statue of a snarling wolf.

On the left was a stone and half-timbered gatehouse. It looked deserted. The gates were open. Welcoming him? He doubted it.

Thunder rumbled again, closer, and his dog quivered. Dominic urged his horse, Hex, up the drive. Shelter from the storm, that's all Wolfestone was to him now.

The castle, when he saw it, took his breath away. Built of the local gray stone, it squatted malevolently, overlooking the valley up which he'd ridden, cold, ancient and forbidding, a house well used to combat and war. And hatred.

His ancestral home. Awe inspiring and ugly. Not worth sacrificing anyone's happiness for.

His mother had almost never spoken of it. The very mention of the place brought that tragic look to her eyes, the look he'd spent his childhood trying to banish, the look that haunted him still. "You'll know if you ever go there, why I cannot speak of it," she'd told him once. He looked at it now and knew.

He would destroy it.

The gravel drive that led to the front door was dotted with weeds. In the front was a stretch of long ragged grass. It should have been a lawn. Dominic frowned.

Movement under a group of oaks caught his eye: three silvery mares, pale and ethereal in the pre-storm light. Beautiful creatures, with gracefully arched necks, sloping shoulders, and large, dark eyes.

Arabians. Valuable creatures. What were they doing running loose in the open? The front gate had been left open. The horses could wander out. Or perhaps they'd wandered in.

One of the mares stood a little apart from the others. She was moving restlessly in a way he recognized. Her belly was stretched almost to the bursting point.

Dominic's frown deepened. No horse should be wandering loose like that, let alone a heavily pregnant mare. Especially when a storm was imminent.

He looked around, but there was not another living soul in sight. It was bizarre. The place should be thronging with servants.

He glanced at the roiling gray clouds and the ominous gloom and urged his horse forward, seeking the stables. Some fool had let those mares out and needed to be told. That pregnant one needed to be under cover, not out in a storm.

He rode up to the front door and yanked on the brass doorbell. It jangled noisily in the depths of the building, but not a soul stirred within. According to the books, wages were being paid, so where were the servants?

He didn't have time to speculate now; he would get to the bottom of it later.

He found enormous stone stables behind the house, but they were deserted, too. His horse's hooves echoed eerily on the dusty cobblestones. From the look of things, neither man nor beast had been inside these stables in months.

Thankfully the stalls were fairly clean and at the front of the stables were some gray-looking bales of hay that, when broken open, proved to be sweet and golden within.

He quickly unsaddled his own horse, Hex, gave him a quick rubdown, gave horse and dog a drink, then prepared several stalls, including a stall for the mare to give birth in, far from the others. Finally he locked his dog in. She whined and scratched on the door but he ignored her.

Cursing his recent run of poor luck, he ventured out to try to catch the pregnant mare at least before the storm hit.

* * *

Grace clung to her leather strap for dear life. Her feet were braced against Melly's seat opposite, Melly's feet were braced against hers. They jolted and bounced and rocked wildly from side to side. The pace was insane.

They must be close to Wolfestone now. Surely.

Lightning flashed and thunder rumbled all around them. Abruptly the carriage lurched, slowing marginally, and swung hard left, nearly tipping over. It was saved by a tall something against which it scraped and banged, then righted itself. Grace caught a glimpse of high stone gateposts with some creature atop them. A dog? No, a wolf.

Wolfestone. At last. Thank God. They might even arrive alive, she thought wryly.

Grace peered out of the window as they hurtled up the gravel drive, trying to catch a glimpse of Wolfestone. And when she did, she just stared. Set against a backdrop of hills and looming clouds, it looked bleak and gray and fascinating. Sprawling, ancient, half house and half castle, it had been extended and added to by various members of the family over generations.

An ugly mishmash of styles, Sir John had called it when delivering a lecture to the girls at the beginning of the journey. But Grace found it fascinating: full of odd angles and strange extensions, turrets, battlements and pointed roofs, arrow slits, and a series of wonderful Gothic arched windows. She hoped there were gargoyles. On such a building there ought to be gargoyles.

On a sunny day the front rooms of the house must be full of light, for dozens of mullioned windows faced south. As she watched, the dark clouds parted and a single ray of afternoon sun caught the diamond panes. They briefly glowed with golden fire.

"How beautiful!" she exclaimed but her words were lost

as lightning slashed down almost in front of the coach. The horses screamed and reared, thunder roared around them, and the coach tipped and crashed over on its side with a horrid splintering of wood. The passengers bounced around like balls, crashing against the walls of the carriage and each other.

Then there was silence, except for the roaring of the storm.

Chapter Two

First appearance deceives many.

OVID

GRACE WAS THE FIRST TO MOVE, SLOWLY AT FIRST. SHE FELT AS IF she'd been given a beating. Her arm hurt and her head, but as her mind cleared she realized she was in one piece. Shaken, bruised, but essentially unhurt.

She turned to her friend. "Melly, are you all right?"

Melly groaned. Grace examined her. Melly groaned again and opened her eyes. "What happened?"

"The carriage overturned. Are you all right? Can you move?"

Melly moved, gingerly. "I-I think so. It hurts, but I think I'm all right." She stretched. "Ouch! I'm bruised all over. Papa—how is he?"

Sir John was conscious and breathing but he looked far from well. His eyelids fluttered and he muttered, "Get me out of this contraption!" in a faint, querulous voice. His breath rasped in and out of his chest in painful-sounding gasps.

"Stay with him, Melly. I'll run for help."

"But what if—" The rest of the sentence was lost as Grace scrambled out of the window. The coach door was underneath them. Lightning flashed again and the heavens opened. Rain pelted down.

The horses moved restlessly, trembling with exhaustion and fear. Lightning flashed. They plunged in fear; she could see the whites of their eyes. One of the horses was tangled in the traces. If they got spooked again, they could drag the carriage with them.

Shielding her face from the lashing rain, she peered around. Surely someone had heard the crash and would come. She saw a still, dark figure lying in the gravel. The postilion. She ran to him and bent tentatively over him. "Are you all right?"

He moved and groaned, then swore drunkenly. He sat up and looked at her. "Whasshappened?" He gave her a bleary half smile, then swore and threw up, just missing her boots.

"Get up, you disgraceful sot!" Grace yelled at him. "You've crashed the carriage and the horses are all tangled in the traces! They could drag the carriage off at any moment!"

"Crashed the carriage?" he repeated stupidly.

"Yes! So get up and help me get Sir John and Melly out!"

The man staggered to his feet, took one horrified look at the upturned carriage, swore, and ran off down the drive.

Grace screamed at him to come back, but he kept right on running. She knew why. He'd probably be jailed, perhaps even transported for his negligence.

The horses plunged again, getting even more tangled in the traces. There was only one thing to do. Grace bent and pulled a knife from her sensible half boot. All the Merridew girls traveled armed but she hadn't had time to borrow her sister's gun. Hiding the knife in her sleeve, she approached the horses calmly and slowly, murmuring soothing words. They tossed their heads nervously, but allowed her to approach close enough to grab their halters, cut their traces and set them free. They galloped toward the trees.

Now to fetch help. She put her head down against the driving rain and started running up the drive to the big gray house. Not a single light burned. Of course, it was still afternoon; the darkness was because of the storm. But it didn't look promising.

She ran up the front steps. There was a snarling wolf's-head knocker and a brass bellpull. She banged the knocker and pulled hard on the door pull. She pressed her ear against the door and could hear a faint chiming in the distance. She waited. She tried again. But nobody opened the door.

It looked like there was nobody in residence. But how could that be? This was Melly's bridal visit.

No time to wonder. She ran round the side, following the drive, and found several likely-looking back doors. She banged on them, but there was no response. Every one was locked.

Had the drunken postilion brought them to the right house? The place was deserted.

Across one side of the cobbled courtyard she could see a bedraggled-looking kitchen garden. On the other was a large stone building with an arched entrance. Stables. Lungs heaving, she ran on.

Inside she paused to let her eyes adjust to the gloom. The building was large and cavernous. Rain drummed on the slate roof. There was fresh hay in a pile by the door and tack hanging on hooks, all covered with dust, except for one foreign-looking saddle and bridle, which gleamed with care. There was a long central passageway, off which lay rows of stalls. Most were closed. Four doors were only half closed: the top half of the door was hooked back. Over the closed lower doors poked the head of a white horse, its eyes large, dark, and intelligent.

Thank God. She could ride for help.

The wind dropped for a moment and Grace heard a whinny and the sound of a man's voice, deep and low. She ran toward it and as she reached the line of open-topped stalls she heard the voice again. It was too muffled for her to make out any words, but it didn't sound like English.

"Help!" Grace called loudly. "Help me, please! There's been an accident and I need help!"

A man looked out over a half stable door. "Where the devil did you spring from?" He spoke with an accent she could not place.

His looks made her catch her breath. No, it was the running, she told herself. He was a disgrace.

He was tall, his face was dirty and unshaven, and his thick black hair was tousled and in need of a cut. His face was severe, all hard angles and planes, lean and . . . hungry.

He stared back at her with strange, cold, yellow eyes, his expression impatient. "I suppose you've come about the mares." His gaze ran over her, lingering insolently on the parts where her wet clothes clung. And the strange golden eyes glowed.

Grace did not care. "I don't know anything about any mares. I need help. There's been an accident."

His gaze snapped to her face. "What sort of accident?"

"Our carriage has overturned. On the driveway below."

He muttered something under his breath. It wasn't English. "Is anyone hurt?"

"No, not really, but they're stuck in the carriage and

the postilion has run away. He was drunk! You must come, now!"

He considered her words. "So, nobody is dead? Or bleeding?"

"No," she said, frustrated. "But the door is blocked by the ground and they cannot get out. You must come at once!"

"Any horses injured?" He came out of the stall.

He might be a gypsy, she thought. He was dark enough for it. He wore no coat. He was dressed in mud-smeared high boots and stained buckskin breeches. His shirt, too, was soiled, the sleeves rolled up over sinewy, tanned forearms. She didn't care. He looked strong and capable and that's what counted at the moment.

"No, they're all right. Please *hurry*!"

"Who did you say you were?" He fastened the door behind him with deliberate care.

She almost wept with impatience. She stamped her foot instead. "My name is Greystoke and who I am is of no importance!"

"Oh, I wouldn't say that. Now calm down, Greystoke. Nobody has been hurt. I'm coming. Everything will be all right." His voice was deep and calm and confident.

She tried to convey some sense of urgency. "Miss Pettifer—in the carriage—" She gestured vaguely down the drive. "Miss Pettifer is Lord D'Acre's affianced wife and soon to be your mistress, so please inform your master, *at once*!"

"I call no man master." His calmness was infuriating. His eyes bored into Grace, wicked amusement dancing in their depths. "But I wouldn't mind a mistress. Are you soon to be my mistress, too, Greystoke?" He hitched up his buckskin breeches. "I could do with a mistress. It's been a while."

Grace was scandalized. But she knew better than to bandy words with a golden-eyed, mannerless gypsy devil. She said crisply, "You have no manners and your mind needs as good a scrubbing as the rest of you! Now *hurry*!"

He gave her a faint, wholly wicked smile and moved purposefully forward. At last! she thought, but then he marched right up to her and suddenly he was close. Too close for comfort and before she could react he had her face cupped in his hands and all she could see was his eyes. They were an odd color, a light golden amber, ringed with a thin black line. They gleamed under slanted black brows.

She was trapped. Like a rabbit facing a wolf. Too shocked to move.

His gaze roamed over her face like a caress. "Are those freckles real?" he asked softly. His voice resonated through her. To her surprise he didn't smell dirty at all, just a bit horsey, which wasn't surprising. And very masculine.

She pushed back at him. "Stop that at once! *There's been a coach accident!*" she reminded him in as stern a voice as she could manage.

"But nobody is hurt," he said and kissed her. It was swift and hard but Grace felt it right through to her very bones.

He released her and stood staring down at her, a blank look on his face. "Now that I didn't expect," he murmured. "Or was it perhaps, a fluke?"

Grace tried to step away from him, reeled and staggered. There was something wrong with her legs. She clutched his arms to steady herself. He was hard and warm and very strong.

Thunder rumbled across the skies.

It jolted her back to reality. She rallied, pulled back, wiped her mouth, and glared at him. Realizing she still held on to his arm, she used it to tug him toward the door. "There has been *a coach accident*."

"Yes, you said. Nobody is hurt and they are stuck in the coach, out of the rain. And in the meantime, I just need to check something." And he kissed her again, a brief, hard kiss that—again—sucked every coherent thought from her brain. And—again—when he released her she was dazed and dizzy.

"So," he said on a long note of discovery. "Not a fluke at all. Well, who'd have expected that?" He steadied her, smiling.

The smile was the essence of male satisfaction.

She kicked him hard on the shin.

The smile widened. "Ouch," he said softly, conversationally.

She kicked him again, harder.

"It would have more effect if I weren't wearing boots," he said in an apologetic tone.

She thumped him on the arm. "Listen, you impossible gypsy! *There has been a coach accident* and—"

He gave a start of theatrical surprise. "*A coach accident?* Well, why didn't you say so?" And before Grace could say another word he'd seized her hand, whirled her out of the door, and started to run. Grace found herself practically flying over the ground, panting and slipping, taking two paces for every one of his.

"So, after this is over, will you give me the good scrubbing you promised me?" he said as they ran. The look he gave her scrambled her brains for a moment.

"No!" she gasped as she flew down the driveway. Her feet barely touched the ground.

"No? Oh well." A slow grin cracked across his dark, unshaven face. "Let me know when it suits you, then."

As they rounded the bend he said, "I can see the freckles are waterproof, so I suppose they must be real." He did not slacken the pace. He was not even breathing heavily.

She was flabbergasted by the irrelevance of it. "Yes. Of. Course. They. Are. Real," she lied. The freckles were an essential part of her disguise.

"Fascinating. I've never seen freckles like that before—all exactly the same shape and color. I'm looking forward to discovering whether they are all over your body or only in . . . selected places."

He was outrageous. He had no sense of proper behavior. How dare he comment on her freckles—real or not—when they were in the middle of a crisis!

Grace only had enough breath to glare and run. A few minutes before she had been soaked, frightened, and tired. Her whole body ached from being thrown around the rolling carriage.

Now she was furious!

And feeling more alive than she'd ever felt before.

Danger did that.

They sped down the driveway, fast enough so her feet barely touched the gravel. She was in no danger of falling; he was very strong and his big, warm hand held her upright. But he kept on looking at her. In a very insolent fashion.

And it made her utterly furious that when she was beside herself with anxiety for her friend and her father that this—this devil should cause her to be distracted for a single second!

As the carriage came into view he slowed in surprise. "Where are the horses?"

"I cut the traces. I thought they might pull the carriage further."

He gave her a sharp look. "Good thinking. What did you use?"

"A knife, of course."

He frowned, but they'd reached the site of the accident and he questioned her no more. Melly thrust her head out of the window.

"Thank God you are here," she gasped when they came close enough. "Papa is ill."

At the other window they could see Sir John slumped, his skin yellowish and clammy. His eyes fluttered open. He looked straight at Grace's gypsy. "D'Acre," he said.

"Sir John," the gypsy acknowledged.

"D'Acre?" Grace exclaimed. "*You* are Lord D'Acre?"

"Who else?" He winked at her. And then winced dramatically as she thumped him on the arm. "Ouch! What was that for?"

"You know perfectly well what for." Lord D'Acre indeed! All that nonsense about mistresses! And then he had the nerve to kiss her, knowing his betrothed—his *betrothed*!—was stuck in the carriage! The wretch!

He gave a swift grin, acknowledging that he did indeed know, then he thrust his head through the carriage window and said in a cold, calm voice, "Miss Pettifer, I'm coming in through this window. Stand back."

To Grace's amazement he swung himself up and went feetfirst through the window. He had to wriggle to get his shoulders through—they were very broad—but she was amazed at his strength and lithe agility.

He poked his head out and told Grace, "Sir John doesn't seem to be injured, but I don't like his color at all. Stand aside. I'm going to kick the side panel of the coach out."

Before she could gather her wits, there was a loud thump, followed by another and another. Wood splintered, then he kicked a few more times and a ragged hole appeared. Another couple of kicks and the whole panel fell out.

"Out you get." With him holding Melly from within and Grace helping from the outside, Melly managed to clamber out.

"Now you, Bright Eyes, in you hop. I need help to get the old man out."

Bright Eyes. That would be her, Grace presumed. She climbed in and was told, "You hold his legs and I'll pull him out from out there."

He jumped out and together they maneuvered Sir John out through the hole and into Lord D'Acre's arms. He scooped Sir John up like a child and strode back up the hill toward the house.

Grace grabbed Melly's hand and they ran after him. The rain intensified, making visibility poor and turning the stone steps slippery. She hurried to the front door. "Oh, there's no one to answer," she said, remembering. "How are we to get inside?"

"Key in my pocket," he said. "Right-hand side."

He wasn't wearing a coat. Grace reached into the pocket of his buckskin breeches. They'd been tight enough before; now they were sopping wet and clung like a second skin. She slid her hand into his pocket a little gingerly; she had never touched a man so intimately.

His pocket wasn't empty, so she had to feel around for the key, past his handkerchief, some loose change, and other odds and ends. The situation was urgent, and yet she was tinglingly aware of his hard, warm flank under the buckskin and the warm, masculine smell of him. It wasn't at all unpleasant.

She thought again of those two brief, shocking kisses. Her cheeks warmed against the cold rain.

She found the key, a large, old-fashioned brass one, and thrust it into the lock. The lock was stiff and she had to struggle to make it turn but after a moment it clicked and she was able to push the massive oaken door open. Sopping wet, they fell into the cavernous entrance of Wolfestone Castle. It was gloomy, cold, and dusty, but at least they were out of the rain.

They paused a moment to catch their breath, and as she glanced around Grace saw the gargoyle she'd hoped for. He was set high up overlooking the entry hall, not stone, but carved in wood, with a strong, benevolent face and sad, wise eyes. He seemed to be looking straight at her. The poor fellow needed dusting.

"Where shall we put Papa?" Melly asked.

Lord D'Acre grunted. "No idea. Find a room with a sofa or something."

Grace gave him a quick look of surprise, but there was no time for questions. She ran to look. The first door she opened led to a sitting room containing a chaise longue under holland covers. She whipped off the cover and he placed Sir John on it.

Lightning lit the room with eery flickers, and thunder buffeted the house. Dominic frowned. The old man looked dreadful. His skin was yellowy gray and flimed with sweat, his eyes were closed, and he was breathing stertorously. Dammit, if the old man died he'd be left with the daughter on his hands.

Miss Pettifer said something, but her words were lost as the storm raged. Rain and wind rattled the windows. She tried again, clutching her little friend's shoulder and shouting in her ear. The taste of the little friend flashed through his mind, distracting him briefly.

"I'll get it," Bright Eyes shouted back. "Where is it?"

His fiancée shouted again, she nodded, hugged her in quick sympathy, and ran off.

Dominic bent over the chaise longue, watching as Miss Pettifer loosened Sir John's tie. Though obviously worried, she tended her father in a calm and capable manner. It impressed him.

The old man looked at death's door. Dominic bent and shouted in the daughter's ear, "I'll fetch a doctor."

She nodded. "As quickly as possible."

Dominic hurried to the stables where he saddled the Arabian mare. He'd only managed to catch two of the mares earlier; the third had disappeared into the rain. Thank goodness he had this one to fall back on. His own horse, Hex, was tired after the long journey.

He glanced in on the pregnant mare. She still hadn't given birth. Probably it would happen in the middle of the night, he thought; most horses gave birth then.

He found a faded black oilskin cloak hanging on a hook, swung it on over his wet clothes, and mounted the mare. He hesitated; he did not know what direction to ride in. He'd ask in the village, he thought, and rode out into the rain.

The mare was a gallant little beauty: she didn't seem to turn a hair at the storm. He rode down the drive and made to pass the coach without a thought when a moving figure caught his eye. He stopped, dashing rain from his eyes, and was flabbergasted to see a slight figure lashed by rain, trying to drag a heavy valise through the mud. Greystoke.

That must be what Miss Pettifer had sent her to do. She was some kind of servant, that had been obvious from the start. No one would willingly choose such a drab outfit.

Her shoulders were hunched against the wind and the driving rain. Wet skirts clung heavily to her slender body.

Dominic felt a surge of fury. To be sent to fetch the luggage in weather like this!

He flung himself off the mare, seized the girl by the shoulders, and shouted, "For God's sake, leave the baggage until the storm has passed! A little water won't hurt it and nobody will come to steal it in this weather." Under his hands, her body seemed small, soaked, and cold. How dare she be told to risk herself in this weather for someone else's belongings!

He tried to shield her under his cloak and pull her back to the shelter of Wolfestone, but to his amazement she resisted and bent to tug again at the heavy leather bag.

"It's Sir John's medicine," she shouted over the noise of the storm. "It's in one of these big cases, only I don't know which, and they're too heavy for me to lift."

He thrust the reins into her hands. "You hold the horse, then. I'll carry these up to the house and be back in a few minutes."

"Were you going to fetch the doctor? Is it far?"

He shrugged. "No idea. I'll get directions in the village."

She looked half drowned. He removed his cloak and wrapped it around her, tugging the hood up over her drenched locks. Her face was pinched with cold and worry. He squeezed her shoulders. "The delay can't be helped. This medicine might be exactly what he needs."

Dominic grabbed a valise in each hand. "You can take the smaller things up when I come back. And as soon as you're inside, make sure you change out of those wet clothes, d'you hear me? I don't want you taking a chill."

He hauled the bags swiftly up the drive, dumped them in the entry hall, and ran back. But when he got back to the coach there was no sign of Greystoke or the mare. Where the devil had she gone?

Surely she couldn't have ridden for the doctor herself?

No. She was some kind of servant. Servants didn't ride. She'd probably dropped the reins and the mare had run off. No doubt the poor little soul was out in the storm trying to catch the blasted mare! He swore. Did she think he'd have her transported for losing the horse?

It wasn't even his horse!

Cursing, he seized the remainder of the baggage and stumped back up the hill. He saddled Hex with one of the old, dusty saddles, put on his big, black Polish greatcoat, and grimly rode back out into the storm.

First he'd find the doctor, next he'd look for the girl.

His run of bad luck was holding.

IT TOOK DOMINIC OVER AN HOUR TO FIND THE DOCTOR'S HOUSE and when he did, he was in a fine temper. The village was full of idiots! Every single villager he'd asked had sent him in a different direction. And when he did find the doctor's house, it was by accident; he'd stopped at a large, neat house to make inquiries, trusting that the inmates would be a cut above the inbreds he'd talked to.

"Where does the doctor live? Here, of course!" the woman at the door had declared, peering at him as if he were the village idiot.

Dominic swore under his breath. The house was on the outskirts of the village, an easy ride from Wolfestone. Why the devil hadn't one of the villagers known that?

"No, I don't know where he went," the doctor's wife told him brusquely. "And before you ask, no, I don't know when he'll be back. It could be a birth or anything. He didn't say. He never tells me anything." She gave him a disdainful look and added, "And he doesn't treat dirty gypsies." And she shut the door in his face.

Dominic swore.

He rapped on the knocker again. The doctor's wife opened it with a bad-tempered diatribe on her lips featuring importunate beggars and dirty gypsies.

Dominic planted his boot in the door and informed her in a cold voice that Lord D'Acre of Wolfestone required her husband's services as soon as possible for an urgent case. Sir John Pettifer had suffered an accident.

The titles made the woman's eyes bulge. "Lord D'Acre?" she gushed in a totally different voice. "Oh, I had no idea he was come to Wolfestone already. And Sir John Pettifer is ill, you say. How dreadful for the poor man! I shall send the boy out to find my husband and send him up to the castle at once. Tell Lord D'Acre that Mrs. Ferguson shall see to it. And please inform his lordship that if there's anything I can do—"

"I am Lord D'Acre," said Dominic silkily, removing his boot from the door. "Of the dirty-gypsy branch of the family." And before the woman could pick up her gaping jaw, he'd shut the door in her face.

"FOLKS ARE SAYING THE DEVIL BE A-RIDIN' THE STORM TONIGHT!" Grandad Tasker eased his bones onto the bench nearest the fire. The village inn was rapidly filling up, despite the rain.

"Aye, I seen 'im, but only through t'window. My missus spoke to 'im."

"She never!"

"She did. Eyes like windows into hell, she told me! Sent him up east, along of the moor, she did."

The listeners chuckled. "Is that right? Clever, your missus."

Another man said, "Big, he was and all dark, and on an 'orse as black as sin. He called a hex on us, 'e did." His friend confirmed it and the listeners shuddered. "We sent him south, toward the church."

"I seen him, too," said a bent old man. "He asked after the doctor. Beelzebub hisself all right, but he didn't fool me." He gave a contemptuous snort. "I sent him west, down to the mere."

All the men had a hearty chuckle at the way the village had fooled the Devil.

Grandad Tasker leaned forward. "You know who else was out a-riding tonight? None other but our own Gray Lady!" He paused for effect as the others exclaimed in mixed amazement and disbelief. "Aye, Granny Wigmore seen the Gray Lady in the middle o' the storm. Spoke to her an' all, Granny did."

"She never!"

"She did. The first sightin' in nigh on seventy years. And you know who the Lady was a-seeking?"

Everyone craned forward to hear who.

"The doctor!"

The audience was amazed. Grandad Tasker nodded. "Aye. She fetched him away to safety, I reckon. T'was our Gray Lady, all right."

"I saw her and all," Mort Fairclough interjected. "Ridin' like the wind she was, on a horse made o' mist and cloaked in a veil o' spiders' silk."

"Spiders' silk?" The murmur ran around the inn.

"Aye, a shinin' cloak o' spiders' silk," said the landlord with authority. "Now, who's for another pint?"

Chapter Three

A sweet disorder in the dress kindles in clothes a wantonness.

ROBERT HERRICK

MINUTES AFTER DOMINIC RODE INTO THE STABLES AT WOLFESTONE, the wind died down and the rain dribbled to a stop, as suddenly as it started. The sudden silence was almost shocking.

"My luck running true," he muttered as small rivulets dripped from his clothing, forming muddy puddles on the dusty cobbles.

He'd seen a black tilbury parked in the courtyard. The doctor? Already? But how?

He went to unsaddle Hex and found his own saddle hanging up and the gray mare safe and sound, dry, watered, and well rubbed down. She'd found the mare then. Presumably the girl was out of the rain, too.

When he went inside, Miss Pettifer came hurrying toward him. "Thank goodness you've returned. Where on earth did you get to?"

He opened his mouth to explain, but she hurried on, "Papa is a little better, but Dr. Ferguson wants him in bed but he can't walk and none of us can carry him upstairs. Would you mind, please?"

"How did the doctor get here so fast?"

Miss Pettifer gave him a puzzled look. "Grac-Greystoke, my companion, fetched him. Didn't you know?"

"No, I didn't," Dominic said brusquely.

"But you gave her your cloak and horse."

"So I did," Dominic agreed coolly. *Greystoke fetched him*—as if it were the most normal thing in the world for a paid companion to ride a strange horse—astride—in a storm.

She opened the sitting room door and a tall, grizzled man stood. "Ferguson, my lord. I'm the local physician." He held out his hand and Dominic shook it.

"How is your patient?"

The doctor gave a swift glance at Miss Pettifer and said lightly, "Not injured at all. Rather shaken up, I suspect. I'll know better once we've got him to bed and stripped down, see just how badly bruised the poor gentleman is." His eyes met Dominic's and a silent message passed between them. Sir John's condition was more serious than his tone suggested.

Dominic nodded. "I'll carry him up, then, shall I?" And then he remembered. The house was a shambles. "Er, I'm not sure where—"

"Greystoke is upstairs preparing a room for my father at the moment."

His brows rose. "Is she indeed? Good for Greystoke," he said tersely. He'd imagined her lost in the storm, wandering frightened and cold. Not only had she fetched the doctor and was home, safe and sound, but she was also wondrously efficient!

And why the devil he should be furious about that was beyond him. He bent to lift Sir John.

"Not yet!" Miss Pettifer shrieked. She blushed and added, "You're all wet!"

Dominic didn't say a word. Her blushes intensified and she averted her gaze as he stripped off his coat and shirt and used one of the chair covers to dry his skin.

"Right, I'm dry enough now—or would you prefer me to remove my breeches too?" Both the doctor and Miss Pettifer made horrified noises, so Dominic scooped Sir John up. "Lead the way then, Miss Pettifer," he said with a sardonic smile.

The little companion was waiting at the top of the stairs. She did not look half drowned anymore, but she was still in her damp clothes. And her eyes were as bright as ever.

"Lord *D'Acre*." She snipped out his name and bobbed a halfhearted curtsy.

So she was still cross with him about that. Seemingly, the fact that she'd been kissed by a lord annoyed her even more than when she thought him an *impossible gypsy*. Dominic's mood lifted immediately.

"Miss-*tress* Greystoke." He inclined his head in an urbane, lordly gesture.

Her eyes narrowed and she said in a tight voice, "In here, please." She gestured to an open door, where he could see a freshly made bed, the glow of a dozen candles, and a crackling fire. It was by far the most welcoming room in the house.

She ran ahead and tugged the bedclothes back. He laid Sir John gently on the bed and straightened. Her eyes widened as she took in Dominic's nakedness.

She did not look away, as Miss Pettifer had, with blushes and pursed, disapproving lips.

Greystoke stared. With wide eyes and softly parted lips. As if she'd never seen a man's chest before.

She probably hadn't.

The thought pleased him.

He said, "Doctor Ferguson and I will deal with Sir John. You two run along and do something useful."

His words snapped Grace out of her trance. She jerked her gaze from his chest. "But—"

"We'll call you if we need you. And, Greystoke—" The strange golden eyes stabbed at Grace. "Change out of those wet clothes."

And without knowing quite how it happened, Grace and Melly found themselves on the other side of a firmly closed door. And before they could say a word, they heard a key click in the lock.

"Well, really!" said Grace, annoyed at being told to run along, as if she were a child. After all she had done.

"But I'm Papa's daughter!" Melly wailed. "He needs me!"

They exchanged frustrated looks. "Mannerless devil though he is, he's right," Grace decided at last. "Your papa wouldn't want two young females putting him into his nightshirt. Let us select bedchambers for ourselves and make up our beds."

They chose a bedchamber for Melly across the corridor from Sir John's room, so she would be close if he needed her in the night. It was a pretty room, a very feminine bedchamber, with faded brocade bed hangings in rose and cream and green. Grace loved it on sight. It looked out over the side lawn area, to an odd mound of rubble, overgrown with masses of red roses, and beyond that, to the mountains of Wales.

There was a large bed and a small one, so, because the house was so big and strange and empty, they decided by mutual consent to share the room. At least Melly's reason was that she was frightened to sleep alone in a big, strange house.

Grace's reason was one she didn't state aloud: she didn't trust the master of the house. Not as far as she could throw him. Him and his wicked golden eyes and his naked, golden torso.

Melly must have read her mind, for as they started to make up the beds she said, "You know, I nearly fainted when he just took off his shirt! He wasn't even wearing an undershirt! I've never seen anything so shocking in my life! I didn't know where to look!"

"Yes, he has no manners at all," Grace agreed. She had looked. She hadn't been able to take her eyes off that expanse of dark golden skin. So smooth and warm and strong. She'd wanted to run her fingers over it. And he'd known it, too, the devil! He'd caught her watching and smiled at her, a slow, wicked smile of . . . of smug masculinity.

She shook her head. He had no business to be walking about half naked. He was an atrocious man! With atrocious manners.

"This place is in an atrocious state!" Grace shook out sheets with a practiced snap of linen. All the Merridew girls had had the basic household skills drummed into them from an early age.

"How could he possibly invite guests here? He ought at least to have the house *cleaned*!" She gestured around her indignantly.

Melly looked embarrassed. "Actually, Lord D'Acre didn't invite us. It was Papa's idea to come."

"What? Without an invitation?" Grace sat down on the bed she'd been about to make up and stared at her friend in amazement. "Melly Pettifer, your father is one of the most proper men I know. What on earth would make him invite himself—uninvited!—to a run-down, deserted house?"

Melly shook her head. "I don't know. I think . . ." Her voice trailed off.

"You think what?"

Melly's embarrassment deepened. "I think Papa thought if he forced Lord D'Acre to marry me here, where it's harder to get away, rather than in London, he might . . ." She flushed and whispered, "Might change his mind."

"Make it a real marriage, you mean?"

Melly gave a despairing half nod. "You know Papa—he has no idea of the real world. He thinks I am beautiful. He says Lord D'Acre will not be able to resist my . . ." Her plump face crumpled. "My *charms*."

Grace hugged her friend. "You do have charms, Melly," she said firmly. Melly was loyal and loving and sweet-natured. She would make a wonderful wife and mother. Only perhaps not with Lord D'Acre . . .

Melly sobbed, unconvinced. After a few moments she gathered her composure and glanced at the door across the hallway. "Do you think they've finished examining Papa by now?"

Grace gave her an encouraging pat. "Go and knock on the door and ask. I'll finish making the bed, then I'll go downstairs and see if I can get some hot water."

"Oh, yes, please, I'd love a cup of tea," exclaimed Melly with a watery smile. "I wonder, who is going to cook us our dinner? I am very hungry."

"I'll see what I can do," Grace assured her. She could manage to make a cup of tea, but she had a sinking feeling about dinner.

Melly had been taught to manage servants; she had no

practical skills except sewing. Grace might be an expert at making a bed, but cooking was another matter entirely.

But they had to eat. Someone would have to do something.

As Melly raised her hand to knock, the door to Sir John's room opened and Lord D'Acre emerged. "The doctor's finished with him. You can go in now, Miss Pettifer."

Melly slipped past him into her father's room, leaving Grace facing Lord D'Acre. Or more accurately, facing Lord D'Acre's spectacularly naked chest.

Or was that naked, spectacular chest?

It was definitely naked. And indubitably spectacular; deep, powerful-looking, and golden. Not that she had anything to compare it with, apart from the chests of statues, and marble simply didn't compare with the fascination of warm, smooth flesh.

He could have used the time to put a shirt on, she thought. His entire upper half was naked. Even more naked than before, for he had no old man in his arms this time. And he was quite shameless about it. Grace forced herself to keep her gaze above his chin, but even so she was aware of a deep chest, an expanse of golden skin, a sprinkling of dark hair and two small . . . She tried not to stare. Did men actually have *nipples*? The thought made her blush.

She stared hard at his nose, trying not to look at his nipples. Her fingers itched to touch them, just to know what they felt like.

His gaze seared Grace and his eyes narrowed. "I was worried about you, you know. Why didn't you tell me you were riding for the doctor?"

She instantly felt guilty. "I'm sorry. It seemed the right thing to do at the time. Sir John needed his medicine and the doctor—I couldn't carry the valise, but I could ride and fetch the doctor."

"I thought the horse had run off into the storm and you'd followed it. So I went back and rode for the doctor on my own horse."

She felt guiltier. "I know. I realized what must have happened when I got back to the stables. I'm so sorry. But I thought you'd understand what I'd done. It was the most obvious thing."

He gave her an incredulous look, but all he said was, "I didn't know hired companions could ride."

She shrugged. "Some of us do." It was very hard to concentrate on the conversation with those nipples winking at her. She stared fiercely at his nose.

He raised his brow. "Astride?"

She shrugged again. "Why not?"

He gave another exasperated look, as if to say it should be perfectly obvious why not. "You should have told me you were going."

"I know—but it never occurred to me you'd be worried. All I could think of was that time was of the essence. And besides, you'd never have let me go, would you?"

"No." He frowned. "Is there something wrong with my nose?"

She blushed and looked at his ear. "No. If I hadn't gone, precious time would have been wasted."

"Speaking of precious time, I thought I told you to change into some dry clothes! You've had time enough to do it."

She gave him an incredulous look. "You can talk about inadequate clothing!" She looked pointedly at his chest. It was a mistake. Her hands itched to touch that golden expanse. She folded her arms.

He shrugged. "My shirt was wet."

The shrug drew her attention to his shoulders, so broad and muscular. How had she never known that shoulders could be beautiful?

"Oh, so you think I should walk about nak—" She broke off hurriedly. She should know not to talk at all when she was . . . distracted.

"I would have no objection at all to that," he agreed instantly.

No, of course he wouldn't! "This dress is woolen," she explained to his chin. "Wool holds the heat, whether wet or dry. That's why fishermen wear woolen jerseys."

"I have not the least interest in fishermen's attire," he drawled. "Nor in the properties of wool. I told you to change and I meant it! Do you need any help with buttons or laces? I'm very good with them, very quick and nimble."

He was outrageous! She forced her mind off those naked, muscular shoulders and said with dignity, "No, thank you!"

He hitched up his breeches, distracting her again. "If I catch you in that damp dress again, you won't enjoy the consequences!" He took two long steps down the hall, then paused and turned. A smile hovered around the mobile mouth. "Or maybe you just might."

His smile reminded her of another grievance. "Why didn't you tell me when we first met that you were Lord D'Acre?"

He raised his brows. "What difference would it have made?"

"None," she declared, cross with what she was sure was his deliberate obtuseness. "Except that you are Miss Pettifer's betrothed, which makes your behavior even more atrocious than I thought it was at the time! Whether a groom or a baron, you are still in need of a lesson in manners!" He couldn't possibly forget that he'd kissed her twice. She couldn't.

His eyes crinkled. "You can give me a lesson in anything you like, Bright Eyes." He made it sound . . . almost indecent.

She sniffed, but it was foolish to encourage such grossly improper talk by acknowledging it. "Which is the quickest way to the kitchen?" she asked. "This house, though charming, is something of a rabbit warren."

His brows rose. "You think it's charming?"

"Yes, very. Why? Don't you?"

"Not a bit. It's ugly and inconvenient."

"Hush, do not say so—the gargoyle might hear you and you will hurt his feelings," she said, shocked.

He raised his brows. "Gargoyle?"

"Never say you haven't seen him? He is downstairs, in the beams above the entry hall. Carved in oak, I think, with the most wonderful face."

"And this gargoyle has feelings, you say?"

"Yes, of course. He is the guardian of the house, you see. At the moment he's covered in dust and cobwebs, so the poor fellow must be feeling a bit lonely and neglected."

His mouth quirked. "Indeed?"

"Oh yes," she said airily. "You can tell just by looking at him that he's not the mean and scary kind of gargoyle, but kind and wise and benevolent. He will bring love to this house, just you see."

His face changed. "I doubt it."

She continued, "And your house is not ugly at all—it's delightfully quirky and a little eccentric and it could be made very beautiful, with just a little care."

He didn't look the slightest bit interested.

She pointed to the stone stairway behind her. "Those stairs, for instance. I love the way they've been worn away by countless feet through the ages and that you and I can place our feet in the dips made by generations of your ancestors. Doesn't that thrill you?"

"Not a bit. It makes the stairs dangerous." He turned away.

"Oh." She was nonplussed by his blunt response. "The kitchen, if you please," she reminded him. "Where is it?"

"I have not the least idea."

"What? But you must. This is your—"

"I've never been here before today."

Her mouth fell open. "But this is your ancestral home!"

"My ancestors'. Not mine. You probably know the house better than I, since you found the bedchamber for Sir John." He frowned as if the purpose of her question had only just occurred to him. "Why do you want the kitchen?"

"I need hot water," she said absently, her thoughts caught up in the conundrum of a man who had never before seen the family—his father's—house. And yet he was the legitimate son—he could not have inherited the title otherwise . . .

"Ah, an excellent move," he said in quite another tone. Distinctly mischievous.

"I beg your pardon?" His tone made her wary.

"You were going to give me a good scrubbing, remember?" He placed his thumbs in the waistband of his breeches. "So let's find the kitchen together and you can start scrubbing me straight away." He winked. "I'll warn you now, though I am, in general, a fine, strapping specimen, there are parts of me that are . . . delicate and should be treated accordingly."

She utterly refused to look at where those large thumbs were hooked. She said with dignity, "The *only* reason I wanted hot water is because Mel—Miss Pettifer wants a cup of tea."

He immediately looked mournful. "So, you won't scrub me?"

"I'd sooner boil you in oil!" she told him sweetly.

He chuckled and strode off down the hall. She watched him go, admiring his long-legged stride. The sight of his naked shoulders and back was magnificent.

Scrub him indeed. She sniffed, trying not to smile. What nonsense the man talked.

The whole time she was searching for the kitchen, her mind mulled over the question: how was it possible for a man to grow to his age—he must be nearing thirty, she guessed, and yet never have set eyes on his father's house? It was a mystery. He was a mystery. One minute all mischief and teasing, the next, withdrawn . . .

And oh, how he appealed to her on every level . . .

EVENTUALLY GRACE FOUND THE KITCHEN AND SURVEYED IT gloomily. A stone-flagged, cavernous room, it was unbelievably old-fashioned. She could easily imagine a medieval feast being prepared here; whole pigs and sheep on spits and huge, bubbling cauldrons. Not any civilized meal. There wasn't even a proper kitchen range. She would have to light a fire and then sling a pot or something over it.

Her sister Faith had once told her about how the soldiers' wives traveling with the army on the Peninsular had learned to live off the land to supplement the unreliable army rations. Faith seemed to think it a fine and clever skill. At the time Grace had not appreciated it.

Now, as her stomach rumbled, she realized what a skill

it was. Melly, Sir John, and she needed to be fed and there were no signs that Lord D'Acre intended to do anything about it.

She remembered the kitchen garden outside. There would be vegetables there. Vegetables could be made into soup. Could Grace march with an army? Could she provide for her family? She could. She was Grace Merridew, soup maker!

She'd watched Cook a hundred times when she was a little girl, though she'd only ever cut out biscuits or mixed cakes under Cook's eagle eye. But how hard could making soup be? It was just chopping, boiling, and stirring. Surely.

She hurried out to the walled kitchen garden. At first glance she could see nothing but weeds. Then she saw some were in fact herbs, wildly overgrown and going to seed, but still useable. She picked chervil and thyme and parsley.

An investigation of a feathery clump of green produced a few odd-shaped carrots. Taking heart, she pulled up more sprawling plants and found some potatoes and a turnip. Combined with the barley and the slightly withered onions she'd found in the pantry, these would make a fine soup.

She took the vegetables into the scullery and scrubbed them clean, then laid them out on the table with a feeling of satisfaction.

She looked at the big, empty grate and realized with a sinking feeling that before Grace Merridew, soup maker, came Grace Merridew, fire builder. Bother. The kitchen had no conveniently set fire, all ready to light, as Sir John's room had. She couldn't even find a coal scuttle or wood box.

She needed to find some fuel. She hoped to heaven it

was not all wet from the storm. She lit a lantern and went back outside to search the outbuildings. The first was horridly cobwebby but in it, to her relief, she found a large pile of dry wood and a stump and an ax. There were a few small chips of wood scattered around the stump, but nowhere near enough for a fire. And the big chunks of wood in the pile were enormous—too big for her to carry.

She looked at the ax in dismay. Then took a deep breath. She was going to travel the world and have adventures. She ought to be able to make a fire. Grace Merridew, wood chopper?

She dragged a chunk of wood over to the big stump, the surface of which was scarred with a thousand ax marks. She put the chunk on the stump, then picked up the ax. She felt the blade. Sharp, but not so sharp it would cut her foot off if she missed. Thank goodness.

She took a deep breath and lifted it over her shoulder in the way she'd seen men do it. Then she heaved it downward with all her might! It came down with a satisfying thunk—and embedded itself in the floor. Bother!

She battled to get the ax out of the floor then tried again, aiming more carefully. Thunk! The ax was sticking into the wood, but otherwise nothing had changed. It obviously took more than one blow.

Grace wrestled the ax out and swung it again. This time it bounced right off the wood, jarring her wrist and arm horribly. It really hurt. She rubbed her wrist and glared at the ax. She would chop wood! She would!

She swung the ax again. Thunk! It hit the wood but didn't split it. Chop! She tried again. And again. And again. Her wrist was very sore, but she was getting better and finally she got it right, as the wood split with a tearing sound. It was almost, though not quite, in two pieces.

Triumphant, she grabbed it and tried to pull it apart but it was stiff and her hand was sore and it slipped. “Owww!” she cried out.

“What the hell are you doing?” a deep voice behind her growled.

Chapter Four

At times it is folly to hasten; at other times, to delay. The wise do everything in its proper time.

OVID

GRACE WAS TOO AGONIZED TO RESPOND. HER HAND WAS ON FIRE. She found herself spun around to face him.

"Why are you chopping wood? That's not work for—" He broke off, frowning. "You've hurt yourself." His eyes dropped to where she was cradling her hand and he muttered something foreign and said, "Let me see."

Irrationally she tried to pull her hand away. He effortlessly prevented her. "Don't be silly. I can help." He gently prised her fingers off the injured hand. "It's a splinter, a big one."

He lifted her hand, examining it carefully in the lamplight, handling her with exquisite care. Grace bit her lip. The trick with pain, she knew, was to focus on something else.

She glanced around. She could focus on the spider creeping along the beam overhead, or she could focus on him.

She didn't like spiders. She focused on him.

Mesmerized by the play of lamplight and shadow over

his strong, narrow face, she let her gaze skim the sculpted planes of his cheekbones, the sharp angle of his jaw, dark and rough with the promise of a beard. He was so close she could see the fine grain of his skin, smell him, a faint exotic fragrance threaded through with the scent of man and horses. His mouth was set in a hard line, his lips compressed, angry perhaps.

It was a beautiful mouth. Even when she thought him an insolent, raggle-taggle gypsy, she'd noticed his hard, beautiful mouth, sculpted in clear, sharp lines by some divine blade. It was bracketed by two sharp lines, cutting deep. Not laugh lines; despite that wicked gleam she'd spotted in his eye on several occasions, he didn't look much like a man who'd gone through life laughing.

He pressed the skin around the splinter gently and she gasped as the pain shot through her. "I'll get it out, don't worry," he said in a deep voice that was meant to be reassuring but which reverberated through her in a most unsettling way.

It was bad enough when he was teasing and being scandalous. Now, when he was gentle and sincere . . .

Thank goodness he'd put his shirt back on.

She managed to say in a light tone, "No, it's all right. You surprised me, that's all." Merridew girls knew how to handle pain. And they knew better than to expose vulnerability to any man, stranger or not. At least Grace did. She was different from her sisters.

His gaze didn't shift; she felt it burning into her for several endless moments. He was so close, she could feel his breath on her skin. For one long instant, she thought he was going to kiss her. She glanced up at the spider on the beam. "Look at all those cobwebs. Your *fiancée*, Miss Pettifer, would hate this place. She loathes spiders." That would remind him.

"Does she?" he said in an uninterested voice and returned his attention to her splinter. Her hand throbbed. She stared at his bent head. His hair was thick and black and waved just a little. It was a little longer than was fashionable. One lock fell over his forehead. Her hand lifted, as if to smooth it back, but she caught herself in time.

Good God. She'd been about to slide her fingers into that thick, inky pelt. Would it be soft to touch or springy? She shivered. She didn't want to know. He was a stranger, her friend Melly's affianced husband. What had come over her?

Exotic, that was the word for him. Exotic and somehow . . . alluring. What nonsense, she told herself. Men couldn't be alluring.

The lines around his eyes, they'd been made by sunshine. His skin was tanned, unfashionably dark. And what ancestry had given him those eyes, those strange, compelling eyes. They were—She jumped as the dark sweep of lashes rose and she found him staring back at her. His eyes, his mouth were only inches from hers. Mesmerized, she stood caught in his gaze for what seemed like forever. She swallowed and licked her lips.

His gaze dropped to her mouth and intensified. She could hardly breathe.

"I don't suppose you have a pair of tweezers on you?"

She gave a shaky laugh at the prosaic question. "Of course not."

The golden eyes heated. He gave a faint, fatalistic shrug. "Then I'll have to do it the old-fashioned way." Without warning his mouth settled over her palm, over her injury, warm and firm.

The unexpectedness of it caused her to curl her hand

involuntarily; she found her fingers cupping his face. Before she could move, he clamped his hand over hers preventing her from moving it away. His gaze locked with hers. She could not break it. She felt helpless, unable to move as she was drawn deeper into that compelling golden intensity.

He was just extracting a splinter, for heaven's sake. She closed her eyes to shut him out.

It was a mistake.

Without that glittering predator gaze on her, her other senses were free. Free? They ran rampant, though she didn't move a muscle. His unshaven jaw was hard and prickled deliciously against her soft palm. His tongue explored her skin, delicately, almost sensuously. Every tiny motion rippled through her body and gathered momentum, setting off strange quivers deep inside her. Her toes, locked in her sensible half boots, curled. A long shudder rippled up her spine and her knees felt suddenly weak. She found herself clutching his arm with her other hand.

He moved, angling his body around her, to get a better grip, she supposed, but oh! He was so close. His big, hard body was half wrapped around her.

She tried not to notice, to block it out as she had with the pain—he was just extracting a splinter—but the intense heat of him seeped into her, making her feel helpless, itchy, restless. His skin was cool but it warmed under her touch. Her fingers moved of their own accord against the hard line of his jawbone, testing that delicious abrasiveness again. She willed them to be still.

Dominic moved, bringing her closer. Slender, soft, and unwillingly aroused. He could smell the moist female scent of her. His pulse leapt in response. He clamped down on it, hard. Now was not the time. Not while she was in pain.

This enchanting little freckled companion would be his. There was no question in his mind.

He breathed in the scent of her again; she was intoxicating. Her small, soft palm cupped his jaw delicately, tentatively. He felt her hesitate, felt her fingers flutter under his, half nervousness and half exploration, and he smiled.

It would be good between them. Better than good. She was shy, she was inexperienced, but he knew: she was becoming aroused. He could sense it.

He closed his eyes briefly and let his mouth and tongue explore her palm, seeking the precise angle of the splinter's entry. The taste of her skin, of her blood, sparked something deep inside him, arousing his more primitive instincts. He forced them back under control.

His teeth bit gently down, pressing the fleshy part just below her thumb, where the splinter was lodged. He knew it must hurt, but she gave no sign. He let his tongue circle the spot, soothing, teasing, pleasuring her shamelessly. Her body softened against him, and he felt the delicate, subtle shivers that she tried so hard to hide from him. He pulled her closer and felt her stiffen, then gradually soften again. Oh yes, she would be his very soon.

He positioned her hand carefully, intensified the pleasure and then, without warning, sucked hard. She gasped at the mixture of pain and unexpected pleasure, and then suddenly he was gripping the end of the splinter between his teeth and drawing it firmly, smoothly out.

He spat it out into his other hand. "A big one. Let's see if anything was left behind." He lifted her hand to the light again. "It doesn't do to leave even the tiniest splinter in. I knew a man who died of a splinter once. Went septic on him and poisoned him in the end."

"Thank you for the reassurance," she said dryly.

He liked that tart astringency about her. She was flushed and flustered, yet determined he wouldn't see it. She would not come to him easily. The predator in him smiled. He liked it that she would be no easy conquest.

He scrutinized her palm with dispassion. "I can't see anything," he told her. "But soak it in hot water, as hot as you can stand, for ten minutes or so. And keep an eye on it. If it gets red and sore, it's infected and we'll need to poultice it."

Grace thanked him and moved shakily to the doorway. Her legs felt decidedly unreliable.

What had just happened?

It couldn't be called a kiss, but . . . oh . . . my. It was a relief to move into the fresh, rain-washed air. She didn't know what had come over her in the darkened outbuilding. Her knees had almost turned to jelly back there when he was . . . sucking on her palm.

She shivered again. Perhaps she was catching a chill after all. She felt hot and shaky and her pulse was tumultuous. He didn't seem the slightest bit unsettled.

She tried to gather her composure.

He straightened his coat. "Now, I'm off into the village. I'll arrange for some villagers to start work here tomorrow. Have you any idea how much help you'll need?"

She blinked at him, but he said impatiently, "Oh, never mind. I'll just send a dozen or so up and you can pick out who you need to help you. Two weeks' work only. I have no intention of setting up house here."

Grace's jaw dropped. He expected *her* to pick out *his* servants?

"And in the meantime, don't let me catch you doing anything so foolish as chopping wood again!"

She bristled at his bossiness. Did he think she was chopping for her own entertainment? She said in a docile-sounding voice, "You said I should bathe my hand in hot water?"

He gave a curt nod. "Yes. Very hot."

"And that I'm not to chop firewood?"

"No, of course not!"

She bared her teeth sweetly. "Then how would you suggest I get very hot water?" She enjoyed the look that stole over his face as it occurred to him belatedly just why she'd been chopping the wood in the first place.

He pulled off his coat and rolled up the sleeves of his shirt. His forearms were as sunburned as any gypsy's, strong and sinewy. His shirt was made of very white fine linen, so fine it was semitransparent. He set a large chunk of wood on its end on the stump.

"Stand back," he ordered and Grace obediently retreated, fascinated by this aspect of him.

Lord D'Acre, wood chopper!

He spat on his hands and swung the ax. Crash! It split the log in half. He picked up the largest piece and placed it back on the stump and swung the ax again. Again it split the wood cleanly in half. He stacked the split pieces in a neat pile to the side, and collected the smaller chips and tossed them onto a piece of sacking nearby.

"You've done this before," she said cleverly.

He gave her a baleful look from under his brows and fetched another piece of wood. He demolished that in one blow. He fetched another. Crash! And another. Crash!

She stood watching him, mesmerized by the swinging ax and the smooth rhythm and pull of his muscles. The fabric of his shirt clung to his body. His face darkened with the exertion and she could see a faint film of sweat on his brow.

He was a magnificent sight; raw, primitive, angry. And exciting.

She swallowed. She had come here to rescue Melly from this man. She watched his muscles bunch and flex, smooth, powerful masculinity in action. Would Melly truly want to be rescued from this?

She thought about the way he'd removed her splinter.

Her hands crept to her mouth. What if she'd got a splinter in her lip?

Dominic was furious with himself. It was his fault she was standing there in her damp and dowdy woolen dress, watching him with big eyes, with a ruddy great gash in her hand. The skin of her hands was so soft, almost silken. She'd never done manual work in her life. He ought to have anticipated the need for fire, for hot water. But dammit, he'd intended to send Sir John and his daughter back to London with a flea in their ears. Arriving uninvited. Forcing Dominic to set foot in a place he'd sworn never to lay eyes on!

And bringing this big-eyed, soft-skinned girl, dammit!

He was all stirred up. And not just by coming here!

He could feel her watching him. She hadn't made a sound while he'd got that splinter out. Not a peep. One gasp when he'd caught her off guard, that's all. Every other woman he'd known—except one—would have wailed and wept all over him.

His mother had been able to take pain in silence, too. It was something some women learned. The hard way.

He swung the ax again and again, splitting each log cleanly in half and half again. It was strangely satisfying.

He needed to do something to dissipate the tension banked up inside him.

He had the scent of her in his nostrils, the taste of her in his mouth. And he wanted more. Dammit! He hadn't planned on this. But Little Miss Freckles, with her soft, silken skin and her big blue eyes fired his blood in a way that no woman had fired it before.

Finally a stack of wood stood in a neat pile and Dominic laid down his ax. He felt sweaty and dirty and not a lot calmer than when he'd started. He bent and collected a pile of wood, bracing it against his chest.

"Take the chips on that sacking," he ordered. "We'll use them to start the fire."

She looped up the four corners of the sacking and ran ahead of him to open the kitchen door. He tried not to watch the sweet sway of her rounded hips and bottom as she moved, but the damp wool clung to her body and he had no choice. His mouth dried, watching.

On the big kitchen table, an array of fresh, clean vegetables were laid out. Dominic frowned. "What's all this?"

"Vegetables from your garden. I hope you don't mind. I thought I'd make soup for supper. There's nothing else."

His eyebrows rose. Was that a faint jibe at his lack of hospitality? The cheeky minx. He dumped the wood with a clatter beside the big, old fireplace. "Hand me that kindling."

She bent gracefully and placed it on the floor beside him. He began to lay the fire.

"Any paper?"

She passed him an old newspaper. Her fingers brushed his and he caught the scent of her again. Damp wool. Damp woman. Dammit!

He crumpled the paper and swiftly arranged chips of

wood over and around it. "I've been meaning to ask you about the cutting of the traces on your coach."

"Why? The horses were all tangled up and they were upset and jumpy. Cutting the traces was the quickest way to free them."

He laid the final pieces of kindling. "I agree. But where did you get the knife?"

"I had it with me, of course."

He gave her an incredulous look. "You carry a knife?"

She raised her eyebrows disdainfully. "Yes, I try never to travel unarmed."

He frowned. "But ladies don't—" He broke off. She wasn't a lady. She was a hired companion, no doubt used to fending for herself. Probably needing to fend for herself. Look how she'd tried to chop the wood.

But she knew what he'd been going to say and took him up on it. "Ladies do so travel armed. My mother always did. So do two of my sisters and my great aunt, and several other ladies I know."

He doubted very much whether the women she spoke of were *ladies* at all. The only ladies he knew who routinely went about armed were ladies of the night. But all he said was, "Not with knives, I'll wager."

"No, they prefer pistols. But my sort-of-sister-in-law and another friend of the family both carry knives." She frowned and corrected herself. "Actually, Elinore's is more of a, a stabbing pin. Cassie's is a proper knife, though."

A *stabbing pin*? Good grief! But he had a clearer idea now of the sort of background Greystoke came from. Some hired companions were women of good family, fallen on hard times. Others, especially the younger variety, were making an attempt to better their situation. Greystoke was of the latter variety, he decided: such small details gave her away. He would be doing her a great favor in removing her from the company of such unsavory women.

He had a sudden vision of her running through the rain, her wet clothes clinging to her body. He could see no place she could have carried a knife. Was she teasing him? "Where did you carry it—your knife?"

"In my boot," she replied carelessly. "Do you need the tinder box now?"

Wordlessly he put out his hand for it. In her boot? He glanced at her feet. The toes of a pair of boots were peeping out from the mud-spattered gray hem. He could just flip the hem up and see if she was teasing or not . . .

"You don't believe me, do you? Well, see for yourself." She thrust a foot out and pulled back her hem just enough for him to see a bone handle protruding from her half boots.

Good God! She did carry a knife in her boot. She also had lovely calves. "That's interesting," he began.

She gave a satisfied nod. "I told y—"

"Not a single freckle on your leg at all." He struck the flint.

She crossly twitched her hem back into place.

"Of course the other leg might be covered with hundreds of them. Unpredictable things, freckles. Pop up in the most interesting places." He struck the flint again.

She made a huffy noise but refused to rise to his bait.

He struck the flint a third time. His fingers felt like thumbs. He was too aware of her. Clamping down on his instincts, he finally got a flame going and lit the fire.

"You're very quick at lighting fires," she commented.

He darted her a glance to see if she was speaking metaphorically. She wasn't. He made a few last-minute adjustments to the fire, and then straightened.

"That should last the rest of the night." He turned toward her with a purposeful expression. *"Now."*

Grace was startled out of her brooding reverie. "What do you mean, *now*?" She didn't trust the look in his eyes.

"I told you to get out of that damp dress."

"And I will, as soon as—"

"I'm not accustomed to having my orders disobeyed, Greystoke."

Grace skittered away, intending to put the big kitchen table between them but like lightning, he reached out and snagged her wrist. "Come with me, Mistress . . . Greystoke." He towed her out of the kitchen and back to the entry hall.

She fumed silently. High-handed wretch. She was getting fed up with being dragged places by him. She had to run to keep up with his long strides.

He stopped in front of the mound of baggage. "Which of these is yours?"

"That one."

He snatched it up and marched her with it back to the kitchen. He dumped it on the kitchen table and flipped it open. Ignoring her protests, he rummaged through her valise, pulling out everything she would need for a complete change of clothes. He didn't even hesitate, but pulled out a pair of lace-trimmed drawers, a muslin chemise, and a lacy petticoat without the slightest qualms. He lifted the lacy white underthings in one big, tanned hand, dangled them in front of her, and raised an eyebrow. "Pretty fancy for a paid companion. I can't wait to see them on you. Or off, as the case may be."

Grace was scandalized. She snatched at the underclothes, but he jerked his hand away and she missed. A wicked look on his face, he held her underclothes high above his head while he rummaged with his other hand for stockings.

She was furious. "Have you no shame?"

The golden eyes glinted. "Not a lot. Do you?"

Blushing enough for both of them, she snatched her unmentionables from him. He laughed softly.

"Now, which dress do you want to wear? This gray thing or this other gray thing. My, my, what a lot of gray. Tell me, do you wear gray because of your name or—"

She slammed down the lid of the valise. He managed to pull his hand back in time. "I can choose my own clothes," she muttered, still furious with him, but a little shocked that she'd almost trapped his fingers.

"Yes, but you didn't," he said with silky menace. "I don't know how many times I told you to change, but—"

"Three."

"What?"

She shrugged. "You told me three times. It might have been four. I forget." She gave him a sweet, mocking smile.

"Then why didn't you change?"

She shrugged again. "You can't tell me what to do. You're not my master."

He placed his hands on the table and regarded her from under lowered black brows. "No, and you're not my mistress—yet! I am, however, the master of this house. And I ordered you to change. And you will find, Little Miss Bright Eyes, that my orders are to be obeyed."

"Oh, stop fussing! And don't call me Bright Eyes! My name is Greystoke. And I told you I never catch cold. I told you I'd change as soon as I have time. But in case it has escaped your attention, Sir John is extremely ill, and this great barn of a house of yours is without servants of any kind. So someone had to make up a bed for Sir John. Someone had to light a fire. Someone has to provide hot water for tea. And that someone is, apparently"—she bared her teeth at him—"the hired companion!"

She waited, expecting him to apologize. He pulled a watch from the pocket of his breeches and flipped it open. "You have ten minutes. I will wait outside while you change."

She stamped her foot in frustration. "Did you hear nothing I said? Sir John is—"

"Being attended to by the doctor. And nobody will expire from lack of tea. Nine minutes," he said calmly and strolled toward the door. "If you are not in dry clothes when I return, Mistress Greystoke, I will strip that ugly gray thing off you, and whatever you are wearing underneath. Then I will dry you . . . thoroughly. Then—eventually—I will put you into those delightful white lacy things and finally, and most reluctantly, I will cover you in another ghastly gray dress."

"Y-y-you wouldn't dare!" His words had conjured up shockingly explicit images in her mind—visions of big, brown gypsy hands smoothing white lace over her bare skin . . .

She shivered.

He turned and shot her a glinting gold look. "Oh I'll dare, Miss Freckles, and having not a shred of shame in me, I will enjoy the exercise very much." His gaze roamed over her. "I've never seen freckles quite like yours, and my mind keeps speculating about whether you have freckles all over your body. Or not. And if not, where do the freckles stop?"

Grace's hands flew defensively to her chest.

His eyes followed their movement. "There, you think?" His gaze trailed insolently down past her middle. "Or lower down? Not as far as your ankles—I know that already." He gave a lopsided, wicked grin. "Well, we shall see."

"Over my dead body you will!"

He laughed softly. "Oh, you won't be dead. You'll be very much alive, Greystoke. Eight minutes." And he shut the door.

Chapter Five

Go to your bosom; Knock there,
and ask your heart what it doth know.

WILLIAM SHAKESPEARE

For fully thirty seconds Grace debated whether to put his threat to the test. He wouldn't really strip her. Would he? He couldn't possibly behave in so scandalous a manner. She was a Merrid—! She stopped in midthought. She was not Miss Merridew, of the Norfolk Merridews. To him, she was just somebody's hired companion. And to many gentlemen, servants were fair game.

He would enjoy it, too, the scoundrel! Her fingers flew to unbutton her wet dress.

Keeping a wary eye on the closed kitchen door, she rummaged in her valise. She refused to wear any of the clothes he'd touched. The mere thought of his strong brown fingers rifling through her lacy underclothes made her hot with—with fury! Her skin prickled with it.

She stripped off her damp clothes and scrambled into dry ones, cursing him with every rude word she could think of. She did not know nearly enough bad words to do his perfidy justice.

She fastened the last button with a mixed feeling of triumph and . . . anticlimax? No, relief. The door had stayed shut. She'd never dressed so fast in her life. She even had a minute to spare, she thought.

She forced a composed look on her face and looked around for something to do. She was not going to give him the satisfaction of knowing he'd flustered her. Soup!

She scraped carrots and chopped them into chunks. It was a bit awkward, cutting with her sore hand. The carrots were quite woody. They'd soften in the cooking, she hoped. She chopped the herbs. Luckily the splinter had gone into her left hand. She picked up the onion and was about to behead it, then put it down. If that black-browed devil saw her with red eyes, he'd think he'd made her cry and she would *not* give him the satisfaction. He did not have the power to make her cry. No man did!

She found a small pot, and transferred some of the hot water into it. She waited until it came to the boil, then tossed the carrots in and stirred them around. They bobbed woodily. She covered them with herbs.

It must be well past fifteen minutes! The fiend! She returned to her vegetables.

After another ten minutes, the kitchen door opened and the black-browed fiend sauntered in. He'd changed into a fresh shirt and coat and another pair of buckskin breeches—thankfully! They didn't cling to his form nearly so much as the wet pair had. His hair had been combed back, but it was overlong and a lock of it fell over his forehead. A drop of water glimmered at the end of it. Not that she cared.

"Miss Pettifer was wondering where her cup of tea is, and the doctor would like his with no milk and two spoonfuls of sugar."

Grace glowered at him. She'd forgotten all about the tea Melly had craved. She seized a brown earthenware teapot and banged it down on the table. He hadn't even mentioned her dress or . . . or anything.

He sauntered toward her like a lazy big predator. Her pulse leapt but she didn't turn a hair. She ladled tea into the pot with as serene an expression as she could muster. She would not let it show, she would not.

A muscle twitched in his cheek. "I gather Miss Pettifer likes her tea extremely strong."

Bother! She'd lost track of how much tea she'd put in. Grace gave him a limpid look. "Yes, she does," she lied. That drop of water was very distracting.

"Twelve spoonfuls is very strong."

"Is it?"

"The doctor prefers his tea weak."

"Does he?"

"But then, I'm sure you'd know how to make tea better than I would. Coffee is more my brew."

It was infuriating, Grace thought, how the right things to say never came when you needed them. She ought to say something clever and cutting about the devil's brew. But she couldn't think of anything clever and cutting, not with that lock of black hair falling over his forehead like that.

"Your hair is about to drip."

He pushed back the lock of hair indifferently. "How is your hand?"

She thrust it into the fold of her skirt. "All right."

He nodded at her soup pot. "What is that you're making?"

"Soup?"

"Really? How enterprising." He strolled over and glanced into the pot. His mouth twitched. "Made soup before, have you?"

"Frequently," she lied. "In any case, there is not much choice, is there?" Hah! That was pretty cutting.

He stood watching her chopping at the turnip. "Would you like me to do that?"

"No, thank you. I can manage perfectly well."

He nodded at her hand, wrapped in his handkerchief. "Is it still hurting?"

"No, it's much better. Thank you."

He gave her an enigmatic look. "You're not cross with me?"

"Good heavens, no," she assured him in a gracious tone. "It's not your fault you were brought up a mannerless wretch with no moral standards whatsoever! For the fire and the wood, I'm quite grateful."

White teeth gleamed. "I don't want your gratitude, Greystoke," he said softly. He prowled two steps closer and before she knew it his hands were on her waist and he was pulling her against him. "I want you," he purred and covered her mouth with his.

Grace stiffened and tried to pull her head away. He took no notice. His lips moved over hers gently, with lazy assurance, as if she were his for the taking. She tried to push him away, but he simply wrapped his arms around her.

She tried to kick him: her brother-in-law Gideon had taught her where to kick a man who was annoying her, but Lord D'Acre blocked her cunning move with ease. Without breaking the kiss he pressed her back against the kitchen wall, covering her body with his in a shockingly intimate move. She could feel every hot, hard inch of him, his mouth firm and demanding, his broad, hard chest crushing the softness of her breasts, his long, hard horseman's thighs pressing against her. His heat soaked into her.

She tried to say something, to protest, but the moment she opened her mouth he took shameless advantage, deepening the kiss, his mouth seeking, demanding a response she hadn't known was in her. She was melting under his heat, spinning, clutching onto him as if he could stop her from falling.

She slid her fingers into the thick pelt of his midnight hair and kissed him back, needing more, more. The taste of him seeped into her, as if it was something she'd craved for for as long as she could remember.

He moved against her restlessly and through the layers of his breeches and her skirts, the hard press of his thighs, of his hips rubbed against her made her legs tremble. It made her want to climb his big, hard body the way a cat climbed a tree, clinging on with her claws, rubbing her soft belly against him.

Her knees buckled and he moved to push his thigh between hers, rubbing and rocking with a rhythm that her body sang to. She moaned and clung and pressed her body and mouth to his, seeking she knew not what . . .

It took her a long dazed moment to realize that he'd released her. A sharp withdrawal of heat that chilled her. Bewildered, unable to take her eyes off him, she touched a shaking hand to her mouth. What had just happened? She was panting like an animal, gasping for breath as if she'd run a mile. He was, too.

His eyes ran over her in a hungry, possessive manner that half thrilled, half shocked her.

She raised a hand to her chest in an automatic, age-old gesture and felt a curl under her fingers. She looked down and suddenly realized her hair had come out of its usual knot and was all over the place. She pulled it back, then realized her skirt was rucked up and caught between her thighs. Thighs that felt trembly and the place between them hot and moist and achy. Hastily she smoothed her dress back into a semblance of order.

Then the realization hit her. She'd just been thoroughly kissed by her best friend's fiancé. *Her best friend's fiancé!* And worse, she'd kissed him back in a way she'd never kissed any man before. With an abandon that frightened her a little. And thrilled her in a way she knew ought to be shocking.

She wiped her mouth with her hand, as if she could wipe away all trace of the kiss. The kiss! Could it possibly have been only one kiss? It had shaken her to the core.

"It won't do any good," he said with soft amusement. "My taste is in your mouth forever, now. As you are in mine."

The shocking claim and the lazy possessiveness in his voice snapped her spine straight. She scrubbed at her lips. "It is not!" It was. She could still taste the hot masculine tang of him. "And—and if it is, a good rinse with vinegar and water will fix it!"

He threw back his head and laughed. Then he said softly, "It won't work. I'm in your blood, Greystoke. And you're in mine. And the only thing to do about it is to follow our instincts."

"Excellent!" she said briskly and when his brow shot up in surprise, she added sweetly, "My strongest instinct is to box your ears!"

He chuckled and shook his head knowingly. "You had that opportunity before, remember?"

She flushed, remembering how he'd caught her hands with such ease, and how later she'd buried her fingers in that thick pelt of glossy hair. His reminder of her weakness flicked her on the raw. "You are a disgrace. You are an engaged man—how dare you make such advances to me while you are engaged!"

"As to that, I suggest you don't fret about what you cannot change," he said. "In any case, my agreement with Miss Pettifer is for a marriage of convenience. It is a business arrangement, nothing more. Miss Pettifer has no feelings for me, I assure you."

She knew that but she was astounded at his casual attitude. "How can you talk of marriage in such a—such a cold-blooded way?"

He shrugged. "Marriage is a cold-blooded institution."

"That's a terrible thing to say!"

Her vehemence seemed to surprise him. "It's a fact of life. People marry for money, for property, for security, to improve their status, and to beget heirs in order to preserve wealth within a family. If that's not cold-blooded, I don't know what is."

"People also marry for love."

He made a scornful sound. "No, that's just what they *call it*. I can give you another name for it—lust! A financial basis is much sounder."

"Only for the man," Grace argued. "Women lose their financial independence when they marry."

"Exactly, which is why I've never been able to understand why so many women so willingly give that up for the sake of being married."

Grace was surprised. She'd never heard a man take that point of view. "They probably believe love is more important that financial independence."

"More fool they."

Grace was inclined to agree with him. It was the way she felt herself—but only for herself. Most women didn't see things her way at all. She thought of Melly. "Most women want children."

He nodded. "True enough. The maternal instinct will out. And men want heirs. Property and heirs, that's what the institution of marriage is for."

Grace thought of Aunt Gussie's second marriage, to her beloved Argentine husband. "No, not always."

She'd never forgotten Aunt Gussie telling her about it: *"He could have married a stunning young virgin—he had the pick of Argentine society."* Aunt Gussie had smiled like the cat who ate the cream. *"But he wanted me. A short, plump, childless English widow in her third decade. Now that was a grand romantic adventure, I tell you. That man taught me the meaning of passion! We sizzled, my dear, positively sizzled!"* And Aunt Gussie had sighed dreamily.

At the time, Grace hadn't been able to imagine any man making her sizzle. She knew differently now.

The way Lord D'Acre had made her feel felt a lot like . . . sizzle.

Then again, he could probably make any female sizzle, the rat! She had to remember he was a lord and he thought her a paid companion. Gentlemen always dallied with servants, careless of their feelings, as if servants didn't have feelings, didn't have hearts that broke. No matter how much he sizzled and made her sizzle, she couldn't take him seriously. He didn't even believe in marriage.

She thought of her sisters, who had all found loving, passionate, loyal husbands. "Some marriages are wonderful, full of love, and happiness, and warmth.

Lord D'Acre snorted. "I'd never have thought a girl who carried a knife in her boot would believe in such fairy tales, Greyst—what the devil is your first name, anyway? You don't want me to call you Bright Eyes, and I can't keep calling you Greystoke . . ." He smiled like a self-satisfied tiger. "Not after all we've shared."

"I don't have a first name. Just Greystoke." She took a determined step away from him and said lightly, "What do you imagine we've shared, Lord D'Acre? You know nothing about me. You are betrothed to Miss Pettifer and even if you know nothing about loyalty—and, and love—I do! Now go away and do whatever you were planning to do before I interrupted you!" She shooed him away.

"You're wrong, Little Miss No-first-name. I know a great deal about—what did you call it?—oh, yes, *love*." The sultry, drawn-out way he said the word was almost indecent! "But if you want to instruct me further—"

"Out!" She pointed at the door. Hands on hips, she waited for him to leave. She could not believe she'd just ordered a man out of his own kitchen.

And naturally he wasn't about to obey her.

He grinned, as if her imperious demeanor amused him, and for a moment she thought he was going to grab her again and kiss her senseless, so when he finally moved, she jumped, expecting him to lunge.

Instead, he fetched a few more loads of wood and stacked them beside the hearth, just to show her who was lord of this castle. And who was the paid companion.

She watched. She wanted to kick him for his obtuseness. And for lighting her fire. And for kissing her. And worst of all, for making her want to kiss him back.

It had all seemed so simple; disguise herself as a companion, and be there to give Melly the courage to tell her father she didn't want a cold-blooded marriage with a cold-blooded lord.

We sizzled, my dear, positively sizzled!

This lord was far from cold-blooded. She watched him stacking more wood on the fire. He was just stubborn, thick-headed, and idiotic! *Marriage is a cold-blooded institution*—indeed!

He made a few last-minute adjustments to the fire. "That should last the rest of the night." He straightened. "Well, I'm off."

He strolled past her. She held her breath and locked her knees. His coat brushed against her and she caught a faint whiff of his scent. He smelled the same as he tasted. Exotic. Forbidden. Wicked. Irresistible.

She wiped her mouth again, as if it could remove the taste of him from her consciousness. *My taste is in your mouth forever.* It was not. It was *not*!

His hand was on the doorknob of the outside door when she remembered to ask, "Where are you going?"

He turned, a sardonic look on his face. "The village tavern does excellent meat pies, I'm told. And after all that wood chopping I've worked up a fine appetite. Good evening."

Meat pies? Grace's stomach rumbled as he closed the door behind him. She looked at the carrots bobbing unsinkably in green-flecked dishwater. *Meat pies?*

Lord D'Acre, spawn of the Devil!

"SO THIS IS WHERE YOU ARE. I HAVE SEARCHED AND SEARCHED AND I couldn't find a soul." Melly entered the kitchen. "The doctor has gone. He said he wouldn't wait for the tea, after all."

"How is your father?"

"Oh, Grace, I'm so worried about him. He looks so ill

and he keeps asking for a . . . for a m-minister." Her face crumpled.

"Oh, Melly." Grace put down the knife and hugged her friend.

"The doctor has bled him and bled him and—" She broke off, wiping her eyes. "I cannot believe it is doing Papa any good. He's sleeping now, but he's so weak—much weaker than he was before."

Grace frowned. Great-Uncle Oswald had strong opinions about doctors and he was scathing on the subject of those who bled patients at every opportunity. "Have you asked the doctor not to bleed him anymore?"

Melly nodded. "Yes, but he took no notice. You know how it is."

Grace did know how it was. "Well, let us see how your papa is in the morning. And perhaps there is another doctor in the vicinity—we could get a second opinion." She picked up the knife and resumed chopping vegetables.

"The doctor said he'd be back in the morning. Perhaps we could talk to him together." Melly frowned as she became aware of the carnage on the table. "What on earth are you doing?"

"Making soup." Grace hacked at a turnip. It was a very old, very tough turnip. Her injured hand throbbed and her stomach kept rumbling. The thought of hot meat pies had set it off. Blast him!

Melly peered at the array of old vegetables dubiously. "I didn't know you could cook."

"Anyone can cook," Grace declared, hoping it was true. "Beside, we have no choice."

"Why not? Is there nothing else to eat? Are there truly no servants? And where is our host?"

The innocent questions made Grace's blood want to boil.

But she couldn't let it boil over poor Melly. She chopped savagely at a hapless turnip. "Our *host*"—*chop, chop, chop!*—"the unmitigated, scoundrelly, callous *wretch*, has left us to fend for ourselves." *Chop, chop, chop!* "He just leapt onto his horse and rode off! To the village inn!" She hurled the turnip pieces into the pot. "Where they make *excellent meat pies!*"

The turnip bobbed woodily with the carrots among flecks of green herbs. It looked nothing like any soup she'd ever eaten.

"How very peculiar," Melly declared.

"Yes, I think the vegetables are too old."

"I meant Lord D'Acre. It's very peculiar of him to go off like that." She gave Grace a half-embarrassed look. "He's not as bad as I expected, you know. Spending hours out in that terrible storm looking for the doctor for Papa—even if you actually fetched him. And helping the doctor get Papa changed. He even told me not to worry, that everything would be all right."

Grace stared at her in incredulity. How could Melly swallow such bland assurances? The same man had just spoken of marriage as a cold-blooded business affair—not that Melly knew that. But she did know that the wretch had just walked out on them to feed his own face while they starved.

Misreading the reason for Grace's incredulity, Melly nodded. "Yes, it was nice of him, wasn't it?"

"Nice of him?" Grace snapped. "There's nothing nice about a man who goes off to eat delicious meat pies leaving his guests to make their own—" She looked at the pot with loathing. "*Disgusting* soup!"

As she spoke there was a knock on the kitchen door. Bemused, Grace went to open it. Outside stood a boy with a large wicker basket. "Please, miss, would you be Mistress Greystoke?"

"I would."

"Then m'lord sent this up for you and the others." He shoved the basket into Grace's hands and gave her a huge grin. "Gave me a shillin' an all, he did, just for bringin' it up here!" he confided joyfully and ran off.

"What is it?" Melly asked from behind. She took the basket from Grace's hands and carried it to the table. The contents were covered by a clean blue-and-white-checked cloth. She pulled it back and the scent of freshly baked meat pies filled the room.

"Mmmmh." Melly inhaled ecstatically. "They must be the ones he told you about—you obviously misunderstood his intentions. And look, there's fresh bread, and cheese and apples and a bottle of port—not that Papa is up to drinking port, but still, it's a thoughtful inclusion." She beamed at Grace. "See, I told you he was a nice man."

Grace smiled and nodded back, but inside she was seething. She hadn't misunderstood—he'd deliberately misled her, the rat! The scent of the pies tantalized her nostrils and her stomach rumbled. The fiend! How could she possibly stay angry with a man who sent her hot pies?

But she had to. Melly was starting to like him, so more than ever, Grace had to keep him at arms' length. Or further.

Only what if Melly fell for him? And he only saw Melly as a cold-blooded business arrangement? It wasn't just her own heart Grace had to protect, it seemed. She sighed and reached for a pie. It was all getting horribly complicated.

DOMINIC SAT ON A BENCH OUTSIDE THE WOLF'S HEAD INN, NURSing a mug of ale. Sheba lay sprawled at his feet, her chin on his boot, her eyes watchful. It was a lovely evening and the scent of fresh, damp earth and leaves rose all around him like perfume. He watched the moon rise over the valley. The valley of his forbears. His despised, unknown forebears.

God, but they'd left things in a state.

He'd never intended to set foot on Wolfestone property, but now he had, it would be some time before he'd be able to leave.

He'd given two letters to the landlord of the inn to go off on the first available post; one to Podmore, the family lawyer and executor of his father's will, and the other to Abdul, his—what would you call Abdul—majordomo? *Agent d'affaires?* There wasn't a word big enough. There was simply nothing that Abdul could not—or would not—do.

He found himself grinning. What would the villagers make of Abdul? They'd really have something to whisper about then!

Each time he'd entered the inn, the taproom had fallen silent. Dominic didn't care. He'd never really belonged anywhere and he had no interest in the villagers' opinion of him. He hadn't intended to know them in the first place, and now, after he'd gotten to the bottom of the situation he'd found here and sorted it out, he'd leave and never clap eyes on them again.

But furtive whispers all around him were irritating, so, since it was a fine evening he sat outside.

He took a sip and grimaced. English ale was not to his taste, yet the innkeeper had been unable to provide him with any decent wine, other than a port that was mellow, but too sweet for his taste. The ale, on the other hand, was heavy and bitter and dark. It suited Dominic's mood exactly.

He'd been angry with Sir John Pettifer and his daughter for forcing him to come here, but in retrospect, it was a good thing he had. How long had Eades been playing out his little scheme? He must have run off as soon as Podmore had instructed him to present himself in Bristol to meet the new heir. He hadn't been warned that Dominic had found anomolies in the estate books. Lucky he had a head for figures, otherwise Eades's embezzlement might not have been discovered.

The estate had been paying for half a castle full of servants for God knows how long. Most of it hadn't been cleaned for years. Eades was the villain, but Dominic knew whose was the real responsibility. His father. He should never have left this place to rot.

Dominic didn't understand him at all. When had he ever? Wolfestone was everything to his father and yet he'd let it rot. What sort of mentality would glory in six hundred years of ownership, and yet think that all that was needed to continue the tradition was a male heir?

Now, having seen the dire state of the estate close up, the mess left by his neglectful father and exploited by his estate mismanager, Eades, Dominic had no choice but to sort it out. He had to get it in a state fit to sell. He hated waste. When you'd started your life with nothing and everything you owned was hard earned, you valued things more, he supposed.

He looked across the valley with a dispassionate eye, at the patchwork fields and rolling hills, golden in the setting sun. It was hard to believe it all belonged to him—after he married Miss Pettifer. This was beautiful country, good, rich land. It would take a great deal of work to bring the estate back to productivity again, but whoever bought it would be well rewarded. The sale of Wolfestone would give him a fine profit.

In the meantime he'd have to live here, for a time at least, in that wreck of a house. The last place on earth he'd wanted to be.

The thought pierced him unexpectedly as it had the first time he'd clapped eyes on his ancestral home, and innumerable times since. *A wreck of a house.* What an irony! What a thrice-damned and blasted irony.

How many times in his life had he sworn to wipe Wolfestone from the face of the earth? And now, here he was, actually planning for a certain amount of rebuilding of the estate . . .

Only until it was in a fit state to sell, he promised himself. For the sake of his mother's memory, he needed to wipe the name of Wolfestone from the face of the earth. How often had he found her weeping, when he was a boy. She never would explain, never would speak of this place, except to say, "You'll understand when you go to Wolfestone."

He understood now, all right. This place was the site and source of all her woes. For Wolfestone, an innocent, unworldly seventeen-year-old heiress had been sold in marriage to a man nearly thirty years her senior. For the getting of Wolfestone heirs his father had forced a young girl to his bed and beaten her when she failed to conceive. For Wolfestone she had been made to suffer most of her young life, and for that her son would destroy it.

Dominic drank some more ale. The inn's pies had been as good as promised, only rather salty. Deliberate, he was sure; salty food meant that patrons drank more.

A faint breeze stirred the leaves of the overhanging beech trees. Autumn was coming, dappling the ground with leaves of gold and russet, like freckles on the earth, like bright new pennies. He smiled.

Thank God for the bright new penny in his life, he thought, his spirits lightening. Who'd have thought he would find her at Wolfestone, of all places, covered in freckles and dressed in an ugly gray gown.

Sheba sat up suddenly and Dominic glanced at the bridge. But there was no sign of anyone. Young Billy Finn wasn't back yet. The boy had earned himself a shilling this evening.

His mouth quirked. He would have loved to see her face when the boy arrived with the basket.

"How on earth did she come to be a hired companion?" he asked Sheba. "Bold as brass and twice as bright. Hired companions are invariably meek and self-effacing. I doubt she even knows the meaning of the words." Sheba thumped a lazy tail in agreement.

Her background intrigued him more than ever: her armed-to-the-teeth female relatives sounded like street-walkers or something of the ilk. And yet in some ways she was so innocent. He grinned, recalling the way she had stared at his chest, nearly going cross-eyed with the effort of not staring, determined he should not see she was as interested in him as he was in her.

A fascinating mix, his Bright Eyes with no first name.

As a hired companion, she had much to learn. She had much to learn about men, too. And Dominic was just the man to teach her.

She had no opinion of lords—that much was clear! He smiled to himself. She'd shown the same amount of respect to him as Lord D'Acre as she had when she thought him nothing but a gypsy groom—little or none! She'd told him what she thought of him in no uncertain terms, those brilliant blue eyes sparking with anger.

Magnificent eyes. His hand wrapped around the mug reminiscently. He could still taste her in his mouth: sweet, warm, fire in his blood. And the feel of her soft young body against his. Her silky smooth skin.

She hadn't so much as squeaked when he'd pulled that jagged great splinter out.

His jaw tightened. Who or what had taught her to deal with pain like that? She was no stranger to pain, to mistreatment. You didn't develop that degree of self-mastery without a reason.

Dominic sipped the bitter brew. And yet her spirit remained undaunted. He thought of how she'd faced him down, again and again with a cheeky air of defiance. Thank God.

"Bold and bright and beautiful," he told Sheba. The dog sat up, pricking her ears, then scrambled to her feet and rushed off into the tangled vegetation opposite.

Paid companion was no life for a woman of Greystoke's mettle. She deserved more. She deserved the world. And Dominic would give it to her.

His mouth quirked. That look on her face when he'd said he was going to eat pie at the inn—Lord, if looks could kill!

Her spirit delighted him. She would not come to him easily. But come she would, he vowed silently.

Greystoke would be his.

A few minutes later Sheba returned, panting, her fur covered in grass seeds and twigs. She laid a dead rat at his feet, her tail a swaying plume of pride. Dominic thanked her gravely. It was not every day one was presented with a rat, after all.

Would Greystoke be as grateful for the basket of food

he'd sent back to the house with young Billy Finn? Somehow, he thought not.

He smiled to himself and lifted his ale in a toast. "Bon appetit, my sweet companion. And to a glorious seduction."

Chapter Six

The desire of the man is for the woman, but the desire of the woman is for the desire of the man.

MADAME DE STAEL

"I WISH WE'D NEVER COME HERE," MELLY SAID SLEEPILY. THE TWO girls were tucked up in their beds. "I'm sure that carriage accident has made Papa worse. And that doctor—he took so much blood from Papa, I felt sick. I couldn't watch."

"Of course you couldn't," Grace murmured soothingly. "But your father is sleeping now and you should be, too. It's been a big day."

There was a long silence. Grace thought Melly had fallen asleep, but then she said, "He's not as bad as I thought."

No guesses as to who she was talking about.

"He's very good-looking, don't you think? Except for those strange eyes."

"Yes." Grace thought his eyes were beautiful, strange but compelling. She hesitated, but it had to be said, "Melly, are you changing your mind about marrying him?"

"No!" Melly sat up and stared across at Grace. "No! Not at all. Just because he's done a few kind things and is good-looking doesn't mean I want to marry him!" She lay down again in the bed. "He's not, not a *comfortable* sort of man. Not *husbandly*, if you know what I mean."

"Not really." Grace thought she did, but she wanted Melly to explain. If there was any likelihood of Melly changing her mind about this betrothal, Grace needed to know before it was too late.

"He's a bit too intense and scary at times and I think he might have a temper. I think I'd always be nervous of him and I think that would annoy a man like that. And besides, he doesn't want me, or children, and that I couldn't bear."

Yes, she'd forgotten Melly's babies for a moment. Though clearly he was the sort of man who liked women. "He might change his mind about that."

"Mmm, he might," Melly said sleepily.

Grace waited for a further comment, but the sound of deep, regular breathing meant that Melly had fallen asleep.

Grace found it much harder to drift off. Her head kept spinning with the day's events, most particularly those involving Lord D'Acre.

She wasn't sure how she felt about him. Her emotions were a jumble of confusion. How could one kiss—well, several kisses—possibly turn everything upside down? Yet that's what it felt like.

She tossed and turned, unable to get to sleep. It was the cheese, she decided. She shouldn't have had it. And those pies, though delicious, had been salty. A glass of water might help her sleep better, but she didn't have one handy. She should have brought a jug up before they retired for bed, but Grace was in the habit of leaving that sort of thing to servants and so she'd forgotten. Now, the more she thought of water, the thirstier she got.

Finally she gave up. She slipped out of bed, put on her

slippers, pulled a shawl around her shoulders, lit a candle from the fire and tiptoed from the room. The house was still and silent.

Shadows flickered eerily as she hurried down the curved stone staircase. She made her way to the kitchen. She glanced out the window as she drank a glass of cold water. Light flickered from inside the stables. What was a light doing there at this hour? It flickered again. Fire? She hurried outside to investigate.

She peered into the stables. The light came from part-way down. Not a fire, but it could be a thief. She glanced around and saw a pitchfork hanging up. She carefully lifted it down and crept forward, her heart thudding.

She came to the half stable door and saw a horse lying down and a dark shape bending over it, silhouetted against the lamplight. Horses hardly ever lay down. Someone was up to no good!

"What are you doing?" she said in as tough a voice as she could manage. "Stand up so I can see you—and be warned: I'm armed."

"And delightfully dangerous." Lord D'Acre straightened and faced her.

Grace nearly dropped the pitchfork in relief. "I thought you were a thief. What are you doing here at this time of night?"

"The mare is giving birth."

"Oh!" She put down the pitchfork and pulled her shawl tighter around her. "Is she all right?"

He said brusquely, "I hope so. She's young. I think it's her first birth. With first births you never know. It might be . . . unpleasant, so if you don't want to witness it, leave now."

He bent over the mare again and Grace was able to see

the whole stall. "Ohhh." She forgot about Melly and Sir John, forgot about the problem of Lord D'Acre, forgot about everything except the drama taking place in front of her eyes.

The mare was lying on her side. She was in some distress, her silvery hide dark with sweat. Lord D'Acre crouched nearby, soothing her with words and touch. Before Grace could say another word the mare's flanks heaved and her tail, which had been wrapped in cloth, lifted. Grace's breath caught in her throat. She could see two tiny hooves protruding.

She watched tensely. She'd never actually watched a mare give birth before.

The mare's flanks rippled and heaved again and the hooves were followed by the shape of a nose and then a head.

Grace held her breath. *Let it live.* Let the mother and baby live, she prayed silently.

In a moment or two, a dark, wet bundle streaked with slime and blood slithered out onto the hay that lined the stall floor. "That's my beauty," Lord D'Acre soothed. He bent over the tiny foal and Grace couldn't breathe. Was it dead or alive?

He made a small exultant sound and she saw one of the tiny hooves twitch, and then twitch again, more certainly. The foal was alive! "There you are, my beauty. You have a fine little son," Lord D'Acre murmured to the mare, then stepped back and quietly left the stall, leaving the mother to get acquainted with her baby.

The mare lay wearily for a moment or two. Grace watched, entranced. The mare had raised her head to sniff curiously at her tiny foal. She moved closer, sniffing him, learning him, cleaning his wet, slimy coat with rough, loving sweeps of her tongue. She stopped every now and then to nudge him gently with her nose and snuff his new baby scent.

It was the most beautiful sight Grace had ever beheld.

The foal squirmed under his mother's tongue. The mare whickered gently and the foal's long ears flicked back and forth as he responded to the first sound of his mother's voice.

Lord D'Acre stood beside Grace, watching over the half door. Grace gave him a misty smile. "It's a miracle," she whispered. "A miracle." Her eyes were blurry with tears.

As she spoke the mare inside whickered again to her foal.

Their eyes met, clung, shared the moment. "Yes," he said slowly. "It is a miracle." He touched her cheek with one finger. It came away wet. "And so are you." And he drew her into his arms and kissed her, a long, sweet kiss.

It was a sweet and simple kiss, tender and quiet, a sharing of feeling, a communion . . . and it stole Grace's heart right out of her body.

After a time, she drew away from him, remembering who she was and who he was. She watched the mare, licking her foal, learning it.

"How does she know just what to do?"

"Maternal instinct," he said quietly. "One of the most powerful forces in the world." He said it almost reverently, and with deep conviction.

"Melly would love this," she murmured.

"She likes horses?"

His question jolted Grace to an awareness of what she'd said. She hadn't meant to say anything—it was for Melly to tell him, not her, but now, by speaking without thinking, there was an opportunity to push things along a little. Should she say something more?

She bit her lip, watching the mother lavish her baby

with care. Upstairs Melly lay dreaming. Melly, overflowing with maternal yearnings, dreaming dreams that would never come true if she married this man. Yes, she should speak up. That's why Melly had begged her to come, to help free her of an unwanted betrothal.

"No, Melly Pettifer doesn't like horses; she's afraid of them. But that." Grace gestured at the mare, nudging her foal gently. "That is what Melly Pettifer dreams of."

He gave her a sharp look. "What do you mean?"

"Motherhood." She met his gaze somberly. "She loves babies. She yearns for the day she can hold her own babe in her arms. I've known her for seven years. She's always wanted children." She pulled her shawl more tightly around her and stepped away from him. "Always."

He reached out to hold her, but she avoided him. "No. It's not me you need to talk to," she said and walked back out of the stables.

GRACE'S EYES FLEW OPEN AND SHE JERKED AWAKE WITH A START. Another dream, she realized. A faint gray light threaded through the curtains. Dawn. She decided to give up on trying to sleep. She knew she must have slept, but mostly the night had passed in tempestuous dreaming: dreams in which Dominic Wolfe played a far too conspicious part. Passionate, toe-curling kisses, jumbled in with phrases such as "Marriage is nothing but a business arrangement." And lurching carriage rides and foals and a dark head bent with unbearable tenderness over a splintered palm. And babies and a silver horse and wood-chopping and a white shirt and wet breeches plastered to a hard, lean frame.

Who was he? One moment he was kissing her with a passion that still curled her toes, a whole day later, just thinking about it. The next he spoke with cool dispassion of marriage being nothing but a business arrangement. And then he labored over a mare and foal with such compassion, and afterward kissed Grace with such tenderness . . .

And what did he want? He desired Grace. That was clear.

And she desired him.

But he seemed to feel no contradiction between marrying Melly and desiring Grace.

Grace glanced across at the mound in the other bed. Melly was still fast asleep, poor thing. She was worn out with worry.

She could not let things continue like this. She'd promised to help Melly, and Melly was her oldest friend. Only what was help? It wasn't as simple as it had seemed in the first place.

If Melly was even the slightest bit inclined to like Lord D'Acre, Grace couldn't in all conscience interfere—not now. Even if—especially if—she wanted him for herself.

And she did. Rake as he was, immoral as he seemed, to her shame, she wanted him.

She'd always thought she was unable to feel the kind of passion her sisters had found with their husbands. She'd thought she could never give herself and her happiness into the hands of a man.

Or so she had always thought until a rake stole a few kisses. And sucked a splinter from her palm. And then kissed her until her very bones were like to melt . . .

In one day he'd turned her world upside down.

And yet he still talked of marrying Melly.

Her plans to travel to Egypt and other exotic places had been based on the assumption that she'd never fall in love. A not unreasonable assumption: she'd been on the marriage mart for three years and had tried very hard to fall in love, even a little bit. And nothing.

She'd thought a man's kisses would never move her. They never had. Even when the nicest men had kissed her, and their kisses had been very pleasant, she'd still felt nothing. Not the sort of thing she knew her sisters felt.

Until now. When she'd kissed a man she didn't even know if she could trust, and who not only didn't believe love and marriage went together, he could see nothing wrong with being betrothed to Melly while kissing Grace.

He should have been all wrong, and yet she'd felt so right in his arms. She'd felt . . . everything. More than she'd thought possible.

No, it was impossible. He seemed determined to go ahead and marry Melly. Melly, though she said she didn't want to marry him, also thought him kind. And good-looking. Now that she'd met him, Melly might become reconciled to the marriage. Grace didn't see how she couldn't. Any woman would want to marry him, she thought despairingly. He was too attractive for his own good. Certainly too attractive for Grace's good!

Lord D'Acre might change his mind about children. He'd said marriage was about heirs. And he seemed to be kind to children. That boy who'd brought the food last night thought him wonderful.

Oh, Lord, she ought to just cut and run. She couldn't betray her friend and she wouldn't stay to be torn apart. She should go to Egypt with Mrs. Cheever, put Dominic Wolfe and his compelling golden eyes and his toe-curling kisses right out of her mind.

Egypt, after all, had always been her dream. Since childhood it had been her ruling passion: to see the pyramids and the Sphinx for herself. To stand there in golden

Egyptian sand and look at—be able to touch—the mystery of the ages.

She'd planned her trip to Egypt the way other girls planned their honeymoons.

She'd attended public lectures on Egypt and the exciting discoveries being made there all the time, she learned everything she could and was even studying Arabic.

She'd met Mrs. Hermione Cheever at one of those lectures. Mrs. Cheever was a wealthy, elderly widow with a similar passion for pyramids and the mysteries of the ancient world. Mrs. Cheever was going to Egypt in the autumn, visiting her poor bereaved cousin Henry Salt, the British consul, and avoiding winter, like the swallows, she'd joked. Why didn't Grace accompany her? It would be such fun!

There was still time. If she left now, she could still join Mrs. Cheever. Grace was nearly one-and-twenty, and Egypt was waiting, as she'd always dreamed of.

But last night she'd been unable to sleep for dreams of a golden-eyed man who kissed like . . . like all the dreams she'd never dared to dream.

Oh it was all too confusing! Going back to sleep was impossible: she needed exercise. And breakfast.

And another good gargle with vinegar and water wouldn't hurt, either.

She dressed quickly. The previous day she'd found an old gray riding habit in a chest of drawers they'd been clearing out for their own use. Grace had tried it on immediately. It had been made for a taller lady, but otherwise it fitted. It was old-fashioned in style but in perfect condition, thanks to the lavender and camphor it had been packed in.

Grace adored riding, but hadn't brought a riding habit with her on this trip. Melly didn't ride and therefore neither would her companion. But Sir John was bed-bound for a time and would never find out, and Melly was asleep and didn't need her, so for the moment, Grace was free to indulge herself.

Holding her skirts high, she skipped across to the stables. Three pale and one dark equine heads poked over the doors curiously. He must have caught the third mare.

The silvery mare she'd ridden yesterday whickered a greeting and tossed her head. Grace was delighted.

"Oh, you remember me, do you, sweetheart?" She caressed the velvety muzzle and fed the mare a carrot. "I'm sorry, it's a bit woody." The mare didn't seem to mind. She crunched it with apparent relish, while Grace fed carrots to all the other horses—extra for the little mother. The foal was standing up, drinking from his mother, his little tail wiggling in delight. Newborn foals were much nicer than newborn humans, Grace thought.

She'd brought a cloth to clean off the old sidesaddle she'd noticed yesterday. It was in better condition than she'd realized. She saddled her mare and slipped a bridle on her. The mare lipped gently at Grace's jacket.

"No, sweetheart, no more carrots. What's your name, I wonder? I can't keep calling you sweetheart." She loved this mare already. "Maybe I'll call you Misty, because you look so much like morning mist. Do you like that name?" She used a manger as a riding block to mount, and rode out.

After the storm the previous day, the world was newly washed and clean and the air was fresh and tangy with the faint promise of autumn.

Her mare was frisky and her mood infected Grace, so first they had a glorious gallop across the fields. The scent of crushed summer grasses and damp earth was intoxicating. Grace didn't take much notice of where she was: all through this valley the gray solidity of Wolfestone was visible, so she wouldn't get lost.

After a while, a field of brown-and-white cows attracted Grace's attention and diverted her path in the direction of a prosperous-looking farmhouse. Where there were cows she hoped there would be milk. And butter and cheese.

There was, and Mrs. Parry, the motherly looking farmer's wife, was only too happy to entertain a young London lady staying at the castle. She ushered Grace into the parlor and gave her a glass of fresh, creamy milk and some of her special gingerbread. And she was delighted to answer all the questions Grace put to her.

Yes indeed, she'd send milk and cheese and butter up to the castle straight away. Young Jimmy would take it right after he'd finished in the dairy. Would miss want some fresh eggs, too, perhaps? And what about a nice pot of honey, and some of Mrs. Parry's damson jam?

Miss would indeed like all of the above. And would Mrs. Parry recommend the best place to buy bacon? And bread? And coffee.

"Oh, the Wigmores are the ones to see for bacon, miss—they killed a pig not too long back, either, so I know they'll have plenty. Just go along this path toward the village and you'll see a cottage with a gate made of a rowan and a willow, all entwined. She be a witch, o' course, old Granny Wigmore—but a white one, so don't be a'feared. A grand healer, Granny be."

Grace nodded. She was well acquainted with country superstition. Her grandfather had despised it, which naturally had made all the Merridew girls sympathize with it, even if they didn't believe. And Great-Uncle Oswald adored trying out folk remedies for his various ailments.

"Most likely Granny will be sitting out the front. She

doesn't sleep much and likes to know what's happening." Mrs. Parry winked. "Now, you'll get bread and coffee in the village. You'll smell the bread baking as soon as you get there, so just follow your nose."

Grace thanked her and got up to leave. "Oh, and Mrs. Parry—if you know of anyone who needs a few weeks' work, you might send them up to the castle."

Mrs. Parry beamed at her. "Ah, miss, that's grand. There's plenty o' folk will be grateful for a little extra. Times have been hard in Wolfestone. I'll spread the news, indeed I will. And my Jimmy will be up wi' everything in a basket for you—and miss, I'll pop in a jar of my best buttermilk, just for you."

"Buttermilk?"

"For your complexion, miss," Mrs. Parry said confidingly. "Bathe it three times a day in my buttermilk and those nasty freckles will fade like you wouldn't believe."

Grace thanked her gravely and left. She'd have to freshen up those nasty freckles with henna in a day or two. And touch up the roots of her hair.

A little further down the valley, she turned a corner and saw the very house Mrs. Parry had described. It was set in the middle of a lush garden of herbs and flowers, and the living archway of entwined rowan and willow at the front gate was unmistakable. It was ancient and gnarled and strangely beautiful.

As predicted, an old woman was sitting in front of the cottage in the early morning sunshine. A sprightly old crone with rosy cheeks and hair in white elflocks, she was on her feet and at the front gate by the time Grace reached her.

"You are Mrs. Wigmore, I think. I am Grace M—" She corrected herself. "Miss Greystoke." Grace slipped from the mare and held out her hand.

To her surprise the old woman took her hand and kissed it, saying, "Welcome, Lady. The sight of ye gladdens my old eyes, it does. Wolfestone needs ye, needs ye powerful bad." She produced a piece of apple and fed it to the mare. "A grand omen that you've returned."

Grace supposed the old lady had mistaken her for someone else. She smiled. "You gave me directions last night to the doctor's, remember? Thank you very much. They were excellent directions. Um, I was hoping to buy some bacon."

"Aye, I have 'un here." The old lady produced a wrapped packet from her apron. "There's enough there for everyone up at t'castle to break their fast. Young Billy Finn'll bring a flitch o' best bacon up later—save ye luggin it on that 'orse."

"But . . ." Grace frowned and unwrapped the cloth. Inside was a beautiful piece of bacon.

The gnarled old hand clutched hers. "Now, Lady, ye'll be wantin' to know which families here have greatest need o' ye."

"Oh, but—"

The old woman ignored her. She described several houses that Grace would find on the way to the village. "The Finns, the Taskers, the Tickels, and all the rest. Just go, Lady, and you mun see. Powerful bad, the folk o' Wolfestone need ye."

Grace shrugged and agreed to go. She might as well recruit workers who really could benefit from having the work, and this old lady would know everyone. She rose to leave. "Thank you, Mrs. Wigm—"

A gnarled, ancient hand shot out to detain her. "I have something more to tell you. Back up the road there and off through the woods be Gwydion's Pool. Ye must not take it lightly, Lady. It be a magical place, but it be dangerous for females. Gwydion be one o' the old gods and if a young girl be so foolish as to bathe in his pool . . ." The old woman shook her head direfully.

"She'll drown?" Grace asked, fascinated by this evidence of ancient folk beliefs.

"Worse! He'll steal her virtue from her."

Grace laughed.

"Ah, young miss, ye don't believe me, but 'tis true. Look at them Tickel girls. Their mam—poor ignorant creature—she be a furriner from past Ludlow and knew no better. She let those girls paddle and splash in Gwydion's Pool when they weren't no more'n babes, and look at 'em now! Not a moral between 'em! Not their fault, o' course, but a warning to the rest o' female kind, they be."

"Well, thank you very much for warning me." Grace got up again to leave.

Again the old woman detained her. "Even so, miss, you need to go to Gwydion's Pool and fetch some o' the water from it."

"Need I? Why?"

"Ye must take a gill o' water by moonlight and bathe yer face in it, morning and night. Them freckles will fade, sure as my name be Agnes Wigmore!" She described the way to the pool in detail, and only then did she release Grace's hand.

Grace thanked her for the bacon and the advice and left. She headed for the village, and because she wasn't in a hurry and had said she would, she went by the curving forest path and stopped at each house that Granny Wigmore had mentioned; the Finns, the Taskers and the Tickels . . .

She was given a warm welcome at each house but the state of the houses shocked her. The people here were in abject poverty. Mrs. Finn lived with five young children in a shack of a house. She took in washing, but her eldest son, Billy, considered himself the breadwinner of the family. Dear Lord, but the child was not yet ten.

The Tickel girls lived with their mother and grandmother, who was bed-bound. They took in washing and the girls went out to scrub and clean whenever work was available.

The Taskers had evidently been prosperous at one time, but, she learned, they'd been unjustly evicted from their farm—the first time in hundreds of years they'd been late—and now they lived in a hovel on the edge of the forest making ends meet as best they could.

Everyone's clothes were worn and patched; there was little evidence of food in any of the houses—Grace was warmly welcomed but was offered water to drink and food that she could see was all there was. The houses were meagerly furnished yet clean and neat. And everywhere she looked there was a need for maintenance and repair—leaking roofs, rotting floors, walls crumbling with damp. Who on earth was the landlord? Grace feared she knew.

Melly had said he was rich.

But at whose expense?

The sun was high in the sky by the time she reached the village, but Grace had much to think on. In the village shop she bought several loaves of fresh, warm bread and a packet of coffee and tea. She left the shopkeeper with an order than left him smiling and bowing her out of the shop like a duchess. She thought of the bare larders of the places she'd just left and vowed she would do something.

Chapter Seven

The voice of conscience is so delicate that it is easy to stifle it; but it is also so clear that it is impossible to mistake it.

MADAME DE STAEL

GRACE ENTERED THE KITCHEN AT WOLFESTONE TO FIND A FIRE blazing brightly and the smell of fresh coffee. He'd certainly acted quickly. Only last night he'd said he would arrange for some help. And here it was.

A stout woman turned away from the hearth as she entered and bobbed her a curtsy. "How d'ye do, miss. His lordship said I was to take my orders from you. Stokes is my name, miss. Good, plain cook I am, with some experience of the gentry. And this here's my niece, Enid," she said as a harried-looking girl emerged from the scullery carrying a large pot. "She's a dab hand in the scullery and will give you no trouble. Give miss a curtsy, Enid!" She poked the girl in the ribs, almost knocking the pot from her hands. The girl bobbed a jerky curtsy and scuttled off.

Grace said, "I'm very pleased you're here, Mrs. Stokes and Enid. However, I think there's some mistake. It should be Miss Pettifer who you will take orders fr—"

"No, miss, excuse me, but his lordship said it was to

be you. Made it quite plain. Miss Greystoke, he said. Small, dressed in gray, and with interesting freckles is how he put it." She hesitated, then said, "I've got an infallible remedy for those freckles, miss, if you'd care to try it."

Grace smiled. "Thank you, Mrs. Stokes, perhaps later. Is that coffee I smell? I would love a cup. And I've brought bacon and fresh bread and—oh, all sorts of things. And there's an order coming up from the village shortly."

"Oh, that's grand, miss. I brought a few things with me when his lordship engaged me last night, the coffee for instance, but I didn't know what was in stock, so—"

"It was very clever of you to think of it," Grace declared.

Mrs. Stokes beamed. "My pleasure, miss. Mrs. Parry's lad brought the supplies up that you asked for, so there's plenty for breakfast." She set a cup of coffee down on the kitchen table, whisked the loaf of bread from Grace's hand, and pressed Grace into a chair. "Now, sit ye down, miss, and I'll cut ye some o' that nice fresh bread. Will ye have honey or some of Mrs. Parry's damson jam?"

"Honey, please," Grace said happily. She took a sip of hot, fragrant coffee. "Oh, Mrs. Stokes, you're a gem!"

Mrs. Stokes, beaming, placed a plate with two slices of fragrant, warm bread in front of her, lavishly slathered with butter and honey. Grace devoured it hungrily.

She was in an excellent mood. Lord D'Acre had hired several servants already. That boded well for her. She hadn't really thought about how he would respond to her own actions this morning.

"Heavenly!" she declared, licking honey from her fingers. "Is there anything better than fresh, warm bread and honey?"

"I can think of a few things." Just the sound of that deep voice sent a shiver down her spine. "Though that does look delicious." The look he gave her indicated he wasn't thinking about bread. She hurriedly stopped licking her fingers and tucked them out of sight, though they were still a little sticky.

"Good morning, Mistress Greystoke."

Mistress. He said it just to annoy her, she knew. Any opportunity to remind her of that first meeting. *I wouldn't mind a mistress. Are you soon to be my mistress, too, Greystoke?*

"Good morning, Lord D'Acre," she said sunnily, determined to be unaffected by rakish looks or innuendo.

He prowled slowly toward her and leaned down. She braced herself. He bent lower and murmured in her ear so she could feel his warm breath on her skin, "There is a most delectable drop of honey just beside your mouth. If you like, I could lick—"

Grace hastily scrubbed at her mouth and glared a silent warning at him over her shoulder. He grinned and winked and held her chair to help her rise. He'd been teasing her; even he wouldn't kiss her in front of Mrs. Stokes and Enid. Surely.

"If you've finished your breakfast—"

"He's going to bleed Papa again!" Melly burst into the kitchen, distraught. "I told him not to but he told me to run along and stop bothering him." She gave Grace an anguished look. "Papa's already lost so much blood. He's so pale and weak! I'm sure it's not good for him!"

"I'll go." Grace dashed out of the room. Lord D'Acre caught up with her at the stairs, hooked his hand around her arm, and took her with him, flying up the stairs two at a time.

They reached Sir John's room just as the doctor was about to open a vein. One glance at Sir John's face confirmed

Melly's opinion. He lay weakly against his pillows, his eyes closed, the skin around them fragile and bruised-looking. His skin was very pale and waxen.

"Belay that, you damned leech!" Lord D'Acre snapped. "Miss Pettifer has already requested you not to bleed her father any more."

The doctor straightened. "I am the physician here!"

"Yes, but when it is her father being treated, Miss Pettifer is the one who gives the orders."

The doctor gobbled with indignation. "I refuse to take orders from some young chit!"

Grace stepped in and said in what she hoped was a calming voice. "Dr. Ferguson, Miss Pettifer is concerned about the amount of blood that you have taken from her father. She feels it is only weakening him, and indeed, that does seem to be the case. If you would just explain—"

The doctor drew himself up and gave her a haughty glare. "I explain myself to no one!"

"Then—" Lord D'Acre strode to the door and held it open. "Miss Pettifer, do you wish to dismiss this fellow?"

Melly looked frightened. She glanced from her father to Grace to the doctor and back to her father, chewing her lip, clearly unable to decide.

Dr. Ferguson decided for her, saying in a sniffy but ingratiating manner, "Well, since you insist, my lord, I will not bleed Sir John today, but be it on your own head. He is seriously ill and I cannot be held responsible if he worsens." He started to pack up his things. "I have other patients to call on, so I will leave you this laudanum, which you can give him if the pain gets too great." He snapped shut his doctor's bag. "I shall return on the morrow—unless he worsens and you send for me. But if you do, I warn you, I shall bleed him, for nothing is so efficacious as bleeding a patient, I find." He stalked from the room, a picture of affronted dignity.

Lord d'Acre watched him go. "Nothing is as efficacious as the prospect of a fat bill being paid."

Melly looked frightened. "But I can't—I don't have any—"

Lord D'Acre cut her off. "Do not trouble yourself about it. I pay for the care of my guests. Now, are you satisfied with the outcome of this discussion, Miss Pettifer?"

Melly gave him a relieved smile. "Oh, yes, thank you, Lord D'Acre. It is most satisfactory. I do believe Papa could not take another bleeding."

He did not seem to notice the glowing smile, but Grace did. It gave her pause for thought.

"Do you have everything you need?" he asked Melly.

Melly looked around the room. "I—I think so."

"Good, then we shall leave you to make your father comfortable. You may order anything you need. Meanwhile, Miss Greystoke and I have a few things to discuss. In private."

"We do?" Grace didn't like the sound of that, but she had no time to question him any further, for he took one of her hands in his, and placed his other hand squarely in the small of her back. She found herself swept from the room like an errant leaf.

"What do you need to discuss? I don't think there's anything we need to discuss. Especially not in private."

He refused to answer, just gave her an enigmatic look and marched her onward.

"Thank you for supporting Melly," she told him.

He rolled his eyes. "The man's a quack."

Grace was inclined to agree. He led her to a parlor,

badly in need of a good dust and polish, seated her, and drew up a chair opposite, uncomfortably close. His knees just touched hers.

She tried to scoot back in her chair, but he leaned forward. "First things first," he said and took her hand in his. "You missed a bit."

And before Grace could work out what he was talking about, he'd lifted her hand and sucked two of her fingers right into his mouth.

She was too surprised to say a word. She tried to jerk her hand back, but he held it firm, his eyes smoldering honey gold above her hand. She scrunched her eyes shut to block off that compelling golden stare but all it did was intensify the sensation of his mouth and what it was doing to her fingers.

He sucked on them in a slow, hypnotic rhythm. Grace had had calves and baby lambs suck on her fingers: they felt nothing like this. Each strong, slow pull arrowed straight to the core of her. Shivers rippled though her with each movement.

At the same time his tongue delicately explored her skin, sending tiny frissons skittering down her arm and backbone. His knees pushed between hers and she felt him move closer.

She felt his warmth, smelled his masculine scent and knew she must resist him.

She recalled that glowing smile Melly had given him and with a huge effort, wrenched her hand from his mouth, and pushed her chair backward.

"What on earth did you think—"

"Delicious honey," he said in a conversational tone, as if he'd hadn't just been outrageous. "Reminds me of the wild honey of the Greek mountains. There is probably a lot of thyme near the hive." He smiled. "And of course there was the added taste of you. Delicious."

She stared at him, dumfounded by his cheek.

His smile deepened. He reached out with one finger and pushed her chin gently up. Her mouth closed with a snap. "Otherwise I'd think you were trying to tempt me into a kiss. Have I warned you I have no resistance?"

"I know that!" The attempt to be scathing failed miserably.

"Yes, and besides, we need to have our little chat. There are people waiting for us."

"People?"

"Yes, a dozen or more people waiting outside. When I inquired why they were there, they told me the Gray Lady asked them to come and work."

"Oh." Grace swallowed.

"Yes, oh, Greystoke."

"Ahh," Grace swallowed. "Yes, I um, met a few people this morning when I went out. And one thing led to another and I, um, offered them work, yes."

He raised a brow. "You hired staff for my household?"

She flushed. "I'm sorry, I know it was presumptuous of me, but I didn't think you'd have time to go out and find staff. And you said last night . . ."

He said nothing. She grew more nervous. "I'm sorry. I thought I was helping. And these people really need the work."

His frown grew. "Do you mean they importuned you—?"

"No, no! They never asked for anything." She bit her lip, wondering whether to be tactful or truthful. Truth blurted out. "But y—anyone can see they are in dire straits if only y—someone—cared enough to look! There is evidence of poverty everywhere."

"Evidence?"

"The children, to start with. All the children are thin and their clothes are worn, made over, and much patched."

He frowned.

"And their houses—the roofs leak, some show evidence of damp and decay, and yet these are tenants, and so not allowed to make repairs themselves."

His frown grew darker. Did he think she was making it up? She redoubled her efforts. "There are people who have worked for your family—the Wolfe family—for hundreds of years! The land is good, so the estate should be prosperous, and yet the people are poor and despairing. Let me tell you about the people waiting outside for a chance to work."

She began to count people off on her fingers. "Jake Tasker is one of your tenants who was evicted from the farm his family has worked for seven generations after a fire destroyed his barn and the livestock in it. His father was killed fighting the fire. They were unable to pay the rent for the first time in his life, but your estate manager—"

"Not *my* manager!"

"Very well then, the Wolfe family's estate manager refused to allow him time to make up the shortfall. Jake Tasker, his mother, and his elderly grandfather now live in a shack on the edge of the forest and Jake and his grandfather take work wherever they can."

She held up a second finger. "The three Tickel girls support—"

"All right, all right," He held up his hands. "I'm not blind. And I imagine you can dredge up some sorry tale for every person on the estate."

She smiled. "Not every person. Just the ones waiting outside." She was relieved he'd taken her criticism of his family so well. Not all lords acknowledged the responsibilities that went with the position. But even Grandpapa, with all his faults, had never neglected his tenants. A thought occurred to her. "Can you not afford it?" she said, horrified. "Because if you cannot—"

"My financial situation is none of your business."

"No, and I know it is very vulgar of me to ask. If you don't want to tell me, just tell me to mind my own business."

"I just did," he pointed out.

"Yes, but I was giving you time to think it over again," she said in a coaxing voice.

He repressed a smile. "Not that it's any of your concern, but I can afford hundreds of damned servants!"

"Oh. Good," she said, relieved.

He said, as if she hadn't spoken, "I don't know how you've discovered so much about the people here in such a short time—"

"To be honest, I don't understand it myself," she admitted. "They all just seemed to think I knew all about them already. They just seem to want to talk to me."

He looked at her with an enigmatic expression. "I can understand that," he said softly.

For a long time he said nothing more. She had no idea what he was thinking. Finally he said, "So you want me to hire all those people outside?"

"Yes, please."

"As a favor to you."

"Y-yes, and because they are your tenants and badly in need. And because the castle needs a good clean."

"But also as a favor to you."

Why did he keep stressing it as a favor? She didn't trust it. Him. She said suspiciously, "If that's how you like to view it."

"Oh, I like. I'll offer you a bargain, then. I'll hire every one of those people waiting outside . . . for a kiss."

Hah! She'd been right not to trust him! Grace slowly licked her lips, pretending to consider his suggestion. His eyes followed the movement of her tongue and she felt a frisson of excitement. Playing with fire.

"A kiss, you say?" She looked at his mouth. He stared at hers. She told herself it was foolish to tease a Wolfe, but she couldn't resist. He was poised, intent. She tilted her head and gave him a speculative, flirtatious look. "For each person you hire?"

"Yes." His voice was a little thick.

"Just one kiss?"

He nodded. The gleam in his eye intensified. He was certain of her agreement.

She purred, "I have an even better idea." She smiled at him.

He smiled back. "I'm always open to new ideas."

"Good." She stood up briskly and gave him a quite different smile. "In that case, I'll pay them myself."

His hand shot out and stopped her. "Pay my workers? Don't be ridiculous! You can't pay them!"

She shook his hand off. "Why not?"

"Why not? Because you're a hired companion yourself, that's why not!"

She shrugged. "I have a nest egg."

"I don't care. I won't allow it. They are my tenants, as you pointed out, and hired to put my castle to rights."

She put up her chin and crossed her arms in a mulish gesture.

He changed tactics. "Come, Greystoke, why be such a little prude? What's so hard about one little kiss per person?" He stroked her cheek with the back of his finger. "A great deal of pleasure and no danger to your precious nest egg."

She jerked her face away from the insidious caress. There was no nest egg—she was an heiress. The danger was to her precious heart. His kisses were just too lethal. "No, your price is too high."

"What about one kiss for the whole lot? It would have to be a very good kiss, of course."

She shook her head serenely. "No, your price is still too high."

"You kissed me for free the moment I met you."

He made it sound like she was a complete hussy, who threw herself at strange men on an instant's acquaintance! "I did not," she said indignantly. "You stole that kiss—those kisses—under false pretenses."

"False pretenses? What pretenses?"

"I didn't know you were Lord D'Acre when you first kissed me."

"No, that's right." He grinned. "You called me an impossible gypsy, didn't you? If that's how you prefer me, I'll be your gypsy lover, Bright Eyes."

"Don't call me that. And I don't *prefer* you at all," she lied. "It has nothing to do with station in life and everything to do with you being betrothed to Miss Pettifer."

He nodded. "I see. But that doesn't explain the other kisses. The ones among the wood chips, and in the kitchen. And in the wee small hours with the foal."

"You stole them, too."

"No, I didn't. You knew very well who I was by then. And you can't deny it, Greystoke, you did kiss me back. With flattering enthusiasm. Or will you deny they were your fingers in my hair, your tongue in my mouth?"

At his words, she felt a wave of heat wash over her.

From the smug look on his face he could see it, too. "Nonsense. I was surprised," she said feebly. "I didn't realize what was happening."

He smiled, a slow gleam of white teeth. "In that case I shall take care to surprise you more often, Greystoke. The results are always so delightful."

And before she could blink, he bent and kissed her full on the mouth. He grinned and licked his lips. "Mmm, wild honey," was all he said. His smile said it all. That and the blood thrumming through her arteries.

"I w-won't—" she began, when she could gather her wits.

But he was already gone. Whistling.

DOMINIC EXITED THE SIDE DOOR WITH A GRIN. SHE WAS SO DElightfully easy to tease. And such a joy to kiss. The faint taste of honey was still in his mouth. His heart felt lighter than it had in . . . years.

The silent group of waiting people caused the smile to fade from his lips. No matter what she thought, he hadn't been blind to the dilapidated cottages, the skinny children in their ragged clothes, or the run-down farms in need of new equipment and modern methods. Ever since he came to Wolfestone he'd thought of little else.

Apart from a small, freckle-faced charmer.

His father's legacy was not what he'd expected. He'd expected a proper Norman-style castle, not some fantastical hodgepodge, part manor house, part castle, part Gothic mansion with a fairy-tale turret thrown in. He'd expected it to be luxurious, filled with beautiful things, not empty, stripped bare, with leaves blowing through empty hallways. He'd expected a flourishing estate, peopled with prosperous tenants who revered the name of Wolfe.

Because everything he'd heard about Wolfestone had suggested just that, and the books and the inventories had confirmed it. Only the books had turned out to be crooked and the inventories no longer accurate.

He'd planned his revenge so carefully. He would sell off the beautiful things, break up the estate, and sell it off in pieces. He would let the Wolfe name die, forgotten, probably despised, and let the famous bloodline end with him.

But his father had already done most of it. The bastard had robbed him once again—this time of his revenge.

And now, looking at the faces of the people waiting in the courtyard, Dominic could not walk away. Not with his self-respect intact.

He moved forward and surveyed them, a dozen or so people with wary hope in their eyes, tamped low against the expectation of disappointment. He could see they'd all made an effort to look their best, the men's hair slicked back with water, the women's tidily knotted. Their clothes were threadbare but clean, and attempts had been made to furbish them up. Every face and hand was clean.

"So, you've come for work," he said.

A broad-shouldered man of about his own age stepped forward. "Aye. The Lady told us to come."

Dominic nodded. "And you would be?"

"Tasker, sir. Jake Tasker." The man held up his head with an odd mix of defensiveness and pride. His eyes met Dominic's steadily.

"Tasker," Dominic repeated the name thoughtfully. She'd mentioned the Taskers and it had rung a bell. The name of Tasker featured on the agent's books and correspondence. "Stand aside, please." He gestured to a bench on which an old man was sitting. "I'll talk to you later. Next?" Dominic looked at a pair of young men, in their early twenties.

A cracked old voice called out from the bench, "Served Wolfes for nigh on six 'undred years, Taskers 'ave." The sound of spitting followed.

Jake Tasker turned with leashed impatience. "Grandad, shut your gob and come home with me. There be no work for Taskers here."

The old man stayed put. "Six 'undred years," he repeated stubbornly.

Dominic ignored him. It was nothing to him how long the old man's family had worked here. Six hundred years, sixty, or six—it made no difference. It was just employment—work for money, nothing more.

"And the Lady told us to come."

He was a very irritating old man. Dominic turned an icy glare on him.

The old man let out a gleeful cackle. "Look at that! Cold as an hoarfrost those eyes be. Ah, ye be a true Wolfe o' Wolfestone, young maister. The blood o' Hugh Lupus runs cold and fast in ye."

Dominic blinked. He'd been perfecting that chilling stare since he was a boy. He must be losing his touch. Not only had it completely failed to abash Miss Greystoke, now it caused an old man to cackle with delight and congratulate him on it!

And he did not want it to be something passed down through generations; it was *his* freezing look, dammit!

Jake Tasker gave his grandfather a burning look and began to trudge toward the driveway. Dominic frowned. He needed to speak with Tasker. There were discrepancies in the estate accounts and Dominic had a feeling this man could help him understand exactly what had gone on. He liked the man's steady blue gaze.

"Tasker, where the devil do you think you're going?"

"Leaving."

"Come back here!" Dominic ordered.

The man hesitated, then said, "No point. I'll not stay to be insulted."

"No one has offered you insult. But I wish to talk to you, in private," Dominic said firmly.

Tasker considered his words, then, with a grudging air, returned and sat himself down beside the old man.

Dominic turned back to the other men. He sent two of them to clear up the kitchen garden, two to chop wood and do whatever Mrs. Stokes wanted them to do, and the rest he set to scything the long grass at the front and cleaning out the stables. He would organize a proper schedule of work to begin tomorrow.

Next were a trio of pretty young girls who bobbed flirtatious curtsies and giggled. "Please, sir," said the tallest. "We be the Tickel girls—Tansy, Tessa, and Tilly—and we be here to clean."

Tickel girls indeed! Dominic kept a straight face.

The smallest added, "And Mam sent some lemons up for the young miss, too." She proffered a string bag of lemons.

Dominic nodded. "Take them in to Mrs. Stokes. She will set you girls to work. You other women." His glance took in the rest. "Report to Mrs. Stokes also."

They all trooped off to the kitchen and his gaze came to rest on the shriveled little frame of Grandad Tasker, sitting on the bench. The old fellow eyed him with beady expectation. Eighty, if he were a day, Dominic thought. What the devil was he to do with such an ancient? "Mr. Tasker," he said.

Jake Tasker rose to his feet.

"I meant Mr. Tasker senior," Dominic corrected. The

withered ancient clambered to his feet and straightened with an echo of a military past.

"A man of your age—" Dominic began gently.

The wrinkled face fell. Dominic cursed himself for a fool and continued, "And experience will be invaluable. I need you to, er . . ." He cast around in his mind for something the old man could do. "Supervise the young men who are clearing the grounds. You know what young men are like."

The old fellow swelled with pride. He gave his grandson a poke in the ribs and said, "See! Six hundred years ain't fer nothin'. The Lady, she told us Taskers was needed agin! I'd better git off and see what them young layabouts is up to!" He creaked off with a sprightly air of importance.

Jake Tasker rose slowly to his feet and fixed Dominic with a level gaze. "My grandad follows the old ways. He believes in the Lady and those others."

"Lady. What lady? You mean Miss Greystoke?"

"According to my grandad she's watched over the people o' this valley for hundreds of years. Harbinger of good times, when the Lady comes, Grandad reckons." He snorted. "Superstitious nonsense, I reckon."

Dominic agreed with him. Greystoke, watching over people for hundreds of years? What rubbish!

"Taskers don't take charity," Jake Tasker said stiffly.

Dominic nodded. "Good. I don't offer it."

There had been mention of Taskers in the agent's records. Something suspicious or damning, only he couldn't recall what. "You had some disagreement with Mr. Eades, I understand."

"I did," Tasker say calmly. His gaze never wavered.

"I will be checking the estate records."

"You do that." The man seemed unworried and Dominic decided to follow his instincts.

"Can you read and write?"

"I can."

"Good, then make up a list of what you think it will take to restore the estate."

Tasker gave him a narrow look. "You're hiring me?"

"Yes, I'll give you a trial of one month in the position that Eades held. My own man will be arriving from London shortly, and I'll listen to his advice, too, but in the meantime, you can see to what needs to be done."

Tasker's eyes widened. "You're putting me in charge? And yet you know what Eades said about me." He shook his head. "I don't believe it."

"My word is my bond," Dominic told him coldly. "I follow my own instincts where men are concerned. And you are here and Eades is gone—that speaks for itself. So, do we have an agreement?" He held out his hand and, after a moment, Tasker shook it.

Dominic felt ridiculously pleased and could not work out why. What difference did it make if Tasker worked for him or not? Dominic was only putting the estate in sufficient order to break it up and sell it. And yet he did feel oddly pleased. The way he usually felt when a new venture had begun.

Tasker hesitated, as wanting to say something.

"What is it?"

"You probably won't have time, but if you're passing by our cottage—"

Dominic's face hardened. Had his instincts been wrong about this man?

"Mam would dearly love to meet Miss Beth's son."

Dominic's head snapped up. "What?" Beth was his mother's name.

Tasker's steady eyes took in his surprise. "My mother

was maidservant to your mother. Very fond of Miss Beth she was. Missed her mortal bad, she did when Miss Beth left. T'would please Mam no end to meet you."

"I'm not sure—"

"Doesn't get out much, Mam. Crippled she is, see."

Dominic nodded. "I'll see if I have time," he said, having no intention of following up on it. His mother had never spoken a word about anyone who lived at Wolfestone. Not one single word, except to say, "You'll know if ever you go there." That told him all he needed to know. He was not going to waste time gratifying some woman's curiosity.

Chapter Eight

For they conquer who believe they can.

JOHN DRYDEN

"How is your father, Miss Pettifer?" Dominic asked Melly as she came out of her father's room.

She started and looked at him as if he were about to pounce. "H-he is resting," she stammered.

"Good, then you and I have leisure in which to chat."

She looked horrified. "Er, I was just going to have a cup of tea."

"This won't take long, and I'd rather our chat was private," he said smoothly and took her arm and led her down the hallway to a small sitting room. He whipped off the holland covers and invited her to sit. She perched on the edge of the chair, looking ready to bolt.

He smiled to make her feel more at ease. She clutched the arms of the chair with white-knuckled hands.

"I have been talking with your companion."

She blanched more. "R-really?" Her voice squeaked.

"She tells me you like foals."

Miss Pettifer's mouth dropped open. "No. I am frightened of horses. Please do not say I must learn to ri—"

"No. Perhaps I mistook her—perhaps she said you liked young creatures." She looked at him blankly, so he made it clearer. "Babies. She said you liked babies."

"Ohh, that is what you're getting at—I mean, yes, I do like babies. Very much." She leaned forward suddenly intent. "Why? Have you changed your mind about a celib—"

"No!" he said hurriedly.

"Oh." She sat back.

There was a short silence as Dominic reviewed his tactics. He needed to learn what she really thought; the trouble was, she was so damned nervous of him. And if he handled it wrongly, it could make everything worse.

"It strikes me that you must have been very young when this arrangement was made between your father and mine."

She nodded. "Yes, I must have been about nine."

"Have you always known of it?"

"Oh, no. I only found out very recently."

"And it did not please you?"

She blushed, glanced down at her knees for a long moment, and then looked up, flat despair in her eyes. "I think most girls would prefer to choose their own husband," she whispered.

"So you don't want to marry me?"

She looked terrified and for a moment he thought she might faint. He frowned. His question had not come out as subtly as he'd intended.

"You may be entirely honest. I won't hold it against you."

She opened her mouth, then closed it, looked longingly at the door, gave him a look full of trapped misery, pulled out a handkerchief, and began to tie it into knots. He waited for her to complete this strange ritual, but the silence stretched and no words were forthcoming.

"Well?"

She jumped as if he'd leapt out from behind a sofa. "D-did Grace-Gracestoke tell you?"

"Tell me what?"

"Th-that, that, that . . ."

He took pity on her and said in the sort of voice he used for nervous horses, "Greystoke told me nothing except that you loved children, babies, to be exact, and that I ought to talk to you about it."

It did not seem to reassure her.

"Since I have no intention of getting you with child and my mind will not change on this issue, I wondered, have you talked to your father about it?"

Her mouth opened and shut and she shook her head. Which enlightened him not at all.

Dominic's patience shredded. "Miss Pettifer, have you told your father you don't want to marry me?"

Her face contorted and he resigned himself to a display of female waterworks. "Yes, of course I've told him, but he is adamant that it is the best thing for me. We are so poor, you see. And now he is so ill, and he thinks he has settled my future securely . . ." She looked about to burst into tears. "I cannot upset him further."

Dominic stood up. "No, of course not." He would have no such scruples. Sir John was the key to this. If the old man could be convinced that marriage to Dominic would make his daughter thoroughly miserable . . .

"I'll speak to him now, see if I can change his mind."

She jumped to her feet, her hands clasped tightly together. "What, now? You won't upset him, will you?"

"Of course not," he lied.

* * *

Sir John lay in bed, propped up with pillows. He looked frail and ill, but his dark eyes were alive with intelligence.

"Fetch me a minister!"

"There is no minister available. The old one has retired and his replacement has not yet arrived. Are you feeling worse?"

The old man gave an irritable gesture. "Worse, better, what is the difference when I'm stuck here in bed unable to do a thing!"

"Would you like to be carried downstairs? The weather is warm and you could sit in the sun on a daybed."

He sniffed. "What good would that do?"

The preliminaries over, Dominic said bluntly, "You know your daughter doesn't want to marry me any more than I want to marry her."

Sir John gave a wheezing chuckle. "Dear boy, I never wanted to marry Melly's mother, either, and she positively disliked me, but marriage has a way of working things out. That woman became the love of my life."

Dominic blinked. It wasn't what he'd expected. "Perhaps, but that doesn't change the fact that I—"

Sir John waved a thin hand, dismissing his unvoiced objections feebly. "My Melly is the dearest, most loving girl. You'll come to love her, D'Acre, I know. You won't be able to help it. I'll lay odds she's the sweetest-natured girl in England."

"I *will* be able to help it! I—"

"Finest achievement of my life, that girl. Apart from marrying her dear mother."

"Sir John—"

"On the road to ruin, I was. Rootless and rudderless. Her dear mother saved—"

Dominic cut across his maunderings. "I understand a large part of your reason for wanting this marriage is to ensure your daughter is financially secure. I am willing to pay a substantial sum if you will release me from this obligation!"

Sir John smiled. "She'll be financially secure if she marries you. *And* she'll have your protection. Needs a man to take care of her, my Melly. Innocent, softhearted little creature. Helpless on her own."

"Well, I won't take care of her. I plan to abandon her at the church door!" Dominic told him.

Sir John gave him a long, shrewd look. "No, you won't."

"I damned well will!"

Sir John shook his head. "Saw that dog of yours. Melly brought her up this morning. I'm fond of dogs."

Dominic frowned, bewildered at the turn of the conversation. "What the devil has my dog to do with this?"

Sir John smiled and closed his eyes wearily. "Mixed breed, ain't she? Mother a purebreed English retriever, father some mongrel at a guess. Pup should have been drowned at birth. Not a gentleman's dog." He opened one eye and said. "Lay you odds she's gun-shy as well." He saw the truth in Dominic's face and smiled complacently. "See? You won't abandon my helpless little girl to her own devices."

Cursing the old fox silently, Dominic rallied. "I won't get her with child, you can guarantee that! I'm told she adores children. Would you condemn this beloved daughter to a barren, lonely life?"

"No." He closed his eyes again and Dominic waited in frustration. Then into the silence Sir John said, "Very feminine little creature, my Melly. You'll fall for her after a time. No man could help it. Comes a time when a man gets tired of chasing after every skirt in town, and the woman he took for granted starts to grow in appeal." He sighed. "She'll get her babies in the end, you mark my words, young feller."

Dominic clenched his fists. The old man was as stubborn as a pig. He was so certain his beloved daughter was some siren, some irresistible beauty, damn it. If he wasn't an invalid, Dominic might be able to shake some sense into him! As it was, he could only leave. He was about to leave, then a thought occurred to him.

He leaned back in his chair and, crossing his leg, changed the subject. "Miss Pettifer's companion, chaperone, whatever she is, what can you tell me about her?"

Sir John opened one eye. "Why d'ye want to know? Not giving trouble, is she? Nice little thing, I thought, though in need of training. Keep her busy, that's the ticket. Get her to clean up or something. This place is a disgrace!"

"It's beyond one small companion's powers I fear."

The old man nodded. "Yes, so I gather. What provision have you made for repairs and refurbishment? You can't expect my Melly to see to it. The place is a shambles. If you don't do something soon, it will end up falling around everyone's ears."

Dominic smiled. "It may fall with my good will."

Sir John's jaw dropped. "But dammit, D'Acre, it's *Wolfestone*!"

"I am aware of that."

"It's the home of your ancestors! For *more than six hundred years*!"

"I'm aware of that, too." So that was part of the old man's plan, Dominic thought. He wanted his daughter to be mistress of Wolfestone. He'd fix that. "I'm selling the estate."

"Good God, man, you can't sell it! An unbroken line of Wolfes have been born here, back to Hugh Lupus and beyond! Every one of the Lords D'Acre since the title began!"

"Not me," said Dominic calmly. "I was born in Italy."

Sir John stared, his jaw agape. "Never have I seen such a disgraceful lack of family feeling!"

"Yes, I know. Another reason for not marrying your daughter to me, I would have thought. Now about Miss Greystoke." Dominic reminded him.

"Eh? Who?"

"Your daughter's companion."

"What's she got to do with this?" His mind was clearly still on the previous part of the conversation.

"I am curious. Is she some poor relation?"

Sir John gave a feeble snort. "Not likely! She's a foundling or orphan or some such. One of Gussie's orphans."

"Gussie's orphans?"

Sir John made a dismissive gesture. "Gussie Manningham as was. Now married to Sir Oswald Merridew."

Dominic frowned, trying to follow this. "The companion is the poor relation of the wife of Sir Oswald Merridew?"

Sir John snorted again. "No, not her! She's no relation to Gussie at all."

"Then why are we talking about Gussie?" Dominic said with great patience. "I asked about Miss Greystoke."

"Gussie is patroness of some orphan asylum for girls. Schools the brats up and trains them to be servants to the ton. Some of them have turned out quite well." Sir John coughed, drank some of his cordial, then resumed his explanation. "Nearly everyone's got one of Gussie's orphans working somewhere in the house. We've got Greystoke.

She's still a little rough around the edges, but we're training her up."

He gave Dominic a sudden suspicious look. "Why are you so interested in Greystoke? I forbid you to shame my Melly by sniffin' around the skirts of her companion!"

Dominic was about to refute the charge indignantly, but paused as he realized it was true. And if it disturbed Sir John so much . . . he could but fan the flames.

He inspected his nails and said in a bored voice. "Pretty little thing. I was curious about her origins. She seems an unlikely type for a companion."

"She is." Sir John fixed him with a glare. "I forbid you to go near that girl! You're betrothed to my daughter, dammit!"

"Your daughter had better get used to it then, hadn't she?" Dominic said in a hard voice. "What was it you said about a man chasing every skirt in town except the one he has at home? If you insist on forcing this marriage, that will be your daughter's fate. Sleep on that, Sir John." He bowed and left the room.

DOMINIC CAME SLOWLY DOWN THE ANCIENT STONE STAIRWAY. SINCE Greystoke had pointed out the dips worn in the stone, he noticed them every time. It was one thing to know his ancestors had lived at Wolfestone for that long; it was another to place his feet in the exact same place where they had trodden. It made him feel . . . connected, dammit!

It would have been better, or at least easier if he'd never come here in the first place.

"'Ere, 'Enry, give us an 'and, will you?" a male voice called from below. A piercing feminine shriek followed.

Dominic raced down the long curve of the stairs, taking them three at a time, then came to an abrupt halt at the sight below him.

The hall was full of people. There was a man on a ladder, using a straw broom to sweep cobwebs away.

"Watch who you be knockin' spiders on top of, Jem Davies!" a woman exclaimed indignantly. That explained the screech, Dominic thought.

Apart from the spider hunter and his victim, there were two other women applying scrubbing brushes to the floor in the far corner. Banging and shouting noises came from the room on the far side of the hall.

"S'cuse us, m'lord." Dominic pressed himself against the stone balustrade as two men carried a large, dusty, three-legged dresser past him down the stairs and out of the house. He ducked as a young boy came hurtling eagerly after them, clutching a pile of long curtain rods and the other leg of the dresser.

"Watch out with them poles, young Billy!" one of the women shrieked, but it was too late. As the boy angled himself to exit, one of the long rods slipped and hit a narrow table on which sat a china bowl filled with roses. The bowl shattered and roses and water went everywhere.

Dominic stared at the roses. He could smell them from here. The scent took him back. He was seven years old and in Naples . . .

"Ye clumsy young—!" one of the women began, but Billy gathered up the errant pole and fled before retribution could be carried out.

Dominic descended the rest of the stairs in a cold temper. He had made it more than clear that the staff he had taken on were to do no more than make the place habitable for his current uninvited visitors. He might be restoring the estate to some semblance of order, but he did not want the house restored in any way!

As he descended, the activity in the hall stopped. The women rose to their feet and faced him, clutching their rags and scrubbing brushes to their bosoms. The man on the ladder snatched off his cap and stayed motionless, above eye level.

"Where can I find Miss Greystoke?" Dominic addressed the room in general.

One of the women bobbed a nervous curtsy. "I wouldn't know, not to be sure, sir. She might be in the kitchen."

"Or up in one o' the attics, mebbe—she's been goin' through things up there."

"Has she indeed?" He stalked out in the direction of the most noise.

A Tickel girl shrieked after him. "Tell her me mam has sent more lemons and they're not to go to Mrs. Stokes this time. They're for miss! *Personally!*"

Dominic ignored her. He did not carry messages for rustics or servants.

By the time he found Greystoke he'd visited almost every room in the huge, sprawling, old house—rooms he'd never intended to enter—and he was more furious than ever. Everywhere he went he saw evidence of the way she'd flouted his orders.

When he discovered her on the second floor, her arms were full of sheets, and she was in the company of two Tickel girls, Billy Finn, and three burly men, each carrying an item of furniture. None of them had experienced the least difficulty finding her, he noted. The blasted servants had conspired to protect her from his wrath, he realized.

He announced his presence in arctic tones. "Miss Greystoke!"

She turned and said brightly, "Yes, Lord D'Acre. What can I do for you?" There was a smudge of dust on the tip of her nose. Her hair was a mess and contained several threads of cobweb. She wore an old-fashioned apron covering her dress and it was far too big for her. And her eyes shone with excitement and the smile she gave him was dazzling.

"I need to speak with you," he told her in a clipped, cold voice.

"Very well, in a moment, then. I just need to get this organized." She turned back to the three men, much to Dominic's annoyance, and said to them, "I think we could use all of these chairs. Start with the ones that need least mending. Take them all downstairs. Tilly and Tessa, you dust them and then, when Jake has mended them, I want them well polished with beeswax. There is nothing like the smell of beeswax to make a house feel homey and clean." She watched as the three men and the two Tickel girls carried a motley collection of chairs from the room, then turned back to Dominic. "Now, what was it you wanted to say?"

"If you recall our conversation of—" Dominic began.

She turned away again, saying, "Oh, Billy, I'd almost forgotten you." She smiled warmly at the young boy, oblivious of Dominic's silent indignation. She had apparently forgotten who owned this house. And who was an uninvited visitor and a paid companion.

"I'd like you to collect all these curtains and take them down to . . . Hmm, who can I get to wash them?" She frowned.

"Me mam could," Billy said shyly. "Takes in washing, Mam does."

"Excellent!" she exclaimed. "Take them to your mother then, and as soon as they're ready you can bring them back up to the house."

The boy scooped up the enormous pile of folded fabric and staggered out. And finally they were alone.

She gave him a bright smile, laced with rueful mischief. "Sorry to cut you off so uncivilly there, but if we're going to squabble, I think it's best to do it in private, don't you?"

"Squabble?" Dominic frowned at the word. Children squabbled.

"Yes. Was I mistaken? You looked like you came here to squabble with me."

"I never squabble," he said haughtily.

She gave a relieved sigh. "Oh good. I was afraid you were cross about something. So, what was it you wanted to *discuss*?"

She gave him one of her dazzling smiles and a moment later he found himself saying, "One of the Tickel girls said her mother had sent lemons for you. But that's not the point—"

"No indeed, I didn't ask anyone for lemons. I wonder why they keep bringing me lemons. Thank you for letting me know."

She started to walk down the corridor.

He clenched his fist. The interview was not going as planned. "I don't *care* about the lemons!"

Over her shoulder she gave him a warm, entirely spurious smile. "No, neither do I. Though they're very good for sore throats, as long as you have honey, which we do, so if you're planning to shout at me, it's nice to know that we have plenty of lemons and honey on hand."

He thundered down the corridor after her. "Don't walk out when I'm talking to you. And I am—" He moderated his tone and finished with quiet dignity. "I am not shouting at you."

She gave him another deceptively sweet smile. "No, of

course you weren't—you just don't know the strength of your own vocal chords. You have splendid vocal projection. If you ever wished to go on stage—not, of course, that you would, I suppose. Barons don't generally, do they?" Her eyes were dancing.

He glowered at her in silence. How had the conversation slipped out of his control to such a ridiculous degree?

She gave him a sympathetic look. "Now, don't look so glum. I know there's a lot of noise, but there's a great deal of work to be done, and it's all going beautif—"

He scowled. "What do you mean, a great deal of work to be done? I don't want *anything* done to this place, bar the bare necessities."

She stopped, her mouth an O of surprise. "Why, Lord D'Acre, you know you don't mean that." And she whipped around a corner and disappeared into a small room lined with shelves and stacked with linen.

He followed her in. "I do mean that. I mean exactly—!"

"Here, take the end of this, and do as I do while we're *discussing*. They are really too big for me to manage by myself." She handed him one end of a bedsheet, indicating he was to fold it with her. Bemused, he found his hands clutching the ends. He glanced at their surrounds. She really should not have enticed him into a linen room.

She hurried on. "Surely you can see there is a great deal of cleaning and sorting out to be done? I know men don't usually care about such things but I assure you—yes, that's the way, now fold it first this way . . . and then like this. That's very good." She gave him an encouraging smile as if he were a child.

He glowered at her and, unruffled, she batted her eyelashes at him. "I assure you it will be over in a trice and then the house will be lovely and homey."

Her assurance was amazing. He preferred her . . . ruffled. "I don't want the house made *lovely and homey*," he grated. "Clean is quite sufficient." Homey was more than he could stand!

She took the folded sheet from him, laid it on a shelf, and sent him a smile that was meant to hoist him on his own petard. It only made him more aware of their close proximity. The linen room was small, cozy, and smelled of lavender and clean linen. Bed linen.

"Is this about Mel—Miss Pettifer?" she asked. "Because if it is, why don't you sit down and talk to her about it. Believe it or not, she's not very happy about this state of affairs, either." She handed him the end of a bundled second sheet. "If you expect Miss Pettifer to feel comfortable here, you need to make this place more of a home."

He found the corners and shook the sheet out with a snap.

"I don't care if Miss Pettifer feels comfortable here or not. Wolfestone is *not* a home. It's not *her* home, it's not *my* home, it never has been, and I don't want it to *look* like a home! It's not anyone's *home* and it's *never going to be*!"

He glared at her and folded the sheet with military precision. The smell of sweet, clean linen reminded Dominic irresistibly of bedrooms. Bedrooms and close proximity to Greystoke . . .

This time when they folded the sheets, he kept possession of the ends and moved closer to her. One step, two. Suddenly he had her pressed lightly against the wall, just a folded sheet between their bodies.

Her mouth dropped open in surprise and she looked suddenly flustered. A state he much preferred her in.

"You know, you shouldn't do that," he said conversationally.

"Do what?"

"Look at me with those big, wide eyes and your mouth just so." And before she knew what he was about, he lowered his mouth to hers.

The moment their lips touched she opened to him. He kissed her slowly, savoring the tastes of her, the shifting textures, the spiraling hunger that he sensed she shared.

He planted kisses from her mouth along her jawline and in a slow, glorious exploration down the creamy column of her neck. His silken-skinned beauty. Her head was thrown back, her eyes closed, crescents fringed in dark gold. He kissed her eyelids and slipped one hand between them, to cup her breast.

It was slight and firm, the nipple aroused. He rubbed it gently and she shivered and pressed herself against him. He was hard and hungry and he wanted her, *wanted* her.

The room was small and private. They could—ouch! His elbow hit a shelf, jerking Dominic to an awareness of where he was and what he was doing. He released her and stepped back, his breath coming in great gasps, as if he'd run a marathon. She looked flushed and flustered and beautiful. He wanted to take her here and now.

No, not here, not now.

When he finally took Greystoke to his bed, he wanted it to be perfect, not a hasty coupling in some cramped little linen room. He folded his arms to stop them reaching for her again and said abruptly, "Don't you have people to organize? Lemons to receive."

She visibly struggled to gather her composure.

He frowned. "What were they for, by the way? The lemons. She said they were personal."

"None of your business." She put her nose in the air and eased warily past his body. "And while I am left to organize people, I shall do it in whatever way I see fit. For, while you might not care about Miss Pettifer's comfort, I do."

She paused in the doorway and looked back at him with mischievous awareness. "Thank you for helping me with the sheets. It was never so . . . interesting when I used to fold laundry with my sisters . . ."

The minx. He watched her go, enjoying the sway of her rounded hips as she hurried away. Now, what had he been going to do before he got sidetracked? Oh, yes, ride to Ludlow.

She had people scrubbing all over the place and they had a tendency to fall silent and gape at him, which was irritating, so he decided to leave by the western door instead. The west wing was in the worst condition and most of the current activity was at the other end of the house.

But when he slipped out the side door, he found five men outside. Three were swinging scythes in a rhythmical line, turning the knee-length grass back into something resembling a lawn. Two more men were clearing weeds and rubbish from a rocky, circular mound that appeared to contain roses—or at least one man was working and the other, the elderly Tasker, appeared to be supervising from a position of sleep. Dominic walked quietly past, hoping not to draw anyone's attention.

"Hey! Yer Lordship!"

In retrospect, silent gaping wasn't too bad. He pretended not to hear and kept walking.

"Yer Lorrrrrdship!" the man bellowed as if Dominic were a mile away instead of only a couple of yards.

Dominic stopped. "Yes?" His faint hauteur was lost on the man.

"What'll we do with this, m'lord?" He brandished what appeared to be a broken stone cupid. "Shall we fix it? Might be able to with a bit of mortar or summat."

"I don't care."

Indifference was lost on the man, too. "And what about the roses, m'lord? It be a bit early to prune 'em, but they need to be shaped a bit. Will I shape 'em up?"

"I don't care," Dominic repeated. "Do whatever you like. Or ask Miss Greystoke."

"Prefer not to take me orders from a woman, sir, if you don't mind."

Dominic gave him a cold look. "Then you'd better learn to like it, for without Miss Greystoke you would have no employment."

He moved off, but an elderly voice called after him. "Yer mam planted them there roses, yer lordship. With her own fair hands, she did." Dominic swung around.

Grandad Tasker had woken and was eyeing him with a cunning expression. "This was 'er special bit o' the garden. Designed the whole thing 'erself."

"How do you know?"

The old man let out a rusty cackle. "A'cos I was the one what 'elped 'er, a' course. Did all the digging for this, I did. Put the stonework in an' all. She told me what she wanted and showed me the drawings she made—quite the artist she was."

It was true. His mother had loved to draw and paint.

"I did all the heavy work, but when it came to them roses, yer mam set every blessed one o' them in the earth with 'er own hands. Loved this spot, she did. Came here every day and sat on that there seat." He pointed to a broken stone seat. He added softly. "A lonely little lass, your mam. Them roses was 'er company, I reckon."

Dominic didn't say anything. There was a hard lump in his throat. He could picture it.

"This was a pretty place once," the old man continued. "When yer mam ran off, yer pa destroyed it. Destroyed a lot of things. A fearsome temper, 'e 'ad. Smashed them statues and 'er seat to bits, 'e did. Slashed the roses to the ground." He gave a toothless grin. "But 'e never managed to kill 'em. Roses might look delicate but they be powerful tough plants. Your mam's roses came back—with a little 'elp." He winked. "Flowered every summer since, they 'ave."

Dominic hadn't known about the rose arbor. His mother had always adored roses. When he was a little boy, trying desperately to bring a smile to her face, he would find her a rose from somewhere and bring it to her. Sometimes she would give him a ravishing, joyful smile, and he'd feel like a knight of old, ten feet tall. But on other occasions she'd take one look, her face would crumple and she would weep, inconsolably. He used to think it was his fault, that he'd brought the wrong sort of roses . . .

"Be grand to put yer mam's garden back t'way she made it, eh, yer lordship?"

"Please yourself," Dominic said finally. "I don't care." But his voice cracked as he said it.

Chapter Nine

What is a kiss? Why this, as some approve: The sure, sweet cement, glue, and lime of love.

ROBERT HERRICK

GRACE PICKED UP A BOX OF ASSORTED BRASS OBJECTS AND WALKED slowly down the stairs, thinking about the kiss, kisses in the linen room. She hugged the box to her, smiling. Her whole body tingled with awareness, with excitement. It felt as though her very blood was fizzing gently, like champagne. And that was just the aftermath . . .

Of course it was wrong of him to be kissing her when he was still betrothed to Melly, and it was wrong of Grace to let him—not that she'd let him, precisely . . . But deep down, it didn't feel wrong.

Melly didn't want him and he didn't want Melly. He just needed a wife so he could inherit the property. As soon as he and Melly sorted out the mess—if they ever did—he would be free to choose . . . someone else.

He fascinated Grace. She purely loved the way those cold, yellow wolf's eyes darkened to gold and lit with a purposeful gleam that both thrilled and alarmed her. There was no mercy in that gleam. It declared his intention to hunt her down. Her mouth curved at the thought. She would be no tame prey of his. She was Grace Merridew—wolf tamer!

She descended the stairs, placing her feet in the hollows made by his ancestors, and thought about his response to the idea that Wolfestone could be made nice and homey. It was a most peculiar reaction. So strong. As if he loathed the very idea of a home . . .

How could anyone think like that?

Grace had never truly had a home of her own. Dereham Court, where she'd spent the first ten years of her life, had been Grandpapa's territory, and she'd never thought of it as home. Home was a place you felt safe in. Grace had never felt safe at Dereham Court.

And since then Grace had either lived with Great-Uncle Oswald and Aunt Gussie, or with one of her married sisters, or else she'd been at school. And while she'd felt safe and happy in all those places, they weren't hers, not really.

After she'd been to Egypt and seen the pyramids and the Sphinx, she planned to make a home, one that was her very own, that she would arrange entirely to her own liking.

She bit her lip. That's what she'd been doing here, she realized. Playing house, as she had when she was a little girl. He had a right to be annoyed. It wasn't her house to play with.

But it was a house built for dreaming, with its fantastical combination of styles, with its fairy-tale turret, its arched Gothic windows, its carved oak paneling and its gargoyle . . .

She glanced up and saw the gargoyle looking down at her, with his wise expression. He was one of the first things she'd had cleaned. He was dust and cobweb free and had been given a coat of oil, which had soaked into the ancient, thirsty wood.

She smiled up at him, suddenly surer of herself. "I don't care if he wants this place to be a home or not—you do, don't you, Mr. Gargoyle? And the house does." She nodded. "For you, then, we'll make this place as nice as human hands can make it. Then it will truly be a place made for dreaming . . ."

DOMINIC TOOK THE SHORTCUT THROUGH THE WOODS, HEADING FOR the Ludlow road. He was enjoying the shade; the open road would be dusty and hot, he knew.

He was in a reverie when a dog shot across the path in front of him. A white dog with liver-colored speckles. Sheba.

He'd left her back at Wolfestone, in the charge of young Billy Finn, who was supposed to be giving her a bath.

Dominic frowned. What the devil was Sheba doing out? Who knows what mischief she might do—killing chickens or chasing sheep. A dog was not supposed to run free in farming country.

He came to the place where he'd seen her cross. A faint, narrow track wound through the trees. He called her a couple of times. Nothing. He whistled. Nothing. He walked his horse a short way down the track. A couple of moments later the trees thinned and he saw the edge of the lake, and a boy and his dog. The dog was covered in mud.

"What the devil are you doing—"

Billy Finn turned, blanched dramatically, dropped what he was holding, and bolted. Sheba began to follow the boy but a word from Dominic stopped her.

"Stop, Billy! Wait—" Dominic began but the boy had fled. The child looked to be in fear of his life. Movement beside the lake caught Dominic's eye and he went to see what the boy had dropped.

A fish. A line and hook lay beside a clump of reeds.

He looked at the fish and then at the path the boy had taken. The look on the child's face had shocked him. Stark fear.

He pulled his watch out and flipped it open. Plenty of time to investigate this little mystery and still get to Ludlow. He picked up the fish and the line, whistled to Sheba, and remounted. "Fetch Billy," he told her, and pointed the way the boy had run. Tail waving like a plume, Sheba trotted confidently down the path. Dominic followed on horseback.

It wasn't long before he came to a tumbledown shack set in a clearing. Sheba bounded joyfully ahead—she'd clearly been here before. Dominic surveyed the building thoughtfully as he dismounted and tied his horse to a tree. He had seen it marked on an estate map as a ruin. But this ruin was inhabited. A thin coil of smoke rose from the chimney and lines of washing were strung between the trees.

He knocked on the door. A worn-looking woman opened it, a toddler clinging to her skirts. Several more young children peered at him, ranging from perhaps eight years old down to four or five.

"Is Billy Finn here?" he asked her.

Her eyes widened. "Billy?" she repeated warily. Her eyes flickered sideways and she thrust the toddler back into the cottage. "No, Billy's not here." She was lying, Dominic was sure.

"He ran down this way."

She shook her head and shrugged. Dominic looked at her more closely. Billy had this woman's eyes.

"You're his mother," he said with flat certainty.

She chewed her lip uncomfortably, then nodded, a tense look on her face.

"He dropped this," Dominic said and produced the fish.

It had a dramatic effect. The woman moaned, and looked as if she was about to faint. She rallied, clutched the door frame tightly and said, "No, no, no, that fish doesn't belong to my Billy. He never touched it, I promise ye, sir. He wouldn't. He's up at the castle, now. The lord, he gave him work." The woman was gabbling.

"I am Lord D'Acre," Dominic told her and she moaned again. Her face was parchment pale under its tan.

"Oh, please, m'lord, don't take him. He's a good boy, my Billy. Oh, please, please, don't take him . . ." To Dominic's horror she threw herself on the ground before him, clutching his feet and weeping. "Please m'lord, have mercy, I beg ye. Don't take my Billy."

Dominic stepped back. "My good woman, I have no intention of taking him anywhere!"

She lay slumped in front of him, weeping and mumbling, "Not my Billy, not my boy."

Dominic was appalled. He glanced at the children watching their mother fearfully. "You there, come out here and help your mother," he instructed them. They took one look at him and ran away, screaming.

Dominic ran his fingers through his hair. Were they all touched in the upper works? Was Billy the only sane one of his family?

She peered up at him through tangled hair and a desperate look came over her face. She knelt, licking her lips, and smoothing her hair. "I'll do whatever ye want, my lord," she told him, "only don't take my Billy." Good God, the woman was offering herself to him!

"I have no intention of taking the wretched boy anywhere!" Dominic snapped. "Now, for heaven's sake, get up, woman!"

Fearfully she clambered to her feet and stood facing him, her eyes downcast and tears rolling down her cheeks. Her hands twisted her apron convulsively.

"Calm yourself!" he ordered her. She gulped and an unnatural look of calm settled over her features. The woman was still terrified.

Dominic sighed. He forced himself to say in a slow, calm voice, "Nobody is taking anyone anywhere. I have no idea what you think I'm going to do to Billy, but whatever it is, it's wrong. Now, go inside and make yourself a cup of tea or something."

She fearfully took a step toward the cottage. "And here, take this blasted fish," he said and thrust it at her.

"No!" she gasped, suddenly defiant. "You'll not plant no evidence on us!"

"Evidence?" Dominic stared. It suddenly fell into place. "You think I'm after Billy for poaching?"

"He's not a poacher!" she flashed at him.

"Calm yourself, woman. I never said he was, and in any case he's a child, for heaven's sake."

She stared at him with painful intensity. "So . . . you're not going to have him taken up and transported?"

"Of course not!"

"You mean it, m'lord?" She read the truth in his face. Tears poured down her cheeks again and she was about to fling herself at his feet in thanks, but he managed to grab her by the arms and fend her off.

"You leave my mam alone!" A small towheaded fury hurtled from the undergrowth and butted Dominic in the stomach. Fists flailing, young Billy Finn hammered into Dominic, yelling, "It's me you want, not my mam!"

Undernourished ten-year-olds were fairly easy to vanquish. Dominic caught the flailing fists and held the boy off so he was out of range of the kicking feet.

"Stand still," Dominic roared. Billy stilled. All the fight drained out of him.

Dominic released the child's fists. Billy gave his mother an anguished look, straightened, looked Dominic in the eye, and said, "It's me ye want, not my mam. Take me, but don't hurt Mam or the little 'uns."

"I have no intention of hurting anyone!" Dominic said evenly. "I was merely curious as to why when I called to you, you dropped your fish and bolted like the devil was after you."

Billy braced himself. "Aye, I took the fish from the lake. Mam never knew I did it."

"I'm not after a confession, you young idiot!" Dominic said, exasperated. "So stop acting as if I'm about to have you dragged off in chains!"

Billy Finn gave him a sullen look of flat disbelief, an adult look far beyond his age. "The old lord had my pa taken fer a fish—and in chains, so why would you be any different?"

His mother caught his arm. "Don't talk like that to his lordship, Billy." She gave Dominic a fearful look. "He doesn't mean to be insolent, m'lord."

Dominic frowned at Billy. "Your father was imprisoned for a fish?"

"Aye. He weren't hanged, though. Transported 'im, they did. New South Wales. Other side o' the world."

"For *fish*? Was he selling them?"

Billy looked indignant. "A'course not. He wouldn't do that!"

His mother said hastily, "No, two years ago, it was, m'lord. We were—it was a bad year, and Will, he had no work and the little 'uns were hungry. My Will, he can't stand the sound o' wee ones weepin' for hunger . . ."

"Will, that's me da's name," Billy explained. "So Da went fishing. And Mr. Eades he caught 'im, and that's the last we saw o' Da." He straightened, a child shouldering a man's responsibility. "I take care o' Mam and the little 'un's now."

And he did, too, Dominic realized. It explained why little Billy Finn seemed to be everywhere, getting underfoot, taking any job he could get. "Well, you have a proper job now, so there's no danger of anyone going hungry."

Billy's head came up? "A proper job?"

"Yes, um . . ." He groped for a suitable-sounding position. "General factotum up at the castle. And um, assistant supervisor of fisheries." He handed the fish over to Billy's mother and wiped his hands on a handkerchief. "That position means you are entitled to take—for your own use—fish from any lakes and rivers on the estate."

Billy's mother surged forward, weeping again, and Dominic hastily stepped back before she could fling herself at his boots a third time. "Now, you clean that fish for your mother, young Billy, and then take Sheba back to the castle. I want to see her gleaming by the time I get back from Ludlow." He turned to go.

Billy and his mother followed. "General what?" Billy asked.

"Factotum. It means you'll do all sorts of different jobs." He mounted his horse. "Like a footman, only more . . . far ranging."

A grin split Billy's face. "Better'an a footman, eh? And will I have a uniform?" His eyes were so excited, so hopeful, Dominic simply didn't have it in him to crush the wretched brat.

"Yes, there will be a uniform." So much for not getting involved with the blasted estate.

"And will I—"

"Don't bother his lordship with questions, Billy," his mother interrupted the flow of questions, much to Dominic's gratitude. She clutched his boot—what was it about this woman and boots?—and said, "Thank you, your lordship. I do beg your pardon if I offended you before, m'lord. I should've known the Lady would bring us good fortune." She gave him a beatific smile. "Saw her the other morning, I did. She has the bonniest smile. Like dawn after a dark night, it was. Nothing but good could come o' a smile like that." Tears dripped onto his boots.

"Yes, yes, I'm sure," Dominic muttered and edged his horse away. "I must get going. An appointment in Ludlow."

He rode off and they both started shouting but he wasn't going to be stopped to be thanked again. His boots were quite wet enough as it was!

He'd gone a good mile and had slowed to ford a stream when a splashing beside him alerted him to the fact that Sheba had followed him. He swore. That's what the Finns had been shouting about. Oh well, it was too late to take Sheba home.

"You will have to run all the way," he told her severely. "For there is no way I am taking a disgustingly wet and muddy creature up on the saddle in front of me!"

Sheba gave him an adoring look. Her tail wagged gently. Her ribs heaved and her tongue lolled.

Dominic sighed and scooped her up in front of him. With any luck the mud would dry before he reached Ludlow and he could brush it off him.

"I WANT EADES CAUGHT!" DOMINIC FORCED HIMSELF TO SIT calmly in the chair opposite his lawyer's desk. Sheba dozed in the corner. "I want the finest runners Bow Street can offer. The bastard has got to be punished for what he has done!"

The lawyer, Podmore, nodded his grizzled head. "So it was as you had suspected, then. Tsk, tsk, it's shocking! Two sets of books—I can hardly credit it. And you say that there was no staff at the castle at all? And yet wages were drawn for them." He made a note. "Embezzlement on that scale—he'll surely hang. Transportation at the very least!"

Dominic shook his head. "I have a strong dislike of being robbed, but that's not the worst of Eades's crimes. All the time he was creaming off the profits of the estate, he was driving hardworking tenant farmers to ruin—I've seen it everywhere. He overcharged on the rent and forced good, solid men off land they had farmed profitably for generations. He pocketed salaries for nonexistent staff and for nonexistent repairs on the tenants' cottages! And you should see the disgraceful state of some of the cottages—cottages for which I must take the blame."

Podmore gave him an odd look. "You actually visited cottages?"

One cottage only, but Dominic wasn't going to admit that. Dominic shot him a look from under his brows. "They're my cottages," he said brusquely. "Why shouldn't I visit them?"

"Why not indeed?" Podmore agreed.

"Do you know what else Eades did?" He fixed Podmore with a freezing glare, "He had a man transported! For poaching *fish*!"

Podmore gave an approving nod. "At least he was not blind to all his responsibilities, then."

"The poacher was the father of five hungry children, for Christ's sake! And they're in even more desperate straits now he's rotting in a penal colony in New South Wales!"

Podmore's brow knotted in confusion. "But what else could Eades do? Poaching is a crime, and transportation a common punishment."

Dominic stared.

"The fish belong to you, my lord."

Dominic clenched his fists. "An entire family ruined for the sake of a few bloody *fish*?"

"I know it sounds harsh, but it is the only way to prevent crime. And lawlessness is increasing everywhere."

Dominic shook his head. "Letting children starve is the crime. The way to prevent increasing lawlessness is to ensure men have jobs so that they can feed and protect their women and children."

Podmore looked shocked. "My lord, never say you are a radical!"

Dominic shrugged. "I was once a lot like that boy. I know what starvation feels like."

There was a long silence. The elderly lawyer looked deeply troubled. "Was it truly so bad, my lord?"

Dominic nodded. "There were times when my mother and I didn't know where the next meal might come from. I did whatever I could to survive—stealing, and worse. And I'd do it again in a heartbeat, if my family was starving. A man is not a man if he does not protect those he loves." Aware he'd shocked the lawyer with his outburst, he moved to the window and looked out. He noticed nothing. He was back in Naples, a skinny, desperate boy, roaming the back alleys and the docks . . .

After a short silence, the elderly lawyer said in a husky voice, "I can sympathize, my boy. I knew your mother, too, recall. A very sweet and lovely lady . . . What happened was a tragedy."

"Not a tragedy—*an outrage*!" Dominic said with quiet savagery. The lawyer didn't know the half of it. He mastered himself and when he turned back, he'd assumed his usual cold expression.

"I want Eades brought to justice."

Podmore said in a soothing tone, "Bow Street will hunt him down, my lord, never fear." He gave Dominic a shrewd look. "Do I gather you've had a reversal of sentiment about Wolfestone since you came here?"

At the question, Dominic jerked his head up. "A reversal of sentiment? Of course not. I despise the place as much as ever!"

Podmore said in a level lawyerly tone, "Forgive me, of course not. It was merely that you sound a little more . . . involved than before." He began to set out papers on the table in front of him. "So you don't intend to repair any of the tenants' cottages?"

Dominic considered the matter. "I'll have to," he said after a moment. "I can't have people living in such disgraceful conditions for something that while not my fault, is nevertheless my responsibility."

"Quite so, my lord. Though I take leave to remind you that if you break up the estate and sell it, the new owner might wish to evict the tenants and demolish the cottages anyway. Modern farming techniques require a larger scale of operation, I understand."

Dominic glanced out of the window, into the busy inn yard. Dammit, he did not want to think about the consequences—he just wanted to be rid of the place. "The new owner might not," he said eventually. "The repairs must be completed before winter. Some of those damned roofs leak!"

"Very well, my lord." Podmore made a note. "Is that all you wanted to see me about?"

"No," said Dominic, continuing to look out of the window. "I wanted to check something about the will. Let us say I break this betrothal to Miss Pettifer and the estate is sold. What is to stop me from simply buying it?"

The lawyer sighed. "I explained it to you in Bristol, my lord. I did fear you were so angry at the time you might not have taken in all the permutations. Your father anticipated this. You cannot buy the property—the will specifies it most particularly. Not you, nor any agent in your employ, nor any blood relative, nor a wife." He shook his head sorrowfully. "I'm sorry, my lord, but your father was furious when you ran off like that. He was determined to bring you to heel in the end."

Dominic clenched his jaw. He would not be brought to heel by his father—dead or not! He said, "Sir John has come down here with his daughter to try to force an early marriage. He's ill. It occurred to me to wonder, what happens if Sir John dies?"

"As long as Miss Pettifer is still unmarried, the will stands."

"And if she chooses to break the betrothal?"

"If she does, the ten thousand pounds originally paid to Sir John by your father on signing the contract must be repaid to the Wolfestone estate."

"What if I choose to waive that?"

Podmore shook his head. "You cannot. The money must be repaid by Miss Pettifer or her father—and you know they don't have it. I'm sorry, my lord, but your father anticipated both Sir John's spendthrift ways and your own reluctance to wed a bride of his choosing."

"What if I give her the money from my own funds?"

The lawyer shrugged. "I would know nothing about that. But the fact remains that, according to the will, you must still gain Sir John's permission to marry—your father, as I said, was determined to bring you to heel—and I was under the impression that Sir John is very much in favor of the match between you and his daughter."

"He is, damn him!" Dominic punched a fist into one hand. The stubborn old fool could not be made to see that Dominic would make a terrible husband for Melly—cruel and neglectful, dammit! He resumed pacing the floor.

Podmore looked coy. "I presume you have some other young lady in mind, my lord."

Dominic looked at him blankly. "No, whatever gave you that idea?"

Podmore shrugged. "An old man's fancy, that's all." He hesitated, then added, "My lord, why do you not simply refuse this marriage and let the estate be sold? Since that is your intention anyway, and since you do not need the money—"

"No! I need to *own* it. It is my *right*! I will *not* be done out of my rights by my damned father's will! If the estate is to be broken up, it will be by *my* will, not my father's, may he rot in Hell!"

Podmore blinked.

Dominic continued, "My mother was sold in marriage for the sake of Wolfestone. She was just seventeen."

"I remember," the elderly lawyer said softly. "She was a beautiful bride."

Dominic nodded. He kept forgetting this old man had known his mother. "My father made her life a misery, so much so that she was forced to flee to the continent in the end. There she lived in poverty for years—and all because of my father and Wolfestone!"

There was a long silence while Dominic battled to swallow the bitterness in his throat. Finally he sat down in the chair opposite Podmore and said, "I promised my mother on her deathbed that I would do whatever it took to ensure Wolfestone came into my possession. She asked me—begged me—to take it back for her sake. And so I will. By whatever means I must."

Podmore heaved a sigh. "Yes, I see. I wish there was some other way to do it, but your father was very thorough."

Dominic set his jaw. If he must, he must. Wolfestone would be his. He changed the subject. "Now, on the matter of the estate, it needs some attention—it's in a shocking state of neglect. I trust I have your permission, as executor, to go ahead with it."

"Of course."

"I've appointed a local man, Jake Tasker, as temporary estate manager, and I've sent for Abdul to come down. He'll take over Eades's position."

Podmore pursed his lips. "Is that wise, my lord? Abdul has no experience in the operation of an English estate."

Dominic raised his brows. "Abdul is a genius."

Podmore shifted awkwardly in his seat. "Yes, but . . . but he is so very *foreign*, my lord. The local people might not take to him. English rustics tend to be very parochial. In these parts they refer to folk from Shrewsbury as foreigners, and that's only twenty-three miles away."

Dominic shrugged. "I have no interest in what they think of Abdul. He is not there to be liked. He is there to do a job—to get the estate in a condition where it will bring the best price at sale."

Troubled, Podmore shook his head. "I fear there will be trouble, my lord. Could you not prevail on him to dress a little less . . . *exotically*? And shave, so that he does not look quite so fierce?"

"No, his attire is his own concern. Now, on that

matter—what progress have you made on the breaking of the entail?"

Podmore absently touched a sheaf of papers in front of him. "It might be as well if I hired your staff then, rather than Abdul. If the place is as neglected as you say it will need—"

"Don't bother. There are upward of fifty people scouring the place from top to bottom as we speak," Dominic informed him. He rose to his feet and resumed his pacing. "And before you start congratulating my initiative, it is a damned nuisance. Miss Pettifer's paid companion has taken it on herself to assemble an army of local people to scrub, mend, and polish."

Podmore's brow wrinkled. "A paid companion has taken on staff?"

Dominic snorted. "Yes, but she's the most unusual hired companion you've ever seen. For a start she has no respect for rank, rides roughshod over my sensibilities, orders her mistress around, and at the same time protects her like a tigress with a cub. She fills my house with local yokels and sets them scrubbing—in *my* house, mind—and when I questioned her, she assured me kindly that if I cannot afford it, *she* will pay their wages!" He snorted again.

"An older woman, I presume?" Podmore inquired delicately.

"Not at all."

"Ahh." Podmore steepled his fingers and regarded them earnestly. "And how old might this companion be?"

Dominic waved a careless hand. "I don't know. Young. The same age as Miss Pettifer, I imagine. Sir John says she's new to the job, says she's one of 'Gussie's gels' whatever that may be—"

"Lady Augusta Merridew. She has an interest in female

orphans and has done some remarkable philanthropic work—"

"—But the way this girl talks to Miss Pettifer, you'd think she'd known her for years. She even calls her Melly half the time! *Melly!* Not Miss Pettifer! No respect at all." Realizing he'd gone into something of a rant, Dominic sat down.

Podmore gave him a long, thoughtful look. "I gather she's pretty."

Dominic frowned. "Pretty? Of course she's—who cares if she's pretty? That's got nothing to do with any of this."

The lawyer smiled. "No, of course not."

Chapter Ten

Telling one's sorrows often brings comforts.

PIERRE CORNEILLE

By late afternoon, Grace was feeling the strain of a long day of putting the house to rights. She was tired of answering questions and solving problems. The more she looked around her, the more there was to do. Her arms and legs ached. It was hot, she was dirty and dusty and weary. What she longed for was a good, long soak in a hot bath, but that would take organization and time to heat the water and there was only the small hip bath and she wanted to wallow. And she couldn't face the raft of questions she knew she'd get about wanting a bath in the middle of the day, and not even on a Saturday.

No, a bath wasn't practical. What she could have however, was a swim. She could swim. When her sister, Faith, had come back from France with her new husband, she'd told all the Merridew girls about the delights of swimming in the sea, and the next summer they'd all learned. It was glorious and twelve-year-old Grace had learned to swim like a little frog. She'd found opportunities to go swimming every summer since, even though it was regarded as a slightly scandalous activity for ladies.

If she slipped away now, nobody would notice. At this time of the afternoon, everyone was occupied. And Lord D'Acre had ridden into Ludlow on business and was safely out of the way.

She knocked on Sir John's bedchamber door and bobbed a curtsy. "Sir John, Miss Pettifer. How are you getting on, Sir John?" Privately, Grace thought he looked even worse. He was thinner and paler than ever. She glanced at his luncheon tray, where a bowl of chicken soup and some thin slices of bread and butter remained untouched. Melly caught her eye and shook her head very slightly. Sir John still hadn't been able to eat anything.

"Can't complain, Greystoke." He shifted and as he did, grimaced in pain. "Gettin' old, that's all. Have you come to play cards with us? I'm fleecing m'daughter of all her beans."

"Thank you, no. I'm here to collect the tray, sir, and to remind Miss Pettifer that she wanted to go for a walk this afternoon."

"Off you go then, Melly," her father said instantly. "You don't want to be hangin' around in a gloomy sickroom with your old father, when you could be out and about on a lovely day like this."

Melly shook her head vigorously. "Oh, no, it's far too hot to be venturing outside at the moment, Papa. I shall go for a walk in the evening, when it is cool."

Her father gave her an indulgent smile. "Worrying about your complexion, eh, puss? Well, such a delicate complexion is worth protecting, eh, Greystoke? Not many of the fine London ladies can beat my Melly in that department." He gave Grace a concerned look. "You ought to be more careful of yours, young Greystoke. In fact, maybe Melly could give you a few hints."

Melly smothered a giggle. She'd helped Grace touch up the freckles the previous evening.

"Yes, Sir John, thank you, Sir John." Grace curtsied and took the tray.

If Melly didn't want an excuse to escape for an hour or so, there was nothing she could do. She took the tray to the kitchen and left, her spirit lightening. She was free to do as she wished.

She could go to the pool in the woods that Granny Wigmore had told her about, the one that was supposed to have magical powers—magical freckle-clearing powers. Grace could have a quick swim and nobody would be any the wiser. And her freckles would be perfectly safe. She was getting quite fond of her freckles, quite protective of them.

She'd had no idea before how freckled girls must suffer. Everyone offered advice on how to remove them. Mrs. Parry sent buttermilk. Granny Wigmore said water from Gwydion's Pool. Even Mrs. Tickel had sent lemons, with instructions that Grace was to bathe her skin in lemon juice twice a day.

And men with wicked golden eyes speculated aloud on where the freckles ended . . .

AN HOUR LATER DOMINIC RODE OUT OF LUDLOW. IT WAS A scorching afternoon, and by the time he rode into Lower Wolfestone, he'd developed a considerable thirst. He was so thirsty, in fact, that the idea of a long draught of the Wolfestone Arms bitter ale appealed. He would not admit, even to himself, that the blasted brew was growing on him.

Deep in thought, he wove his way between the people

gathered in the taproom, vaguely noticing that there seemed to be rather a crowd, but not bothering to wonder why. A voice pierced his reverie.

"Wolfe! Dominic Wolfe! I say!" A hand thumped him between the shoulder blades, almost hard enough to make him stumble.

He turned and beheld a lanky young man dressed in neat dove-gray trousers, a pale gray-and-white-striped waistcoat, and an elegant black jacket, only slightly worn at the lapels.

Dominic's jaw dropped. "Frey—is that you? Good God!" He seized the man's hand and wrung it heartily. "Frey Netterton! Here of all places! Come outside and we'll have a drink."

His friend glanced around the taproom and wrinkled his long nose. "I quite agree. I gather soap has yet to be discovered by our companions."

Dominic grinned. Some things never changed, thank God, and Frey was one of them. His friend might be as poor as the proverbial church mouse, but he was as fastidious as ever. "I can't believe you're really here, Frey. But what has dragged you to the wilds of Shropshire? I'd swear you didn't know I was here. Very few people do."

"Yes, you blasted hermit. When I think how old Jenkins used to wax lyrical about your penmanship, it's a disgrace that you never put it to use in keeping in contact with your friends." He ran a finger delicately around his collar to loosen it without disturbing the exquisite arrangement of his neckcloth. "Not to mention letting them perish of thirst in this blasted heat."

Dominic laughed and arranged for drinks to be brought to the shady bench outside. "It's only ale, I'm afraid. They don't cater to toffs here."

Frey seized a brimming pewter tankard and took a long draft of the brew. "Ahh, that's better. Now, who are you calling a toff, *Lord* D'Acre, owner of all he surveys?" He looked around critically. "The village is part of the estate, ain't it?"

Dominic surveyed his tankard of ale and pulled a face. "Yes, but I don't actually own any of what you see, yet. I have yet to secure the estate."

Frey frowned. "What do you mean, secure it? Your father's dead, ain't he? And you're his only son."

"Yes, but his will is rather . . . complicated."

Frey snorted. "You mean he's still trying to make you dance to his tune, even from the grave!"

Dominic relaxed. He should have known Frey was one of the few people who'd understand. "Yes, you have it in a nutshell. My father tries to pull my strings even from the grave and so I must earn my inheritance."

Frey sipped his ale thoughtfully. "Dashed good ale, this. And how are you supposed to earn it?"

"By being the dutiful son and heir. By marrying the girl he so kindly picked out for me when I was sixteen."

Frey's jaw dropped. "You never told me that!"

"He never told me, either. I only found out a few weeks ago." He grimaced. "He wants me to breed sons for Wolfestone, but I'll not do it."

"You'll refuse to marry?" He shrugged. "Fair enough. Not as if you need the land or the extra income.

Dominic shook his head. "No, I'll marry, damn him. I won't let the bastard deprive me of my rights! But he won't have it all his way!"

"So, it's parson's moustra—" Frey broke off with an unconvincing cough. "Er, holy wedlock for you! Who's the lucky girl? Is she pretty? Does she love you already?"

"Not at all. She's plain, dull, and doing it for the money."

His friend stared. "Good grief! Why saddle yourself with a female of that sort? If I was going to saddle myself with a wife, I'd make sure she was dashed pretty. Not that I can—saddle myself with a wife, that is. Not till my blasted uncle turns up his toes."

"Still hanging on to the purse strings, is he?"

"As tight as if they were a lifeline," Frey said gloomily. "Keeps me—and thus my mother and sisters—on an absolute shoestring. How he expects the pittance he allows us to support myself, my mother and sisters, *and* scrape enough together for the girls' coming-outs is more than I can fathom."

Dominic nodded in sympathy. Frey's uncle controlled the huge family fortune with miserly righteousness, as if poverty was a virtue. "Let's not talk about such things here." He jerked his head back toward the inn, where anyone could be listening. "Why don't you come up to Wolfestone?" He frowned. "You never did tell me—if you didn't know I was here, why have you come?"

Frey gave him a sheepish look. "The vicar of St. Stephen's Church is old and ill and has retired to live with his daughter in Leeds."

Dominic didn't follow. "And how does this vicar concern you? Is he a relative of some sort?" Dominic drank deeply from his tankard. He was slowly developing a taste for this ale.

Frey flicked at a nonexistent spot on his jacket, "Ah, no. No relation at all." Then with an air of faint embarrassment, he added, "Actually, I am the new vicar of St. Stephen's Church—and didn't your mother ever teach you not to spit ale on a vicar? It is uncouth and disrespectful.

Luckily as your new spiritual shepherd, I can take you in hand." He wiped off the drops of ale that Dominic, in his surprise, had splattered over him.

"You're a vicar? *You?* You're joking."

Frey said with an air of great dignity, "Show some respect for a man of the cloth, heathen! I'll have you know I was ordained by the archbishop of Canterbury himself several years ago."

Dominic let out a sharp laugh. "Poor fellow was hoodwinked then! A rogue like you dressed in sheep's clothing."

"Sheep's clothing?" Affronted, Frey adjusted the lapels of his coat. "It may not have been tailored especially for me, but this is very fine merino cloth, you ignorant clod! As for calling me a rogue, you were always the wolf in our pack."

Dominic shook his head. "You—a parson? But why, Frey, why?"

His friend shrugged. "Got to earn the readies however I can. Never did have a head for business, can't afford to get killed in the army—then Mama and the girls would be left utterly destitute after my uncle passes on—am too shatter-brained to be a diplomat, so the church it must be."

Dominic laughed. "I can't seem to take it in. You, the new vicar of—where?"

"St. Stephen's. Just for a few months—I hope—until they find someone permanent. It's reputed to be one of the poorest livings in Shropshire."

"And where is this St. Stephen's?"

Frey shook his head in mock reproof. "Right here in this village of yours, you heathen!"

"Good God!"

"Exactly. I am glad to hear you know that, at least!" his friend said severely. He put down the tankard and rose to his feet. "Thanks for the drink, Dom. Now, I must get on to the vicarage. I'll be conducting my first service on Sunday. You'll come, of course."

Dominic rolled his eyes and heaved a long-suffering sigh.

"Excellent," Frey clapped him on the shoulder. "I knew you wouldn't let an old friend down." He held out a hand to shake and said softly, "You know, it really is *dashed* good to see you, old friend. I've missed you."

Wordlessly, Dominic wrung his old friend's hand. He was damned pleased to see Frey, too. His eyes fell on a pile of baggage that had been loaded into a rustic handcart. Shabby, old-fashioned, yet stamped with the Netterton family crest, it could only belong to Frey.

"Didn't you drive your curricle?" It was Frey's pride and joy.

Frey shook his head and said in a stuffy ecclesiastical voice, "A village vicar can't swan around in a vehicle more suited for sport than pastoral visits." He resumed his normal voice. "Came by stage. I had to sell the curricle and the pair anyway. Beautiful steppers they were—you should have seen them, Dom. But—" He sighed. "Needed the money. And so the bishop is lending me his ancient gig." He pronounced the word with some distaste, and pulled a face as his friend let out a shout of laughter. "It should arrive some time this week."

"And in the meantime?"

"I walk," said the Reverend Netterton with dignity. "And pay rustics to carry whatever I cannot manage. D'you know, a wretched urchin tried to wrest my baggage from me the moment I alighted from the stage! Wanted sixpence for it! As bad as London! I sent him off with a flea in his ear."

"You came by *stage*!" Dominic was shocked. Things were worse than he thought.

Frey sighed. "Bishop's orders. Privation is supposed to do my character good," he admitted. "Though I don't see how anyone becomes a better person by living in squalor. Seems to me people just get meaner and more desperate—but try telling the bishop that!"

Dominic laughed and strolled over to where his horse stood, hitched to a post in the shade. "Here, take my horse for today, at least." He tossed his friend the reins.

"Won't you need it?"

"No, I can take a shortcut through the woods. It'll only take me fifteen minutes. You can use Hex to get around the district until your gig arrives."

"I will then, and to hell with bishop's orders. But . . . Hex?" Frey raised his brow. "Not delving into witchcraft, are you, Dom? That would really be pushing things with the bishop."

Dominic smiled a slow smile. "No, but the horse is a stubborn brute. Good-looking, but not too bright. His full name is Hexton."

Frey glanced more closely at the horse and grinned. "A gelding I see. The next time I see Hexton I'll tell him you've named a horse after him."

"Only the rear end."

Frey spluttered with laughter. "Hexton is a rising star in government, you know."

"See? Told him at school he'd come to a bad end and I was right." Dominic stretched. "Come up to the house and dine with us this evening. See what my doting papa left me—or not as the case may be. Country hours. Spartan conditions, which will delight your bishop. I gather the bishop in question is your uncle."

Frey nodded gloomily. "Yes, Uncle Ceddie, rot his purple stockings! He's always had it in for me, ever since I put glue in his mitre. No sense of humor at all! Little did I know he'd turn even more ghastly with age. Should have put an asp in the mitre instead!"

Grace followed Granny Wigmore's directions to the fairy pool and found the pathway with no trouble. It was narrow and soft with leaf litter. The forest was quiet; probably all the creatures were sleeping through the afternoon heat. Grace trod quietly, not wishing to disturb the peace.

Much as she'd quite enjoyed marshaling the troops in the Battle of Wolfestone, it was wonderful to be away from the endless questions and to be alone with her thoughts.

The beech trees grew more densely here and the sunlight pierced the leaf canopy in golden shafts in which dust motes danced. It looked glorious against the deep green.

Beech trees gave way gradually to alders, and she knew from Granny's directions that she must be getting close. And then suddenly she was out of the gloom with the pool before her, half its surface dark and in shadow, and the other half rippling and dancing as it caught the last of the afternoon sunlight.

The pool was fed by a small brook that burbled down from the hills, tumbling out through a collection of rocks opposite Grace. The water looked clean and cool and wonderful; a fairy pool indeed. According to Granny Wigmore she should bathe her face in it on the rising of the new moon. It would help rid her of the freckles she said. The pool was a special place: magic.

It was hardly the rising of the new moon, but Grace didn't care. She was going to bathe more than her face and she devoutly hoped her henna freckles survived the dip. If they didn't, she'd have to renew them. She sat on the narrow border of soft green grass and pulled off her shoes and stockings. She quickly undressed, stripping off until she was down to her chemise and drawers.

Leaving her clothes in a pile on the grass, she stepped into the pool and shuddered deliciously as water lapped at her ankles. The floor of the pool was soft and her toes squished deliciously in the mud. She waded out another few steps, flinching as the cold water embraced her hot flesh. It seemed freezing, but experience had taught her that once in, it would not feel so cold. Grace's sisters liked to take forever to get into the water, wading in by inches, jumping as each new inch was wet. Not Grace. She was an all or nothing girl. She closed her eyes, took a deep breath, held her nose and submerged herself.

She bobbed to the surface gasping, her whole body tingling with exhilaration. It felt glorious, but cold. She decided to swim to the rocks on the other side, where the sun still shone. She crossed the pool swiftly, enjoying the ripples that spread out in front of her as she swam, pushing her arms out ahead of her and kicking like a frog. She reached the rocks and climbed out. They were smooth, sculpted in strange flowing shapes from years of being washed by the water and surrounded by ferns and mossy crevasses. She caught the clear, spurting water in her hands and drank deeply of it. It was the best water she'd ever tasted.

She sat on the rocks for a while, dangling her feet in the spring, enjoying the contrast of the hot rocks and the cool water. It wouldn't do to stay in the sun too long: she didn't want to develop real freckles, so she slipped back into the deep water.

Halfway across she stopped and floated on her back a moment, enjoying the sensation of weightlessness.

Melly must be so hot in all those clothes. Grace should teach her to swim. Her father wouldn't allow her to swim in the sea, but here, in the privacy of the forest, they could swim and be private and Sir John wouldn't be any the wiser.

How deep was this spring? Granny had called it bottomless. She took a deep breath and dived down as far as she could but she didn't touch the bottom. Bottomless indeed. Maybe it was magic, after all. She returned to her floating.

IT WAS HOT AND HIS RIDING BOOTS HAD NOT BEEN CONSTRUCTED for walking. Dominic peeled off his coat and swung it over his shoulder. The woods were shady, but not a breath of air stirred the leaves. Beside him, his dog trotted, panting. She came to a faintly marked offshoot of the pathway, ran up it a short way, stopped, and looked back.

"Oho, so that's your plan, is it?" Dominic said.

Sheba's tail wagged. Her tongue lolled.

"Yes, it is hot, I agree. Very well then, since you insist."

Chapter Eleven

Chance is always powerful. Let your hook be always cast; in the pool where you least expect it, there will be a fish.

OVID

GRACE WASN'T SURE HOW MUCH TIME HAD PASSED BUT SHE thought she heard a splash. She opened her eyes and looked around but could see nothing, so she closed her eyes again, moving her arms and legs lazily, just enough to keep from floating into full sun. It was simply bliss floating here, cool and calm and free of—

No. It was definitely a splash. She looked again and this time she saw the shape of a dog among the reeds on the shallow end of the lake. She started to relax, then the dog moved clear of the reeds for a moment. A white dog with liver speckles. Lord D'Acre's dog, Sheba, who was rarely far from her master . . .

She narrowed her eyes against the glare of sun on the water and, shading her face with one hand, scanned the shore more carefully. That was when she spotted him, standing on the edge of the lake, leaning against a tree, arms folded, watching her in a leisurely manner. In his buckskin riding breeches, dark green jacket, and brown riding boots he'd blended perfectly against the forest background.

A couple of feet away from him was the neatly folded mound that was her clothing. Most of her clothing, thank goodness, not all.

"How long have you been there?" she called, treading water.

He stepped forward. "Good afternoon, Greystoke. Perfect day for a swim, I quite agree." He pulled his cravat free.

Grace glanced around but there was no place she could climb out of the lake. The bank was too steep on this side. "Have you been there long?"

"Long enough." Without taking his eyes off her he shrugged himself out of his coat and laid it beside him. On top of her pile of clothes.

Long enough for what? she wondered. She was decently enough covered by the water at the moment—only her head was visible—but what about when she'd been floating? She'd worn only her chemise and drawers and she knew from experience that they were almost transparent when wet.

He sat down on the grass and began to pull off his boots.

"What are you doing?"

"Taking off my boots."

"I can see that, but why?"

He gave her a look, as if to point out the banality of the question. "Because I don't want to ruin them."

He couldn't possibly be going to do what she thought he was going to! She watched as he pulled off first one boot, then the other. He drew his stockings off, tossed them down beside the boots then stood up. He unbuttoned the top buttons of his shirt and pulled it over his head. Again, he was not wearing an undershirt.

"Stop that right now!" she ordered.

"Stop what?" he asked politely, and began to unfasten his breeches.

"Don't you dare!" she yelled from her watery position, helpless with frustration.

"Don't I dare what, Greystoke?" She couldn't see the glint in those wicked eyes of his, but she knew perfectly well it was there.

"Don't I dare swim, is that what you mean? You needn't worry on my behalf, I am accounted an excellent swimmer." He finished unfastening his breeches and pushed them down his legs. Grace covered her eyes with her hands. "What about you, Greystoke? Are you also an excellent swimmer, or have you only mastered floating?"

She kept her hands firmly over her eyes. He couldn't possibly see from there that she was peeping through the cracks. The devil. He was still wearing his drawers. "If you wish to swim, then turn your back and I will come out."

"Oh, there's plenty of room."

"That's not the point." Mixed bathing was scandalous—unless it was husband and wife, and even then, it was very daring.

He shook out his breeches and tossed them over her clothes. They sprawled in lewd parody. "Now don't fuss, Greystoke. Nobody can see."

That was a lie for a start. She could see! Hands clamped across her eyes, fingers parted every so slightly, she couldn't take her eyes off him.

He stretched as if to loosen tight muscles. Her mouth dried as she watched, even though she was surrounded by water. He was magnificent; spare and hard muscled, broad shouldered, deep chested and narrow hipped. His legs were long and powerful, and the contrast of his white drawers against his tanned skin only served to draw her eyes to where the fabric bunched.

He was tanned all over. He probably swam naked most of the time. Even as the thought crossed her mind he hooked his thumbs in the waistband of his drawers.

"Don't you dare!" she screeched.

He grinned, a white flash of teeth. "Greystoke, you naughty girl, you were watching after all. Tsk, tsk, tsk."

She felt her face flame and bobbed under the water to cool her heated cheeks. When she surfaced he was still standing on the bank, watching her. His legs were braced apart and the fabric of his drawers seemed to be bunched even more. She promptly turned her back.

"Don't turn around on my account. I don't mind you staring. I'm flattered that you want to watch me undress."

"I don't!" she gasped, scandalized by his words, even though a tiny part of her knew it was true. "And I wasn't staring! I just peeked for a second, and the only reason I did is because I don't trust you!"

"Not trust me?"

"No! Now please turn your back and let me out."

He instantly stepped back and made a courtly gesture of invitation. "If you want to get out, then don't mind me. In fact I'll help you out. The mud of the bank looks quite slippery." He moved right to the edge and held out his hand to her, as a footman held out his hand to help a lady climb out of a carriage. Only no footman was ever so naked. Nor a lady so inadequately dressed.

"You know very well I won't get out with you standing there half naked. Go and swim in that section of the lake and when you're there, I shall get out." She pointed to the far corner of the lake.

"But why do you want to get out? It's my lake. I don't mind sharing."

"I won't bandy words with you a moment longer," she said snippily. "Now, I want to get out, so just go!"

"But you bandy them so delightfully." He frowned. "Are you cold?"

She seized on the excuse thankfully. "Yes, I'm cold and I want to get out. Now please move!"

"Yes, certainly. If you're cold, you need to be warmed, instantly," he said and dived in.

Grace took advantage of the moment and swam as fast as she could toward the lake's edge—not the section where her clothes were, but a closer shore. She did not want to risk bumping into him as he surfaced from his dive. She would climb out and then use branches to screen her modesty while she skirted the lake back to her clothes.

He did not surface immediately, and she made good progress in closing the gap to the shore, but the closer she got, the more she started to worry. He had been under a long time. Had he hit his head? Was he caught in some underwater snag, some drowned tree roots, or perhaps a thick clump of water weeds?

She slowed and stood up. The water was only waist deep. She scanned the surface, but all she could see were ripples. He had dived in a good distance from her and the glittering surface of the water made it impossible to see beneath it.

How long had it been? One minute? Two? It was hard to tell. She was seriously worried by now. Nobody could possibly hold their breath for such a long time. He was in trouble! She started to flounder her way across to where he'd dived in.

"Missed me?" With a whoosh of water, he surfaced directly in front of her.

"Wha—" She had no time to say another word, for he wrapped his arms around her, holding her hard against him, and hugged her tight. She was so relieved that she actually hugged him back for a moment. He held her hard against him, one arm locked around her waist and the other rubbing gently up and down her back. Floating in the cool water, his skin cold, his body hot, she could feel every breath he took, and every beat of his heart.

And then his hand closed over one buttock and squeezed and she came to her senses.

She was almost naked, dressed in her underwear and he was as close to naked and she could feel every hard muscle of him pressed against her. She tried to push him away.

"No, no," he said, pulling her tighter. "You said you were cold, so I'm warming you. I can feel you shivering."

She shoved at him again. "Warming me, my foot! You're being perfectly shameless!"

He loosened his hold on her, but kept his arms linked around her waist. His eyes danced like sun on the water. White teeth glinted. "You are trembling, you know." His smile was pure male satisfaction.

She thumped him on the arm and then crossed her arms defensively against his prying eyes. "If I'm trembling, it's because I thought you might be drowning! Where did you disappear to? You couldn't possibly have stayed under the water so long."

"I could. I did."

"But it was minutes." Her heart was still thudding from the fright he'd given her.

"I told you, I'm an excellent swimmer." His fingers crept between the space between chemise and drawers and caressed the tender skin in the small of her back. It sent tingles up and down her spine.

"But my brother-in-law Nicholas is also an excellent swimmer and even he couldn't stay under that long." She held on to his shoulder with one hand; she was a little out of her depth. Her body bumped gently against his.

He shrugged. "Nicholas probably didn't spend his childhood diving for pennies thrown from rich people's boats. You develop an ability to stay down longer." His voice was deep and quiet, creating a small intimate space of the stretch of the lake.

"What? Why were you diving for pennies?"

"Pennies add up. Sometimes I got enough to buy a meal."

"A meal? You mean you needed the money *to eat*?"

"Everyone needs money." He smoothed back a damp lock of hair from her eyes.

Not like that, she thought. It meant he was in danger of starving! "Where was this?"

"Naples, mostly. And a couple of times in Alexandria for fun." He looked down into her eyes and said softly, "Don't look so horrified, Greystoke. I quite enjoyed it at the time. I was very competitive and I outdived and outswam the other boys, so my efforts were quite well rewarded."

She put a hand to his cheek, knowing it was futile to wish to comfort a boy who no longer existed. "Poor little boy," she whispered.

"Nonsense," he said gruffly. "I was a tough little urchin." He turned his face and kissed her inner palm. She felt it clear to her toes. They curled in the depths.

"I ruled the street urchins." His hands kept sliding up and down over her waist and hips, but she was so distracted by his story that she forgot to push them away. Besides, it felt so good.

"In Naples? And Alexandria?" She stared at him, trying

to see in his face some sign of a young boy who needed to dive for pennies to make ends meet. "But how could that be? You were—you are—the heir to Wolfestone. The lords of D'Acre have never been poor. Did your father not—"

"I was born in Italy and grew up abroad." He'd cut her off. She'd noticed before that he didn't like talking about his father. Dimly she realized his hands were under her chemise and against her naked skin but she couldn't seem to care.

"Yes, and that's why you didn't know where anything was that first day."

"You remembered." His teeth glinted. "It's also why I am so good in the water," he murmured and slid his hands around to cup her breasts. His thumbs rubbed across the tips of her breasts. Her lower body curled up as if to meet him, and something deep within her clenched. He rubbed them again and her whole body convulsed in a shudder. She was so surprised she nearly sank. She clutched his shoulders tightly.

"Wrap your legs around my waist," he told her. "That will make you more secure."

Dazed, she obeyed without question and it wasn't until she felt his warm, hard body pressed against her inner thighs that she realized how exposed this position made her. She started to shift, but his hands dropped to her thighs and stopped her.

"Stay where you are," he growled softly, cupping her thighs and then her buttocks. "You're quite safe here with me."

Safe was hardly the word. She felt open, exposed, vulnerable. But before she could say a word, his mouth captured hers, taking possession with a gentle, searching tenderness that completely undid her, as if he was learning her, worshiping her.

Her eyes were shut and she could see the sun glowing redly through the closed lids, then a shadow fell over her face and he kissed her eyelids with a tenderness that made her want to weep.

She opened her eyes and looked at him, drinking in the features of his face anew, as if she'd never seen him before.

Golden eyes burning into her, he bent and kissed her again, as softly as before. She did not want to be worshiped, was not yet ready to be possessed quite so completely. She clutched his head with both hands and kissed him back, softly, carefully. She had some vague notion that she could exercise some command—of herself at least, if not of him or the situation.

It was a foolish notion. The moment she returned his kiss he gave a fierce growl, deep in his throat—exultation, triumph, satisfaction perhaps, and deepened the kiss and she was swept away by the unleashed power of his wanting her. It vibrated through his body; the very air around them thrummed with it.

He kissed her as if she meant all the world to him.

She had no resistance to him. She was his creature, his being. And she gloried in his every caress.

Her body clung to him, molding her curves to his hard-muscled strength. She kissed, licked, nipped, oblivious to anything but the taste and feel and smell of him.

His hands held, caressed, squeezed and suddenly she realized her chemise had come undone and her breasts were bare and bobbing in the water. She opened her eyes, in time to see the flare in his as he beheld them.

"Such a beauty you are, my love," he murmured and cupped them, smoothing his big thumbs back and forth over her engorged nipples. She shuddered and clenched around him, flinging her head back, her eyes closed to the sky. Her world had shrunk to this moment, these feelings, and this man. He stroked and caressed her until she felt she could bear no more and then he lowered his head and his hot mouth closed around a cold and tender nipple.

She made a soft, high sound deep in her throat and convulsed, gripping his waist hard with her thighs, as if trying to take him into her. She shuddered and thrust against him in need, silently demanding he take her, blind to everything.

The blood roared in him and for a moment Dominic forgot—forgot his resolution to make love to her the first time in a bed, forgot that they were out in the open, standing in a lake.

Her legs straddled him, and he could feel the warm nakedness of her against his belly. He slipped his hand down between them and cupped her there, where the slit in her drawers exposed her to him. Not for the first time he applauded the practical design of women's drawers.

He cupped and stroked her soft, warm folds and she trembled against him, urging him with her thighs and making breathy little squeaks of abandon. He circled the hard little nubbin with his thumb and watched the sensations take her as it built and she arched and climaxed against him.

He was hard and aching and his cock was hot and nudging at her entrance when the sound of frenzied barking and splashing nearby distracted her. His own blasted dog!

Her eyes flew open. She looked around dazedly, clutching his shoulders and as he watched, her eyes widened with awareness of the position they were in. She stared blindly at where Sheba had startled some creature and was barking excitedly and splashing through the shallows and reeds at the far end of the lake.

She turned back and stared at him, panting. He was breathing nearly as hard as she was. He saw confusion and then panic dawn in her eyes as she worked out exactly what was pressing against her so intimately.

One quick thrust and she would be his. It took all of Dominic's self-control not to do it.

She must have seen it in his eyes, because she said, "No!" It came out in a gasp. She loosened her grip on him and pushed herself away, almost going under as she'd forgotten she couldn't stand. He caught her by the arm. "Steady, you're all right now."

She blinked and looked away. She was embarrassed, he saw. A surge of tenderness washed over him.

"We did nothing wrong," he assured her quietly.

She made a small sound of disbelief.

"We are free agents, you and I," he reminded her.

She froze, her back still to him, then whirled, "No, *you* are a betrothed man!" she said and began to swim to shore.

Grace was mortified. Admittedly their lower regions had been hidden by the water, but what she'd been about to do shocked her.

She swam as fast as she could, seeking to put as much distance between them as possible.

What had come over her? His hand had been inside her drawers, touching her in the most intimate way a man could touch a woman. Almost.

As the thought occurred to her, she felt her body clench deep inside, and an echo of pleasure rippled through her. She swam harder.

Granny Wigmore had warned her she'd lose her morals if she bathed in Gwydion's Pool.

FREY RODE SLOWLY UP THE DRIVEWAY LEADING TO DOMINIC'S home. No, not Dom's home, he corrected himself—

Wolfestone. Lord, but the entire estate had seen better days. He wondered what plans his friend had for it.

Somehow he couldn't see Dom settling down to contented domesticity. He'd never settled anywhere. The original rolling stone, that was Dom.

He dismounted at the front entrance and when no one came running to fetch his horse, he espied a couple of fellows working on repairing a window and gave them a whistle. One looked up and Frey gestured him to approach. The moment the man was close enough, Frey tossed him the reins.

"Take this beast to the stables, will you and make sure he's well watered and gets a good rubdown." He pressed a copper coin into the man's hand and horse and man trotted off happily enough.

Frey rang the doorbell. It was opened by an urchin, the same urchin who'd tried to make off with his luggage earlier, only now he had dirt on his nose and hair full of cobwebs. Frey wrinkled his nose fastidiously. "I'm here to see Lord D'Acre," he said.

"Sorry, 'e's not 'ere," the urchin said and made to close the door.

Reluctantly, for they were his second-best boots, Frey stuck a foot in the door and prevented him. "Listen, you scrubby bra—" Luckily he remembered he was now a vicar and as such was above squabbling with urchins. He reopened the conversation in a more dignified tone. "My son, I am here to visit Lord D'Acre. He is expecting me."

The urchin frowned. "I'm not your son and I told you a minute ago, Lord D'Acre's not 'ere."

"It's a figure of speech," Frey explained testily. "I'm the new vicar and I will come in and wait. I spoke to Lord D'Acre not an hour since and he invited me here. He told me he was on his way home." He pushed open the door and entered. He glanced around at the grim, gray hallway. Dom had told him conditions were spartan, but really!

He looked down his nose at the boy. "And who might you be?"

The child threw out his chest. "Billy Finn. I'm Lord D'Acre's personal gen'ral factotum!"

"Good God!"

The brat scowled at him. "You wouldn't talk to me like that if I 'ad me uniform!" he muttered.

"No uniform could lend luster to a boy with hair full of cobwebs," Frey declared austerely. "Now, conduct me to a sitting room and fetch me some refreshments."

The boy combed at his hair with his fingers, wiped his hands on his breeches, then sulkily threw open a door. "In 'ere, then."

"Such grace and style." Frey was about to enter the room when a soft voice behind him said, "Are you looking for Lord D'Acre? I'm afraid he's out at the moment."

He turned and coming down the stairs was a girl who seemed to Frey to be all softness and curves. She descended the stairs carefully, with an earnest expression that charmed him. She had a round, soft face with a quantity of brown curls, simply drawn back and pulled into a loose knot from which dozens of tendrils had escaped. She saw him watching her and blushed. Her hand went to her hair. "I'm sorry, things have been at sixes and sevens this afternoon and my hair is a mess—"

"You look charming," Frey assured her.

She gave him a doubtful look. "Billy, dear, would you please ask Mrs. Stokes to send us a pot of tea and some of her lovely lemon biscuits—" She turned to Frey. "Or would you prefer coffee? Or something stronger?"

"Tea and lemon biscuits would be delightful," he said, surprising himself. He hated tea. He watched her organizing the urchin. He supposed he'd have to get used to drinking tea. It was the sort of thing vicars were forced to drink.

"Please, will you take a seat?" she invited. "I'm sorry, I didn't catch your name."

He bowed instantly. "Humphrey Netterton at your service. I'm an old friend of Dominic's—Lord D'Acre's I should say."

"And I am Miss Pettifer." She said it as if he should know who she was. She held out her hand and he took it in his. Like the rest of her, it was small and very soft. Her eyes were brown and exactly matched her hair. Her skin was like cream.

They stood there, staring at each other until Frey recalled himself enough to fill the silence. He said, "I am also the new vicar of St. Stephen's."

"Oh." Her face crumpled. "I am v-very p-p-pleased to meet y-you," she managed and burst into tears.

There was only one course of action a man could take under these circumstances, Frey realized. He drew her against his chest, put his arms around her, and let her sob her little heart out all over his exquisitely arranged neckcloth.

She sobbed against him, quivering in his arms like a little mouse. He held her and patted her back and made soothing noises. Her curls tickled his nose. He inhaled the scent of her. She smelled of . . . he frowned, trying to place the scent. Something sweet and uncomplicated . . . like soap and . . . pansies? Did pansies have a scent? He wasn't sure, but that's what she reminded him of, a pansy.

"I'm sorry," she managed to say on a hiccough after a few moments. "I don't know what came over me."

"There, there," he soothed. "You said things had been at sixes and sevens."

She looked up at him, her eyes swimming. "My father is very ill. The doctor is with him."

His arms tightened around her. "Hush now, I'm sure everything will be all right."

"I—I think h-he's going to—going to—." She could not say it. Her full lower lip quivered.

Without thought Frey cupped her chin, tilted her face up, and kissed her gently. She tasted of sweetness and peppermints.

"It will be all right."

She blinked and gave him a watery smile. "You're very k-kind, but I fear the worst. Papa has been asking to s-speak to a m-minister for days. I think he wants to make his p-peace with God, b-before . . . before . . ."

She looked at him with tragic eyes. "And now y-you are here and he can and s-so I fear he will d-die soon." Her face crumpled again, and she sobbed anew into his neckcloth. It was ruined anyway, Frey thought, rubbing her back in soothing circles.

Poor little soul. If her father was dying . . .

Good grief! *He* was the minister who was expected to help Miss Pettifer's father make his peace. Frey swallowed. He'd never given comfort to the dying before. He hoped she was mistaken.

She clutched at his sleeve. "Will you do something for me, please?"

Frey found himself saying yes.

"I don't want you to see Papa yet. I am afraid . . . afraid, that once he has spoken to you . . ." She broke off, unable to go on.

That he will give up the ghost, Frey supplied silently. "Yes, if you think it's best, I will stay away. But if he starts to fail, you know I must go to him."

She nodded, tearfully. "Yes, of course. Thank you." She looked a little guilty. "He is bedridden, so . . . he will not know you are here unless anyone tells him. But I promise you if he—if the worst—"

Frey took her hand. "I know." He closed his eyes to pray for her father's rapid recovery.

Instead, he found himself remembering the taste of those soft, sweet lips . . .

He hadn't meant to kiss her. He didn't know what had come over him, actually. It was most uncharacteristic. Thank God she hadn't reacted badly. It would have been frightful if she'd set up a screeching.

Come to think of it, she'd hardly reacted at all. His technique must be slipping.

Well, of course the girl hadn't reacted, he told himself. Her father was dying. What did a kiss from a relative stranger matter when she was facing the unimaginable. He knew how he'd felt when his father had died. Poor little thing. His arms tightened around her.

She was so wonderfully soft . . .

Chapter Twelve

Thou strong seducer, Opportunity!
JOHN DRYDEN

GRACE REACHED THE SHORE OF THE LAKE AND BEGAN TO CLIMB OUT. He moaned and she turned to see what was the matter. He moaned again.

"Are you in pain?" she called.

"Agony," he said, but he didn't look like a man who was ill. His golden gaze roamed over her, gleaming with enjoyment. She clapped her arms over herself, striving for modesty. "Turn your back."

"Not humanly possible."

She turned her back and scrambled for her clothes. He moaned again. "Like a peach wrapped in tissue paper," he said when she bent over.

She snapped upright, holding her clothes against her. "Will you stop that nonsense?"

"It's not nonsense, it's poetry. You are living poetry." He began to wade out of the water and she got a glimpse of what she must look like to him. His drawers were almost transparent, clinging to his body, as he said, like tissue paper, only not around a peach . . .

She tried not to stare, but could not help herself. It was not material bunching after all . . .

"Stop there," she croaked.

His eyes glimmered with amusement. "Willingly," and promptly posed for her like a Greek statue, changing poses rapidly. Only none of Lord Elgin's marbles looked a bit like this man. He was bigger, more masculine, and he lived and breathed. The taste of him was still in her mouth.

"Stop it," she spluttered with reluctant laughter. "Cover yourself."

"Can't. My drawers need to dry first, otherwise when I return to Wolfestone they will be all wet in certain places and people will wonder what on earth I have been doing." He looked at her and added, "And they will see damp patches on your dress, too, and they will add two and two . . ."

Grace bit her lip indecisively. She wanted to be securely covered from head to toe, right now, but he was right.

"As I see it, you have two choices—you can take off your wet clothes and put the dry ones on over a naked body." He looked at her from under his brows. "In which case you will have to somehow hide your underclothes as you walk up to the house. I could put them in my pocket and carry them for you."

There was no way in the world she was giving him her underwear.

"Or you can sit in the sun and let your underclothes dry and then you can get dressed. That's what I'm doing." He stretched out on the grass and she steadfastly avoided looking where she most wanted to look.

"Very well, I'll do that, too," she decided. He patted the grass beside him, but she shook her head. "No, I'll sit over here." She sat down on the other side of a bush where she felt securely screened.

"Ah, like Pyramus and Thisbe," he said. "How sad."

"Not at all like them," she retorted. "We are not star-crossed lovers!"

"But we are lovers," he said and stepped around the bush.

She sat shielding herself from him, knowing it was futile after what they'd done in the lake. She was silent for a moment, then said, "I can't."

He sat down a short distance away from her. "It's all right, I know. You're not ready for me yet. I can wait."

She shook her head. "There's no point waiting, I'm not going to change my mind."

He just smiled. She shivered inside. It wasn't from cold. Or fear. She turned her back on him. She could still feel his warm gaze slipping over her like a touch, a caress, but at least she couldn't see him. She sat on the fresh green grass, hugging her knees, rocking back and forth. Her emotions were in turmoil.

They were not really star-crossed. Melly didn't want him, but her betrothal was still official. Grace wanted him, but he acted like a free man, and he wasn't. That disturbed her.

What did *he* want? To make love to her, yes. A few moments of passing pleasure, yes. But what else?

She didn't know him very well, and what she did know wasn't encouraging. He didn't want a home. He didn't want children. Ever.

There'd been no talk of marriage between them. Or even love. He'd called her "my love" once, but that was just an endearment, and he'd been in extremis at the time.

Her breasts still tingled from his caresses. She hunched over them.

He thought she was a hired companion. Men had a double standard toward women of different classes, she knew. For all she knew he might be just wanting to tumble her as lords had tumbled servant girls for centuries. Droit du seigneur.

Of course she could tell him who she really was; there was no need to keep up the imposture now that Sir John was so ill. But she didn't want to. Yet.

She'd never been in this position before, where a man reacted to *her*, to Grace herself. Not to Miss Merridew, a diamond of the ton, or Miss Merridew, heiress, but to simple, ordinary Grace, a girl who'd grown up in a cold, miserable house, and who, like her sisters, had nourished herself on dreams.

But dreams could deceive.

Two of her sisters had allowed their dreams of love to deceive them. Both Prudence and Faith had made disastrous mistakes at first, mistaking their own deep yearning for love as the real thing and falling for men who were unprincipled rogues.

They'd let their dreams of love blind them into taking terrible risks, giving themselves and their happiness into the hands of unworthy men. Both their lives had nearly been ruined forever. Luckily they hadn't, but it made Grace wary.

She was not yet ready to take the same risk. Not for a man who she'd only known a few days, and who, despite his soft words and caressing ways, might turn out to be just another untrustworthy rake.

She needed more than soft words and tender caresses. The taste of ecstasy he'd shown her in the lake couldn't be allowed to affect her.

Or that when he kissed her it felt like he was a man who'd come out of a desert and she was his first taste of water . . .

No, that couldn't be allowed to matter.

He might seem to be the embodiment of all her secret dreams, but she couldn't trust her feelings yet. Not while he remained betrothed to Melly. Not while she knew so little about him.

"I have other plans," she told him at last. She rose to her feet and went behind a bush to don her dress.

"Do you want help with your corset?" he asked.

"No, thank you," she said crisply. She had, in fact, left off the corset when she decided to come swimming but she didn't want to alert him to the fact.

As she emerged, fully dressed, he said, "Ah, I see you've left off the corset. How delightful." He'd dressed very rapidly, too.

She crossed her arms across her breasts and fought the blush.

"Why hide what I've already memorized, already tasted?"

His soft words threatened to melt all her resolve. She turned and hurried down the path.

He followed her. "What other plans?"

It took her a moment to realize what he was asking about. The way he'd looked at her made her so . . . flustered. "I want to travel. I want to sail into Venice at dawn, I want to see the moon rise over the pyramids, to stand in front of the Sphinx and know how small and insignificant I am. I want to sail in a felucca down the Nile and to ride a camel." She turned and began to march down the pathway.

He followed. "A camel?"

"Yes, why not? I think it would be very exciting to ride a camel. A ship of the desert, isn't that a wonderful expression?"

"Camels smell, they spit, and they sneer."

"Sneer?" She laughed.

"No man on earth can sneer as well as a camel, I promise you," he said. "And they're vilely stubborn! And as for the ship of the desert, that no doubt comes from their rocking gait, like a ship on a rough sea. I hope you don't get seasick."

She ignored that. He was just teasing, she could tell. "Have you ridden a camel?"

"Many times. And I'll tell you now, I'd take a horse any day."

"Yes, but a camel is so exotic."

"Not in Egypt."

She beamed at him. "Exactly." They reached the castle driveway and he took her hand and tucked it under his arm.

She told him, "If I hadn't come here with Mel—Miss Pettifer, I would be packing now to leave for Egypt with the cousin of the British consul general."

"Really?"

"Yes, it was all arranged. We were going to sail to Alexandria . . ." She looked at him shyly. "Would you tell me about Alexandria, please?"

He said nothing. He stopped and frowned as if in deep thought.

"Not, of course, if the memory is painful," she said quickly.

"Oh, it's not painful. It's just that I remembered something more important." He turned to her and said in a solemn tone, "Do you know, your freckles stop just below your neckline. There's not a single one below here." He traced a finger along the round neckline of her dress, leaving her skin tingling. "I was"—he darted her an intense look—"distracted at the time, but I've just realized it. Isn't that fascinating?"

"Not a bit." She stepped away from him. "I told you I had other plans. I'll tell you something else, Lord D'Acre—I don't dally with the *fiancés* of other girls. I don't dally with husbands, either. In fact I don't dally at all." She bared her teeth in a smile. "So, now you can ignore me completely."

"I don't want to ignore you, Greystoke," he murmured.

She made a careless gesture. "Then don't. But if it's dalliance you want, I believe the Tickel girls thrive on it, so you could try them."

"I don't want a Tickel girl."

"Are you sure? They're very pretty. I think Tansy is the prettiest, but Tilly has the lovelier smile and her complexion is a dream."

"I prefer freckles. Especially where they stop."

She blushed and tried to carry it off. "Oh, of course it must be Tessa; she's by far the most curvaceous of the three. I know men set great store in curves when it's a matter of dalliance."

"Do they?"

"So I'm led to believe." She was getting a little flustered by his stare.

He gave her an enigmatic look. "I have no interest in any Tickel curves. Nor Tickel smiles or complexions or any Tickel quality whatsoever. I like small, gray spitfires with freckles."

"Well, you can't have them—us—me!" She hurried up the driveway alone.

"Oh, can't I?" He called after her. "I'm a Wolfe—we

don't wait for invitations. We choose our prey and hunt it down. Consider yourself warned, Miss Prey."

When Dominic arrived at the house he found Frey ensconced in a parlor eating lemon biscuits and sipping gingerly from a teacup, which Miss Pettifer refilled as he arrived. Dominic's lips twitched. He'd heard Frey before on the subject of tea.

Frey rapidly explained his mission. "Sorry to thrust myself on you so dashed early, Dom, but the vicarage is in a mess, I'm afraid."

"In what way?"

"Storm a few days ago, I'm told. Seems to have blown off half the slates. The roof has leaked, quite badly. Everything is wet and rotting—the stink is frightful. Dashed inconvenient, but act of God, y'know. I was hoping to prevail on your hospitality, Dom, and stay at Wolfestone."

"Of course, Frey. You are very welcome, of course, though conditions here are rather more spartan than you're used to."

"Oh, not so spartan—Miss Pettifer here has made me very welcome." He smiled at her, almost fatuously, Dominic thought.

She blushed and murmured something inaudible.

"I see you've met my betrothed," Dominic said.

"Eh?" Frey's jaw dropped and he spilled tea all over his dove-gray inexpressibles.

Mrs. Stokes outdid herself at dinner that night, triumphantly serving up trout with almonds, a fricassee of chicken, green beans, rice and veal soup, potato pie, roasted quails, something she called a fidget pie, made up of bacon and apples, which tasted surprisingly good, a grand salad, several jellies, a plate of lemon curd cakes, and a trifle.

"Well, miss, I'm trying me best to tempt Sir John into eating something," she said when Grace complimented her on the meal. "He doesn't eat enough to keep a bird alive."

Grace raised her brows. "I would have thought chicken soup would have been more the thing for him."

Mrs. Stokes blushed. "Ye've caught me out, miss. I did send chicken soup and bread and butter up to Sir John—not that he touched it, poor soul. 'Tis the vicar," she confided. "Such a skinny, long lad he be, anyone can see he be in need o' some good Shropshire home cooking."

Grace laughed. It seemed they would all benefit from Mr. Netterton's lanky build.

But despite the lavish spread, nothing seemed to appeal to Melly, she noticed. She picked at her meal, merely nibbling on a morsel of chicken and some green beans. She even refused the lemon curd cakes, which Grace knew for a fact were her favorites.

"Are you feeling ill, Melly?" she whispered as the final course was removed.

"No," Melly said, surprised. "Why, do I look it?"

"It's just that you're not eating."

"Oh, that." Melly avoided her eyes. "I'm just not hungry tonight, that's all."

Grace frowned. Sir John's loss of appetite was bad enough. She hoped Melly was not falling prey to the same illness. But apart from refusing food, she looked in good health—glowing health actually.

It was the worry, Grace decided. Melly's father was not making any visible progress—in fact he was fading away to a shadow of his former self. Of course Melly was getting increasingly worried. They all were.

"GRACE." THE WHISPER CAME OUT OF THE DARK. "ARE YOU awake?"

"Yes," Grace responded. "What is it, Melly?"

"Oh, nothing. I just wondered if you were asleep yet." There was a long silence, then Melly whispered, "You like Lord D'Acre, don't you?"

How was she to answer that? Grace thought. Like was entirely the wrong word. There were times when she could happily throttle him. And times when she ached for him. "He—he's an interesting man."

"I saw you when you came in this afternoon. Your face was glowing."

"Too much sun," Grace muttered.

"No, Grace. He came up the drive just moments after you. You'd been with him, hadn't you?"

Been with him? Grace pressed a hand over her mouth. What did Melly mean by that? "I ran into him down at the lake," she said in what she hoped was a careless tone.

"I saw your face. And I saw the way you two looked at each other through dinner. You're in love, aren't you, Grace." It wasn't a question. Melly was one of her oldest friends. The two of them had whispered of love for years.

Grace sighed. "Oh, God, Melly. I don't know. All I know is that I've never felt like this. I never imagined . . ."

There was another long silence, then Melly said, "I'll talk to Papa. I'll make it right for you, Grace. I promise."

* * *

"AH, HERE YOU ARE. I THOUGHT YOU USUALLY DID YOUR GRAMMAR study in the library." Dominic strolled out onto the terrace where Greystoke was curled up in a chair, basking in the morning sun, a book in her lap. Her feet were tucked under her and her shoes lay askew on the stone flags of the terrace.

She looked up and smiled at him and, as always, he felt a catch in his chest.

"I know, but it was such a lovely morning, I thought I'd sit out here for a little while. Only I can't seem to concentrate. The sun is making me sleepy," she confessed. She closed the book and sat up in a more decorous manner, slipping her feet to the floor and fluffing her skirt out over them to hide the fact that she was barefoot. "I might try again later in the day."

"You're still determined on traveling to Egypt?" He watched her feeling surreptitiously for her shoes.

"Yes, indeed." She was determined to be sensible.

He strolled over and knelt down in front of her. "It seems an awful lot of bother to swot over an Arabic grammar book, just to look at the pyramids."

"What are you doing?" she squeaked as he reached under her skirts.

"Fetching your slippers for you." He located the errant slipper and wrapped his hand around her bare foot. Without taking his eyes off hers he took her toes into his mouth. She gasped with shock, then found herself melting at the incredible sensation. He sucked them gently at first, just playing with them, and then gradually the sucking became hard and rhythmic, and he watched the look of arousal steal over her face, softening her features.

The sound of gardeners arguing nearby recalled her to her surroundings and he felt her try to pull back. He kissed the sole of her instep, making her foot curl, and slipped the shoe on.

"I can't believe you did that!" She fussily tucked her skirt around her feet.

He grinned at her actions. "Out of sight is not out of mind, Greystoke. I know what's under your skirts, remember? And your toes taste as delicious as the rest of you."

She looked aroused, flustered, and trying hard to look disapproving. "What did you come out here for?"

Casually he dropped a small leather-bound book on the table beside her. "I found it the other day in the library and thought of you. Might be more interesting than a grammar book to read."

She opened it. "It's in Arabic," she exclaimed. "It looks like poetry . . . It is poetry!" She read some and her face lit with pleasure. "And beautiful poetry, too." She glanced up at him, her face glowing. "Did you read any of it?"

He shook his head. "That sort of nonsense is of no interest to me," he lied. "It's yours now, to keep."

Her smile dazzled him. "Thank you, I'll treasure it always," she told him softly. She hugged the book to her bosom briefly and then returned to examining it. "Oh, look, there's an inscription here in the front—the back as we think it. The ink is faded, but perfectly legible: *'To my dove, my heart, my beloved, ever yours, Faisal.'*" She sighed dreamily. "How romantic. I wonder who Faisal was. And who his beloved dove was? And how did it get here, to Wolfestone?"

He shrugged. "No idea. I have to go. Meeting with Jake Tasker." Before she realized his intent, he bent and kissed her swiftly on her soft, unwary mouth. "Enjoy the poems."

* * *

"You were surprised yesterday when you discovered I was Lord D'Acre's betrothed," Melly said to Mr. Netterton. Her father was sleeping so she'd ordered a pot of tea to be brought to them in the drawing room.

"Me? I suppose I was—I mean I didn't expect a conveni—" He broke off and cleared his throat. "Yes, a bit surprised."

"You were going to say something like you didn't expect his convenient bride to be someone like me, weren't you?" she said with dignity. "You must think me very odd."

"No," said Mr. Netterton, sipping his tea mistrustfully. "I was wondering why my friend Dominic, who I always thought was a clever chap, could be such a fool—"

Melly bit her lip. She must learn to become inured to such careless insult.

"—As to waste someone like you in a white marriage," he finished.

Melly closed her eyes in embarrassment that he even knew the conditions of the agreement. Her biggest humiliation: that Lord D'Acre didn't even want her as a brood mare.

And then his words penetrated.

Melly blinked and looked at Mr. Netterton in surprise. "You think it would be a waste?" she whispered.

"I'd say I do," he said and reached for a biscuit. "Any red-blooded man would agree with me. Dominic's a fool."

Chapter Thirteen

And listen why; for I will tell you now
What never yet was heard in tale or song.

JOHN MILTON

DOMINIC WALKED TO HIS MEETING WITH JAKE TASKER WITH A SMILE and a jaunty step. The look on her face when he'd sucked on her toes . . . He grinned. He was going to introduce her to a whole world of new pleasures.

But when he spoke to Tasker the smile dropped from his face. "Tour the estate? Good God, no! That can wait till Abdul gets here."

"No, m'lord," Tasker insisted. "You must learn the estate and its people. And they must meet you."

"Abdul is the one who'll deal with that sort of thing. The tenants can meet him. I just want to be kept informed."

But Tasker was made of sterner stuff. "Like your pa was kept informed by Mr. Eades?" It was a low blow.

Dominic compressed his lips. "The books will tell me all I need to know. It was through my examination of the books we discovered what Eades was up to."

Tasker snorted. "Us folk here could tell he was bent

from the first. By the time you found he'd been fiddling, a deal o' damage was done and honest folks ruined."

Dominic was irritated by such blunt, plain speaking, not the least because he knew the blasted fellow was right. He made one last effort. "Abdul, on the other hand, is a man I've known for ten years and is completely trustworthy. He can get to know everyone."

Tasker looked skeptical. "Aye, p'raps folk will take to some furriner, I dunno, but they'll not take kindly to him unless they've met their lord first. 'Tis a matter of respect, m'lord. You respect them and they'll respect your man. But they'll not have a bar of him unless they hear it from you."

"You don't know Abdul! I've never seen him fail."

"And Abdul ain't never worked wi' no Shropshiremen, either," Jake said simply. "Stubborn as pigs, we be, and set in our ways." He said it with pride. "Six hundred years we been here, and six hundred years Wolfes have been tellin' us what to do. That's the way it's always been, and no clever furriner will change that. If you want the estate back on its feet, m'lord, ye need to get them all behind ye. And that means ye must meet 'em, every man jack of 'em, an' listen to what they've got to say."

Dominic sighed and sent for horses to be saddled. Dammit, he'd never wanted to come here, let alone get . . . involved. This would be a superficial visit only. He would meet all the most important people, give them a nod and listen to a few opinions and that would be the end of it. Then he'd hand them over to Abdul and forget about them all.

To his surprise the first place they stopped at was a run-down hovel on the edge of the woods. Tasker dismounted and reluctantly Dominic followed suit. "Why are we stopping here."

"Thought it only right, seeing as it's on the way."

Stubborn as pigs was right, Dominic thought. Tasker had a clear idea of what he wanted Dominic to see and he wasn't going to bend to suit his lord or to curry favor during his trial period. Dominic might be irritated at having to do what he would prefer not to, but he was also pleased—he'd judged the man aright.

Tasker knocked and the hovel door was opened by a woman in her fifties, neatly dressed in a worn blue gown and a clean white apron. She leaned heavily on a stick and she looked at Dominic with a steady blue gaze that he recognized. Tasker's mother.

"Miss Beth's boy," she said softly. Her eyes filled with tears. "Oh, m'lord, I'm so happy to meet you at last. I was your mam's maid, and more—I was her friend."

To his consternation she hobbled forward, reached up, and stroked his cheek softly, as if to check he was real. Dominic set his jaw. His mother used to stroke his cheek in just the same way.

Mrs. Tasker led him into the hovel. The family must all live in one room, he saw. A stone fireplace in the corner provided heat as well as being the kitchen area; there was a bench over which a blanket had been folded, two beautifully whittled chairs and a table, and that was all. Two corners were curtained off—sleeping areas, he assumed. It was small, smoky, and cramped but ferociously neat and clean. Jake set about making tea.

Mrs. Tasker made Dominic sit beside her on the bench. "She must have been so proud of you. Longed for you, she did. Wept every month when she knew there would be no baby."

"My father needed an heir for Wolfestone," Dominic agreed gruffly, wishing he were miles away.

"Him." She dismissed his father with a contemptuous

wave. "That wasn't it at all, m'lord. I mean—he did want his heir, but that wasn't the only reason why Miss Beth wept. She wanted a babe for herself, see? A lovin' little lass, she was, and longing for a wee babe of her own. She'd visit all the young mothers on the estate and play wi' their babes for hours."

Dominic stared straight ahead of him, fighting for control. *A lovin' little lass*—it conjured up such an image of his mother.

She stroked his cheek again, and uncannily, it was as if his mother was doing it. "Glad I am that she had such a bonny boy. And you looked after her, didn't you, lad?"

Dominic forcing unwanted waves of emotion back, nodded. He had, as best he could.

Mrs. Tasker smiled. "Aye, I can see you did. You have your da's eyes, but there's a sweetness in you that's all Miss Beth."

Dominic felt something inside him, some tension, unravel.

"Did she have a happy life in the end, lad?"

He nodded and said in a voice that cracked, "Especially in the last ten years." There was no point in telling this woman how dreadful the first eight years had been.

She nodded. "I'm glad. She got a letter to me, after she'd escaped." She smiled at his surprise. "I was her friend. Did you think I didn't know how it was between her and your da?" She shook her head. "I nearly went with her. That was the original plan, only it weren't to be." She rubbed her leg absently, as if it pained her. Tasker brought over the tea, and she looked up and gave him a loving smile. "And if I had gone with her, I wouldn't have married Jake's dad and had a bonny lad o' my own, so things worked out for the best, I reckon."

The tea was weak and tasteless, the leaves used, dried, then used again. Poor people's tea. Dominic drank it in silence. The taste recalled his childhood.

"Fetch him out the album, son."

Jake set down his empty cup and from a small wooden chest by the wall took out a wrapped bundle and handed it to Dominic. Bemused, and not a little apprehensive, Dominic removed the oilskin wrapping to reveal a brown pigskin folder, about twelve by sixteen inches. He glanced at Mrs. Tasker, who gave him an encouraging nod, so he opened it.

The album turned out to be paintings, fine, delicate watercolors of Wolfestone from every angle, a place he wouldn't have recognized, with flowers spilling over the harsh angles of stone. Paintings of the rose arbor, of various people, of children playing, of a dog sprawled in sleep, painted with delicacy . . . and love.

"Your mam's paintings," Mrs. Tasker told him. "That's me." She pointed. He would never have recognized her. The girl in the painting was pretty and full of life, not tired-looking and with a face aged by pain.

"The album's yours, lad," she told him. "I been saving it for you, ever since I heard you'd been born. I knew after Lord D'Acre died, you'd come home to us in the end. I'm just so sorry you couldn't bring Miss Beth home with you." Her eyes flooded with tears and, forgetting he was a lord and she an impoverished tenant, she hugged him.

Dominic sat frozen through the hug, and when it was over, he thanked her gravely for the tea. As he said his good-byes, she stopped him. "I hope you don't mind, m'lord, but I just have to do this, for yer mam's sake." She pulled his head down and kissed him on the cheek.

Dominic gave her an awkward nod and walked in frozen silence to his horse. He tucked the precious oilskin bundle into his saddlebag and mounted his horse.

"You didn't mind Mam hugging you like that, did you, m'lord?" Tasker asked after a moment or two.

Dominic shook his head curtly. He couldn't trust himself to speak. His emotions were in turmoil.

"Powerful fond of your mother she was," Tasker explained. "She wept for days when Mr. Podmore told her Miss Beth had died."

Dominic's head whipped up at that. "*Podmore* told her?"

"Oh, aye. Mr. Podmore, he always makes a point of looking in on Mam. Sweet on Miss Beth, Mam reckons he was, and liked the opportunity of talking about her with someone else who loved her. Mam reckons there's comfort to be had in that."

Dominic bit his lip. She was right. He hadn't spoken of his mother since the day he'd buried her, for no one he knew had known her. Now, since he'd come to Wolfestone, he'd met two people who not only knew her but had loved her. And in the pain of talking about her, there had been comfort as well.

What irony, to find them both at Wolfestone, the place he'd sworn to destroy.

After a few miles had passed he said to Jake, "How did your mother hurt her leg?"

There was a short silence. "You don't know?"

A sense of foreboding filled Dominic. He shook his head.

"It got busted up badly the night Miss Beth run off. When your pa found out she'd gone, he was wild with fury." He rode on a few paces more and then added, "Mam wouldn't tell him where Miss Beth had gone, so your pa threw her down the stairs."

* * *

GRACE SAT IN THE LIBRARY, READING THROUGH THE SLENDER volume of poems Dominic had given her. After Dominic's discovery of the little book, she'd searched all through the shelves in the hope of discovering more texts in Arabic, but she hadn't found a single one. How strange to have just one book in that language.

But what a wonderful one to have. She hugged it to her bosom. Such a romantic inscription. The more she read, the more she could see that Faisal had loved his dove very much.

One of the poems in the little leather book had already become her all-time favorite poem. Written a thousand years before, it was still fresh and lovely enough to make her weep.

> And she came like bright dawn
> opening a path through the night
> or like the wind
> skimming the surface of a river.
>
> The horizon all around me
> breathed out perfume
> announcing her arrival
> as the fragrance precedes a flower.

The door opened and Mr. Netterton entered. "Oh, terribly sorry. Didn't mean to disturb you, Greystoke. Miss Pettifer has just gone back up to tend to her father and I thought I'd snatch a few moments to write some letters . . . well, actually . . . a sermon."

He looked rather self-conscious. "Thing is, I've never actually conducted a whole service before, not by myself. Oh, don't look so surprised, I know all the rote stuff, it's the sermon I'm worried about. Thought I could crib a few ideas. Bound to be books of sermons in that lot." He gestured to the shelves of dusty old books.

"Yes, I can see that it would be a bit nerve-wracking," she agreed. "Your first time, and I imagine you'll want to make a good impression on your new flock."

"*Flock*." He pulled a face. "I don't feel like anyone's shepherd. And if you want to know the truth, I think I've slept through almost every sermon I've ever heard. Dreary stuff."

She smiled at him. "Then you know exactly what to do."

He looked puzzled. "What do you mean?"

"Well, you know how *not* to write a sermon. Why don't you write the sort of sermon that you would have liked before you, er, found your vocation."

He snorted. "The only sermon I would have liked was one that was as short as all get out, maybe with a joke or two and with no jaw-me-dead moralizing."

She laughed, surprising herself. "Exactly. It's your sermon, after all."

His jaw dropped. "Oh, I say, what a good idea. If you don't mind, I'll make a few notes while your suggestion is fresh in my mind." He sat down at the desk and started to write.

They stayed like that for some time, Grace lost in the beauty of medieval poetry rising fresh and lovely from the page a thousand years after it was first penned, Mr. Netterton scribbling rapidly, filling several sheets of paper, then screwing them up and starting again.

After a while Grace became aware that he'd finished writing and was staring blankly at a wall of books.

"Finished?"

He started. "Yes. Yes, I think so." He looked doubtfully at the sheet of paper in front of him. "It's very short."

She laughed at the expression on his face. "Don't worry. I'm sure everyone will be grateful. What's the subject?"

He looked a bit embarrassed. "Er, it's a sort of fable, not from the Bible, actually. About the dog in the manger—not Jesus's manger, of course, another sort of manger entirely. In a different country. In a different time."

"It sounds just the ticket," she assured him. "A nice rural theme for a rural parish. In any case, you'll be writing sermons for the rest of your life. There's no hurry. You'll get the hang of it eventually."

He looked appalled. "It's just like school," he said mournfully. "Hated essays then. Why the dev—er, deuce did I choose a career that involved writing?"

It was an opening Grace couldn't resist. "You knew Lord D'Acre at school, didn't you? What was he like then?"

Frey grinned reminiscently, glad to be changing the subject. "He was a bit of a savage at the beginning. Spoke English with a slight foreign accent and would fight anyone who looked sideways at him. That's how we met, actually. We had a good old punch-up—forgotten what it was about—but we slogged into each other until neither of us could stand, and ended up best friends." He said it quite matter-of-factly.

She must have looked as horrified as she felt, for he laughed and said, "Can see you haven't any brothers, Greystoke. Boys are like that. Uncivilized young brutes. Perfectly normal to punch the living daylights out of each other and wind up friends. Happens all the time."

"I'll take your word for it," Grace said.

"Anyway, after that we were inseparable. Did everything together—games, lessons, mischief . . . Would have spent the holidays together, too, if we'd been allowed." His smile dimmed. "Bad show, that."

"What was?"

He looked uncomfortable. "Not sure he'd want me to be telling this stuff."

"But it's all in the past. What can it hurt?" Grace coaxed. She wanted to know all about him. "And besides, I won't tell a soul."

Mr. Netterton thought for a minute and then nodded. "Thing is, it was his father had him brought to England and to Eton. Hadn't known about the boy for years, but someone spotted him with his mother and, well, Dom is the spitting image of his father, so there's no doubt of his blood! As soon as the old man found out, he wanted him trained for the position he would one day take—heir to Wolfestone and the D'Acre title, that sort of thing. His mother was in . . . Egypt or somewhere I think. Too far, anyway, for Dom to go to his mother's for holidays—not that his father would have allowed it. Once he'd got his hands on Dom, he wasn't going to let him leave England again. Kept him short of funds the whole time. Poorest boy in Eton, he was—or should have been. Thing about Dom is, he has this knack for making money—amazing he is!" He pondered this for a moment. "Where was I?"

"Holidays," she prompted him.

"Yes, well, my parents would have been happy to have Dom spend his holidays with us. Keep us both entertained. M'father wrote to old Lord D'Acre for permission." He grimaced. "Turned m'father down. Dom wrote and asked, too. Said no, every time."

"I expect he wanted Dominic to spend them with him."

Mr. Netterton shook his head. "No. Dom only ever met his father twice in his life. Never spent more than an hour in his company."

"What? Not even for holidays?"

"No. Fixed it that Dom wasn't allowed to leave the school at all. Not ever. Think the old man was afraid that Dom would try to escape—and he wasn't far wrong at that."

"Wasn't he happy at school?"

"Not that. He was worried sick about his mother. Hadn't heard a word from her since he set foot in England. And d'you know why?" His voice rose in indignation. "That father of his had stopped all her letters. Dom found out eventually from his father's lawyer—old Podmore. Fellow was acting for his father, but seems to have had a soft spot for the mother and thought that old Lord D'Acre was doing the wrong thing by the boy."

"I should think so, too!" Grace declared, feeling quite upset by the thought of young Dominic incarcerated in a school in a foreign land—and then forbidden letters from his mother.

"The school was under instructions to send his mother's letters to the lawyer, and the lawyer was under instructions to destroy them, which he did."

Grace was horrified. "Destroy his mother's letters! How could anyone be so cruel?"

Mr. Netterton winked and tapped his nose. "Cunning beggar, Podmore. Copied the letters first, didn't he? Burned the originals as instructed. Sent the copies to Dom, passing them off as his own letters. School wasn't told to stop Dom getting letters from his pa's lawyer."

Grace clasped her hands together. "What a wonderful man!"

"The fellow saved Dom's sanity, I believe. Stands to reason, a boy who's spent the first twelve years of his life looking after his mother isn't going to abandon her just because some father he's never met tells him to!" He made a scornful noise.

"His father must have been a very unfeeling sort of person," she said thoughtfully. At twelve a boy was still very much a child and needed his mother. Her heart bled for that boy.

"He was a right ogre," Mr. Netterton agreed. "Wouldn't even let Dom spend Christmas or Easter with any of his friends. Never had a proper English Christmas, Dom, poor beggar. The first few years he used to ask me all about it—you could tell he was dying to experience it for himself. In Egypt and Italy they don't do Christmas like we do in England, with all the trimmings. He used to hang on every tale, at first . . ." He broke off, shaking his head.

"Tell me," she prompted softly.

"Well he hoped, you see. Every year his father let him think there was a possibility he might be asked to Wolfestone for Christmas . . . Dom would get all excited—not that he'd say anything, but he'd get . . . I don't know, keyed up. Well, stands to reason—your first family Christmas, meet the relatives, clap eyes on Wolfestone, the place you're going to inherit . . ."

"And?"

"Every year it was called off at the last minute. Year after year. One year a coach came with his father's crest on it and you should have seen the look on Dom's face! Those odd eyes of his fairly blazed with excitement. All his Christmases coming at once—literally." He clenched his fist. "Turned out to be a footman bringing him a set of new clothes—someone must have reported that he'd outgrown all his others—and a history of the Wolfe family for him to study over the holidays." He gave her a somber look. "Bastard even set him a test, afterward."

"Did his father not realize what he was doing?"

"I don't think he cared. I don't think he ever thought of

Dom as someone with feelings. He was just the heir."

"What an inheritance." She knew now where his intense bitterness about Wolfestone had come from.

Frey nodded. "Yes, and after that Dom just sneered at the mention of Christmas or holidays. Said they meant nothing, that he couldn't care less, that it was a stupid English custom, and that he had better things to do."

"People do cover up when they're hurt," Grace whispered. "Poor little boy cut off from all comfort and joy . . ."

"Stupid of his father, trying to cut him off from his mother and keep him locked up in the school."

"Criminal!" she said fiercely.

"That, too. But stupid most of all." He considered it a moment and added, "Taught me a lot, come to think of it. Never can force things of that sort. Loyalty. Allegiance."

"Love," Grace added.

He nodded. "Has the opposite effect if you try." He sat back in his chair. "The day he finished school, Dom was to go to Wolfestone. His father had instructed the school that he wasn't to go up to Oxford—though unlike me, he would have made a fine scholar—he was to go to Wolfestone and learn how to manage the estate." He grinned. "Only one of the masters made the mistake of telling Dom in advance."

Grace sat forward, excited. "What happened?"

"His father's carriage arrived to collect him, but Dom had left in the night. He'd amassed enough money for a fare to take him home."

"To Egypt?" Grace was stunned. "By himself?"

Mr. Netterton nodded proudly. "All the way to Egypt, crossing the continent entirely on his own. He crossed France in the middle of Boney whipping the frogs into a new frenzy, and he missed Waterloo by a couple of weeks! Amazing journey!"

"His mother must have been so happy to see him after all those years."

"Ah, well . . ." Mr. Netterton's face fell. He looked uncomfortable. "That was the biggest tragedy of all. When he got there, he found her deathly ill. He did all he could but she died in his arms just one day after he got there." He was silent a long while, then added, "He never set foot on English soil again until the old man was dead." He pulled out a clean, white handkerchief and handed it to her.

Grace took it mechanically, not knowing why he'd given it to her.

"Your cheeks are wet," he explained.

She rubbed at her cheeks and eyes, feeling angry and upset on behalf of the child who had been Dominic. No wonder he seemed so hard and cynical at times and tried so hard not to show he cared about anyone or anything. His father had left him a bitter legacy indeed.

Chapter Fourteen

Love seeketh not itself to please, nor for itself hath any care, but for another gives its ease, and builds a Heaven in Hell's despair.

WILLIAM BLAKE

"My boots are ruined," Dominic growled at Jake Tasker. The estate tour was taking a great deal longer than he'd expected or wanted. At every farm and every cottage, he'd had to dismount and tramp over every inch of the blasted property.

Tasker eyed the boots with scant interest. "Look all right to me. A bit muddy, mebbe, but mud'll brush off. Now, tell Lord D'Acre what you were tellin' me last week, Seth."

Dominic listened while the tenant called Seth explained his ideas for the renewal of the estate.

Tasker had gotten every farmer and tenant they'd met to explain everything: problems, needs, possible solutions, and despite himself, Dominic found it all fascinating. He was starting to see a pattern, starting to form ideas about how the estate could be brought back to full productivity and prosperity.

Dominic probably could have come to exactly the same

conclusions by looking at the books and talking to Tasker. And it would have been a damn sight easier to make the sort of decisions that ought to be made!

That's why he wanted Abdul here. Abdul could be the one to get interested, Abdul could listen to the problems and discuss solutions. Abdul was a ruthless business man. He could make the tough decisions. His eyes wouldn't stray to ragged children and thin, worn mothers and be pierced with guilt and anger by the sight.

It wouldn't rip Abdul apart every time some old woman spoke kindly of Dominic's mother and what a sweet young bride she'd been, and how she'd brought them fruit when the baby was born.

And if Abdul met one more young woman who'd been named Beth, "After your kind lady mother, m'lord," he wouldn't get a hard lump in his throat making it impossible to talk. Abdul would just eye the woman's curves and make some flirtatious remark.

He wouldn't feel any sense of connection at all with these blasted people, dammit! He'd just ruthlessly haul the estate into a state fit for a profitable sale.

Dominic wished he'd never come. It was as if carefully healed scars were being picked apart. In the kindest possible way. It was unbearable.

At one o'clock he made some excuse to take lunch at the village tavern, refusing the offer of a meal at one of his tenants' homes. He wasn't hungry; he'd had refreshments offered him at every stop. He just needed a drink, and a respite from all the . . . whatever had left him feeling so stirred up.

Besides—he seized on the excuse—he had letters to post.

The village postmaster glanced though them curiously. "I allus get a thrill from seeing letters go out, m'lord," he confided. "To think something that's been in my own hands here, will end up in . . . ooh, Italy." He looked at the next. "And Egypt . . . and New South Wales and, what's this, oh, just London," he said, disappointed.

But lunch and the post could only take up so much time, and then it was back to the estate tour.

It was nearly dark when Dominic rode wearily back to Wolfestone. He wasn't even halfway through the tour and already his head was stuffed full of farming information, of names and faces, of people who'd smiled at him, and touched his hand, who'd welcomed him, unbearably.

Unbearably because while he'd been prepared to be seen as the next heir of Wolfestone, he hadn't thought that so many people would remember his mother; asking after her with genuine kindness and expressing sadness and sympathy at her death, so many years ago.

He'd never shared his grief with anyone; he'd just mentioned her death to a few friends in letters. None of them had known her.

Now, in a country far from where she'd died, and more than ten years after she'd died, in the place where he thought she had been so unhappy, the place he'd learned to hate, her life had been celebrated, truly celebrated in small, sincere, heartbreaking ways.

Children had been named after her, small kindnesses remembered, stories shared with her son. Her death seemed as fresh to these people as if her funeral had been today.

Dominic had not wanted this tour: he'd been braced to receive hostility, greed, demands. He'd prepared no defense for kindness, sympathy, and . . . an overwhelming feeling of belonging . . .

It tore him apart.

He left Hex in the hands of a groom, checked the foal

almost mechanically, and then entered the house by a side door. He didn't feel like company.

He had taken half a dozen steps when she came hurrying around the corner, her arms full of some fabric. He stopped dead and just looked at her. He stiffened, trying not to let his feelings show, determinied to disguise how shattered he felt.

Grace took in the rigidity and tension of his big, strong body, the clenched jaw, and the knotted fists. Every inch of him declared his lack of desire for human contact. She was about to turn away when she saw his eyes. Golden, anguished. Wounded.

That look drove every other thought from her mind. She made a small sound in her throat, dropped the bundle of fabric, bolted down the corridor straight as an arrow and hurled herself into his arms.

They locked around her wordlessly. He couldn't speak, could do nothing except hold her. In silence he held her, wordlessly fighting his long-buried, freshly torn-up grief.

In silence she held him, hugging the small boy who'd been torn from everything he knew and loved, and the youth who'd been set adrift, ever since. The man who'd never belonged.

Until today.

"I'm sorry," he muttered against her skin. "It's just—"

"Hush," she told him and kissed him on the jaw, on the mouth. His mouth covered hers, devouring her like a man starved of nourishment. His arms locked around her, crushing her against him, then his grip shifted and he swung her off the floor as if she weighed nothing at all. Still locked together in a kiss, he carried her into the small salon and kicked the door shut behind him.

Keeping her clasped hard against his chest, he half sat,

half sprawled on a long sofa. He said not a word, just buried his face against her neck, his chest heaving as he grappled for control. Grace clung to him, stroking his hair, his strong neck, his shoulders—any part of him she could reach.

She could feel his big, warm hand moving over her, holding her, caressing her, seeking and exchanging wordless comfort.

Time passed: she did not know how much. It was enough just to be here with him, feeling the heat of his body soak into hers, the hard muscles closed implacably around her.

Frey's revelations about Dominic's life had just about broken her heart. This man, this big, powerful, complex man had been alone most of his life. From what she could make out, he'd taken care of his fragile mother since he was a small boy. And then, no sooner had she found love and security than young Dominic had been whisked away to another country. At school he'd been different, foreign. And on holidays he was shut out from his own family and not allowed to be accepted into others.

Alone he'd forged a place in the world, amassed a fleet of trading ships, made himself independent of everything—except the past. This quest for revenge on behalf of a dead mother. Guilt was a terrible burden. Did he blame himself for her death, too?

Grace knew from her oldest sister Prudence that when a child was burdened with responsibility too young, it burned into her soul. It was years before Prudence stopped feeling responsible for her sisters' happiness and well-being. Even now, it still cropped up from time to time and they had to remind her.

But at least Prudence's sisters were alive . . .

His grip on her finally loosened. He raised his head. "I'm sorry," he said in clipped tones. He was embarrassed, she saw. "It's been a . . . difficult day. Unexpected."

She leaned back into his embrace and rubbed her cheek against his jaw. "Tell me."

His arm tightened around her again. "I was so certain . . ." He stopped, his brow furrowed.

"Certain of what?"

"Certain I knew what she wanted me to do with this place."

"Your mother?"

"Mmh." He nodded, deep in thought. A ripple of pain crossed his face. "She may as well have been exhumed today."

She held tight to him, unable to find words of comfort.

There was a long silence and then he muttered, "I thought she hated Wolfestone, but now . . . I'm not so sure."

Suddenly Grace had had enough. He was so mired in the past. It wasn't healthy. She sat up. "You cannot keep guessing at her reasons and intentions."

He said nothing, so she gave him a small shove. "If you go on like this, you'll drive yourself mad." He made to speak but she covered his mouth with her hand. "Hush, let me finish. You keep talking about your father and mother—and I'm sorry for such blunt speaking—but they are both dead. And whatever plans and dreams they had for you or this place have died with them. You cannot know what they intended. It doesn't matter anymore to them. You cannot be bound by the dead. You are here. They are not. You are alive. What matters now is you and your future—*your* hopes, *your* plans, *your* dreams."

He stared at her.

"So, Dominic Wolfe, what are your dreams?"

There was a long silence while he thought about what she'd said. Grace waited tensely. While she'd been speaking he'd moved away from her slightly, breaking the contact between their bodies. Deprived of his heat she felt suddenly chilled and nervous. She'd been very blunt—almost rude. She'd trampled on his sensibilities at a time when he was shaken by the emotions of the past. Had she offended him?

At first he looked blank, almost shocked. Then a ripple of tension passed through his body and his eyes started to glow. She *had* offended his sensibilities.

His powerful hands took her by the shoulders; his golden gaze pierced her.

"You want to know my dreams?" His fingers tightened their grip. He took a deep breath. She braced herself.

"You." He pulled her back into his arms. "*You* are all I dream of. All I want is you." And his mouth clamped tenderly, fiercely, possesively over hers.

Grace melted. In a heartbeat all her doubts and fears dissolved. Under the heat of his hunger, his ravenous, driving need, all her resolutions about keeping him at arm's length evaporated. She wanted him. More, she needed him.

And he needed her.

"Dominic." She flung her arms around his neck and kissed him back with all the yearning buried deep inside her.

Their tongues tangled, sliding sensuously back and forth, back and forth in an ancient rhythm her body unconsciously echoed. At the wine-dark, heady taste of him, her blood thrummed, thrilling in dark anticipation of what she'd already decided. Her body molded itself against and around him, curves seeking hollows, her softness craving his hardness, her skin itching, craving to be closer still, quivering deep within.

Dominic clamped down hard to control the passion that surged within him. She was beautiful, eager, and despite her tangible innocence, generous. Too generous. Dangerously generous. It made a man lose control.

And he was not going to lose control—yet. When he took her he wanted it to be perfect. So not here, not now, he told his rampant body.

His hands caressed her feverishly, running down her back, her sides, her buttocks. Each time a shudder of pure desire rocked him, he felt an echoing response rippling through her. He ached to take her.

He opened the front of her dress and caressed her breasts, half hidden by her stays. Her nipples pushed against the stiff fabric and each time his hand brushed across them she quivered and he felt it in his loins.

He pushed her skirts higher, caressing the long, slender legs. They trembled and opened to him. He groaned and caressed her through the white cotton underwear.

She rubbed against him feverishly. "Yes, Dominic, yes."

Her hands flew over him, stroking his shoulders, his chest, and down his front to his breeches. Her fingers explored him, feeling the hard ridge, the evidence of his desire.

"May I touch?" Without waiting, she started to explore the fastenings of his breeches and he couldn't bring himself to tell her to stop, even though he knew it would spell the end of all his noble resolutions.

Resolutions? They went up in smoke. Dominic was in flames.

She was fumbling at his breeches. He started to help her when he became aware of a growing din outside. He paused, distracted. It sounded like an army was charging at the house. Groaning, he lifted himself off her and glanced out of the window.

He frowned, closed his eyes, and swore softly. "Visitors."

"Now?" she said, and then repeated crossly, *"Now?"*

If he wasn't in extremis himself, he'd have laughed at the expression on her face. He kissed her on the nose. "Yes, now. And we must go and greet them, so button up, my love."

They hurried to restore their clothing. Her hands were shaking and Dominic had to help her.

In a few moments respectability was restored and together they strolled out to the front entrance, meeting Frey and Melly at the door. Most of the household, drawn by the unaccustomed noise, had drifted to the front of the house as well.

"It's Abdul!" Dominic explained.

As always, Abdul made an entrance worthy of a prince royal. A veritable cavalcade swept up the driveway: several carriages laden with baggage and a string of horses following, led by several mounted grooms, the whole procession accompanied by armed outriders.

Abdul leapt from the first carriage and strode into Wolfestone with all the arrogant swagger of a warrior arriving home. He was a magnificent sight. He was huge—even taller than his master—about six foot three or four, Grace guessed. Broad shoulded and walking with pantherish grace, he looked the very embodiment of an Ottoman warrior prince.

On his head he wore a brilliant multicolored turban, with a huge glittering stone set into it. His face was swarthy and narrow, and was bisected by a bold hawkish nose. He had an enormous black mustache and a firm, square jaw. His eyes were dark and liquid deep, with the tragic expression of a martyred saint in an Eastern icon. He wore a long-sleeved coat of magnificent embroidery, a yellow silk shirt opened to reveal part of his chest, and a pair of gathered red trousers, tucked into high boots that were exotically curved at the toes. Around his waist he wore a black-and-silver sash with a curved dagger thrust through it.

Behind Grace, Dominic murmured in a voice only she could hear, "You'd never believe he was born a slave, would you?"

She turned, shocked. "He's a slave?" She didn't approve of slaves.

"Not anymore," Lord D'Acre said mildly. "I actually bought him to save his—man—er, life. I freed him, of course, but he chose to stay and work for me." He saw the look she was giving him and added, "At a not-inconsiderable salary."

Grace was intrigued by the way he'd cut himself off. "What was it prompted you to buy him? What did you save?"

He continued as if she hadn't spoken, "And don't imagine that outfit is anything you'll see anywhere else in the world. Abdul has dressed to impress the natives."

If he had, it was working, Grace observed. People had appeared from everywhere, crowding into the hall, craning their necks for a sight of the enormous foreigner and speculating about him in audible tones. The three Tickel girls stood in a line, eyes popping and jaws agape, smoothing their hair and skirts and sending coy glances the big man's way.

He never so much as glanced at them. He seemed, in fact, magnificently indifferent to the sensation his arrival had created.

"Part of his tactics," Dominic murmured in Grace's ear. "He makes it clear from the start that he's outside any frame of reference they have; thus he cares nothing for popularity or fitting in. If we were in Turkey now, he'd no doubt be dressed as an English gentleman, only it would be some unique and bizarre arrangement of English attire, so that nobody would mistake him for a genuine Englishman. In Arabia he once dressed as a Russian. The costume varies. Only the mustache is constant."

"Why doesn't he want to fit in?"

"He's establishing his authority."

"His authority?"

"Abdul is my—there is actually no word that adequately describes his work, but majordomo might cover it. He will take charge of the household. He may take charge of the entire estate—it will depend on his opinion of Jake Tasker's abilities."

"Abdul decides?" She was amazed. "Don't you have any say in it?"

"Of course, but I've learned it is better to let Abdul have his way. His methods are unorthodox but invariably effective, and he puts my interests first, last, and in between. He is that rare gem, an incorruptible employee."

And then Abdul was there in front of them, bowing fluidly before his master. To her amazement, he addressed Dominic in Arabic. Grace was thrilled at the sound. She'd studied the language, but she'd never heard a native speaking it. Unfortunately he spoke too fast for her to understand.

Lord D'Acre inclined his head and said in English, "Welcome to my father's home, Abdul. As you see, it is in need of your talents."

Abdul straightened and glanced at the other inhabitants of the room, then returned his gaze to Grace, fixing her with a narrow-eyed piercing look. She raised her chin a little, feeling self-conscious under his scrutiny, and examined him with equal thoroughness. The black eyes sparkled, he looked from her to Lord D'Acre and back, then cleared his throat deliberately.

"This is Miss Greystoke," Lord D'Acre said obediently.

Grace held out her hand and to her surprise, Abdul took it and, bowing low, carried her hand to his forehead in a reverent gesture. She said in careful, self-conscious Arabic, "Greetings, Abdul. Peace be with you."

He shot her a surprised look, then his swarthy face split in a dazzling grin. He responded, slowly enough for her to follow. "Thank you, *sitt*, and peace be with you also." *Sitt* was Arabic for lady.

Grace was delighted. Her first real Arabic and it had worked! Maybe with Abdul, she could practice more so she would be ready for Egypt. She glanced at the man beside her. If she went to Egypt. He'd turned her plans upside down.

After Lord D'Acre had introduced him to Melly and Mr. Netterton, Abdul turned and scanned his surrounds with an enigmatic look, apparently unaware of the audience that had gathered. "You permit?" he asked Dominic.

Dominic nodded. Abdul strode off toward the gawking crowd. Without making a sound and without, as far as Grace could see, making any actions, he swept them all before him, back to the domestic regions like a flock of silent chicks.

"What's he going to do?" she asked Dominic.

"Take charge," he responded. "By tomorrow evening he will have inspected the house from top to bottom, will know every person here, what they do, and how. And then he will make it better. And then he will do the same to the estate. He's a genius."

"How interesting. And what will you do?"

"Nothing further, thank God. I brought Abdul in so he could bring the estate and house into a state sufficient to make a good profit on its sale. It's what he's good at."

"You are still planning to sell the estate?" Grace asked, shocked.

"Why would I not?" he said, and left the room. Dismayed, she watched him go.

After a night of fitful dreaming, Grace rose early, dressed, and slipped downstairs, heading for the stables. The house was so much nicer these days—everyone's hard work was showing results. Gleaming woodwork, well-beaten rugs, a faint scent of roses in the air. How could he still be thinking of selling the estate?

She saddled Misty in thoughtful silence and rode out into the morning, trailing the heavy weight of dreams behind her, breathing in the chill morning air fragrant with a hint of autumn, making breath steam and noses cold.

She headed for the hills, where the sun struck first. It was going to be another glorious day. The farmers might need rain, but it was hard not to enjoy the sunshine. Sunshine was a gift to treasure.

The sound of hoofbeats coming up behind her disturbed her reveries. She looked back. She watched the mist drifting low in the valleys and a tall man with golden eyes approaching on his big, black horse.

Without thinking she urged Misty to a gallop. Hooves thundered over the fresh, damp turf. It was exhilarating, this unexpected challenge. She loved the sudden call to action and the feel of flying over the fields. She relished the sensation of the horse's hooves beneath her, thundering over the ground, tossing up clumps of turf and mud, while brisk cold air scoured her lungs and made her skin tingle and her eyes water and her blood sing.

And she loved the sensation of the big, black horse pounding along behind her, gaining slowly, inexorably on the smaller mare.

I'm a Wolfe . . . We choose our prey and hunt it down. Consider yourself warned, Miss Prey.

Laughing, she reached the top of the hill a breath ahead of him. She flung herself off her horse and stood there, hands on hips, panting, laughing, and crowing victory. Dominic leaped off Hex and caught Grace by the waist, swinging her around in an exuberant circle, then pulling her hard against him. And then they were kissing, kissing as if they could not stop, kissing and touching as if it had been weeks, not hours since they parted.

"I didn't sleep a wink," Grace told him breathlessly between kisses.

"Me, neither." He cupped her face in his hands, kissing her mouth, her cheek, her eyelids, covering her with kisses.

After the first rush of emotion, they fell apart and simply stood there, facing each other, panting, and staring into each other's eyes. "I'll fetch my coat, shall I?" Dominic said.

She knew what he meant. Her mouth dried. "Yes, the grass is still damp." She wiped her hands against the skirts of her habit. She wanted this, had tossed and turned all night dreaming of it, but now, suddenly she was nervous.

He fetched the coat that he'd rolled up and strapped to his saddle. He'd planned ahead. Prey indeed. She tried to smile and felt it wobble.

He noticed. "You don't have to do this, you know." He looked chagrined. "I promised myself our first time would be in a bed."

He was nervous, too. The thought relieved her. It was momentous for both of them. She smiled, leaned forward, and kissed him softly on the mouth. "I *want* to do this. I want you, Dominic Wolfe."

At her words his eyes blazed bright. He spread the coat on the grass, then sat on it and held out his hand to her. "Come to me, love."

And she came. In silence they kissed and touched and explored. He unbuttoned the jacket of her riding habit and caressed her through the silk shirt she wore beneath it. He unbuttoned the shirt and smiled. "Front-laced stays—clever girl."

She smiled. "Indeed, but I wasn't planning for this when I dressed this morning." She made a rueful moue. "If I had, I might have put on prettier underclothes."

"I'm all for pretty underclothes," he told her with a grin, "but I'm much more interested in the person in them." He planted a kiss between her breasts and started to unlace her corset. She saw how he was looking at her and suddenly her underclothes didn't matter. He was eating her with his eyes and she felt beautiful. More than beautiful, she felt powerful.

All nerves fled and she sat up and started to unbutton his shirt. And suddenly it was another race. Laughing, their hands tangling and dueling as they flew to undo buttons and laces. She pulled his shirt off at the same instant as he unlaced her corset. They stared. He was more naked than she, because under the corset she wore a light muslin chemise.

"You are beautiful," she whispered, laying her palms on the hard planes of his chest.

"No, this, this is beauty," he said and cupped her breasts, caressing the tight nipples with his thumbs. "You are beauty." The heat of his hands as they created friction between the thin muslin and her highly sensitized skin soon had her moaning in pleasure. His mouth soon followed, hot, seductive, compelling. He took her aching nipple into his mouth and played on first one, then the other, with his tongue and teeth. She writhed beneath him, hungry shudders racking her body, centering on the hot, aching core of her. Her hands raked his body, kneading, scratching, demanding more.

He pulled off her chemise and she gloried in the sensation of skin against skin: hot, damp. Her legs were thrashing with a need she didn't know how to assuage.

But he did.

She felt a coolness against her legs and dimly realized he was pushing her skirts up. His hard, warm palm soothed her, caressed her, slid under the cotton of her drawers and cupped her intimately, then slid his fingers across, around, between. She arched against them, whimpering softly with need. His mouth closed over hers and he kissed her deeply, his tongue subtly mimicking the movements of his fingers and she jerked and shuddered around him uncontrollably.

He moved over her and she stiffened as she felt the hot, hard bluntness pushing at her entrance. "Hold fast, love," he murmured, pleasuring her again with his fingers. She felt herself softening and melting around him again, and suddenly he thrust and she arched in shock and froze, gasping.

"That's it, love, now relax," he murmured.

"Relax?" It came out as a squeak. "How can I—"

His fingers moved again, soothing, pleasuring her as he had done before and she felt her body slowly adjust to the unfamiliar . . . occupant. He was inside her body. She could feel him. She was all around him. And nothing was broken.

Experimentally she flexed her inner muscles and immediately he groaned. His head was flung back in a rictus of agony . . . or ecstasy.

The feeling of pure feminine power surged back through her. She flexed her muscles again. Again he moaned.

"I think you're relaxed enough," he ground out and started to move inside her.

Her breath fled as he moved, rocking her whole body with each movement. Without conscious volition her legs embraced him, locking around him, pulling him tight and hard against her, pulling him deeper.

His big, powerful body surrounded her, cradled her, surging into her, carrying her with him as wave upon wave juddered through her, skin to skin, inside and out, blood thrumming. All awareness faded as exquisite tension built and built and built, and it was like his blood was thundering through her, and hers through him, and together they were . . . they were . . .

"Look at me, love."

With an effort she pulled back from the brink and forced her eyes open. He made one last mighty thrust and she heard, as if from far away, a high, thin scream.

And he held her gaze as she shattered into oblivion around him. And oblivion was pure, incandescent gold.

It seemed like hours later she opened her eyes and awareness gradually trickled back. She was lying, half naked on top of him, her back naked, warmed only by his arms and the morning sunshine. And by the golden glow of his eyes as they watched her come back to her senses.

They flared the moment she realized they were still

joined together. Her inner muscles clenched and he jerked within her. He smiled, and the smile was both triumphant and possessive.

"I don't think you're ready for me again just yet," he said softly. He was, she could feel him, hard and hot and ready, deep within her.

"You have no idea how noble of me it is to do this," he said as he withdrew from her.

"Pooh to your nobility," she murmured. "I never asked you to."

He grinned and kissed her. "If you're not just yet, you'll be feeling a little bit sore soon enough. The next time I want you to enjoy it even more."

She was feeling a bit sore, a bit swollen and sticky, too, but she didn't care about that. She felt too good to care. "There's more?"

He laughed and refastened his breeches. "Yes indeed, you insatiable wench."

"Good," she said. "In that case I'll agree to wait."

He stared at her a moment, then laughed and snatched her into his arms, kissing her exuberantly, then tenderly. "My dream."

Afterward, they rode home slowly, talking in spurts, of small, inconsequential things. And all the way, the attraction hummed between them, powerful and insistent, springing up at a glance, a look, a touch.

For two pins, Grace thought, she'd push him off his horse and have her way with him again. She couldn't stop smiling. And from the way he kept looking at her, he felt the same.

They reached the crest of the hill that overlooked Wolfestone and by mutual unspoken accord, stopped to take in the view. They could see the castle, the village, Frey's church, and a myriad of patchwork fields and coppices.

"It's so beautiful here," she murmured.

He was silent. She turned and looked at him. "You don't really mean to sell all this, do you?" Grace asked.

He shrugged. "Why not?"

"I thought you'd changed your mind since . . . since you discovered how the people here remember your mother."

He shrugged again. "You were right, all that's in the past. All I want is to secure ownership and then I'll sell the damned place off—to a dozen different buyers if necessary! Then we can travel, you and I, to all the places you have dreamed of."

"Break up the estate?" Grace said with all the horror of one whose ancestors had one main purpose in life—to acquire and hold as much land as possible in perpetuity.

"Why not?"

"But if you break it up, it will destroy Wolfestone. It will be the end, the end of six hundred years of tradition."

"Exactly," he said with satisfaction.

"But why? Why would you want to destroy something when you could make something wonderful of it instead? If you break the estate up and sell it, the people here will end up worse than the way your father left them. I couldn't possibly enjoy our foreign travels, knowing that the people here were suffering."

He stared at her. "That's ridiculous. You can't possibly mean that."

"I do. Wolfestone isn't just land, it's a living, breathing community. The people here depend on each other and they depend on you."

"Then it's time they stopped and learned to stand on

their own feet. They are ignorant and superstitious and backward and—"

"And if they are, whose fault is that?"

He stared at her.

She continued. "Your ancestors! And though you can deny the responsibility all you like—"

"I do. I had nothing to do with—"

"You cannot and should not take responsibility for their past, but the responsibility for their future lies squarely on your shoulders, particularly if you intend to sell their homes and their farms from under them!"

He said nothing for the longest time and Grace wondered whether she'd upset him. After all, it was wonderful of him to be planning to take her on foreign adventures, but he had to see that he had a place here. He belonged here. He could go on foreign adventures, but he also needed a home to come home to.

"Would you really want to live here?" he asked.

"Yes. It's beautiful. And I've never had a home, not a real one of my own."

"You'd live here with me? And help me rebuild the state?"

She nodded. "We could make it something really special, Dominic."

"You're sure about this?" His eyes bored into her.

She smiled. "I'm sure."

He took a deep breath. "Then that's what we'll do."

"And what about Sir John?"

"I can deal with him," Dominic said. "As long as you're mine, I can do anything." He looked at her and his eyes gleamed possessively. "And you are mine, aren't you, love?"

The look and his words thrilled her. "Yes, and you're mine."

They rode back to Wolfestone hand in hand. Grace didn't think she'd ever been happier in her life.

She was in love. At long last.

Chapter Fifteen

Gather ye rosebuds while ye may, old Time is still a-flying.
And this same flower that smiles today, tomorrow will be dying.

ROBERT HERRICK

As they entered the front door, Melly came flying down the stairs, wild-eyed and frantic. "He's killing Papa! He's bled him again and Papa has collapsed, insensible! Help me! Oh, please help me!" She turned and raced back up.

Grace and Dominic followed.

In Sir John's bedroom, they found the doctor fending off Melly, who was nearly hysterical. Beside him was a basin containing a quantity of fresh, bright blood.

Sir John lay back, unmoving, his skin almost as pale as the pillows on which he rested. As Grace watched, his thin chest rose and fell very slightly. "He's alive!" she said. "Melly, calm yourself. He is alive and we will keep him that way!"

Melly burst into tears.

Dominic, having ascertained that Sir John was indeed still breathing, turned on the doctor. The doctor, seeing his face, took an involuntary step backward. "I told you to desist from that practice!" Dominic said in a quiet, chilling voice.

"I—I—it was necessary," the doctor blustered. "He has a swelling—see?" He pulled back the bedclothes and revealed an angry red swelling on the upper right-hand part of Sir John's abdomen.

"But he has already lost so much blood! And he hasn't eaten in days," Melly interrupted passionately. "He's too weak to be bled. I think you just enjoy bleeding him. You're nothing but a butcher!"

Grace tried to calm things down. "Isn't there any other way to treat that?" She gestured at the swelling. "Without bleeding him, I mean?"

But the doctor was incensed at Melly's accusations. Huffily, he tossed his things into his bag. "I'm leaving! I'm not staying here to be insulted any longer!"

Melly looked shocked. "But what about Papa? You can't leave him like this!"

The doctor sniffed. "There's nothing I can do for him anyway. He's dying!"

There was a stunned silence.

"Dying?" Melly whispered. Grace put her arms around her.

The doctor jerked his chin at Sir John's swollen abdomen. "His liver's hugely swollen. My guess is it's cancer of the liver. That or consumption. If he coughs blood, you'll know which. Either way, there is absolutely nothing anyone can do."

"But we can't do nothing," Grace said.

He shrugged. "Give him laudanum for the pain. In increasing doses as the pain worsens."

"If there is *absolutely nothing anyone can do*, then why were you bleeding him?" Dominic asked in a cold voice.

The doctor looked uncomfortable.

"You did enjoy it, didn't you?" Grace accused him.

"I'm leaving now," he blustered.

"Yes, you are," Dominic agreed. "You're leaving Wolfestone."

The doctor gave him an uncertain look.

"Leaving the entire district," Dominic clarified. "I don't think you're any sort of doctor at all. And I won't have a man who enjoys the drawing of copious quantities of blood treating my people."

Grace noticed the word if no one else did. *My* people.

The doctor's eyes bulged with shock. "You can't do that!"

Dominic fixed him with a cold golden stare. "I am Lord D'Acre and I won't have a bloodsucking leech on my land, mistreating my people. You have two weeks."

"How dare you—"

"One week, then. And if you're still there after that I'll send my men around to remove you and your charming wife!" He paused. The man was staring at him in shock. Dominic added, "And if you're not gone by the time I count to three, I'll give in to my overwhelming desire to throw you bodily down the stairs. One, two—"

Abdul loomed up behind the doctor, crooning in a sinister voice, "Give the bloodsucker to me, I beg of you, sir. In my land we know what to do with such as these." He gave the doctor a terrible grin. "It will be my pleasure to—"

The doctor gave a frightened screech and scuttled from the room.

Abdul winked at Grace. "That got rid of him." He turned to Melly and said in a solicitous voice, "Now, who shall we bring in to look after your father, Miss Pettifer? Do you have any preference?"

Melly's blank look showed she hadn't thought about it.

From the door, one of the Tickel girls piped up, "Granny Wigmore's the best healer in these parts."

Abdul nodded without turning. "Thank you, Tansy. What do you think, Miss Pettifer? Shall I send for this Granny Wigmore person?"

Melly looked at Grace for guidance.

"She can't be worse than that doctor," Grace told her. "And she's clean and knows more about herbs than anyone I know. Plus I like her, Melly. She'll be very comforting to have around."

Abdul bowed. "Then Tansy will run like the wind to fetch this herbal granny for you, *sitt*." And Tansy did.

Granny Wigmore took one look at Sir John and muttered, "The consumption he said it was, did he? Or cancer? Well it might be, and it might not be."

She lifted an eyelid and peered into Sir John's eye. " 'E looks proper liverish to me." She looked at the inflamed swelling on his stomach and wrinkled her nose. "That 'un be the source o' the problem, I reckon. It might be a boil, or it might be sommat worse. We must wait and see. I'll poultice it and we'll see if aught comes out."

"What might come out?" Melly asked nervously.

The old lady wrinkled her face up. "Whatever's ailing yer pa, young miss. Whatever's ailing yer pa. I hope."

Sir John opened his eyes and said in a weary voice. "Then get on with it, woman."

Everyone heaved a sigh of relief. Sir John was back in the land of the living, for now, at least.

Under Abdul's eagle eye, Mrs. Stokes, on her mettle, put on an even more excellent dinner that evening and the next, but still Melly just picked at her meal. Grace watched her, concerned. It was not like Melly. Her father had grown no worse under Granny Wigmore's treatment and he at least was taking liquids.

At the end of the meal, Mrs. Stokes's niece, Enid, knocked on the dining room door and entered looking worried. "Excuse me, m'lord, Reverend, ladies, but I've just now come from Sir John's chamber, collecting his dinner tray—"

Melly jumped up. "Is something the matter—"

"Oh no, miss, he's—he's the same as ever. Didn't eat nothing, but Granny's been makin' him drink herbal tea all day, and he has kept that down, which is a change. Apart from that, he's just as he was this morning. Only . . ."

She twisted her apron nervously. "Only I was chatterin' on a bit, meaning no harm—he's an easy old gentleman to chat to. But—" She glanced at Abdul and then Frey. "I was talking about Mr. Abdul here, and then I let slip that we had a vicar in the house as well as an 'eathen. And now he wants to see the vicar. Alone and at once."

Melly gasped and Grace and Dominic exchanged glances.

Enid added, "I'm sorry, miss. I know I wasn't s'posed to say." Abdul waved her out.

Grace moved to sit beside Melly. She took her hand. "Melly, there is no reason to think the worst—"

Melly started to sob.

Frey set his napkin aside and rose from the table, saying in a calm voice, "Now, Miss Pettifer, there's no point fretting when you don't know what he wants. I'll go up and speak to him—it was remiss of me not to have introduced myself when I first arrived. Just you sit there and have a nice cup of tea. I'll talk to you when your father has finished with me."

To Grace's amazement, Melly valiantly gulped back her sobs and nodded. "Tea would be nice," she managed, and Grace signaled to Enid to fetch a pot at once.

Frey went upstairs and introduced himself to Sir John. He'd never met the man before, but though he was shocked at how thin and fragile the elderly gentleman looked, he was also encouraged by the alertness of the old man's eyes.

"Can I get you anything, sir?" he asked.

Sir John waved the offer away with a grimace of pain. "Pull up a chair, my boy. I'll have some of that filthy stuff later." He gestured to the little bottle of laudanum on his bedside table. "Addles my mind though, so I'll wait till after I've said m'piece."

Frey sat down, folded his hands, and waited. Sir John gave him a thorough inspection. "Netterton, eh? I knew a Humphrey Netterton slightly when I was young. Your father?"

Frey nodded. "Yes, sir. I am named after him."

"Good fellow, your father. Sorry to hear how he died." Sir John sniffed. "Knew your Uncle Cedric better in those days." He shook his head. "Never would have believed it when he became a parson, of all things. Not Ceddie Netterton."

"He's a bishop now, sir."

"Good God! What's the world coming to?" He grinned at Frey. "Is he frightfully pompous?"

"Frightfully." Frey grinned back.

"Still a parsimonious old lickpenny?"

"Indeed he is, sir." Frey was starting to like this old gentleman very much.

"Ah well, he hasn't changed as much as all that, then.

Neither have I, more's the pity. I can't hang on to money, he can't spend it. So, about this business with m'daughter."

"Sir?"

"I want you to call the banns on Sunday. Her and D'Acre. It's all arranged."

Frey frowned. He hesitated, but he couldn't not speak up. "Sir, please forgive me if this sounds impertinent, but—"

Sir John waved a thin hand. "You're goin' to tell me Melly doesn't love D'Acre, and he doesn't love her? I know all that."

Frey opened his mouth to speak again and again, Sir John interrupted, "You're going to tell me it's not fair on my girl to arrange a marriage when she was a child to a fellow she doesn't know, that she ought to be able to choose her own husband."

"Well . . . yes, sir."

"Well, don't. I know all that but I have my reasons." He gave Frey a candid look. "I'm all rolled up, my boy. Skint. Not a shillin' to m'name and in debt to the eyebrows. If I'm to save Melly from the consequences of my folly I have to get her married. Prefer not to force the issue, but needs must . . ."

"I see." Frey saw only too well. Poverty was a trap and he couldn't blame Sir John from wanting to keep Melly out of it.

But Frey felt he had to persist, make a push to see if he could sort things out. It was—it was his duty as a minister. "Do you realize that Lord D'Acre has no intention of making a normal marriage? It's to be a convenient marriage, he tells me. A white marriage."

The old man shrugged. "Told me the same. He'll come around. And if he doesn't—" He broke off. "Can you see my Melly trying to scrape a livin' as a governess or some such thing? Fending off the randy sons of the middle classes?"

Frey was horrified by the picture. "No, sir."

"So even if it is a white marriage, could be worse. D'Acre is young, good-lookin', and has a kind heart. Even if he doesn't come to love her, he won't mistreat my girl."

Frey said heavily, "Yes, I know."

Sir John's eyed him shrewdly. "How d'ye know?"

"I was at school with him. We're friends."

"Ah, then you think she'll be safe with him, too?"

"Yes," Frey admitted reluctantly. "Safe, but not happy."

Sir John dismissed that with an impatient gesture. "From where I'm sittin', my boy, happiness is a luxury."

"Yes, sir," Frey agreed bitterly. It was the same from where he was sitting.

Sir John gave him a hard look, but all he said was, "So on Sunday you'll call the banns, then."

"If Lord D'Acre agrees—"

"He'll agree. Call the banns."

"Yes, Sir John."

Frey returned to the dining room. He glanced at Dominic, then back at Melly, and ran his finger around between his neck and his collar, as if it was too tight. "He wants me to marry Miss Pettifer to Lord D'Acre as soon as possible and wants me to call the banns."

"What?" came from the throats of the three people listening.

Frey continued. "He has written to your local minister, Miss Pettifer, instructing him to commence the calling of the banns in your own parish also. I have it here, countersigned by me as witness. I shall post it as soon as possible."

Melly burst into tears and ran out of the room. Grace

followed her. Dominic swore and strode to the window. He stood, staring out into the night, then swore again.

"He looks shocking, Dom." Frey said. "I think he's dying and he knows it. He's making a push to secure his only child's future. You can't blame him for that. Her circumstances are such—"

Dominic flung him an opaque look. "I know her circumstances, dammit!"

The two men stood side by side staring out into the night.

"He wants me to start calling the banns on Sunday."

Dominic swore again. "Dammit, I'd settle a house and an income on her, but the stubborn old fool won't listen to me and she won't try to talk him round. He thinks she can't look after herself."

"Well, she's very young and sheltered—"

"Don't give me that. My mother was young and sheltered and she had to look after herself and a baby in a foreign country!"

"And look how that ended. She knows he's dying, too, Dom. You can see it in her eyes. She's agreeing to this in order to give her father peace of mind."

Dominic flung him a hard look and resumed his pacing. "Blast it, she can't possibly be willing to sacrifice herself and her future happiness—and me!—for her father's peace of mind!"

"She's a noble creature!"

Dominic made a rude noise.

"Then what are we to do?" Frey said.

Dominic resumed his pacing with a brooding expression. "For God's sake, I told him the girl would be taken care of—what is there to complain of in that?"

"It's all very well to speak of settlements, Dom, but

Miss Pettifer would still be the butt of many sly and nasty comments."

"What?" Dominic frowned.

"It will be bruited about that you took one look at her and paid out good money to avoid marrying her."

"What rubbish! I mean the girl is plain, but there is nothing to disg—"

"*Plain!* Are you *blind*? How can you call such creamy skin, such melting dark eyes plain? And there is a sweetness of expression that—" Frey broke off.

Dominic was regarding him with raised eyebrows. "I see," he said slowly. "You're right, she's not plain."

"No," Frey muttered. "She's not. And all he's trying to do is provide for his daughter."

"By condemning her to a loveless, childless marriage!"

Frey clenched his fists and stared out into the night. There was just no answer to some problems. Or rather, money was the only answer.

They fell silent for a long time. After a while Frey said, "I understand why you're unhappy about this marriage, but what are we going to do, Dom? Her father is adamant. He has instructed me to commence the calling the banns on Sunday."

"Then I have until then to turn this thing around," Dom said heavily. "And if I fail, call the banns and to hell with us all!" As if in some macabre toast, he and Frey drained their glasses.

"I THOUGHT YOU WERE GOING TO TALK TO YOUR FATHER," GRACE said into the darkness.

"I did," Melly said after a moment. "I tried, Grace, I truly did." Grace could hear her despairing sigh from across the room. "I talked to him again just now, but he won't listen." She added with a sob, "I'm sorry, Grace, I'm so sorry." The darkness filled with the sound of muffled sobs.

Grace hugged the pillow to her, biting her lip.

The banns were going to be called on Sunday. Melly Pettifer and Dominic Wolfe's intention to marry would be announced to the world on Sunday.

Only Melly had the power to change her father's mind. And she was too paralyzed with fear to even try.

Melly feared that if she opposed his will, her father would die. She also feared that he would die and she'd be left alone and destitute. Melly could not think past her fears.

Grace could and it brought her no comfort at all.

She lay in bed, the thoughts spinning round and round in her head.

Her grandfather's old vicious whispers taunted her. *"Not you, Grace. Never you. You'll die alone and unloved . . ."*

She pulled the pillow over her head to block it out. It didn't matter. She had been loved, even for just a fleeting moment. He hadn't said a word, hadn't declared himself, but she'd tasted ecstasy and passion in Dominic's arms.

Most people never tasted ecstasy their whole lives.

She had. So what if it had been snatched away again? She had her plans to fall back on. She would still get to see the moon rise over the pyramids.

But the moon was distant and cold, not hot, intense, and golden like his eyes. And the pyramids were stone, not hard, warm flesh.

And he hadn't ever actually said he loved her.

Slow tears welled, soaking Grace's pillow. She scrubbed them from her cheeks and thumped the pillow into a different shape. She would not cry. She would *not*!

She would plan and think and *try*.

In the room across the hall a frail, old man tossed and turned, racked with pain and anxiety, fearing to sleep lest he die before his daughter's future was secured.

Chapter Sixteen

Many women long for what eludes them, and like not what is offered them.

OVID

"HOW COULD YOU AGREE? AFTER ALL YOU SAID TO ME YESTERDAY morning, how could you just turn around and agree to let Frey call the banns next Sunday?" Grace and Dominic had met the next morning in the place where they'd first made love.

He frowned. "I know. It's a damned nuisance. I had hoped to escape it. But it won't affect you and me." He caught her to him and kissed her. "Good morning, love."

She pushed him away furiously. "*Not affect you and me?* What are you talking about? Of *course* it will affect us!"

"Well, if it upsets you so much, we shall leave immediately after the wedding."

She stared at him, confused. "Which 'we' are you talking about?"

"You and me, of course. You've told me of your dreams: I'll take you traveling. We'll sail into Venice at dawn on the most beautiful yacht you've ever seen. I'll take you to

Egypt, and together we'll watch the moon rise over the pyramids and—"

"After you've married Melly Pettifer?"

He nodded. "Purely for convenience and in a white marriage."

Grace was thunderstruck at the barefaced audacity of him. "You expect me to become your mistress!"

He grinned at her. "Not become, love. You already are my mistress. Or have you forgotten yesterday morning already?"

She wanted to scream.

"Is that it? Do you want me to remind you?" He stepped forward and she thumped him as hard as she could on the chest.

He rubbed it. "Ouch! What was that for?"

She stared at him in disbelief. "I presume you don't mean to insult me—"

He looked horrified. "Insult you? No, of course not! Is that what you think?" He reached out and hauled her against him. "I promise you there is no insult intended." She tried to wrest herself out of his embrace but he effortlessly restrained her.

"I'm not letting you go until you understand."

"I'll *never* come to that sort of understanding," she flashed.

"I don't know how you think a mistress will be treated, but I promise you, you don't understand. Just *listen* to what I have to say."

Grace wasn't sure he understood at all. But she was willing to listen, at least. "Why would anyone choose to be a mistress?"

"My mother was much happier as a mistress than as a wife."

"Your *mother*?"

He nodded. "It's a long story, but put simply, my mother married well, or so society thought. But she was utterly miserable as a wife. My father was a brute, and she was trapped. To cut a long story short, she ran away and much later, she fell in love with a man, also trapped in a marriage without love. He was a rich man and he begged my mother to become his mistress. She used all the arguments you used just now, but he wore her down, and she loved him and was lonely so eventually she agreed to become his mistress. He loved her for herself, not for what she could bring to a marriage, and . . . It was a love for all time. A love such as the poets and minstrels celebrate."

She swallowed.

"When he died, losing him broke her heart, and within a few months she, too, died. She could not live without him."

She closed her eyes. She could not bear to see the pain in his, knowing she would only add to it.

"This is what I offer you: my heart. Not some tawdry exchange of money for favors, but a love with no fetters and legalities, where we can choose each other freely, regardless of birth or wealth. I will bestow a settlement on you at the start, free and clear. You would have no financial obligation to me, and no obligation to stay unless you want to stay. You will be wealthy enough to leave me if you want and to live well for the rest of your life. All that will bind us to each other will be love."

She withdrew her hands from his clasp. They felt cold. "I'm sorry, I cannot be your mistress," she said softly and pushed him away.

He grabbed her back. "Think about it. Don't reject the idea out of hand. We could have a wonderful life together—better than a marriage."

She thought about it for half a second and shook her

head. "I can't possibly be your mistress—especially not if Melly is your wife."

He dashed the question of Melly away with an impatient gesture. "Don't worry about her. This is about you and me!"

"It's not just about Melly. I don't want to be just your mistress—I want more from life—from you!—than that."

"There's no *just* about it. You would be, you *are* everything to m—"

She laid a finger over his mouth and said sadly, "No, I love you, Dominic, but I want *everything*. I want to marry you, to live with you, to build something together with you, here at Wolfestone, to give you children and grow old with you."

"You don't understand," he said urgently. "Mistresses are much better off than wives."

Grace shook her head. "You're wrong. You don't know who I really am. I'm not really a hired companion—I'm Melly's friend. We went to school together."

"I suspected as much. But—"

"I'm not poor, or an orphan, either. And my name is not even Greystoke. It's Grace, Grace Merridew." He was silent, so she added, "Of the Norfolk Merridews. My grandfather is Lord Dereham of Dereham Court in Norfolk, and my great-uncle is Sir Oswald Merridew. Lady Augusta Merridew is my great-aunt by marriage, not my sponsor. One of my sisters is married to a duke, another to a baron, and a third to a baronet. I'm an heiress and—" She stopped, knowing she was babbling. "So there is no question of me living with you as your mistress."

"I see." Dominic swallowed. "But why—"

"I disguised myself to come down here and boost Melly's moral courage so that she could break her betrothal to you." She added bitterly, "We neither of us understood the situation properly. And Melly has no moral courage!"

She pressed her lips firmly together until she'd mastered herself, then said in a voice that wobbled, "I'm sorry, that wasn't fair. I know Melly has tried. It's her father who's so stubborn. But whatever the reason, I can't be your mistress.

"Though it might suit some women perfectly, it's not enough for me. You say marriage can be a trap, but to my way of thinking, it's a half life you're offering me, Dominic Wolfe. And so I must say thank you, but no, thank you."

He sat staring at the ground for a long time. Finally he said, "Why didn't you tell me all this earlier? About who you really were? I knew you were an unusual companion, but all sorts of women become companions and I just thought you were a unique sort of companion." His eyes darkened. "You are unique."

She hung her head. "I thought of telling you so many times. I wanted to, but . . ."

"But?"

She hesitated, wondering how to explain. She was going to sound horridly conceited. "Every man who's ever shown an interest in me knew before he met me who I was, who all my relations were, and what my fortune was, almost to the last guinea—I am an heiress, did I mention that?"

He glared at her. "I couldn't care less if you're the richest woman in the world! That's not what I want from you."

She gave him an uncertain smile. "I know, and that's why I didn't want to tell you. You're the only man who's looked at me and seen . . . *me*. Not an heiress, or a beauty, or a well-connected aristocrat. Just me. Ordinary Grace Merridew. It was . . . irresistible."

"You're wrong about that, actually."

She looked puzzled.

"I do see a beauty when I look at you. And there's nothing ordinary about Grace Merridew."

She bit her lip. "My hair is dyed this ugly color and these freckles are false."

He just looked at her in a way that was breaking her heart, so she added almost desperately, "You said yourself my freckles were odd."

"That's true," Dominic said softly. He'd had enough of her keeping him at arm's length. "Odd, but delightful. How did you make them?" He wasn't even going to try to understand the rationale behind the freckles but he'd feign interest in anything if it got him close to Greyst—Grace again. He peered earnestly at a freckle.

"Henna. It's this stuff you paint on and it dries and stains your skin. See, they're fading now."

He moved closer, pretending to look at her skin. Frowning intently he cupped her face in his hands to get a better look. He ran his thumbs along her cheeks. "So smooth and silky," he murmured. "And the freckles do seem to have faded a little. It wasn't the lemons from Mrs. Tickel that did the trick, then? Or the buttermilk from Mrs. Parry?" He winked.

Her skin warmed under his fingers. "You knew about that?"

Dominic nodded, gazing down into her face. God, she was lovely.

The tension in her face eased for a moment and she gave a rueful smile. "Half the ladies of Wolfestone have offered me remedies. I never knew there were so many methods of getting rid of freckles. Do you know, one lady even told me to wash my face in the dew collected from a gravestone!"

"So these freckles will eventually disappear?" He touched them one by one. "This one and this one and this one?"

"Yes." She went all shy on him, turning her face away.

"That would be a pity; I'm very fond of these freckles," he murmured and began to kiss them, one by one.

She went stiff and for a moment he thought she was going to pull away again, but then he felt her soften and sigh against him, and his pulse leapt and his arms tightened around her. He kissed a few freckles on her face, then kissed her long and deep on the mouth, then a few more freckles, then another long, drugging kiss.

She gave a soft little moan and kissed him back, her hands running up his neck and into his hair, clutching at his head, pulling him closer. She kissed him back with all the fervor any man could dream of.

This was what he wanted. This was *all* he wanted. Greyst—Grace in his arms. It made no difference to him who she was.

Why could she not see it as simply as he did?

He pressed her back onto the grass and his hand went to her bodice. She smacked it hard, pushed him off, and sat up, flustered and angry.

"No, Dominic. I won't be your mistress! You've agreed to marry Melly Pettifer so it's over between you and me."

He lay there and watched her straighten her clothes and hair. She was so lovely when she was flustered.

"It's not over at all, Grace," he told her softly. "I keep what's mine and you, my love, are mine."

She stood over him, glaring, her fists clenched and every lovely line of her braced for a fight. He didn't move a muscle, and he watched in amusement as she wrestled with her sense of fair play and decided not to kick him while he was down. She stalked over to her horse and seized the reins and he was hard put not to laugh out loud when he saw her realize she needed him to help her back into the sidesaddle.

She refused to look at him and bent her knee without a word. He caressed her calf so quickly and lightly she didn't have time to complain before he'd tossed her into the saddle. He admired her seat as she galloped crossly off.

She didn't have a hope against him. They'd said all that needed to be said yesterday: she was his and he was hers. She might have given up on him, but he wasn't giving up on her, not by a long shot.

MELLY WAS STILL NOT EATING, JUST PICKING AT HER FOOD. GRACE was worried that Melly might be doing it to punish herself. She could see how guilty Melly felt, but it wasn't her fault. She'd tried to talk to her father and he'd refused. That was no reason for Melly to starve herself.

But whenever Grace tried to talk to Melly about it she changed the subject, looking self-conscious and a bit annoyed.

"I'm all right, Grace. It's not as if I'm fading away to a shadow, am I?" she said bitterly.

"No, but, Melly—"

It was no use. Melly had walked off, leaving Grace frowning after her. This was not the Melly she knew and loved. This whole thing was driving a wedge between them. It was horrible.

If she couldn't talk to Melly, someone should. If it was worry that stopped her from eating, that was one thing, but if it was illness . . . or guilt . . . She decided to talk to Frey about it. That was part of a vicar's job, after all, listening to other people's worries.

"You can't say she doesn't have a lot to fret about," Frey said. "Apart from her father's condition, you could cut the atmosphere here with an ax at times."

"But she never refuses food, not in all the years I've known her." Grace had told Frey who she really was, as well. No point keeping it secret any longer.

Frey frowned. "You don't think she's in danger of going into a decline, do you? I wouldn't be surprised. Would depress anyone's spirits. I've done my best to get her out of that blasted sickroom. It's no place for a young lady to spend all hours of the day in."

"Yes, I noticed you've been taking her for a walk every afternoon. It's very good of you."

He gave a self-deprecatory shrug. "Pooh, nothing else to do. Waiting for the vicarage to be fixed, sermons to write, parishioners to visit—to be honest I look forward to that walk. Highlight of my day." He looked suddenly bleak. "I'm a bit worried that Dominic will want me to officiate at this—this wedding. My oldest friend, you know. If he does ask me, I'm not sure I can refuse. But I'd rather not do it."

Grace didn't know what to say.

"You're not happy about it, either, are you?"

She shook her head.

He sighed. "Stubborn brute, Dominic. Don't like to be done out of what he believes is rightfully his. Comes of the poverty he endured as a child, I expect. What's his is his."

She glanced at him, but he was talking about the estate, not Dominic's outrageous claim to own her. She nodded. "Melly's father is just as stubborn. He's the cause of all our anxieties."

He patted her awkwardly on the shoulder. "I'll talk to Miss Pettifer. See what's putting her off her feed."

* * *

He broached that question the next afternoon, after their customary walk. It had become her habit to order tea and cakes. Frey was almost beginning to like the filthy taste of tea. As long as there were plenty of cream cakes to be washed down by it, and Mrs. Stokes was the best maker of cream cakes he'd ever come across. Normally he and Miss Pettifer cleared the plate, but lately, he realized, she hadn't touched the cakes at all. Miss Greystoke was right. Melly was fretting.

"You're not eating any cakes," he observed.

"No." She blushed. "I'm not hungry."

"You hardly ate a thing at dinner last night, nor the night before. And now no cakes, when I know you how much you like them."

She hung her head.

He leaned forward and took her hand. "What's the matter, Melly?" he asked softly. It was the first time he'd called her Melly to her face.

She kept her face averted. "I'm trying to slim," she muttered.

"Slim?" He didn't understand.

Her blush intensified. "To lose weight."

He stared at her. "Good God, why would you want to do that?"

"I'm too fat," she muttered.

"Too fat?" He stared at her, utterly dumbfounded. "Whoever told you that is a blind fool," he said at last. "Look at me—a scrawny, unattractive bundle of bones, whereas you—you're a, a vision of delicious feminine curves, the kind of warm softness a man dreams of sinking into and finding paradise."

His words hung in the silence. Frey felt himself going red. She was blinking at him, flushed, her rosy lips parted in astonishment.

"Good God, what am I saying?" He rose from his seat and took a couple of agitated steps around the room. "I'm a clergyman, for heaven's sake! I'm not supposed to think this way!" He sat down again. "You're a parishioner, a member of my flock." He stroked her cheek. "My little lamb." He bent and kissed her. To his amazement he felt her arms wrap around his neck, and her fingers slide into his hair. Her mouth opened shyly to welcome him. The kiss deepened and his arms tightened around her.

After a moment he released her, breathing heavily. He glanced hungrily at her soft, lush bosom and ran a finger around his tight collar. "If Uncle Ceddie knew what I was thinking now, he'd send me to Outer Mongolia."

"Why?"

With an effort he walked away from her and stood next to the mantelpiece. "The thing is, Melly, I'd—I'd do something about this blasted situation"—His eyes burned—"But I'm so damnably poor."

"I'm poor, too," she told him, adding hopefully. "I don't mind being poor. I've never been anything else."

He shook his head. "No, it's more than that. I'm the sole support for my widowed mother and two younger sisters. I can't afford to get married. I probably never will."

"Never?" she said sadly. "I wouldn't mind waiting." She blushed. "If someone wanted me to wait, that is."

He eyed her hungrily, battled with himself, and then shook his head. "No, it's not possible. One day—when I'm a hundred and eight, no doubt—I will be rich beyond my wildest dreams!"

"A hundred and eight?"

"That's how long my Uncle Ceddie will live for, I bet. I'm his sole heir and while the estate is rich enough to support the entire family in luxury, down to the last third cousin, Uncle Ceddie won't part with a penny if he can help it. He keeps us all on the most stringent allowance—my mother can barely make ends meet. Almost all I earn in this job will go to her and the girls—Lord knows what we'll do once the girls are old enough to get married." He looked into her soft brown eyes. "So you see, there is no chance I can ever marry. No matter how much I might want to."

"I see," she said in a doleful voice. She sat there quietly, her hands folded in her lap, the picture of quiet hopelessness. "Will you be there when I am married to Lord d'Acre, then?"

He shook his head. "I couldn't bear to watch."

"Mr. Netterton says he won't be able to officiate at the wedding, Papa," Melly told him that evening.

"Why ever not?"

"I—I'm not sure. He just said he wouldn't be able to be there."

Sir John pursed his lips. "I suppose we'd better get another parson, then. It's a damned nuisance."

"Yes, Papa." She smoothed the sheets and pulled the bedclothes straight. He watched her face with a troubled expression.

"You do understand why I'm doing this, don't you, puss?"

She sighed. "I understand your reasoning, Papa."

He patted her hand. "It will turn out all right in the end. Trust me, Melly. It will be all right in the end."

"Yes, Papa." Her voice was almost inaudible. "Don't worry."

"You've been putting quite a lot of work into getting the estate to rights, haven't you?" Frey commented that evening. The two men were playing billiards.

"Mmm." Dominic squinted down the cue and potted his ball.

"That Abdul fellow seems to be running everyone ragged in an effort to bring the house up to scratch."

"Mmm." Dominic considered the best angle for his next shot.

"I suppose you and Miss Pettifer will spend a good deal of time here after the marriage."

"No." Dominic's cue ball glanced off Frey's, then struck a red ball, which rolled toward the pocket, teetered on the edge for a second, and then dropped in.

"Good shot! What do you mean, 'no'?"

"I'm going abroad." He made another shot, but missed. "Miss Pettifer, Lady D'Acre as she will be, will live wherever she wants—somewhere in England, I presume. Your turn."

Frey chalked the end of his cue thoughtfully. "You mean you're not going to live with her?"

"Good God, no! I plan to have nothing to do with her after the ceremony."

"What? Never?"

"No," said Dominic in a cheerful tone. "She will be free to do as she wishes. The marriage is merely a means to gain my inheritance. Do you think you have enough chalk there or shall I send for some more?"

Frey started and shook the excess chalk off. He'd used

half the piece. "You mean you're going to abandon her?"

"Abandon? You can hardly talk about the generous settlement she'll have as abandonment. She'll be *free*," Dominic corrected him.

"But she'll be alone."

"Nonsense. She'll have plenty of money to hire servants. And a companion."

"Old ladies hire companions—not young women not yet one-and-twenty! Who will look after her?"

Dominic raised his brows. "Oh, you mean that sort of companionship?" He shrugged. "I imagine that, too, will be easy to come by—"

"I didn't mean that at all. She's a nice, respectable girl! She wouldn't—"

"I'm in the process of purchasing her a house near the docks. After that she is free to do whatever she likes."

"But that's a terrible area. You can't leave a shy little creature like Miss Pettifer in that district—she'll be too nervous to leave the house."

Dominic shrugged. "Better than no house at all. And besides, it'll keep her out of mischief."

"Mischief? What sort of mischief do you think she would get up to? Do you know her so little? She's a virtuous little soul."

"Good, then it will keep her safe from the consequences of any foolishness."

"What do you mean?"

"I don't care if she takes lovers—she can have strings of 'em for all I care," Dominic said carelessly. "As long as she doesn't fall pregnant."

"Good God, she's not the sort to take lovers!" Frey exploded. "And even if she was, why should she not fall pregnant—you don't want her, so what do you care?"

Dominic inspected the end of his cue. "I won't have a cuckoo in the Wolfestone nest, that's why. I'll have her watched, of course. The first hint of pregnancy and she's out on her ear! Without a home, and with no income. I'm not one of your English gents who shrinks from the public fuss and disgrace of divorce. I was brought up in a part of the world much less rigid about that sort of thing, recall."

"That's inhuman!" Frey exploded.

"You think so?" Unconcerned, Dominic lined up his shot.

"Of course it is. What sort of a life is that for a young girl on the verge of womanhood?"

"Rather a dreary one, I imagine." Dominic potted the red ball.

"She'll be lonely and frightened and alone! You can't do it to her, Dom!"

Dominic gave a careless shrug. "She's doing it to herself, Frey. Nothing to do with me. I just want my inheritance. I'd prefer not to have to marry at all, as you know."

"You callous bastard," Frey gasped. "I never thought you'd turn out to be such a swine, Dominic. It goes to show, the apple never falls far from the tree. You're as bad as your father!" He threw down his cue and stormed from the room.

Dominic set his cue back in the rack and smiled.

Chapter Seventeen

Oh fateful night!
Hold back the hour of sundering!

IBN SAFR AL-MARINI

"I HEREBY PUBLISH THE BANNS OF MARRIAGE BETWEEN DOMINIC Edward Wolfe, Lord D'Acre, of Wolfestone Parish and Miss Melanie Louise Pettifer of the Parish of Theale in Reading. If any of you know cause or just impediment why these two should not be joined in Holy Matrimony, ye are to declare it. This is the first time of asking."

As Mr. Netterton finished the announcement, an audible ripple of speculation ran through the church. The locals who had crowded into the church in order to get a look at the new vicar were getting their money's worth.

"That's not 'er name," Grace heard someone mutter to a neighbor.

"No, 'e's got it wrong, the silly clunch. It's one thing to be nervous, but gettin' the name wrong—well!"

"Who's Miss Melanie Louise Pettifer?"

"The other one. Her friend."

Grace felt her face reddening. If she could hear the speculation, then so could Melly and Dominic, who sat on either side of her. They should have been sitting together, of course, looking like a couple, but as they'd entered the church to support Frey through his first solo sermon and hear the banns read, Dominic had been detained by someone or other, with the result that she and Melly had been sitting together in the Wolfe family pew, and he'd slid in at the last minute to join them. Next to Grace.

She glanced at Dominic. His face was granite and unreadable. She looked at Melly to see how she'd taken it. She looked pinched and miserable and desperate. Grace squeezed her hand in sympathy. Poor Melly, caught between two stubborn men.

Poor Grace, caught in the same trap.

As they filed up to the altar rail to take Communion, Grace tried to block the sympathetic smiles and grimaces from the villagers. They all seemed to think she was the one who should be marrying Dominic Wolfe. It was not just embarrassing, it was agonizing.

Because she happened to agree with them. And it was just not possible. And though her heart was breaking, she had to smile and be polite. She would put a bright face on this if it killed her.

She couldn't bear pity. What a fool she'd been to let herself believe that true love had at last found Grace Merridew! She could just imagine Grandpapa sniggering.

After the service, Frey was held up chatting to his new parishioners. As Melly, Dominic, and Grace filed inconspicuously past, they could hear him trying gracefully to parry invitations to Sunday dinner from several quite forceful ladies and gentlemen—all with marriageable daughters—who had traveled a good way to hear and meet the new bachelor vicar. At the same time, he was attempting to deal with just as forceful and much more blunt statements from the locals, pointing out his error in the banns.

In between repeated variations of "So sorry, very kind of you to ask, but alas, previous engagement at the castle. Yes, another time would be delightful," and "No, I did *not* make an error in the names, dash it all!" Frey was looking quite harassed.

Dominic began to lead them to the carriage. He felt numb, furious, cold.

"What of Mr. Netterton?" Melly asked.

"What of him? He can follow on later," Dominic told her.

Melly looked worriedly at Frey being mobbed by his flock and nudged Grace.

"Oh no, it would be too cruel to leave him there," Grace declared. "Why don't we give him fifteen minutes to chat and do the polite thing, and then Lord D'Acre can stride up and claim him in a lordly manner."

She was being so brave, he thought. Smiling and smiling and chattering brightly, while all the time in her eyes he could see how devastated she was. If she could be brave, so could he. He gave her what he hoped passed for a quizzical look. "Claim him in a lordly manner?"

"Yes, you know, with that ruthless, cruel, lordly look you do so well. Leaving poor Mr. Netterton no choice but to come with you or suffer a horrid fate."

"Oh, that look." He narrowed his eyes at her.

"Yes, that's the one," she said approvingly. "Utterly terrifying." She linked arms with him in a friendly fashion and looked up at him with swimming blue eyes and Dominic fought the urge to sweep her into his arms and comfort her with promises he could not keep.

She said brightly, "Well, we need some sort of spectacle

seeing as how Abdul has disappointed everyone so badly."

"He's what? How?"

"By not turning up. Mr. Netterton thinks it's him they've all come to see, and that's probably true, as far as the gentry is concerned, but most of the villagers are here to see a real live Turk."

"Real live Turks don't usually attend Anglican services."

"Nonsense, this is England. Half the people here are chapel, not church, but it hasn't stopped them coming today in the hope of seeing Abdul. Besides, before the Ottomans, Constantinople was the center of the Catholic church. It stands to reason some of them must have remained Christian."

"Not Abdul. I don't think he follows any particular faith, as it happens. And in any case he's not a Turk—he's a man of many races. His mother was the daughter of a Circassian slave girl, his father an Egyptian of Greek extraction, and the further back you go, the more complicated it gets. He says he's pure Ottoman—representative of every part of the empire."

He turned to offer his other arm to Miss Pettifer, but she was in close conference with Granny Wigmore. He waited a moment, but the conversation seemed quite intense and likely to take a while, so he and Grace started strolling through the churchyard. He pressed her arm against his side and covered her hand with his and, as always, her touch soothed him.

They strolled in silence for a few minutes and gradually he felt less desperate. He could feel the tension seeping from her, too. "Dreadful how they wanted to correct poor Frey, wasn't it?"

She didn't respond. He slipped an arm around her. "Don't worry so much, Grace. It will be all right, I promise you." It had to be. He'd risked things on a gamble before.

They walked on. After a while he asked her, "How do you know these things—like them wanting to gawk at Abdul? You've been here as long as I have and I never know what the villagers are thinking."

She said with an enigmatic air, "It's a mystery. Some call it a gift."

"Indeed?" he said dryly.

She smiled and said, "In the last few days I've lost track of how many villagers have asked me if it was true that his lordship had a real live Turk up at the castle. The people here have long memories, it seems."

"Too damn long," he agreed feelingly. "But what the devil do long memories have to do with Abdul? He's only just arrived."

She primmed her lips and his heart clenched as he saw how gallantly she tried to cheer him up. "Well, first there was talk of how much you resemble your ancestors. Figuring large in collective village memory is some fellow called Sir Simon Wolfe who fought with Richard Coeur de Lion in the crusades and became the first Lord D'Acre."

He grunted, fed up with reminders of his ancestors. "So?"

Her smile was genuine this time. "So, Sir Simon also brought back a real live Turk as prisoner. The villagers are thrilled you are continuing the tradition."

"Oh, for heaven's sake!" he said, disgusted.

She giggled and his heart lifted. They strolled on. He felt suddenly more positive. The feel of her small, firm hand tucked into his arm felt so right, so good. He adjusted his steps to suit her shorter ones; she was lengthening hers to suit his. As they walked, their bodies brushed against each other, just a touch, a reminder, a promise of things to come.

He would find a way.

"Oh, look." She stopped in front of a plaque set into a lichen-covered stone edifice with an angel on top. It was set in a large railed-off section of the churchyard. She read the inscription: *"Martha Jane Wolfe, Lady D'Acre, wife of Gerard Wolfe, Lord D'Acre of Wolfestone."*

Beneath the main inscription were six smaller ones, each only recording a name and a date. Her hand tightened on his arm as she read the names and realized the significance. "Poor lady, to lose so many babies . . . She died so young."

He looked at the stone. Another of the innocents sacrificed for Wolfestone. Well, no more. He steered her away.

"Will you go through with it?" she asked him after a moment. The connection was clear.

"I don't want to talk about it." He knew what he wanted. People didn't get everything they wanted.

She pulled her hand out of the crook of his arm. "But you must make a decision."

"Must I?" He glanced back at Frey and his parishioners. "Things are in train."

Unable to bear the look in her eyes, he drew her away. He would drag Frey away from his parishioners and get the hell out of this place. He dropped her arm and strode toward the group gathered around Frey. Grace was left staring after him.

Melly was waiting quietly at the back, watching Frey with an expression that broke Grace's heart.

Poor Melly, caught on the horns of a terrible dilemma and quite unable to take action of any sort.

Grace could not imagine what it would be like to live with the knowledge that you'd not only disappointed your father dreadfully but caused his death, as well.

The whispery voice echoed in her head. *"You killed your mama, Grace."*

Well, yes, actually. She could. And she would not wish it on anyone, let alone a tender innocent like Melly. Only what were they to do?

All Grace knew was that she could stand this no longer.

After church Grace knocked on Sir John's door. Melly was walking with Frey around the garden. She could see them from her upstairs window. They were deep in conversation.

The calling of banns had made up Grace's mind. She could stand this stalemate no longer. It was simply too painful. She would leave before they were called again, leave Dominic Wolfe and Wolfestone and everything that was ripping her apart. She would go back to London and pack to leave for Egypt with Mrs. Cheever.

But before she did, she would talk to Sir John.

"Yes, Greystoke," he said. "What is it?"

"It's not Greystoke, Sir John." She walked up to his bed. The clean scent of herbs could not quite disguise the stench of sickness. She tried not to pull a face. "It's Grace, Grace Merridew. I was at school with Melly, remember?"

Sir John's brow wrinkled in confusion. "How can you be Grace Merridew? You're Greystoke!"

"Look at me, Sir John, I dyed my hair and painted freckles all over my face." Grace tried not to stare at the large lump high on Sir John's abdomen and visible through his nightshirt. Of course, she told herself, if Granny was poulticing it, the poultice would make it look larger.

She could see the truth dawn slowly in his eyes. "I do recognize you. You deceived us? But why?" He looked shocked and bewildered and for a moment Grace suffered qualms about upsetting an old man who was so unwell. She steeled herself. It had to be said.

"Melly knew who I was all the time." She took a deep breath. "In fact Melly begged me to do it."

"But why?"

"She's desperately unhappy, Sir John. She doesn't want this marriage. Neither does Dominic Wolfe. You know that."

"They don't know what's good f—"

"They know what they want! And what they don't want. For a start, Melly would probably deny this, but it is my opinion that she's become very fond of Frey—Mr. Netterton."

"I'm fond of the lad myself," Sir John told her. "But he's as poor as a church mouse. And supporting his widowed mother and sisters. I'm not going to condemn my Melly to a life of poverty by letting her marry Frey Netterton."

"He won't always be poor. He's his uncle's heir and his uncle is very—"

Sir John cut her off with a dismissive gesture. "Long-lived family, the Nettertons. Ceddie will live to a hundred, I'll lay odds. Doesn't drink, smoke, or gamble." He shook his head in disbelief. "When you think of the wild youth I knew . . . A dead bore now, of course."

He recalled himself and shot Grace a mulish look. "I won't have my Melly scrimping and saving in the vicarage when she could be the lady of the manor, living a life of ease."

"Not even if she's happy scrimping in the vicarage?"

"Pshaw! Marriage doesn't guarantee happiness. But money guarantees comfort and security."

"You would make guarantee she is miserable by marrying her to a man who doesn't want her."

"D'Acre might not want her now, but—"

"He loves me. *Me*." She let that sink in. "And I love him."

He gave her a shrewd look. "But he's agreed to marry my Melly."

"Yes."

"For the money."

"Not for the money," she flashed proudly. "For his *home*. For the place his family has lived for six hundred years."

"He doesn't care about—"

"Oh, he cares, believe me. He just hides things deeper than most." She tried to think how to get through to this old man. "He *belongs* here. He's only just discovered that, but he needs to be part of Wolfestone as much as the Wolfestone people need him . . . And so I am leaving."

"Good."

She was speechless. "I thought you loved Melly."

"I do. And I'm doing what's best for her, even if she doesn't know it. Yet." He lay back on his pillows and closed his eyes. Argument over.

Grace said bitterly, "Then this is good-bye. I—I cannot claim to bear you no grudge, Sir John. But I will pray for your recovery. But know this—you are *wrong* to force this match, more deeply wrong than you will ever know."

Part of the night I spent
embracing her
and part kissing her
until the banner of dawn
summoned us to leave
and our circle of embraces
was broken.

Oh fateful night!
Hold back the hour of sundering!

With shaking hands Grace closed the little leather-bound book of poems. This poem, "Night of Love" by the poet of Andalusia, Ibn Safr al-Marini, was her favorite. So beautiful and so sad.

She was curled up in the big overstuffed armchair in the library. Dinner was over. It was her last night at Wolfestone. She'd made arrangements to leave at dawn. She hadn't told Dominic. She knew he'd make a fuss and she couldn't bear it. But everyone else knew. She'd said her good-byes.

Melly, caught up in helpless misery and guilt, had made an excuse and gone upstairs to sit with her father. It was an excuse, Grace knew, because her father was always asleep by this time. So Grace had retired to the comfort of the library and her beloved book of medieval poems.

Hold back the hour of sundering indeed, Grace repeated in her mind. But it was too late. Their circle of embrace had already been sundered. Dominic was marrying Melly. In a few more days the banns would be called for the second time.

She could not bear to stay and watch. She was not noble enough for that.

She looked around the room. Hard work had brought it from dusty neglect to beauty. She closed her eyes. She loved this place. She loved Dominic. How could she bear to leave?

How could she bear to stay?

Her body prickled with awareness. She looked up. Dominic had entered silently and stood watching her with an intense expression.

"I can't decide if your eyes are more beautiful when they're dancing like the sun on the sea, or when they're like bluebells bathed in the morning dew." By the time he'd finished speaking he stood in front of her. She couldn't move. Her legs seemed to have tangled beneath her.

"How long have you been standing there?"

For answer he bent and kissed her full on the mouth. She tasted passion and tenderness and desperation.

She closed her eyes and kissed him back with all her heart. The last kiss.

When he finally pulled back for a moment, she pressed her hands to his shoulders, saying, "No more."

"Why not?"

"Because I cannot bear it just now. No, I don't want to talk about it, just tell me why you have come here."

"Come upstairs with me. Come upstairs and lie down with me and we will talk."

"No, I cannot. There are too many people here. We would be discovered and I would be ruined."

He sighed, and turned on his heel and walked away from her. For a moment she thought he was leaving her and her heart was in her mouth. She didn't want to leave him like this.

But he was only going to lock the door. He returned and scooped her off her chair, carrying her in his arms as if she weighed as little as a child. Her pulse pounded.

With as much strength as she could muster, she said, "I said no, Dominic." It came out feebly.

With an innocent look he sat down with her on the sofa, only it could hardly be described as sitting. He leaned back against an arm of the sofa and she lay across his lap, half sprawled along the hard length of his body. She made a halfhearted attempt to sit up, but he pulled her back down, and to tell the truth, it was heaven being here in his arms.

Heaven and hell combined. He was marrying Melly, she reminded herself. As always the thought tore at her.

"I can't bear to see you fretting," he said.

"I can't bear this situation."

He kissed her. "I know. But the only simple solution is to shoot Sir John and Melly. Which, of course, I would do. Only then I'd have to kill Frey, which would be more difficult—my oldest friend, you know, and he's a devilish good shot himself, so it would be tricky. And then there's all the possible witnesses, and of course I could shoot them, too, but then there would be all those bodies to dispose of and I *hate* digging."

Unwillingly she laughed.

"You may laugh, but I really loathe it," he assured her. "But you are thinking, of course, that I am lord of this manor and I could just order a few peasants to do it, but what you haven't considered is that to cover up my awful crimes I would have had to kill all the peasants, too, so there would be nobody left to dig. Except me." He pulled a face. "And that would be terrible. I love you, Miss Merridew, but though I would kill for you, digging is quite another matter!"

By then, of course she was laughing. And crying at the same time. "You are ridiculous. I don't know how you can be so flippant at a time like—"

He kissed her. She kissed him back with all the love in her heart, all the yearning and dreaming and heartache.

And then she slipped from his arms and unlocked the door.

She paused at the door and said, "Good—good night." And before he could react, she'd slipped out of the door. She leaned against it a moment, whispered, "Good-bye, my love," and raced upstairs to her bedchamber.

She had to get away from him. When he looked at her

like that, with yearning and desperation in his eyes, she weakened. And if he kissed her again, which was only a matter of time, she would be lost.

She understood now what he meant when he'd asked her to be his mistress. It was no insult, no second best—not in his mind. He had offered her his heart.

But it was not enough for Grace. Children, the society of friends and family—was she willing to give them up for him? No. If there was no other way, perhaps she might consider it.

The marriage with Melly could still be stopped. He would stop it, she was sure, if he did not still believe in his heart of hearts that love and marriage could not co-exist.

But he didn't, and she couldn't think of any way to show him how wrong he was. And so she had to leave.

Egypt and the pyramids called. Her first, most reliable dream.

GRACE WAS WOKEN BY THE PREDAWN BIRD CHORUS THAT WOKE HER most mornings. She lay a moment, savoring it. The birds seemed to sing more sweetly here, she fancied. She slipped out of bed in the chill, gray half-light, dressing as quickly and quietly as she could. Melly was a still, silent mound in the bed. Grace wasn't sure if she was awake or not, though she rather thought she was; but Melly didn't say anything so Grace didn't, either.

She felt a rush of sadness. There was such a gulf between the two of them now. One day Grace might be able to understand, but right now, it was not in her to be understanding. She was too angry and unhappy.

She'd made her farewells with Melly last night as they'd

gone to bed. They'd wept—as much for their friendship as anything else.

She would go to London, where she knew her sister Prudence would be. Grace loved all her sisters, but right now, it was Prudence, the oldest, she most wanted.

Prudence had been like a mother to Grace for most of her life. These days she shared that role with Aunt Gussie, but when Grace was heartsore, or sick or angry, or grieving, it was Prue she turned to, as she had turned to her all her life. And right now Grace was heartsore and angry and grieving and in sore need of her big sister's comfort.

Her valise was downstairs already. She packed her nightgown and a few things in a small bag. She'd arranged with Abdul to borrow one of the chaises he'd brought down with him and a driver and groom. She'd offered to pay, but he'd waved it aside with a lordly air.

She'd made her good-byes last night. She just wanted to slip away quietly. She didn't want to see . . . anyone.

She was angry with Dominic, too, though she knew there was nothing he could honorably do. He was trapped.

She hated what this situation was doing to her, turning her into a virago. She was even angry with Sir John, and that wasn't fair at all—the poor man was staring death in the face and was desperate to secure his daughter's future.

She wished she'd never come here in the first place. It was so much easier dreaming of love than being caught in its toils. Love was torture. Why had nobody told her that?

She closed the door behind her and tiptoed downstairs, foolishly unable to resist stepping in the dips his ancestors' feet had made. *Torture*.

To her surprise Mrs. Stokes was already at work and had Grace's favorite breakfast waiting for her; a slice of bacon and a poached egg on toast, followed by coffee and toast with honey.

"You don't think me and Enid would let you go off on some long journey without a good breakfast inside you? Now, eat it while it's hot, miss."

Grace stared at the honey pot and memories assailed her. *Torture*. "Is there anything else, apart from honey? I don't feel like honey today," she told Mrs. Stokes. Or ever again.

"There's whimberry jam, if you like, miss. A Shropshire specialty. The whimberries were picked on the hills just yesterday by young Billy Finn, and I made the jam myself," Mrs. Stokes told her. "Very good for what ails ye, whimberries are."

"That would be lovely, Mrs. Stokes. Thank you," Grace managed, though no jam could fix what ailed her.

After breakfast she took some apples and carrots and slipped out to the stables to say good-bye to the horses she'd grown so fond of. In the courtyard, the grooms were buckling the carriage horses into their traces. She hurried inside.

The mares were waiting to greet her, as they did every morning, their heads poking expectantly over the half stable doors, whickering a greeting. She went first to say good-bye to the foal, but he ignored her, his head buried in his mother's flank, drinking hungrily, his little tail wriggling with pleasure. She laughed and fed an apple to his mother and her sister in the next stall.

She gave a carrot to Dominic's horse. "Look after him, Hex." He took the carrot but when she tried to pat him, he threw his head back in alarm. "You are well suited, you two—both big, handsome, noble-looking and thick-headed!"

She heard the carriage being driven around to the front

and hurriedly said good-bye to the dainty silver mare she'd come to look on as her own. "Good-bye, Misty, my darling. I'll miss our morning rides." Misty took the apple delicately, crunching it with relish, as Grace stroked her velvet nose and hugged her good-bye.

She left with lagging steps. It would be so easy to change her mind, to saddle Misty and ride off as usual . . . only . . . *Torture*.

Abdul was waiting for her in the hall. "You honor me, Abdul," she told him.

His smile was wry. "Perhaps, *sitt*. I am here to argue with you as well."

"Argue with me?"

"You are running away, but you need to stay and fight."

"There is nothing I can do."

He threw up his hands in exasperation. "I cannot understand how it is that the English have come to rule most of the world! You, he, and that other girl—and each of you say, 'I can do nothing.' So you all be miserable. Pah! I say kill the old man and be done with it!"

He couldn't be serious. She smiled, shook her head, and made to step around him, but he caught her by the arm. "*Sitt*, I have known Dominic Wolfe for ten years—since he came to manhood—and I say he has never, *never* looked at a woman the way he looks at you! Always he has pursued women he cannot have—women with old husbands, or absent husbands—women who will never want more of him than he is prepared to give."

He gave her arm a little shake. "*Never* has he yearned after a young virgin!"

She blushed at his bluntness. She was no longer a young virgin. She pulled her arm away. "You are talking to the wrong person, Abdul."

He flung up his hands again. "Bah—he is like a mule! But behind the mulishness, young *sitt*, he is in—how you say it?" He made a rapid rolling movement with his hands.

"Turmoil?"

"Yes, in turmoil. It is not just that he pursues a young virgin. Never has he involved himself in any lives other than his own—only when he first buy me, and that was to save my manhood." His hands rested briefly over his male parts. "Thanks be to God and Dominic Wolfe. I was to be made a eunuch. You understand eunuch?" He made graphic cutting movements with his hands.

She nodded, blushing furiously.

"Every time I lie between the thighs of a woman I rejoice in the compassion of Dominic Wolfe—and I am a lusty fellow, so I rejoice often! But him—he has dark shadows. Too many, and I say to myself, Abdul, that is your task. But he is like a leaf that blows." His hands imitated a leaf drifting aimlessly in the wind.

He made an emphatic gesture and his dark eyes flashed with excitement, "But now, suddenly, in this place he says he does not want to be, he takes an interest in this young boy, that old man, this woman and her family, that farmer with his broken roof, and on and on and on. He has me working all hours to rebuild the estate—and this was the place he swore he would destroy."

"I'm glad." She bent to pick up her bags.

He snatched them away. "Pah! Ask yourself what has caused this change, *sitt*!"

She shook her head, deliberately obtuse.

He made an exasperated sound. "You, only you! You touch something inside him, wake a part of him I have never seen! And so you must stay and fight; fight for your happiness, for this estate, and for the heart and happiness of Dominic Wolfe."

She looked at him a long moment. "I have already given my heart to Dominic Wolfe," she said quietly. "It changed nothing. And now I must go, if you please."

"But of course, *sitt*," he said smoothly as if the last few minutes had never been, and he carried out the bags.

She looked up at the gargoyle. "Good-bye, Mr. Gargoyle," she whispered. "Take care of him and the people of this estate. Make him see how much he belongs here." Tears prickled at her eyelids. "Make him happy."

She hurried outside and stopped dead. Every servant had gathered on the front steps to farewell her. It was only just after dawn.

Mrs. Stokes and Enid stepped forward and gave her a basket. Mrs. Stokes's face was stiff and red, Enid was weeping openly. "Just a few things in case you get hungry on the way, miss."

The three Tickel girls gave her a bag of apples and some more lemons from their mother, "For them lemons have done a power o' good to yer freckles, miss." They burst into loud sobs.

Billy Finn, dressed in a uniform of slightly oriental design, was clutching a ragged bunch of wildflowers, which he thrust at her, saying, "There's rosemary in there, miss, so ye don't forget to come back to us."

She thanked him and gave him a hug. "I'll miss you Billy," she whispered.

They all lined up to farewell her, shaking her hand, pressing small gifts on her and wishing her a safe journey. Even old Grandad Tasker creaked forward and pressed a rose in a pot on her. "Tis the same rose as his lordship's mam used to grow. She loved them roses and I reckon you do, too," the old man said. She thanked him brokenly.

Finally there was Granny Wigmore, looking bright and rosy. Of all the people there, she was the only one not visibly distressed. She hugged Grace. "Farewell, Lady. You'll come back to us at Wolfestone, never fear. I know it here." She touched her heart. She handed Grace a small silken bag. "Sleep on this, Lady, and it'll sweeten your dreams." It smelled of roses and herbs.

Grace kissed Granny on the cheek. "Look after him, Granny."

"I will, lass. I will."

Abdul handed her into the carriage, which was just as well, for she could hardly see for tears. "Could you tell Lord D'Acre good-bye for me, please?" she told him. "I couldn't tell him last night."

"Of course, *sitt*." He added in Arabic, "God grant you a safe and pleasant journey." He tucked a travel rug around her and safely stowed away the various bits and pieces she'd been given, leaving her only Billy Finn's flowers, which she refused to give up. The whole time she stared out of the window, looking at the faces of the people who had become so dear to her in such a short time.

She glanced up to the windows above and saw Melly in her nightgown and shawl, watching miserably. Grace lifted her hand. Melly's face crumpled and she pressed her palm to the glass.

A few windows across from her, Frey stood, dressed in a gorgeously embroidered dressing gown. He must have been awoken by the noise of the carriage. As their eyes met he lifted his hand in a solemn farewell and made the sign of the cross, a blessing for her journey. She thanked him silently, then with a jerk, the carriage moved off.

Her eyes clung to a third window, but it remained cold and blank and empty. There was no movement, no sign of a tall dark man with intense golden eyes.

She waved good-bye to the others blindly. Billy Finn ran after the traveling chaise for several hundred yards, but she lost sight of him as they turned the corner. She looked back, but Wolfestone and its people were nothing but a blur of tears.

Chapter Eighteen

Thou art my life, my love, my heart,
The very eyes of me:
And hast command of every part
To live and die for thee.

ROBERT HERRICK

THE CARRIAGE DROVE BETWEEN THE WOLF-MOUNTED STONE gateposts and her sobs grew louder. She wiped at her wet eyes and cheeks with her hands.

"Here, use this." Dominic proffered a handkerchief from the dark corner of the coach.

She leapt about a foot in the air. "Where did you come from?"

He slid along the leather seat and, cupping her chin in one hand, proceeded to dry her face for her. "I was here the whole time. You were too busy looking out of the window to see me." He smiled tenderly at her. "Your eyes are like drowning violets."

"Last time they were dew-spangled bluebells," she said tartly, snatching the handkerchief from him and moving to the opposite side of the carriage, out of his reach. "Why are you here?" She scrubbed at her face with his handkerchief.

"I'm coming with you."

"But I'm leaving you."

"Yes, I know. That's why I'm coming with you." He took the handkerchief from her and proceeded to dry her eyes. "You don't imagine I'd let you leave me without coming with you, do you? No, if you're running away, we'll run away together."

She snatched the handkerchief back. "I can do it myself. And I'm not running away."

"No? Looks like it to me." He retrieved the handkerchief and said softly, "Stop fussing, love, and let me do this."

She wasn't sure what he meant—come with her or dry her cheeks. "But you can't come with me when I'm leaving you."

"You're my dream, remember? I have no choice."

Fresh tears flooded her eyes. He blotted them tenderly. She pushed his hands away saying, "But . . . what about Wolfestone? What about Melly? And Sir John?"

"What about them? If they want to come, they can get their own carriage. We only have room for us."

"But today Frey will be calling the banns for the second time."

He shrugged. "Frey must do what Frey must do."

She stared at him in disbelief. "What about Melly?"

He examined her cheeks and found another spot to dry. "I don't think she'll mind me taking a trip to London, do you?"

"I won't be your mistress."

He gave her a shocked look. "Perish the thought! I wouldn't insult you so by asking—even though I believe it's a very fine position, but only for some women. Not for you."

She scooted across the seat and frowned at him suspiciously. "What are you up to?"

"I'm going to London to visit the queen."

"Be serious!"

He smiled and said softly, "I'm escorting you to your family." He sounded quite sincere.

"Truly?"

"Truly. It's a long trip."

She thought it over a moment. "You promise there will be no funny business?"

He heaved a mock sigh. "Spoilsport. All right, I promise."

She tried not to smile. Then she thought of something. "If we travel together, and especially if we stay at the same inn, my reputation will be in shreds. I'll be ruined."

"Ruined?" He shook his head and said firmly. "I wouldn't harm a hair of your head, let alone ruin you. I've thought it all out. We shall stop overnight at Cheltenham and stay with friends of mine there. Married friends."

"But I'll be alone in a closed carriage with you for nearly two days."

"Nonsense. I've brought along another female to chaperone you. Not to mention a driver and two grooms."

She looked around the carriage pointedly. "Well, where is this female then?"

He waved a hand, "She's up the front, out there with the driver. She'll only travel inside if it's raining. Mostly she prefers enraging other dogs who we pass and having the wind in her face."

"Other dogs—you don't—you can't mean *Sheba*?"

He grinned.

"You're using your *dog* to chaperone me?"

He said indignantly, "She's a very good chaperone. She's never let a cat come near me!"

She stared at him, biting her lip, but she could not prevent a giggle escaping. He was outrageous.

He immediately pulled her into his lap. "Now just relax, my love. I'm not letting you go alone, so let us just enjoy the trip."

Grace gave in. She lay against Dominic's chest and wrapped her arms around him. She didn't know what he was up to, coming with her like this. It didn't make sense to her. But she'd been offered a short reprieve and she didn't have the strength to send him away again. Not just yet.

"I hereby publish the banns of marriage between Dominic Edward Wolfe, Lord D'Acre, of Wolfestone Parish and Miss Melanie Louise Pettifer of the Parish of Theale in Reading. If any of you know cause or just impediment why these two should not be joined in Holy Matrimony, ye are to declare it. This is the second time of asking."

This time there was hardly a ripple in the congregation. The absence of Lord D'Acre and Miss Greystoke had been noted. Most people knew by now that they'd gone off in a carriage at dawn earlier in the week. No, that was old news.

But this congregation was just as thrilled as last week's, possibly more so, for this Sunday the Turk had, in his master's absence, escorted Miss Pettifer to church.

What's more, he'd escorted her to the Wolfe family pew, bowed, then retreated to a nearby commoner's pew and remained throughout the service, sitting between two Tickel girls.

It had been rare entertainment, the village agreed afterward, for the three Tickel girls had almost come to blows over who was to sit beside the big foreigner. Tansy had lost, and had flounced off and sat with her mother, pouting and glaring throughout the service.

He, amazingly, had not turned a hair—and they could

tell, for today he wore no turban, but a colorful, foreign-looking hat, which he'd removed, very properly, before entering the church. His hair was very black and very thick and curled around his collar in a heathenish manner.

He'd stood for hymns and even sung, he'd knelt for prayers and as far as anyone could tell, he hadn't put a foot wrong, except that he didn't utter a word of the prayers, even though both Tickel girls were holding prayer books for him. And he hadn't gone down to the rail for communion.

The congregation paid little attention to the sermon; it was busily speculating on whether the Turk was a heathen or some sort of odd foreign Christian, and whether they should welcome him or not. Since he was bigger than most of the men present, it was decided that he should be welcomed into their midst. After all, not many villages had a real live Turk to boast of.

They filed out of the church in the wake of the minister and altar boys, well pleased with the day's offerings.

Grandad Tasker spoke for them all when he said as he shook his minister's hand, "A grand service, Vicar. Not too long a sermon and plenty to look at!"

Outside, Abdul waited to escort Miss Pettifer to the carriage. "I'll walk if you don't mind," Melly said. She was still a little nervous of the big man. Every time he looked at her she read disapproval in his eyes. "It's such a lovely morning. Mr. Netterton will escort me."

She looked at Frey, who nodded and said, "Yes, I'll escort Miss Pettifer."

Abdul bowed and strode away. As he reached the Tickel family, he paused and raised both elbows ever so slightly. There was a brief scuffle and he continued serenely on his way, a Tickel girl triumphantly hanging on each arm. Tilly hung back in the rear, looking sulky.

He turned and looked back at her. "Tilly," he commanded in a deep voice. "There is enough of me for all of you." Giggling, Tilly ran to catch up.

The villagers buzzed, delighted to be horrified at such openly scandalous behavior. But, well—you couldn't blame 'em. What did Turks and Tickel girls know of respectable folks' ways?

Melly stood next to the church door, waiting while Frey chatted to his parishioners. She didn't mind waiting. It was pleasant in the morning sun, and besides, it was interesting hearing what people had to say.

A young woman walked up with a baby wrapped in a blue blanket. Melly had heard it crying in church. The young woman had left. She shifted the baby from one arm to the other. Melly stared, fascinated at the tiny curve of fuzz visible from the shawl.

She could not help herself. Without conscious thought she gravitated to the young mother. "May I see?"

Proudly the mother drew back the blanket to reveal a tiny infant, with button nose and the sweetest little red bow of a mouth.

"Oh, he's beautiful," Melly breathed. "What a dear little treasure. Oh, yes, you are," she told the baby. "A precious treasure."

The child stared solemnly at her with big blue eyes. One tiny hand waved aimlessly in the air and Melly caught the little fist, marveling over the perfect tiny fingernails.

"Would you like to hold 'im for a bit, miss?" the mother said. "I need to talk to Vicar a moment."

"May I?" Melly was thrilled. Carefully she gathered the child in her arms, rocking him and murmuring gently so as not to startle him. Vaguely she heard the mother and Frey arranging for the child to be christened the following week, but all her attention was on the baby who lay so trustingly in her arms, staring up at her.

She planted a kiss on the fuzzy crown, on the silken cheek. She cradled him against her breast. The heavy, warm, weight of him felt so perfect, so right. She closed her eyes and breathed in the pure baby smell of him, crooning to him gently. She so ached for a baby of her own.

"I'll take him now, thanks, m—" The woman broke off. "Are you all right, miss?"

"Yes," Melly assured her, puzzled.

The young woman stared. "It's just that you're crying, miss."

"Oh!" Hastily Melly wiped her cheeks. "Sorry. It—it's nothing. The, um, the flowers in church sometimes have this effect on me."

The woman gave her a long look. Melly avoided her eyes.

"You'll have a bonny wee babe of your own, one day, miss, don't worry," she said softly and squeezed Melly's arm.

Melly turned away. She didn't want anyone to see how her eyes had flooded. She stood there, groping blindly in her reticule for her handkerchief.

"What did she say to you?" It was Frey's voice, fierce, angry. He seized her by the shoulders and tried to turn her toward him.

"Nothing. She said nothing." Melly tried to hide her face from him, knowing her eyes would be red, her face blotchy.

"I saw it, Melly," he said sternly. "She made you cry!"

"No, no, she didn't." She tried to pull away.

He didn't budge. "I'm not letting you go until you tell me why you're in tears. She must have done *something*!"

"It was the *baby*! The baby made me cry!" she told him in despair.

"The *baby*?" He stared down at her. "Don't you like babies?"

At that she looked up at him, and fresh tears filled her eyes and spilled down, and suddenly Frey saw it all: all the tender yearning, all the flat despair. "Come here," he said and pulled her into his arms.

"We'll be in Cheltenham soon," Dominic murmured in Grace's ear. She stirred sleepily. Earlier, they'd been watching the moon rising through the chaise window and she'd fallen asleep, snuggled against him.

The journey had been swift and uneventful. Recent light showers had dampened down the clouds of dust that usually accompanied summer travel. They hadn't been heavy enough to make the roads boggy with mud, so the roads were dry and hard and perfect for travel.

The hooves of the horses beat out a steady rhythm, the chaise rocked gently—a testament to excellent springs. It was as if they'd managed to steal a moment out of time.

"I almost wish we didn't ever have to stop," she murmured. "It's lovely just being here, with you. No difficulties, no arguments, no horrid decisions to be made, just the moon, and the clip-clop of the horses and us."

His arm tightened and she lifted her head and turned her face up to be kissed. And he was more than willing to oblige.

The horses slowed a little, laboring up a hill. He glanced out of the window and stiffened. She followed his gaze and saw twinkling lights winking in the darkness.

"Cheltenham," she said in a sad voice. "We're back in the real world again. I wish . . ." She gave him an anguished look and kissed him with a desperation and sweetness that pierced him, wrapping her hands around his head and kissing him as if it was the last time. When the kiss finished she held him tightly for a moment, her silken cheek pressed against his rough one, before moving back to take the seat opposite him.

"Tell me about these friends of yours we're staying with," she said.

"Ah . . ." He thought for a minute. "Before I do, could you give me a definition of exactly what you meant by 'funny business'?"

And then he told her about his friends.

"A *harem*? You are joking, surely."

"No, it's a genuine harem."

Her eyes sparkled. "In *Cheltenham*? Are you sure?"

He laughed at her amazement. "Yes, we're staying in a house in Cheltenham that contains a harem. It's the home of Tariq bin Khalif, a very old friend of mine. I've known him since we were boys together in Alexandria. He's immensely rich—a silk merchant, among other things—and every year he comes to Cheltenham to drink the waters. They helped cure some ailment he had in his youth. This year he has brought his wives with him for the first time."

"A real harem? How exciting!" Then she laughed. "Oh, but if this gets out—first he chaperones me with his dog and then he takes me to a harem!"

"You won't be ruined," he assured her. "A harem is designed to safeguard the virtue of the inmates."

"Oh."

He laughed at her disappointment.

It looked just like any other Cheltenham house from the outside, with a green door, a brass knocker, and wrought-iron railings. The only difference was that the windows of the upper story were covered also, though not with railings, but carved wooden screens just inside the windows. You had to look closely to see them.

Dominic rang the bell. The door opened smoothly and a servant dressed in western clothes, but wearing a white headdress, bowed to Dominic and ushered them inside. He did not acknowledge Grace by as much as a flicker of an eyelash.

The owner of the house came down the stairs to meet them, an olive-skinned man of medium height, dark browed, black bearded, and with dark, almond-shaped eyes. He was dressed entirely in western clothes.

He said in heavily accented English, "Peace be with you, old friend. Welcome to my house, and welcome, too, to your lady." He shook Dominic's hand and inclined his head toward Grace.

"Miss Merridew, this is my friend Tariq bin Khalif."

Grace curtsied. "Thank you for offering us your hospitality."

"Dominic's friends are my friends. I have had rooms prepared for your visit and all is ready for your comfort." He hesitated, uncertain of how she felt about other cultures. "Would you be willing to meet my wives?"

Dominic laughed. "Try and stop her."

"If you, and they, would be so gracious," Grace said in careful Arabic.

The black brows flew up. He responded in the same language. "The lady speaks our tongue?"

"A little only and not well," she replied.

"She also reads it," Dominic said quietly, and Grace thrilled at the note of quiet pride in his voice. "She has a fondness for the poetry of Ibn Safr al-Marini."

"The celebrated poet of Andalusia? I am impressed and my wives will be well pleased. They were, you understand, a little nervous of meeting an English lady." He clapped his hands and a large, fat, soft-looking man in Arab clothing appeared soundlessly in the doorway. "Conduct this lady to the women's quarters," Tariq ordered. "She speaks our language."

The large man bowed and indicated that Grace was to precede him.

"A eunuch," Dominic murmured inconspicuously in Grace's ear.

Grace's eyes widened. So this was what Abdul might have become? She followed the man. He led her past the main stairs to a staircase at the back of the house.

The women's quarters were on the second floor at the rear, separated from the rest of the house by an exquisite carved screen that blocked the passageway. The large man opened the door and bowed, indicating to Grace that she should enter. She entered, her heart beating rapidly. She was eager to meet the ladies of the harem, but a little nervous, too.

He opened a door and it was like stepping into another world, an exotic world of scent and color and rich textures and intricate patterns. The air was scented: sandalwood, perhaps, Grace thought. Some sort of incense anyway, musky and exotic and exciting. Thick Persian carpets covered every inch of the floor, sometimes several layers thick and laid higgledy-piggledy, without regard to color or design, quite different from the careful balance sought in English style.

The windows were covered by delicate carved wooden screens and framed by lavish drapes of brilliant gold silk, but silver lamps swung from the ceiling, bathing the room in golden light, and casting shadows in the corners. Light also reflected from mirrors; gilt-framed mirrors in all sorts of shapes and sizes almost covered the walls—a surprise to Grace, who'd grown up in a house without mirrors and thought one mirror plenty. She'd never seen so many mirrors in one room. Patterned hangings and embroideries filled the few spaces left.

Five ladies stood staring at her, their hands clasped nervously. Grace, recalling what Tariq had told her, smiled and curtsied. "Peace be with you," she said in Arabic. "I thank you for inviting me to your home."

There was a flutter, a murmur, and the ladies gathered around her, chattering excitedly in Arabic.

Laughing, Grace held up her hands and explained that she was not yet very good with their language, that she could read it better than she could speak and understand.

One by one the ladies introduced themselves. The oldest wife came first, Fatima, an elegant woman who Grace thought would be in her late twenties, then came Kadije, round-faced and jolly, and Mouna, an exquisite dusky beauty who looked about seventeen. These were Tariq's wives.

The other women, it was subtly made clear, were servants. A fourth wife had remained in Alexandria, to give birth. Mouna demonstrated with a graphic demonstration and a giggle.

They invited her to sit. There was little furniture—several low divans, mounds of sumptuously covered cushions and a few low tables and chests made of cedar, patterned heavily with inlaid mother-of-pearl. Grace sat on a divan and found herself sinking into lush softness.

Fatima clapped her hands and the servant girls appeared, one bearing a tall silver jug, which proved to contain a fruit drink, oddly perfumed, but delicious. The other carried a huge tray and the low table was soon covered with dozens of silver dishes containing foods Grace had never before seen. The ladies urged her to eat, and waited with interest for her reaction to each dish and pelted her with questions. Grace even managed a few of her own.

It was the ladies' first time in England and they found it very different, they told her: quite cold and damp, even though it was summer.

By the time she'd tasted a little of everything she was full to bursting. She was in the middle of thanking the ladies when she exclaimed in English, "Oh, heavens I almost forgot!" Recollecting herself, she said in Arabic, "I brought you some small gifts."

As soon as Dominic had told her where they would be staying the night, she'd ransacked her luggage for anything she thought might please harem ladies: a couple of ladies' magazines, lavishly illustrated, a box of homemade toffees, and some cosmetic creams and lotions—though she was fairly sure they would have their own. She had no idea of their tastes, of course, but she imagined that harem ladies would be interested in the same things she and her sisters had longed for when they'd lived with Grandpapa, cut off from the rest of the world.

She also gave them a few things she'd bought for her sisters' children; a box of spillikins, a dissected map puzzle, a French doll, and a kaleidoscope. She presumed the ladies had children.

The ladies exclaimed excitedly over the gifts, turning the pages of the magazine back to front and poring over the illustrations, particularly the fashions. To Grace's amazement they fell on the children's toys with equal delight. They loved the French doll, with clothes that could be taken off and put on. They took turns peering into the kaleidoscope and exclaimed over the beautiful patterns.

They peered dubiously into the box of spillikins and looked at Grace with puzzled faces, as if to say, *you brought us a box of sticks?*

She cleared the low table and demonstrated how to play the children's game. Soon all four of them were seated around the table, laughing and competing fiercely at spillikins.

At the end of the third game, they were fast friends.

"I wish you could meet my sisters," she told them.

The younger two looked to Fatima for an answer. She smiled, "We would like that very much."

Grace was surprised. "But I thought you were always locked in," she blurted. "All those locks and bars."

They laughed. "No, any locks and bars are for our protection," Fatima explained. "We can go out, as long as we are escorted." It was much the same as English girls of good family, Grace realized.

Mouna was examining the French doll. "Do you wear all this under your clothes?" she asked Grace.

"Not exactly the same, but yes."

"Show me." Mouna bounded up and waited in clear expectation.

Grace blinked. "You want to see my underwear?"

All three ladies nodded eagerly.

Grace felt herself blushing. She'd never undressed in front of strangers before. Well, except for mantua makers. And Dominic Wolfe. It was harmless, she told herself. These ladies were just curious, and she was just as curious about their clothes. She swallowed and stood up. "Very well, this looks like a dress, but in fact it is a skirt and a bodice, and the join is hidden by this belt." She spoke in

English, emphasizing the words "skirt" and "bodice" and "belt" and they supplied words in Arabic, which she tried to remember.

"And underneath the skirt is a petticoat." She lifted her skirt to allow the ladies to see the petticoat, but in seconds they had unfastened the skirt, the better to see how it was made. It was passed around the servant girls as well.

It was a source of amusement and interest to them that the petticoat belled out around her without touching her legs. They examined the hem minutely and she showed how rope was inserted into it to make it stand out better. They thought that very ingenious. The petticoat, too, was removed and passed around.

Then they turned to look at her pantalettes. "These are my pantalettes." Grace placed her hands over the drawstrings to indicate she was not taking them off!

Mouna had removed the pantalettes of the French doll and poked her fingers through the slit in the crotch, a question in her eyes. Grace nodded, blushing. Trust the French to be totally accurate. But she was not going to show the slit.

There was some discussion as to the purpose of this slit, and some embarrassing gestures made. Grace was instantly transported back to the moment in the lake when Dominic had caressed her through that very slit. Blushing, she shook her head. People might do such things, but it was not the main purpose of the design. Eventually Kadije squatted in imitation of relieving herself and Grace nodded in embarrassed relief.

The ladies thought that very strange and rather unpleasant. They wore loose, gathered pantaloons which were held up with a drawstring and easily dropped—as Kadije demonstrated. They were all quite blunt and matter-of-fact about nakedness, Grace saw. And why not? They were all female.

"This is a corset." She unbuttoned the bodice to show them, but Mouna drew it off her, indicating they wanted to examine the darts and design. They were all fascinated by the corset and nothing would do but that they unlace it, too, and examine it, so Grace was left in just pantalettes and a chemise, which, when she thought about it, was much the same as they were wearing.

The ladies each tried on the corset, with much laughter. Only Mouna could fit. They were intrigued by the way the corset pushed her breasts higher, and thought the whalebone inserts a most odd and interesting device.

When they discovered the polished bone busk pushed into its little pocket they drew it out with excited exclamations, but seemed disappointed when they saw it. Fatima explained that from the shape and feel of it, they'd expected it to be a knife.

Grace laughed and tried to explain that she knew one lady who did carry a sharp instrument there for protection, but that most of them didn't. The ladies nodded. What were men for, if not for protection?

"Now," Fatima told her while Mouna was being buttoned and laced into Grace's clothes, "we shall dress you in our costume."

Servant girls brought forward a pile of shimmering fabrics. They surrounded Grace, Fatima said something and before she knew it, her chemise was replaced with a blue silk top—like a tunic, except it was extremely sheer.

Grace, looking down at herself, was a little taken aback at how sheer, but saw they were bringing a bodice and she relaxed. However when they fastened the bodice, an exquisite thing of gold and blue and red embroidery, she found it didn't help. It covered her back very well, but the front consisted of a tight band that went under her breasts—to push them up a bit, like a corset, Fatima explained.

What it did was make the near nakedness of her breasts more apparent, Grace thought.

But then they brought a hip-length shirt with long sleeves to button over it and then a waistcoat sort of thing and she felt a lot less self-conscious. Fatima explained the clothes came from different countries, as did they—she was from Alexandria, but Kadije was from Turkey and Mouna from the green hills of Lebanon. Their husband traveled widely, she explained.

"One must travel far to find such treasures," Grace responded and the compliment delighted them all.

The ladies were intrigued by the faded marks of her freckles. Henna, she told them. They nodded as if it confirmed something and explained that they painted their feet and hands with henna and used it to brighten hair, but never had they made such dots on the face, neck and hands! Was this a popular look in England?

"No," Grace told them. "I'm letting them fade."

Fatima said something and a servant girl ran out, returning in a few minutes with a small phial. "It will hasten the fading," Fatima told her. Grace smiled as she accepted it. Some things, it seemed, were universal.

They let her keep her pantalettes on but slipped on a pair of soft, loose trousers in pattered blue-and-red silk over them, and a loose, sheer skirt in yellow over the top. Kadije drew a line of blue kohl around her eyes and painted her lips with some red paint. Mouna, dressed in Grace's clothes, presented her with a small, embroidered cap and showed her how to drape a sheer veil from it, and then Grace fetched her large-brimmed flowered hat and placed it on

Mouna's head, showing her how to use hat pins to hold it firm.

They stood, side by side and gazed at themselves in the mirrors. "I look wonderful!" Grace exclaimed. "Completely exotic. Oh, how I wish I could show my sisters!"

"But of course you can," Fatima said. "These clothes are our gift to you. They are for indoor wear, naturally, but there is a robe for outside."

Grace demurred, but the ladies were insistent. She looked at Mouna, still primping in front of the mirror. "Would you like to keep those, Mouna?" she asked. "And my hat, too? I know they are not new, but—"

Mouna embraced her with a shriek of delight and went spinning around the room, her skirts flaring out in a bell.

Fatima ordered coffee, which was poured into tiny cups and was unlike any coffee Grace had drunk, being strong and very sweet and thick and muddy. It was accompanied by tiny pastries, dripping with syrup and filled with nuts, and *loukoumi*—Turkish delight.

As the last dishes were cleared away, a servant announced, "The *hamam* is ready, mistress," and Fatima rose. "Come, Grace," she said. "This will be a very special treat."

"Oh, I couldn't eat another thing!" she exclaimed.

They laughed. "Come. We planned this when we heard you would visit. Your lord requested it. It is the perfect thing after travel. We were not sure if an English lady would like it, but now that we know you, we think you will."

In a dubious frame of mind, Grace allowed herself to be taken downstairs, still on the women's side of the house, and through a doorway, into a small anteroom where she was—slightly to her consternation—divested of her newly acquired clothes—again, she retained her pantalettes—and wrapped in a large muslin sheet. The three wives did the same, much to her relief. Then they put on strange wooden shoes, raised off the ground, and entered a large circular room, attached to the back of the house.

No Englishman had built it, that was clear; made of stone, it had a domed roof and was lined throughout with tiles decorated in the oriental manner. Inside it was hot and steamy and there was a deep pool in the middle and a fountain bubbling on the side.

"Turkish bath," explained Kadije. "Built for me," she added proudly.

A bath? Dominic had requested they *bathe* her?

Chapter Nineteen

Thyself: cast all, yea, this white linen hence,
There is no penance due to innocence:
To teach thee I am naked first; why then
What needst thou have more covering than a man?

JOHN DONNE

FEMALE SERVANTS SURROUNDED THEM AND WITHOUT WARNING Grace's sheet was twitched off her, her pantalettes whisked off, and she was doused in warm water and soaped from head to toe—even her hair was undone and washed.

"This, you want it dyed dark again?" they asked her. She flushed, realizing they'd noted the contrast with her pubic hair. "No," she said.

"You want the same color?" They pointed, unembarrassed, at her pubic hair.

"Yes."

A girl ran off and came back with something that they rubbed into Grace's hair, a noxious-smelling ointment that they left in and wrapped in a towel.

Grace thought she was clean, but then the scrubbing started—from her ears to her toes, she was scrubbed with a rough-surfaced mitten until her skin felt raw and tingling. They indicated she could do her private parts herself, and she washed them thankfully. She'd wanted an exotic experience, she told herself! Beside her Mouna, Fatima, and Kadije were all getting the same treatment.

They rinsed her down, soaped her again, and rinsed her a second time. "Now, get in," the servants told her and pushed her toward the pool. It had steps leading down to it and the water was deliciously warm. Grace felt like she would melt, it was so relaxing, but after fifteen minutes or so, they wanted her out again to rinse and scrub her hair again. They plastered it with some other lotion and put her back in the pool. More time passed blissfully in the warm pool then she was hauled out for her hair to be rinsed and scrubbed a final time. They sluiced with cooler water, then a large elderly woman beckoned to her.

"Oh no!" she exclaimed. "Not more scrubbing. I'm as clean as anyone can be!"

"Turkish massage," Kadije told her. "Make you feel very relax, very nice."

The old woman dried Grace down as if she was a baby and laid her, front down, on a tiled bench covered with a thick cloth. Warm liquid spilled between her shoulder blades and the scent of roses filled the air. The old woman started massaging her, pulling and pushing and kneading her muscles. Her hands were strong, as strong as a man's. It took a few moments to get used to, but once she did, Grace felt like a cat, stretching and purring under the experience. Now she really was dissolving.

The massage went on and vaguely she noticed Fatima, Kadije, and Mouna climbing out of the pool, drying off, and going into the next chamber. Silence fell, the only sound the tinkling of water in the fountain. Grace didn't care; the powerful hands of the old woman were working magic.

In the distance she heard a door close, but the kneading and smoothing went on uninterrupted and Grace floated.

Hands worked along the tense muscles of her shoulder and neck, circling, squeezing, unraveling her, sending her into a state of bonelessness.

The rose scent of the oil was intoxicating. Now that all the kinks had been smoothed out the strokes of the massager changed subtly, stirring her senses, and making her want to arch against the movements of the big, powerful hands. Truly like a cat, she thought vaguely. Pleasure, rather than relaxation. Awareness prickled at her senses, but she was too relaxed to move.

But the massage was becoming too pleasurable, she started to think after a moment. She was becoming aroused, just the same as she had with Dominic. She started to stiffen and the soothing hands urged her to relax, but it didn't feel right, to feel this way from an old woman touching her. She started to sit up, but the big hands pressed her down, stroking down her back and over her buttocks.

Then something warm and moist pressed briefly against the nape of her neck and at the same time a hand glided between her legs in an intimate caress.

She twisted, kicking in outrage.

"Relax, Greystoke. It's only me," a deep, amused voice said. Dominic.

Only me, indeed! Now she understood why she'd become aroused. Her body had known him, even if her mind hadn't yet worked it out. The sneaky rat—he'd substituted himself for the old woman without so much as a whisper of noise or a break in the rhythm of the massaging hands. "How did you get in without me seeing you?"

"There's a separate door for men." The whole time he kept massaging, caressing, stroking. She was naked under his big warm hands. If she moved she would be more naked still.

"You taste delicious," he growled and nipped her shoulder gently between his teeth. Her toes curled almost painfully and her stomach clenched, low down.

His hands stroked and caressed her thighs and buttocks while he planted hot, moist kisses in the nape of her neck.

She moved languorously. She could feel everything, everywhere he touched her, everywhere her skin touched anything; the friction of the towel on which she lay, against which her breasts, full and aching, were pressed, the cold, hard marble bench beneath.

His hands slipped between her legs again and she jumped and jammed her thighs tightly together. Mistake. His hand stayed trapped there. He pressed a hot kiss to the base of her spine, then ran his tongue the length of her spine and she arched in response, pleasure radiating from his touch like music rippling harp strings.

"You promised no funny business," she managed to gasp.

"Relax. This is not funny, it's pure pleasure." He ran his tongue around the shell of her ear and her insides curled with pleasure.

Relax? Not possible. She was all raw nerve endings screaming for release. She felt a half-hysterical laugh bubble up, but his fingers and tongue kept moving and her concentration . . . dissolved.

Her bones were turning to liquid, thick, viscous, like honey. Between her thighs his fingers moved, stroking rhythmically, relentlessly. Shudders of pleasure rocked her in waves. Her fingers flexed and curled like a cat's claws. She writhed under the pleasurable torment and of its own volition, her backside lifted, pushing against him in jerky rhythmical movements. Demanding more.

"Turn over," he murmured and she twisted under him, wanting to see him, hold him, touch him.

He kissed her and the familiar spicy taste of him surged through her blood. He'd branded her that first day. *"My taste is in your mouth."* And it was. And would probably be for the rest of her life, she thought. As would the sight and the feel of him.

He was almost naked, too. His only garment was a pair of loose white cotton trousers of oriental design, held up by drawstrings. They rode low on his hips. His chest and arms and stomach were bare, bare and beautiful.

His eyes glowed topaz dark as he gazed down at her. "Your hair has changed color," he said and fingered a damp curl.

"The women here did something to it."

"It's pretty, like corn silk tinged with rose." He pressed his face between her breasts and inhaled deeply. "You smell good enough to eat." He looked up suddenly and gave her a white, wicked smile. "You always did, Grace. Even unperfumed, you are completely . . ." He nibbled on her skin. "Deliciously . . . edible."

He rubbed his jaw lightly against the tender skin of her breasts. Her skin, already sensitized by the scrubbing she received, felt every faint rasp as a wash of pleasure. He placed the tip of one finger on her hard nipple and caressed it, scraping delicately back and forth across the straining nub. It was heaven. It was torment. He continued caressing her breasts as he kissed his way down her stomach. She was boneless with pleasure and rigid with anticipation.

He touched her belly button. "A sultan would fill this little hollow with a ruby or an emerald, or perhaps a sapphire to match your eyes." He bent and ran the tip of his tongue lightly around it, making her shiver deliciously.

"I am not a sultan," he murmured against her skin, his

breath warm, like a desert breeze. "I think it is perfectly beautiful just as it is, unadorned and perfect." He kissed it. "Just." He kissed it again. "As." Kiss. "It." Kiss. "Is." And he plunged his tongue in and she arched against him.

"You are perfect," he told her in a low, husky voice. And kissed her lower and lower. And then his fingers were in the triangle of red-gold curls and he parted them, parted her, and kissed her there.

She stiffened in surprise, but his mouth devoured her, each movement sending sharp spears of pleasure through her. Her body shuddered, out of her control, and she was vaguely aware that she was twisting and writhing and that all the time his mouth was on her and suddenly it was as if she was going to explode or die or shatter—and she knew no more.

When she was more in control of her mind, she looked down and saw him watching her with a fierce, exultant look.

"What . . . is that?"

"The French call it the little death. Did you enjoy it?"

She blinked and stretched her limbs and relishing the friction of skin against skin. "Enjoy is too tame a word for such a feeling," she said at last. "Did you feel it, too?" He did last time, she was sure, but last time they were joined.

"I felt other things." He kissed her breast.

She could feel him, hard and erect and pressing insistently against her leg. Instinct and logic told her he hadn't felt what she felt.

He was going to give her all the pleasure, she realized, and take no satisfaction himself. Because he'd given her his word there would be no funny business. Only pleasure.

He suckled her and she felt every pull deep within her, shuddering and writhing against him. She felt sated and dreamy and—awareness flooded her—full of female power. She felt like purring. She flexed her claws.

She didn't like uneven bargains.

"My turn." She pushed him back and sat up. Bemused, he watched her slide off the bench. His eyes drank in the sight of her. "Lord, but you're beautiful," he said.

"So you said," she answered briskly. She felt so alive, so full of energy. And oh, how she was going to enjoy this. "Now, lie down there and close your eyes for a minute. I have a surprise for you."

"A surprise?" he frowned. "I'm not sure—"

She pressed him back on the bench and tossed a towelette over his face. "Just stay there and keep your eyes closed. I told you, it's my turn now."

She went to the shelf where a range of colored-glass phials stood. One by one she took off the stopper and sniffed the contents, wrinkling her nose at some and smiling at others. "There is rose oil, sandalwood, or a nice citrussy one. Which would you prefer?"

He relaxed. "As long as I don't walk out of here smelling like a rose, I don't mind which."

"I like the citrus one," she decided. There were several other items on the shelves and she picked out the two largest and most impressive and carried them back to the bench where he lay, supine, relaxed—well, almost. One part of him was still very rigid. Grace smiled to herself.

She knelt down beside him on the bench. "Dominic," she purred seductively in his ear.

"Hmm?"

"I'm finally going to do it."

His eyes flew open. He stiffened all over. She hadn't thought it would be possible, but his penis grew a fraction more. "What?" he croaked.

"Close your eyes," she ordered and instantly he obeyed.

She trailed her fingernails from his chest down his stomach and stopped just below his belly button. "I'm going to do what you've wanted me to do for such a long time."

He groaned.

"Will that make you happy?" she murmured.

He made a sound of incoherent affirmation.

"I thought it would," she purred. She climbed on top of him and sat astride his thighs. She tucked his hands under her knees. She brushed a hand over his erect flesh. He gave a moan. "Am I too heavy?"

"No," he said gruffly.

She picked up the three items she'd selected, along with the citrus oil, and set to work getting them ready for use.

He frowned, trying to work out the unfamiliar sounds.

"Are you ready, Dominic?" she whispered.

"Bloody hell, yes," he rasped.

"Then open your eyes."

He opened his eyes, then blinked. He stared at what she had in her hands, as if unable to take in the sight. "What the devil—?" He tried to move, but she had his thighs and hands pinned under her.

"It's what you begged me to do, remember? Several times."

He stared, appalled, at the two large, extremely bristly scrubbing brushes she held, poised and soapy, barely an inch above his manly parts.

"That very first day, you wanted me to scrub you, remember?" she cooed. "Are these the delicate parts you warned me about?" She lowered the brushes until the bristles rested lightly against his most delicate skin.

He twitched as they touched him. "Don't!" he said hoarsely. "I've changed my mind."

Laughing, she threw the brushes away. "If you could have seen your face" she said between giggles and hugging him.

"You little witch!" he growled, kissing her fiercely.

"I know. But when I went to get the perfumed oil, I saw those scrubbing brushes there, and the notion just flew into my head. I couldn't resist." She tilted her head. "Will you trust me to massage some oil into you now? It's not even boiling."

He gave her a baleful look. "Yes, but behave yourself!"

"Behave myself?" She smiled a feline smile. "You mean I should get off you and go and get dressed?"

"No, minx, you know very well what I mean!"

She laughed. She had no intention of behaving herself. He'd made her feel wonderful, and she was going to return the favor.

She slathered him in oil, which had the faintest hint of citrus, and rubbed it in, enjoying the sensual experience as much as when she'd been massaged. "I never realized men were so beautiful," she murmured.

Dominic couldn't believe she could talk such rubbish. Men weren't beautiful. "I'm the one looking at beauty," he corrected her. He stroked her breasts languorously as they swayed above him. She seemed fascinated with his body, examining him with an innocent sensuality that flooded him with a mix of lust and protectiveness and helpless awe.

She straddled his thighs unself-consciously, massaging oil into his skin, seemingly unaware of how open she was to him. The taste of her was still in his mouth; honey and roses and tart, sweet woman.

His cock strained, his balls ached, and he groaned with the effort of maintaining his rigid control. Every time she moved, her inner thighs brushed against him. One thrust and he could be buried inside her.

He'd given his word he wouldn't seduce her. He'd meant to finish this after he'd brought her to climax before. He should never have agreed to let her massage him. He closed his eyes.

As long as she didn't touch his cock, he would manage.

Her small hands stroked and rubbed, her nails scratched gently over his nipples in imitation of what he had done to her. Since the scrubbing brushes, her hands hadn't dropped below his waist, thank God.

Heaven and hell on earth. Tantalus in Paradise.

Those damned scrubbing brushes. He smiled. His silken-skinned little witch. Naked, skin to skin with him and smelling of roses, wild honey, and aroused femininity.

Her hand closed around his cock. He groaned and shuddered beneath her as she explored it with the thoroughness she'd shown to his nipples.

He strained against every one of his instincts. They were screaming at him to act, to mate with her. He held himself rigid. He wasn't going to make it. Dammit, he would, he could control this.

"That's enough—" he began.

"I want you, Dominic," she said at the same moment.

He stared at her. "I promised—"

"I know. But I want you inside me. Now." And she guided him to her entrance and pressed herself inexpertly against him.

He groaned. If they were going to do this, he'd do it right. He reached between her thighs and caressed her. She was all heat and softness and wild female honey. He continued to caress her and she flung her head back with a frustrated moan that matched his own.

"Now!" she demanded impatiently and he could hold back no longer. He entered her with one long, powerful thrust and she moaned and clasped him deep within her. And then he thrust again and she moved with him, trying to catch the rhythm.

"Ride me," he gasped.

Her eyes widened; she moved experimentally and he arched under her, moaning, and suddenly she'd caught the rhythm. She rode him like he'd never been ridden before, her head back, abandoned, and he moved in her and with her and together they went spiraling, surging, soaring . . . to a shattering, perfect climax.

HE LAY WITH HER CLASPED TO HIM, THEIR SKIN TOUCHING, their breath mingling, their heartbeats slowly returning to normal.

An echo of familiarity tugged at his recollection. He inhaled deeply and closed his eyes and suddenly the connection was there. Rose with a hint of citrus. He smiled. "You know, together we smell of the roses at Wolfestone."

"They are the most beautiful roses. I've never smelled roses like that anywhere else." She rubbed her cheek against his jaw. "Let's not talk of Wolfestone."

He sighed and caressed her with the back of his fingers. "All right." Wolfestone didn't matter. She was his.

They lay there a long while, and then gently he lifted her off him and sat up. He reached for his trousers, and chilled by the sudden loss of contact between them, she wrapped herself in her linen wrap.

He pushed his feet into the Turkish slippers and sat for a minute, thinking. He gave a big sigh, and when he turned to her there was such a light in his eyes it made her want to sing and dance. He grinned at her, and for the first time since she'd known him, he looked young and boyish and full of excitement.

He grabbed her and swung her around until she was dizzy, then kissed her fiercely. Then they dressed and left the *hamam* through separate exits, heading for separate bedrooms. Grace would sleep in the women's quarters.

It was a timely reminder: one rule for men, another for women. It was the way of the world.

And she would not be his mistress.

THEY LEFT EARLY THE NEXT MORNING. GRACE HARDLY ATE ANY breakfast. She longed to be home, to have dear, familiar family around her. But once she was home she would have to tell Dominic to leave.

She was farewelled warmly by Fatima, Kadije, and Mouna, who insisted Grace keep the Ottoman clothes they'd dressed her in. They pressed several more gorgeous items of clothing on her and to please them, she'd worn a pair of splendid, curly-toed golden silk slippers.

She said her good-byes and thanked the ladies repeatedly, hugging them as if she'd known them for ages. Misreading the distress in her eyes, they hastened to reassure her. "Don't be sad, Grace," they told her. "You will come back and visit us again. Dominic will bring you. He is a fine man, your man."

She smiled and nodded. "I know." There was no point in trying to explain. Harem wives would never understand her dilemma.

Tariq farewelled them both solemnly. As they left the

house, it started to rain and to Grace's delight, Dominic swung her into his arms and carried her to the carriage to save her exotic silk slippers.

Sheba had been sitting up proudly in the front of the carriage with the driver, her nose pointed eagerly toward the road, but as soon as the rain started, her ears flattened. She scrambled down from the driver's seat and sat beside the carriage steps, looking up at Dominic in mournful appeal.

He laughed. "Ever seen a water dog who hates the rain? Meet my Sheba." He snapped his fingers and she leapt into the carriage and lay happily at his feet.

They waved good-bye to Tariq and his wives as the carriage rolled away. Silence fell as Cheltenham slowly disappeared from sight.

"Are you all right, Grace?"

She looked at him and suddenly she was in his arms and they were kissing again. Their last day together. Their own special mobile world.

"How did you know about the harem?" she asked him a long time later.

"Tariq and I have a history going back to when we were boys. You might almost say we are related."

"Related?"

He settled her more comfortably against him and began the story. "One of the places I lived in as a boy was Napoli—Naples. Even now I have mixed feelings about it. We'd pretty much run out of funds by then—my mother had managed to eke out an existence by the sale of her jewels, the only thing she took with her when she fled from my father. I spent a lot of time down by the docks. There were opportunities for a quick-witted boy who was also prepared to work hard."

She hugged him, remembering the boy who had dived for coins.

"One day a boy—not one of us, a rich man's son—was accidentally knocked into the water when men were loading cargo. Nobody else saw him fall. I watched and he didn't come up—he must have been hit on the head. So I dived in and pulled him out."

"You saved his life."

He nodded. "That was Tariq. His father owned the ship that was being loaded. He took me aboard and fed me and then, for some reason, decided to thank my parents in person." He grimaced. "I did everything I could think of to stop him coming—my mother was embarrassed by the way we lived—but he insisted."

He was silent for a long moment, remembering. "It was love at first sight. Tariq's father and my mother." His arms tightened around her and he rubbed his jaw against her curls. "When the ship departed for Egypt, my mother and I were on it. He bought her a beautiful house in Alexandria and we never lacked for money again."

"But wasn't he married? I mean, he had a son."

"Oh, Faisal was married, with several wives. My mother became his mistress and he treated her better than my father ever treated his wife. She owned the house he bought for her—the deed was in her name. He gave her a large sum of money and paid all the household expenses and settled an annuity on her. Security for her lifetime."

Faisal. "The poetry book?"

He nodded.

His mother was *"my dove, my heart, my beloved."*

"But it wasn't about money—Faisal adored Mama and treated her like a princess. And she loved him. I never saw her so happy. He was a good man. He even arranged for me to be schooled with Tariq." His voice hardened. "Until my father got his claws into me and had me brought to England to be schooled. I wouldn't have let them take me if Mama wasn't safe and happy."

There was a long silence in the carriage. "It broke her heart when Faisal died."

The horses' hooves clip-clopped on the road. A dog barked from a nearby farm. Grace remembered what Frey had told her, how Dominic's mother had died in his arms. She held him tight.

The rain pelted down.

Chapter Twenty

How blest am I in this discovering thee!
To enter in these bonds, is to be free;
JOHN DONNE

"THAT'S ALL VERY WELL, YOUNG GRACE," SIR OSWALD DEMANDED crossly. "But what the deuce are you doin' travelin' all the way—overnight!—to London alone and unchaperoned—and no, the dratted dog doesn't count!—with some strange feller I've never met before today, when you're supposed to be at some dratted country house party with Sir John and Melly Pettifer?"

Grace swallowed. She'd prepared her little speech, and it had sounded quite good in the carriage, in her head. But Great Uncle Oswald hadn't swallowed it at all.

Worse, Prudence and her husband, Gideon, in London were not the only members of her family visiting Great Uncle Oswald and Aunt Gussie. So were all her sisters and their husbands. And none of them looked at all impressed with what Grace had had to say.

Except for Aunt Gussie, who was eyeing Dominic with quite blatant, not to say embarrassing, admiration.

Dominic, however, didn't look a bit embarrassed. Nor

did he look the slightest bit concerned about Great Uncle Oswald's questions. Or the threatening looks being given him by her four large, angry, and muscular brothers-in-law. She glanced at Edward and amended that to three large, angry, and muscular brothers-in-law and one medium-sized, cross duke, her brother-in-law Edward.

Dominic was apparently so unconcerned about Great Uncle Oswald's rant that he kept looking from her to her sisters and back, quite clearly comparing them for family similarities. And once, she'd actually seen him give Aunt Gussie a wink.

They were going to tear him limb from limb.

And if they didn't, she was going to. Her speech would have worked perfectly well if Dominic hadn't kept interrupting with his "helpful" explanations, reassuring them that Sheba was an excellent chaperone, and that a harem wasn't nearly the den of vice people would imagine.

"Aunt Gussie," Grace's brother-in-law Gideon interrupted smoothly. "Why don't you and the girls take Grace off somewhere more comfortable and have a little chat with her. We gentlemen will have a quiet word with D'Acre."

"Excellent idea, my dear boy," Lady Augusta declared, and in a trice had swept all the ladies from the room, leaving Dominic to face a gaggle of angry aristocrats.

Three of the brothers-in-law faced him with tight, cold faces and clenched fists. He knew what to expect. It was not the first time he'd faced a gang of England's finest bullyboys. The only difference was that he was no longer a schoolboy.

Gideon, Lord Carradice, spoke first. "So, D'Acre. I think you have some explaining to do."

Dominic inspected his nails.

"Out with it man! Speak up!" snapped Blacklock, another brother-in-law.

Military background there, thought Dominic. He picked a piece of fluff off his sleeve.

"Fellow needs a good thrashing," growled the one called Reyne.

Dominic shrugged. He shrugged out of his coat and started to roll up his sleeves.

"What the devil do you think you're doing?" Carradice demanded irritably.

"Preparing to defend myself."

"What?"

"In my experience the sons of *gentlemen* don't usually like to listen. But I quite enjoy a fight, so we might as well get it over with."

"Well, *we* intend to talk. Or rather, listen. We're not at all clear on what's going on here, so before we give you the thrashing you probably do deserve, we want some answers."

Dominic frowned. Carradice almost sounded ironic.

The duke asked in a quiet, dignified voice, "What are your intentions toward our sister-in-law?"

Dominic shrugged. "I'd have thought even a blind man could see that."

Gideon rolled his eyes. "Dammit, man, stop fencing or I will be forced to thump you!"

Dominic shrugged again. "I've done my level best to get her to agree to be my mistress."

Four men clenched their fists.

Carradice eyed him narrowly and held up his hand to ward the others from precipitous action. "You either have a wish to die young, or . . ."

Dominic said, "I'm going to marry her, of course." Why else did they think he'd brought her to London?

Carradice raised his brows. "Just like that? And if she refuses you? Or her family opposes you?"

Dominic examined his nails again.

"I expect you've heard rumors that she's an heiress," Reyne commented.

Dominic said, "Her fortune is of no interest to me. I doubt it matches mine."

"I suppose you know she's stubborn and argumentative. All the Merridew girls wear their husbands to shreds," said Carradice.

Dominic looked them over, each one relaxed, healthy, and almost smug with happiness. "Yes, you all have the look of henpecked men. Ah well, we must all bear our crosses in life."

"Do you love her?"

Dominic gave him a flat, unblinking stare. He had no intention of responding. That was for him and Grace alone.

Carradice gave him a shrewd look. "When you first met Grace," he said slowly, "what was it about her that struck you?"

Dominic thought for a moment. "Her foot."

"Her foot?" they chorused.

"Yes." He gave an insolent smile. "She kicked me. Twice!" If that didn't make the fists start flying, nothing would.

"Kicked you?" Gideon glanced at the others in triumph and said, "The Limb *kicked* him! I knew it! We have a love match on our hands!"

Dominic couldn't believe his ears. "I think you misunderstood," he said. "I told you she *kicked* me!"

Carradice smiled at his confusion. "Yes, she did the same to me the first day we met. It's why I call her the Limb. It's an excellent sign. You see, dear boy, we thought she'd been broken of the habit long since. She must have been keeping it in reserve for a special occasion."

Carradice and the duke both shook his hand and left.

Dominic stared after them. "But I deserved the kick. I kissed her. Twice."

Blacklock and Reyne laughed. "Let me give you a tip," said Blacklock as he passed. "Once you've kissed a Merridew girl . . . there's no point fighting."

Sir Oswald Merridew glared at him from under beetling white brows. "Well, come on, D'Acre, don't stand there like a stump! If you're goin' to marry m'great-niece, we have settlements to discuss! And I'll tell you straight, they'd better be good!"

"I wouldn't have it any other way," said Dominic stiffly. "I have no wish to touch a penny of her money. It shall be in the settlements that she retains everything."

Sir Oswald raised his bushy white brows. "Happen t'know your estate's in a bad way."

"It's not your concern. It shan't affect her. I have my own private fortune that is unaffected by my father's will."

The old man nodded, then creaked to his feet. "That's what my informant said, too."

He chuckled at Dominic's look of surprise. "Y'don't think I was fooled by Grace's little strategems do you? Gel I've known since she was ten years old? I knew what she and Gussie were up to all along. Had you investigated on the off chance. Some sort o' guardian I'd be if I didn't keep an eye on who my gel's mixin' with."

An hour later he ushered Dominic to the front door. "Come back tomorrow mornin' and you can pop the question to the gel herself."

* * *

"I'M SO SORRY, DOMINIC."

She came to him, glowing and beautiful and dressed in a shade of blue that exactly matched her eyes. Currently very distressed eyes.

"What has upset you, love?"

"I don't know what they said or did to you last night, but whatever it was, you don't have to do this."

"Do what?"

"Marry me."

He frowned. "Dammit, woman, that's my line."

"What?"

He sank down onto one knee and said, "Grace Merridew, will you marry me?"

She was silent for a moment. "Don't, Dominic. I can't bear it."

His grip on her hands tightened. "Marry me, Greystoke."

"Stop it! I know you never wanted this. But much as—"

"This is a very cold floor," he interrupted in a plaintive voice. "Will one of you—Grace or Greystoke—please say you'll marry me so I can get up."

She bit her lip. "Are you sure, Dominic?"

He smiled. "Of course I'm sure." He stood up and pulled her into his arms. "Why else do you think I brought you here? I told you I wasn't going to lose you."

"But you don't believe in marriage."

He smiled wryly. "I didn't, but you do, and if anyone can make me believe, it will be you, my love. Now, for the third time, will you marry me?"

"But what about Wolfestone? You'll lose Wolfestone if you marry me." Tears flooded her eyes. "Oh, Dominic, we made all those plans . . ."

He squeezed her hands. "We'll make new plans."

"I don't want you to lose Wolfestone."

He made a dismissive gesture. "I never had it in the first place, love. You can't miss what you've never had."

"But you need Wolfestone, Dominic. And Wolfestone needs you."

He swore. "What I need, Greyst—Grace, is *you*, dammit! I don't need a moldering old castle and a run-down estate—the Wolfestone people will survive as they have for six hundred years. Someone else will own the land. With any luck it will be someone good. But it won't be me." His voice softened. "I will be with my love, watching the moon rise over the pyramids, or sailing into Venice at dawn.

"Come now." He leaned forward and took her hands in his and said in a coaxing voice, "You've always wanted to go traveling, haven't you? And I'm the man to take you. I've traveled the world all my life."

Grace was distraught. He'd offered her what she most wanted in life . . . But it was at the expense of his own dreams, his fragile, newborn dreams. Could she let him do that?

"Of course I'll marry you. I ought to refuse you. You need—"

"I need my silken-skinned girl in whose eyes a man could happily drown. I need the woman who makes my heart pound and my blood sing. I need my beloved girl to tell my heart to, and to hold in my arms through the deep stillness of the night. The girl to gallop with in the crisp dawn air, the girl to hold in the night while outside the storms rage."

Her eyes filled with tears. This was more beautiful than any poem.

He pulled her against him and held her tight. "I'm sorry.

I didn't mean to make you weep. You're tired." He kissed her gently.

Outside a small bell rang. "Oh," she said, "that's the bell for luncheon."

"Go, my love. Go and dine with your family." He smiled ruefully. He wiped her cheeks gently. "I have no business asking you anything while things are still in a mess. I will go hom—back to Wolfestone—"

The correction was smooth, but she heard it and it cut deep. Wolfestone was no longer his home.

"Don't worry, I'll straighten things out with Melly and Sir John. I'll settle a sum on Melly; she won't have to worry about finances. And I need to make sure the repairs I've started get finished, so the tenants will be dry and warm through the winter. And I'll see the trustee, Podmore, and tell him to put the estate up for sale and to draw up the marriage settlements."

Grace bit her lip. He looked after everyone, this man of hers. Everyone except himself. He spoke in such a matter-of-fact way, but she knew how deeply it wrenched him. If she hadn't pushed him into contact with the Wolfestone people, hadn't shown him how much he belonged there . . .

"Don't look at me like that," he growled, kissing her on the mouth with brief, exquisite tenderness. "I won't be gone long."

"No, it wasn't—"

"I'll be back before you know it. And then, Miss Grace Merridew—" He gave her a smile that was a pale shadow of the wicked smile he'd first given her, when she thought him a raggle-taggle gypsy and fell for him anyway.

He cupped her cheek and his golden wolf eyes glowed. "And then, Miss Grace Merridew, I'm coming after you.

Wolves mate for life, you know, and I've found my dream, my one true love." The kiss he gave her now was hard and possessive and she clung to him, kissing him back. She wouldn't, couldn't refuse him; she didn't have the strength to resist him. She wanted him more than anything in life.

But the knowledge of what he was giving up for her tore her up inside.

GRACE ENTERED THE DINING ROOM SHORTLY AFTER SHE'D WATCHED Dominic leave for Wolfestone. The table was set for a celebration, she saw. "Sorry I'm late," she said, slipping into her usual place.

Everyone was there: Prue and Gideon, Charity and Edward, Hope and Sebastian, Faith and Nicholas, and Cassie and Dorie. Everyone was smiling at her so joyfully, Grace couldn't bear it. "Where are the children?" she asked.

"Upstairs in the nursery," Charity said. "We'll go up and see them all after luncheon."

"Now, enough fussin' over the children," Great Uncle Oswald declared, beaming at her. "I'm about to fire off the last of the Merridew Diamonds! I've got my best elderberry wine here and Gussie insists on offerin' everyone champagne as well, so take your pick, young Grace—which one shall we toast your happiness in?"

Grace looked at the elderberry wine and the champagne, and then at all the beloved faces smiling at her. She burst into tears and ran out of the room.

"Go after her, Prue," Aunt Gussie said, but Prudence was already gone.

The rest of them sat looking stunned. Charity voiced what was in all their minds. "Has she refused him?"

"I thought—I was sure she was in love with Lord D'Acre," Faith said. Her twin nodded.

"And I would have wagered my best team that D'Acre was head over heels in love with her, too," Gideon added.

By the time Prudence came back, more than an hour later, the luncheon dishes had been cleared away, virtually untouched, and only the men of the family remained in the dining room. They were drinking brandy.

"Gussie and the gels have just popped upstairs to see how the children are behavin' themselves," Great Uncle Oswald informed her. "Now, don't go runnin' off after them yet, Prudence! What's up with young Grace?"

"They love each other, all right," she reported. "And she has accepted him. But there's a problem." She explained the situation, which took a long time, as Great Uncle Oswald, her husband, and brothers-in-law kept interrupting her with questions. She told them everything Grace had told her: the will, the way Dominic had been brought up, how his hate for Wolfestone had slowly turned to love, and the plans for it he and Grace had made.

At the end of her explanation, Great Uncle Oswald snorted. "Most edifyin'! Now pop up to the nursery and tell your sisters and Gussie that luncheon will be served in another half hour and fetch Grace down to join us. I'm not havin' the gel sobbin' her little heart out while we starve! Her whole family is here and we'll dine together or not at all—and tell her I said that!"

Thirty minutes later the family reconvened around the luncheon table. Grace joined them, pale and heavy-eyed.

Great Uncle Oswald sent the butler around to fill everyone's glasses with either elderberry wine or champagne. Great Uncle Oswald raised his glass of elderberry and said, "Well, we have a weddin' in the family to be celebratin', so charge your glasses—even in dratted champagne—and drink a toast: to Grace and D'Acre! And Grace—"

Grace looked up.

"We've decided on your weddin' present!"

Grace glanced around the table. Everyone was beaming at her. She couldn't bear it.

Great Uncle Oswald waved his glass at her. "Stop lookin' so tragic! Young Sebastian saw the solution even quicker'n I did. You'll marry the boy and we'll buy the estate and give it to you for your weddin' present! We've all agreed."

"You'll *buy* Wolfestone?" Grace was dumbfounded. "But . . . It will cost an enormous sum."

"Pshaw! D'ye think we're the kind of nip-farthin' family who'd set a price against your happiness, you foolish gel?"

"But Dominic could have it for nothing . . . if he married Melly Pettifer."

Great Uncle Oswald set down his glass with something of a snap. "Saints deliver me from young women in love! What the devil would he want Melly Pettifer for when he could have you!"

"Besides, Mama promised us *all* love and laughter and sunshine and happiness, remember?" Prudence reminded her. Grace had told her upstairs what Grandpapa had said and Prudence had refuted it utterly.

"All of us," Charity agreed firmly. "*Especially* her darling baby girl." Prue must have told her sisters, too.

Grace could say nothing. She sat there, clutching her glass, tears rolling down her cheeks.

Great Uncle Oswald said, "I would've been happy enough to buy the blasted place m'self, only the others wouldn't have it. I've seen each one of you gels happy and I'll be damned if I let the last little darlin' sacrifice herself for a paltry bit of land!" He pulled out a large handkerchief and blew into it noisily. "So it's settled. You'll marry the boy and we'll give you the estate as a weddin' present! So charge your glasses—to Grace and D'Acre!"

"To Grace and D'Acre!" They all drank.

"And if you can get that wretched boy to go a bit slower on the refurbishin' of the place, we might even get it at a bargain price."

"Oh my God!" Grace exclaimed in horror. Everyone looked at her. "He's just gone down to put it on the market!"

"Then we'll just have to go after him and stop him, won't we?" Gideon said calmly.

"Who's 'we'?" Great Uncle Oswald demanded.

"Whoever wants to go with Grace," he said.

"That's the village!" For the last half hour Grace had traveled with her head half out of the window, craning for her first sight of Wolfestone.

The cavalcade of Merridew traveling coaches swept through the village at a decorous pace. Grace had remembered the chickens. No Wolfestone chickens would die under her coach wheels. She saw Billy Finn outside the inn and waved happily at him.

He ran up to the carriage, shouting. "You're late, Lady! The wedding's already started."

"What wedding?" She shouted to the driver, "Stop the coach!"

"Miss Melly's, o' course! She looks a treat, she does."

Great Uncle Oswald thrust his head out of the window. "Where's D'Acre?"

"At the church, o' course," Billy said with withering sarcasm at such a stupid question. "Everyone's there. All except me." He pulled a face. "Don't like weddings. Me mam cries."

"Where's the church?" Great Uncle Oswald demanded.

Billy pointed. Great Uncle Oswald leaned out of the window and shouted to the five coach drivers. "To the church! That way!"

Five traveling coaches hurtled up the narrow lane and came to a halt in front of St. Stephen's Church. Five carriage doors flew open and five men leapt down without waiting for the steps to be lowered. And without even waiting for the ladies to descend, five men stormed toward the church.

Great Uncle Oswald, having arrived in front, led the rush. He flung open the church door with a crash. There was a bishop in his gorgeous vestments and tall mitre; there was the bride in creamy white lace. There was an enormous Turk glarin' at him from under an enormous turban. Great Uncle Oswald blinked and checked to make sure his eyes were not deceivin' him. No, it was a Turk all right.

The Turk moved and Great Uncle Oswald snarled. For there, shameless as a harlot, holding the bride's hand and looking magnificent in his finest formal wedding attire, stood Lord D'Acre.

"Stop the weddin'," roared Great Uncle Oswald. "Unhand that woman, D'Acre, you despicable hound!"

If a pin had dropped at the moment it could have been heard by every single person crowded into the church.

"I beg your pardon," the bishop boomed in the sort of voice bishops develop with practice.

Great Uncle Oswald bellowed back at him. "So you dratted well should. Marryin' this—this louse to this woman when he's already betrothed to my great-niece!"

The bride turned around and regarded him with shock.

Great Uncle Oswald gave her a friendly nod. "Afternoon, Melly. You look lovely, m'dear."

The bishop turned puce. "How dare you storm into my church and fling baseless accusations around! This is my ceremony and—"

"Baseless accusations? I'll have you know—"

A lanky, elegant young man stepped forward and peered at Great Uncle Oswald. "I think there's some mistake—"

"Don't you start tellin' me what's what, young feller! What's it got to do with you?"

"I'm not betrothed to your great-niece. I don't think I even know your great-niece."

Great Uncle Oswald stared at him. "I never said you were."

"I think you implied it."

"I did not! It's that despicable hound who's betrothed to my great-niece!" He pointed dramatically at Lord D'Acre.

Every eye swiveled to Lord D'Acre. He bowed.

"Yes, and I'll be happy to marry her—today if you like—just as soon as I give Miss Pettifer here away in marriage to my good friend Humphrey Nettterton." His lips twitched as he indicated the lanky young gentleman.

"Ah," said Great Uncle Oswald. "So you're givin' the bride away, eh, D'Acre?" He nodded. "Good, good, then I have no objection to the weddin'. Parson, you may continue." He waved his gracious permission.

"I, sir," thundered the bishop, "am a bishop!"

"Well, stop wastin' time tryin' to impress us and get on with marryin' this couple," Great Uncle Oswald retorted, unabashed. "And after that you can write us up a special license. My great-niece is marryin' D'Acre there and we'll need a special license." He turned to Gideon, who was convulsed with silent laughter and explained, "Only use for bishops I've ever been able to see."

MELLY GLOWED. "HE LOVES ME, GRACE," SHE DECLARED WITH SHY pride. "Loves *me*! And I love him." Outside in the great hall of Wolfestone, the wedding reception was in full swing. Melly and Grace had stolen a few moments in the library to catch up.

Grace hugged her friend. "Oh, Melly, I'm so happy for you both! But when did this all happen?"

"Just after you and Lord D'Acre left. Apparently Frey and he had an argument about the plans Lord D'Acre had for me after our wedding. Frey said he just couldn't get them out of his mind. He was absolutely furious. And then last week at church, he realized what the matter was."

Grace smiled. "That he loved you and wanted you for himself."

"Yes. I can't believe it. He wants *me*!" She clutched Grace's hands tightly and said in a stunned voice, "Grace, he says he thinks I am *beautiful*."

Grace looked at Melly's glowing face. It was as if someone had lit a candle inside her. "And so you are beautiful, Melly, love." But she was still puzzled. "But I have to say, I'm surprised your father allowed it."

Melly sobered a little. "Well, that day after church, Frey was still in a temper. He just strode into Papa's room and shouted at him. Frey told Papa it was wicked what Papa was doing to me and he said he loved me and wanted to marry me, even though he didn't have any money." She sighed dreamily.

"So what happened then?" Grace prompted.

"Well, nothing. Papa said no. But three days later Frey's

uncle, the bishop, arrived out of the blue. Frey had no idea he was coming. And the bishop spoke to Papa for a long time and when he came out he told Frey he was going to increase his allowance to a much more generous one—and make a separate allowance to Frey's mother. And then Papa agreed to let me marry Frey. And then Lord D'Acre arrived, and Papa told him he should marry you, and he said yes, he was going to."

"How amazing," Grace exclaimed. "What do you think the bishop and your father talked about?"

"Well Frey did ask Papa afterward, and Papa just tapped the side of his nose and said something about youthful sins coming back to haunt the bishop and causing a sudden surge of generosity." She wrinkled her nose. "It made no sense to me at all, but Frey thought it was very funny."

Melly heaved a sigh of happiness. "So everything has turned out wonderfully well. Even Papa's health has improved. Soon we think he will be well enough to leave his bed."

"Excellent! I'm so happy for you, love." Grace embraced her friend and stood up. "Now, let us return to your party."

Chapter Twenty-one

The horizon all around me
breathed out perfume
announcing her arrival
as the fragrance precedes a flower.

IBN SAFR AL-MARINI, POET OF ANDALUSIA

DOMINIC SPENT MOST OF THE NEXT DAY OUT SEEING TO VARIOUS arrangements—legal matters, estate matters, wedding arrangements, guest accommodation, and organizing his honeymoon.

Grace spent most of the day with her sisters and Aunt Gussie and a London modiste brought down especially for her wedding dress. It might be a short engagement period and a wedding in an obscure village church, but Aunt Gussie was not going to allow the last of the Merridew Diamonds to be married in anything less than the best.

Grace, however, took a little time out to make a few arrangements of her own with Abdul and the Tickel girls.

It was extremely late by the time Dominic got home.

At the front entry hall he paused. What was that on the floor? When he'd first arrived this entryway had been adrift with dead leaves. He bent to see what was scattered across the marble flags. Rose petals. How peculiar.

He picked up a few and smelled them. Rose with a hint of citrus. He smiled.

He glanced up at the gargoyle. "Do you know anything about this?" Dammit, even he was talking to statues now.

He turned to climb the stairs and saw more rose petals, one or two on each step. They led all the way up to the top; a wavering line of rose petals. Like a pathway or trail.

He followed them, his feet stepping in the hollows made by his ancestors.

They led along the passageway and stopped at the door of his bedchamber. He opened it, and saw his room had been turned into a tent. Swathes of colorful, gauzy cloth hung from a centerpoint in the ceiling, and fell in graceful sweeps to the walls. Rose petals led to an entrance.

He followed them and slowly parted the curtains.

Curled up on his bed on an acre of white cotton sheeting lay Miss Grace Merridew, clad in nothing but rose petals. His heart was full to bursting, but he managed to say, "Is this a houri which I see before me?"

"No, it's me," Grace answered. "And hurry up. These rose petals are actually quite clammy!"

With a joyous laugh Dominic bounded into bed.

"THEY *WHAT*?" DOMINIC SAT UP IN BED, SHOCKED.

"They planned to buy Wolfestone. And give it to us as a wedding present."

"But they couldn't!"

Grace smiled. "Of course they could. They're not related to you at all."

"I didn't mean that, I mean—It would cost a huge sum."

"They're all rich."

He raked his fingers through his hair, confused. "But why would they do such a thing?"

She stared at him, puzzled. "So that we could get married, of course."

"But we were getting married anyway!"

"Yes, but they didn't want you to lose Wolfestone."

Dominic grappled to make sense of his feelings. "Why would they care?"

She stared at him confused. And then it hit her. He had a great deal of pride. And a different experience of family. She slipped her arms around him. "They're my family, Dominic. They wanted us to be as happy as they are. Great Uncle Oswald is really disappointed he can't buy us an estate now. He loves grand gestures."

Dominic chuckled. "So I noticed in the church yesterday."

She giggled.

"Frey will have standing room only in his church for months to come," he told her. "Do you know, Grandad Tasker congratulated him—told him that going to church at St. Stephens was as good as a circus."

Around midnight Grace stretched like a satisfied cat and said, "I'm hungry. I wasn't hungry before—only for you—but now I'm starving."

Dominic sat up. "I'll fetch some food from the kitchen."

"I'm coming, too." She climbed out of bed and donned an assortment of clothing and like naughty children, she and Dominic tiptoed hand in hand down the hallway. As they came to the stairs they heard odd sounds from above.

"What's that?" Grace asked.

"Oh, Abdul has taken up residence in the turret," he informed her. Deep masculine groans accompanied by feminine laughter drifted down. At least two different feminine laughs. Possibly three.

Dominic frowned. "What the devil is he up to?" he muttered.

"I know," she informed him. "Abdul is *rejoicing*."

"Rejoicing?" Puzzled, he looked at her.

" 'Rejoicing in the compassion of Dominic Wolfe,' " she quoted and laughed. "Come on, hurry up. I want food and then I might *rejoice* with Dominic Wolfe myself."

DESPITE THE FACT THAT IT WAS A HURRIED AFFAIR, THE WEDDING was the finest affair the village of Lower Wolfestone had seen in generations. The castle was crowded with guests—more toffs in their fine London hats than Grandad Tasker could poke a stick at.

Abdul the Turk had even moved out of the tower apartment in order to make room for the guests. That's what Abdul claimed, anyway. The village was of the opinion that it was to avoid scandalizing the London toffs. Easily shocked, toffs were, it was agreed.

Abdul and all three of the Tickel girls had taken possession of the gatehouse. 'Twas a scandal all right, the village agreed, but what could ye expect of a heathen Turk and the poor, lost Tickel girls who'd been robbed of their morals when they were wee babes and washed in Gwydion's Pool.

Besides, if there was going to be a scandal in a village, it might as well be a good, big, juicy one, they agreed. And the Tickel girls were nothing if not juicy!

The new vicar didn't perform the service–well, him only being married for a week himself, it was understandable. His uncle, the bishop, stayed on and married the Wolfe and his Lady, as well. Two weddings in a week!

The Lady's sisters were there, each one more beautiful than the last, and the ones called Miss Cassie and Miss Dorie were her bridesmaids, with the vicar's wife matron of honor and the vicar being best man.

The vicar's father-in-law was there and all, in his wheeled chair. Granny's poultices had brought up a lovely tumor and once it busted, the old man was on the mend again. And there was a gaggle of young flower girls and pageboys—the lady's nieces and nephews.

Something odd happened in the service. After the bishop had declared them husband and wife, and let no man put them asunder, he held out his hands and said, "And let us now all *rejoice*," and the bride fell to giggling and couldn't stop for ages.

When the bride and groom came out of the church everyone chucked rose petals. Word had gone around they were her favorites, so everyone had been saving them for the occasion. Lovely they were, too.

A small squabble had broken out among a few of the women after the bride passed by with her veil back so you could see her proper. Mrs. Parry reckoned her buttermilk was responsible, but Mrs. Tickel reckoned 'twas her lemons that done the trick. Granny shut them both up—it was water from Gwydion's Pool, she said—and Granny knows!

After the church there was feasting and music and dancing—one party for the villagers in the castle courtyard and one inside for the toffs as well. Grand, it was.

But the best thing about the wedding was the end. The bride and groom came out from the castle, all ready to go off on their honeymoon, and what do you think was waiting for them? A camel! A proper one with a hump and all.

The beast got down on its knees and the Wolfe and his

Lady climbed up on it—the Lady giggling fit to bust and kissing her new husband like she'd been bathed in Gwydion's Pool and all! And then the great beast rose to its feet and off it went with the Wolfe and his Lady, riding off into the sunset, laughing and waving . . .

Alexandria, someone said they were off to. Up past Shrewsbury, someone said that was.

Epilogue

Live well. It is the greatest revenge.

THE TALMUD

"EVEN THE EMINENTLY SENSIBLE SWALLOWS GO *FROM* ENGLAND *to* Egypt in the winter," Dominic said. "And yet we go the other way around! It's freezing! Why you wanted to leave glorious, sunny Egypt to come back to cold and gloomy old Wolfestone is beyond me!"

She smiled from her nest of rugs. "You'll see."

She peered out of the window eagerly. "Look, there's Granny Wigmore's. And there's a sign hanging at her gate. What does it say?"

They pressed against the window to read it.

GRANNY WIGMORE
POTIONS TO THE GENTRY

Grace giggled. "Potions to the gentry! What on earth does that mean?"

The coach and four reached the open iron gates and

passed without a pause between the two snarling stone wolves.

As they turned the last corner, Wolfestone came into sight, blazing with light in the late December gloom. Candles burned in every window, the doorway was festooned with greenery, and the wolf 's head knocker was surrounded by a wreath of fresh holly and ivy.

"What the devil—?" Dominic began.

The door was flung open and golden light spilled out, welcoming them. Sheba came first, a streak of white, wriggling and ecstatic at her master's return, followed by a throng of happy well-wishers. For a moment Dominic wondered whether his honeymoon had been a dream—all of Grace's family was here.

But he and Grace had watched the moon rise over the pyramids. And they'd sailed into Venice at dawn. They'd kissed in front of the Sphinx. Not a dream, but a dream come true.

"Happy Christmas, Dominic," Grace told him as they were swept inside. To Dominic's amazement, all of Grace's family was there, even the children. And every single one of them hugged or kissed him as if it was perfectly normal, as if he was part of their family.

"I hope you don't mind us invading you," Prudence told him. "But we always have Christmas together and Grace told us she wanted to spend her first Christmas with you here at Wolfestone."

"You're most welcome," Dominic managed to say.

The inside of his house was festooned with greenery. A huge yule log was burning in the sitting room. The air was filled with the scent of pine and spices.

"Hot mulled wine coming up," declared Gideon as he plunged a red-hot poker into a large bowl of spiced wine.

"Dinner will be in an hour," Prudence told them. "I'm so glad you got here in time. We were worried that snow might prevent you from getting here."

After dinner the whole family sat around the fire, watching the yule log burn and singing Christmas carols. Dominic didn't know the words. Ten-year-old Aurora watched him for a while, then climbed off her father's lap and plopped herself on Dominic's, saying, "Here, Uncle Dominic, I'll help you," and for the rest of the evening she showed him the words from her little book of carols.

It was a scene of perfect peace and family togetherness and as the last carol came to a close, young Jamie Carradice called out, "Look, everyone, it's snowing!"

Through the windows they could see snow drifting down light and powdery. And it was Christmas Eve.

Dominic passed the next day in a daze. He spent what time he could in the library, going through the correspondence that had accumulated in his absence.

After church, everyone came to dinner. Frey brought Melly, rounded and beautiful, glowing with early pregnancy. Sir John came in a bath chair, declaring his determination to live to meet his first grandchild. The house rang with children's shouts and laughter.

People hugged Dominic and kissed Dominic and gave him presents. And he ate like he'd never eaten before.

And after dinner there was snow to be dealt with—a snowman to be made and snowballs to be thrown. The air was filled with the sounds of shrieks and giggles and splats. And after that it was back inside for hot chocolate and Christmas cake.

Dominic's first English Christmas, with a family that made it clear he was a valued member, and in the house he'd hated most of his life but which had, miraculously, become the home of his heart.

That night in bed, he held his wife tight and gave thanks for the greatest gift of all—Grace.

The next day was Boxing Day and it turned out Grace had also left instructions about that, before they'd left on their honeymoon: a party for everyone on the estate.

"And we give each family a Christmas box," Grace explained to him. She showed him. "In each is a little money and perhaps some food or clothing—a little something to help them through the winter months, and to give thanks."

Dominic saw the box with "The Finn Family" written on it. "Don't give that one out until last," he said and hurried off to the library. He found the official-looking letter with the government seal on it and slipped it into the Finns' box.

The villagers came and the party was a great success. Dominic let Grace give out the boxes; the villagers loved their Lady; it was right that she gave out the boxes.

Granny came up to fetch hers. "Not sure I need no box, though I'll take it with thanks. Did ye see me sign? I got toffs coming from London to ask me advice and buy me potions!" she told them proudly. "Pay a fortune they will, for herbs I pick for naught! That Sir John, he writ letters to everyone!"

"That's marvelous, Granny!" Grace hugged her.

Jake Tasker came diffidently up to receive the box for his family. It was a lot smaller than the others. He took it from Grace and shook it, frowning. Suspicion writ large on his face, he opened the small box and took out a key.

"What's this?"

Dominic stepped forward and looked at it. "Looks like the key to the estate manager's house."

Jake gave him a hard look. "And what would I be wanting with a key to Mr. Eades's house?"

Dominic said, "The house doesn't belong to Eades, it belongs to the man who is managing my estate."

Jake frowned. "But I've been doing that."

"Exactly." As the realization dawned on Jake's face, Dominic grinned.

Dominic raised his voice slightly, well aware that all the tenants in the hall were stretching their ears to follow the conversation. And this was news they all needed to hear. "Besides, Mr. Eades won't be needing it. In fact Mr. Eades is not allowed to have any keys where he is."

"Where is he, m'lord?" shouted Grandad Tasker.

Dominic looked around the room, at the eager faces of all the Wolfestone people. The people whose fates were tied with his own. *His* people. He announced it loud and clear: "Mr. Eades is rotting in Newgate Prison, awaiting trial for what he did to you all—us all. Most of what he stole from the estate has been recovered and will be used to make improvements on everyone's land. Wolfestone estate is going to be a force to be reckoned with."

A huge cheer went up.

After the noise had died down, Dominic continued, "And I'd be well pleased if Jake Tasker would accept the position of estate manager permanently."

Jake shook his hand fiercely and said over the renewed cheering, "I will and all, m'lord. Thank you!"

There was only one box to go. Billy Finn waited with his mother and brothers and sisters, eyeing it excitedly. Every box that had gone to a family with children had contained sweets as well.

"Merry Christmas, Mrs. Finn," said Grace as she gave the gaunt woman the box. Mrs. Finn opened it and bemused, took out the big, official-looking letter. She looked fearfully at Grace. "It ain't an eviction, is it?"

"No, of course not," Grace reassured her. "I don't know what it is, but I promise you no one on the estate will be evicted."

Mrs. Finn looked at it anxiously. "Nothin' good ever come in a letter that looks like that. Is it a lawyer's letter?"

Billy took it from her hand. "Let me see it, Mam." He opened it, frowned over the heavy paper with a government seal on it, then unfolded a much smaller, more ordinary piece of paper. He read a few lines, then looked straight at Dominic and asked with a mixture of hope and truculence, "This be a joke or not?"

"It's real, Billy," Dominic said quietly.

Billy swallowed and said to his mother, "It's from the governor of New South Wales, Mam. And a letter from Da." When the exclamations had died down, he read:

"My darlin Annie, I hope this finds you and the nippers well. I'm writin' to tell you I'm a free man. I been pardoned. Lord D'Acre writ a leter to the governor and told him I were wrongly convicted. He told him I never did nothing wrong at all."

Mrs. Finn gave a great sob and hugged the nearest child. Billy continued, his voice a little husky:

"I can't go back to England, but New South Wales ain't what we feared. They be short o' farmers here and they need food, so I been granted land. I'm a farmer, Annie, on my own land."

"His own land!" The murmur ran through the crowd.

"Life here be clean and good, so I am saving money to bring you and the children . . ."

Annie started sobbing and clutching the children. "All that way! It'll cost him a fortune."

"Look in your box, Annie," said Dominic quietly.

A hush fell as Annie slowly opened her Christmas box. In it was a purse of money. When she opened it and saw how much it was, she nearly fainted.

"It will buy you and the children a passage to New South Wales. Or you can use it to support your children here, if you don't want to go."

She raised a glowing, tear-streaked face to him. "Not want to go? Not want to go and be with my darlin' Will again? Oh, we'll go all right, m'lord, as soon as we can." She grabbed his hand and tried to kiss it, but Dominic would have none of it. "Thank you, thank you, m'lord."

"Nonsense," he said gruffly. "I'm only putting right the wrong done to you through my father's lack of care."

Billy folded the letter and turned to face the marveling crowd. "See—I *told* you he was a good 'un!" he yelled jubilantly.

THAT EVENING DOMINIC AND GRACE, ARMS AROUND EACH other, walked slowly up to bed, stepping in the hollows his ancestors' feet had made. Dominic looked down at her. His heart was almost too full to speak.

"Look up there," Grace told him.

He looked up and there above them was the Wolfestone gargoyle, his wise old face wreathed with mistletoe.

"I think he wants us to kiss, don't you?"

And so they kissed. And it was a perfect kiss.

Enter the rich world of historical romance with Berkley Books.
Lynn Kurland
Patricia Potter
Betina Krahn
Jodi Thomas
Anne Gracie
Love is timeless.
penguin.com